Caroline

ALSO BY SARAH MILLER

Young Adult Non-Fiction

The Borden Murders: Lizzie Borden and the Trial of the Century

Young Adult Fiction

The Lost Crown

Miss Spitfire: Reaching Helen Keller

Caroline

Little House, Revisited

Sarah Miller
with the full approval of
Little House Heritage Trust

An Imprint of HarperCollins*Publishers*

None knew thee but to love thee,
Thou dear one of my heart,
Oh, thy memory is ever fresh and green.
"Daisy Deane"

CAROLINE. Copyright © 2017 by Sarah Miller and Little House Heritage Trust. All rights reserved. Printed in the United States of America. No part of this book may be used or reproduced in any manner whatsoever without written permission except in the case of brief quotations embodied in critical articles and reviews. For information address HarperCollins Publishers, 195 Broadway, New York, NY 10007.

HarperCollins books may be purchased for educational, business, or sales promotional use. For information please e-mail the Special Markets Department at SPsales@harpercollins.com.

FIRST HARPERLUXE EDITION

ISBN: 978-0-06-268810-1

HarperLuxe™ is a trademark of HarperCollins Publishers.

Library of Congress Cataloging-in-Publication Data is available upon request.

17 18 19 20 21   ID/LSC   10 9 8 7 6 5 4 3 2 1

One

Caroline's wrist turned and flicked as the steel tongue of her crochet hook dipped in and out, mirroring the movement of the fiddle's bow. With each note, the white thread licked a warm line across her finger. Her pattern had just begun to repeat, chorus-like, as the tune ended. She smoothed the frilled cluster of scallops against her cuff and smiled. So long as she could keep ahead of the mending, a pair of lace wrists would freshen her second-best blue wool before snowmelt. There would be no time for a collar—once the trees began to bud, she must turn her hands to the tedious seams of a new set of diapers, bonnets, and gowns.

Charles rested the fiddle on his knees and primed himself with a breath.

"What is it, Charles?" Caroline asked, plucking a slouching festoon of thread into place.

"I've had an offer for this place," he said.

Caroline's hook stilled. "An offer?"

"Gustafson's agreed to pay one thousand twelve dollars and fifty cents for our half of this quarter section."

The sum swept her mind clean as a gust of wind. "My goodness," she said. One thousand twelve dollars. And the delightful absurdity of fifty cents besides, like a sprinkling of sugar. They could use it to buy a week's worth of satin hair ribbons for Mary and Laura. "Oh, Charles." Caroline clasped her hands before her lips to hide their eager trembling. "And the same for Henry and Polly's half?"

Charles grimaced. "Gustafson can only afford eighty acres. Your brother isn't going."

Going. The image her mind had already begun to embroider unraveled. Such foolish greed; she had let herself imagine that money as though it were sitting in her lap, beneath this very roof—not as the lever that would pry her loose of it.

She need not ask where they would go. All winter long Charles had talked of Kansas, its free, level land and bountiful game. Even Mary and little Laura could repeat his reveries of the mighty jackrabbits and tree-less acreage as easily as the words of "The Gypsy King." The West was a song Charles wanted a hand in composing.

A subtle tightening, as though she were taking hold of the cabin and everything in it, passed over her. To move westward was nothing new, but always, she had traveled from the sanctuary of one family to another: from Ma and Papa Frederick's house in Concord to Father and Mother Ingalls's farm, and from there to this quarter section they had bought together with Henry and Polly, just seven miles east of the Mississippi.

And yet beneath that apprehension, a twinkle of ex-citement. Caroline remembered the thrill, after three years of married life spent under others' roofs, of buy-ing this place and making of it a home all their own. Within six months she had been pregnant. How might it feel to do the same on land that bore no mark of an-other family? Such a place would belong more thor-oughly to them than anything had before.

"We stake our claim, make improvements on the land while Gustafson makes his payments, and by the time the Indians move on we can clear the mortgage on this place and preempt a full one hundred sixty acres with upward of five hundred dollars left to spare," Charles went on, pulling a blue handbill from his pocket. "The settlers put up such a fuss that the government's finally reneged on the railroad interests. The Indian Territory is there for the taking—a dollar and a quarter an acre. We only have to be there when the land opens up. The sooner we arrive, the sooner we've put in our fourteen months' residency." He leaned forward for her reply.

The arithmetic alone spoke for itself: twice the acreage, none of the debt. Cash in hand, where before they had banked with pelts and crops. She should not hesitate at such a gain. Yet how to weigh that against losses that could not be measured? Departing before the Mississippi thawed would not leave time enough to bid her own mother goodbye. She did not answer yes or no. "We will have an increase in the family well before then," she said instead.

Caroline tucked her lips together. She had not intended to tell him for another month yet, not until she was certain the child was safely rooted. But Charles looked at her as though it were the first time, and she went rosy in the glow of his happiness. "When?" he asked.

"Before harvest."

He combed his fingers through his whiskers. "Should we wait?"

Her conscience rippled. She could say yes, and he

would give her the year at least, restaking himself to this land without question or complaint. Another year with her sisters and brother, with Mother and Father Ingalls, with plenty of time to visit Ma and Papa Frederick one more time. One final time. Were she to answer on behalf of the coming child, it might even be an unselfish thing to ask. Yet she'd had no sense of its presence—only the absence of her monthly courses coupled with an unaccountable warmth in her hands and feet—nothing to signal it as separate from herself.

Caroline's eyes roved over the place where her china shepherdess stood gazing down from the mantel. The silken glaze of her painted dress and body seemed at once so hard and smooth as to render the little woman untouchable. If she indulged herself by claiming this time, Caroline thought, Charles would treat her with almost unbearable awe and deference. No matter that carrying a child made her feel no more fragile than a churn full of cream. Staying would only make for a year shadowed with lasts—one vast goodbye shattered over innumerable small moments. "Better to travel now," she decided. "It will only be harder if we wait."

He leaned back, grinning, until the chair was on tiptoe. Her news had dyed the fabric of the coming year twice as brightly for Charles. He took up the fiddle and played softly, so as not to wake the girls.

> There's a land that is fairer than day,
> And by faith we can see it afar.
> For the Father waits over the way,
> To prepare us a dwelling place there.

Caroline laid her morsel of lace aside and rocked herself deeply into the long notes.

Two

"Long as those hickory bows are curing, I might as well make a trip into town," Charles said, shrugging into his overcoat. "We still need oakum to caulk the wagon box and canvas for a cover."

"Get a good heavy needle and plenty of stout linen thread," Caroline reminded him. "And check the post office," she added, silly as it was. The letter she'd sent into town with Henry the week before could hardly have reached her mother in Concord by now. Charles winked and shut the door, whistling.

Caroline stood in the middle of the big room with a burst of breath puffing out her cheeks. Charles always saw the beginning of a new start, never the loose ends of the old one that must be fastened off.

The cabin had not seemed overlarge before, but it

was more than would fit in a wagon box—the straw ticks alone would fill a third of it. Every object she laid eyes on suddenly demanded a decision of her. To look at it all at once made her mind swarm. *One thing at a time,* Caroline told herself. She pulled the red-checked cloth from the table, and the shepherdess from the mantel. Some few things, at least, there was no question about.

In the bedroom, Caroline opened her trunk and lifted the upper tray out onto the bed. In one of its shallow compartments lay the glass ambrotype portraits from their courting and marriage, and her three school-books. She opened the reader. Its cardboard cover shielded her certificate of good behavior and the little handwritten booklet of poems she'd sewn together as a youth. She slipped a fingernail between its leaves and parted the pages. "Blue Juniata" stood out in Charles's writing. She smiled, remembering the cornhusking dance where she had first heard Charles play the tune. He had not sung the words correctly, and she had been so bold as to tell him so. "That's the way we Ingallses sang it back East," he'd said, and his eyes twinkled at her. They'd twinkled again when she asked him to inscribe his version in her booklet. "Now no matter which way I sing it, it'll be by the book," he'd teased.

She did not hear Mary and Laura come pattering down from the attic until they stood in the doorway.

"What are you doing, Ma?" Mary asked. "Can we help?"

"May we," she reminded, secreting the fragile booklet back into the reader.

"May we, Ma?"

Laura was already peering over the rim of the trunk. A tongue of frustration licked at Caroline's throat. She could not let children of five and three pack her best things, yet they would make themselves busy getting underfoot if she did not give them something to do. She smoothed back a sigh. "Very well. Mary, please bring me the scrap bag, and Laura, you may fetch the newspapers."

Into the bottom of the trunk went her books, together with the family Bible and the volume of Sunday school lessons her mother had given her. The lap desk just snugged in beside them. Caroline slipped the ambrotypes beneath the trunk's lid and cushioned them with a length of flannel Mary fished from the scrap bag.

"Now, Laura, we must fill all the cracks and corners with newspaper. Pack them tightly, so nothing can wiggle."

While Laura crumpled and crammed newsprint

into every cranny, Caroline showed Mary how to roll the silver spoons up in squares of felt. The girls occupied, she packed a sturdy cardboard box with her thin china teacups, leaving a hollow in the center for the shepherdess. When Laura finished, Caroline folded her wholecloth wedding quilt with the red stitching and squared it over the layer of books.

"Now Mary and Laura, please bring me the good pillows." She let them put one at each end of the trunk, then nested the box of porcelain amongst the goose down. Her pearl-handled pen and the breast pins she slipped into the red Morocco pocketbook before tucking it into the lid compartment.

The delaine, shrouded in soft brown paper and tied with string, came last of all.

"Please, Ma, can't we see the delaine?" Laura begged. Her mouth fairly watered for its strawberry-shaped buttons.

Caroline could not help remembering her mother's broad hands sewing those buttons onto the rich green basque by lamplight. Just now, she did not want to unwrap that memory any further, even for her girls.

"Not today."

"Aw, Ma, please?"

Caroline raised an eyebrow. "Laura." Her tone dwindled the child into a half-hearted pout.

Over it all Caroline smoothed the red-checked tablecloth, then lowered in the tray and latched the lid. *Tck* went the latch, and the band of tension broke from her chest. "There now," she said, and felt herself smiling. "Thank you, Mary and Laura." With such things out of sight, she could begin imagining them elsewhere and other people's possessions in their places.

By the time Charles came back from town, she had packed one of their two carpetbags tight with trousers, calico shirts and dresses, sunbonnets, and cotton stockings. At the bottom waited her maternity and nursing corsets with the baby gowns Mary and Laura hadn't worn out. The other would hold their spare sets of woolens, along with their nightclothes and underthings. At the sound of Charles's boots on the floor, the girls abandoned their half-folded pile of dishcloths, napkins, and towels and scampered to him for their treats.

"Sweets to the sweet," he said, handing them each a sugared ginger cookie. "And something for your ma." A quick little inhale betrayed Caroline's hopes for a letter. She looked up eagerly as Charles flopped a drab bundle tied with twine from his shoulder onto the bed. The *whoosh* of its landing fluttered her stacks of linens.

"There you are, Caroline—thirty yards of osnaburg canvas and the stoutest thread goods in Pepin."

She sat back on her heels. "Thirty yards!"

"Fellow in the dry-goods shop said four widths ought to be enough to stretch over the wagon bows, and it'll have to be double thick. Need extra to double-sack all our dry provisions besides. How long will it take to make?" Charles asked. "Lake Pepin's solid as a window pane, but the cold can't hold out too much longer."

Three doubled seams more than twice as long as she was tall, plus the hemming and the sacks. If each stitch were a mile, her needle could carry them to Kansas and back dozens of times over. Caroline's fingers cramped to think of it. "No longer than it will take you to bend those hickory bows and fit up the wagon," she told him.

He chucked her under the chin. "Got some extra crates for packing, too," he said.

On mending day, she gave herself over entirely to the wagon cover. Laid flat, it stretched from one side of the big room to the other. In the time it took Caroline to fetch her papers of pins, Laura had already taken to tunneling under the carpet of canvas.

"Mary, be a good girl and take Laura upstairs to play with your paper ladies," Caroline said after she'd scolded Laura. "There isn't space to have you underfoot down here. If you play nicely until I've finished, you may cook a doll supper for Nettie on the stove to-night."

Mary needed no more enticement than that. She took her sister by the hand and marched Laura to the ladder. Caroline straightened the lengths of fabric and settled down to her long chore. With every stitch she pictured the journey in her mind, envisioning the views the hem now before her would soon frame.

When the pads of her thumb and forefinger grew rutted from the press of the needle, Caroline laid the canvas aside to dip the steel knives and forks in soda water and roll them in flannel to keep against rust, or to melt rosin and lard together to grease the outside of the bake oven, the iron spider, and Charles's tools. With the leftovers she would waterproof their boots and shoes.

By noontime the close of the center seam was less than an arm's length away. She might have finished it before dinner, if not for a burrowing sensation low in her middle that would not be ignored. Caroline pinned her needle carefully over her last stitch and stepped out from under the stiff blanket of fabric. Her forearms were heavy with fatigue from holding the everlasting seam at eye level.

"Girls," she called up the ladder into the attic, "I'm going to the necessary. Keep away from the fireplace and cookstove until I come back."

"Yes, Ma," they sang out.

It took longer than she intended; where before the slight pressure of her womb had driven her to the chamber pail three and four times between breakfast and dinner, now the child had taken to making her bowels costive.

She could not hear the girls' voices overhead as she stripped off her shawl and mittens in the narrow corridor that led in from the back door. A twist of unease tickled the place she had just voided. "Mary? Laura?" she called. Giggles in return, muffled. Caroline cocked her head, not entirely relieved. "Girls? What are you up to?"

She strode into the big room and stopped short. Her rocking chair stood twisted halfway around, bare of its canvas cloak—they'd dragged the wagon cover over the table and benches and made themselves a tent of it. Her needle dangled in a widening gap that formed the flap of their door.

Caroline threw up her hands and dropped into the rocker. *A woman can resolve that, whatever happens, she will not speak till she can do it in a calm and gentle manner,* she recited to herself as she waited for the flare of temper to ebb. *Perfect silence is a safe resort, when such control cannot be attained.* "Come out of there, the both of you," she said evenly after another moment.

They crawled out on hands and knees. "We're playing 'going west,'" Laura explained. "I'm Pa, and Mary's Ma, and this is our wagon." Laura was so earnest, Caroline pinched back a smile in spite of herself. Mary stood by, sheepish.

Caroline made herself sober. "You know better than to tangle with my mending," she said, mostly to Mary. "Our wagon cover must have good strong seams to keep us safe and dry. You may not play—"

"Aw, Ma," Laura mourned.

"Laura. It's very rude to interrupt. You will have more than enough time to sit under it when we go west." She looked again toward Mary. "There will be no doll supper tonight."

"Yes, ma'am," Mary said.

"And no bedtime stories from your pa," she told Laura. Caroline stood and gathered up the span of canvas. "Now set the table for dinner and sit quietly in your places while I repair this seam."

Caroline felt as though she needed a good starching. Dinner had not been started, the wagon cover still lay in pieces, and already her body simmered with exhaustion. Well, there was no great loss without some small gain—at least she would not have to hover over the cookstove with Mary and her pattypans.

"Ready?" Charles asked.

Caroline nodded. Together they leaned over the side-boards of the wagon and took the corners of the folded sheet of canvas from Mary's and Laura's outstretched hands, pulling it square over the hickory bows.

"Best-looking wagon cover in Wisconsin," Charles proclaimed. He tossed Laura and then Mary up over the tailgate and cinched the rear flaps down so tightly they could barely peek through. "There we are—snug as a tent!"

Caroline could not deny it was handsome, all clean and close-fitting as a new bodice. It was easily the largest thing she had ever sewn. And yet it looked to have shrunk. All that canvas, which inside the cabin had seemed vast enough to set a schooner afloat, now enclosed an area barely the size of the pigpen. "I declare, I still don't know how it's all going to fit," Caroline said as the girls ran whooping up and down the length of the wagon box.

"I'm whittling a pair of hooks for my gun. Tell me how many you need, and I'll make you enough to hang anything you like from the bows."

"That will do for the carpetbags, but we can't hang the bedstead and straw ticks."

"I'll lay a few boards across the wagon box to

make a loft for the straw ticks right behind the spring seat," Charles said. "The girls and the fiddle can ride there, with the extra provisions stowed underneath."

But there was still the medicine box of camphor, castor oil, laudanum, and bitter herbs. The willow-bough broom, sewing basket, scrap bag, sadirons, soap and starch; the kerosene, candles, tinderbox, and lamps; the chamber pail. The whole of the pantry must go into the wagon, from the salt and pepper to the churn and dishpan. Always there was something small and essential turning up that must be wedged into a box—packets of seeds, scraps of leather and balls of twine, the little box that held Mary's rag doll and paper ladies, the matches screwed tightly into a cobalt blue medicine bottle. And yet there must be room for Charles's things: chains and ropes and picket pins, the metal tools and traps, his lead and patch box and bullet mold. It was a mercy the buckets and washtub could hang outside the wagon.

"Don't worry about the furniture," Charles added. "We'll leave all that. Once we get settled I can make more."

Caroline pulled her shawl to her chin, stricken. Over and over again she had imagined her things arranged in the new place Charles would build, until the picture felt familiar, almost beckoning. All at once there was no place to spread the red-checked tablecloth, nowhere to prop the pillows in their embroidered shams. Even her cozy vantage point—her rocker before the hearth—now vanished from the image. "That will help," she said weakly.

Charles loosened the rope and stuck his head inside the wagon. "Any Indians in here?" he called to Mary and Laura. Caroline measured the wagon one last time with her eyes, then left Charles and the girls to their play.

The cabin still smelled of the linseed oil she'd used to cure the canvas. Boxes, crates, and bundles leaned in the corners, encroaching on her sense of order no matter how neatly she stacked them. Turning her back to the disarray, Caroline went to the hearth and lowered herself into the embrace of the rocking chair, listening for the accustomed sigh of the runners across the floorboards. Charles had fashioned this chair for her of sugar maple just before Mary was born. In the last days before the birth, its sway had soothed her nerves as much as it soothed the baby afterward. Beside it sat Charles's own straight-backed chair and Mary's and Laura's little stools, like a wooden family. Charles had built them all, and he would build more. Caroline stroked the arms of her rocker. Her fingers knew the grain of their curves as well as they knew the coiled knot of her own hair. The work of Charles's hands might make a new chair familiar to her touch, but it would not be the same.

Three

In the grainy dark before dawn, Caroline woke to the pull of her stomach drawing itself taut. Before opening her eyes she resigned herself to it; better to let her muscles express her dread of this day than give voice to it.

Already the room had changed. Neither Charles's clothes nor his nightshirt hung on the nail beside her own, though the usual sounds of him putting on his boots and taking up the water pail came from the back door. She lay still a moment more after the door shut, letting herself collect the feel of the roof and walls around her one last time before kneeling alongside the trundle bed to pray.

As she fastened her corset, Caroline marked the faint rise of her waist, like the dome of a layer cake peeking over the pan. The quickening would follow before long. She was more impatient for it this time than she had been even with Mary. After spending weeks packing boxes and crates, it was disquieting not to have felt her own body's cargo. Caroline flattened her palms below her ribs and drew a breath. Not a flicker, yet the steady press of the steels along her core eased the quiver of her nerves. With each successive breath she stretched her lungs deeper still, until she was nearly within reach of her accustomed cadence.

Caroline took her dress down from its nail and the bedroom turned gaunt—stripped and scoured down to the last bare inch. Vinegar still stung the air, sharpened by the cold. It crowded out the familiar traces of Charles's shaving lather and rosemary-scented bear grease. Caroline washed her face, then with her damp palms smoothed the length of her braid before pinning it carefully up. Last of all she dipped the comb into the basin of cold water and slicked down the loose strands between her forehead and the nape of her neck.

A fresh pail of half-melted snow already waited beside the cookstove for her. Caroline stoked up the fire and set the draught as deftly as Charles tuning his fiddle. She filled the coffeepot and skillet with snow, draped the girls' underthings over the back of the rocker to warm, then went to fetch the last of the salt pork.

At the threshold of the newly emptied pantry she hesitated. A score of years had passed since she'd faced such a barren set of shelves, yet the sight was enough to waken the old tremors of unease. The few things she had not been able to make room for—the last half-dozen jars of preserves, the eggs in their big barrel of salted limewater—beckoned to be packed as persistently as the bedstead and rocking chair. Tightly as they'd loaded the wagon, Caroline could not help wondering if hunger would find a place to lodge among the crates and bundles.

Caroline shook herself free of such thoughts. This morning at least, they would have their fill of eggs and empty an entire jar of tart cherry jelly onto their corn-bread.

As she stirred milk into the cornmeal, her mind ran counterclockwise. Their first meal in this cabin, Caroline remembered, she had nearly cried. She'd forgotten the sugar—somehow forgotten it entirely when they'd loaded the wagon with their share of the provisions at Father and Mother Ingalls's house that morning. She was just pressing the cornbread into the pan when she'd realized.

Charles had looked at her, with her hands caked in cornmeal and her face on the verge of falling, and said, "I don't see how sugar could make that cornbread any sweeter than the prints of your hands already have." That night in bed, he'd kissed her palms instead of her cheeks.

Once the salt pork was parboiling and the cornbread was in the oven, she dried her hands and went in to wake Mary and Laura. Caroline smiled as she crouched beside the trundle bed, at the harmony of their breaths beneath the patchwork quilt. She nudged them from their dreams, then sat back on her heels to watch for the moment she delighted in, when their faces seemed almost to shimmer as their minds began to stir. And then the way the girls looked first at each other, as though the sight of the other was what made the world real to them.

When both had taken their turns with the chamber pail and washbasin, Caroline led Mary and Laura to the stove. They yawned and rubbed their eyes as she buttoned the bands of their flannel underwear over their stockings and layered them with woolens. She combed their hair until it lay straight and soft as corduroy, then sent them back into the bedroom to put their rolled-up nightdresses into the carpetbag and pull the linens from their bed while she finished breakfast.

Charles stepped in. "Anything to take out yet?"

Caroline split an egg against the lip of the skillet and opened it onto a saucer. Still fresh, though its white was tinged pink from the preserving barrel. "The second carpetbag is packed," she said. "As soon as the girls have stripped the trundle bed the straw ticks will be ready. The chamber pail and basin may both go once they've been emptied and rinsed. And my trunk." She dropped the eggshell into the teakettle to take up the lime, wondering aloud how long it would be before they would have eggs again.

"Indian Territory's swarming with prairie hens," Charles promised.

Caroline's fork jittered in the skillet. "I wish you wouldn't call it that," she said as gently as she could manage.

"What?"

"Kansas. Indian Territory." She pricked at the curling strips of pork as she spoke. "I don't like to think of the Indians any more than I have to. I saw enough of them in Brookfield."

"The Potawatomis never did your family any harm."

"Just the same, I've had my fill. I'll be thankful when they've moved on."

Around the edges of the skillet, a dribble of egg white was beginning to form a skin like the rim of a pancake.

Caroline's stomach shuddered as the smell suddenly unfurled, thick and brown, saturating her nostrils.

"Are you all right?" Charles asked.

She swallowed hard, remembering that she had not taken her usual glass of warm water to insulate her stomach against the skillet's odors. "It will pass if you'll fill a mug from the teakettle for me, please." Caroline dragged the skillet to the side of the stove and scraped the crusted membrane of egg loose before sinking onto the bench.

Charles held the steaming mug by the rim as Caroline hooked her fingers through its handle. She leaned into the vapor and drew its blank scent through her nose and mouth. Immediately the steam began to melt her queasiness like a breath against a frosted windowpane.

As each sip expanded her throat, Caroline became aware of Charles standing over her, silent but breathing quickly. He had seen her ill this way before, yet the pitch of his anxiousness was keen enough to draw the girls from the bedroom.

Caroline raised her eyes over the rim of the mug. All three of them stood poised before her, waiting, and suddenly she understood that without a word she could stall their going. A simple shake of her head would send Charles to unload the wagon. But it was not going she dreaded—only leaving. Waiting would wind the dread more tightly. Once the break was made she would be all right. She held them with her silence a moment longer before saying, "Thank you, Charles." And then with a nod toward the bedroom doorway where Mary and Laura hovered, "Go on with the packing. I can manage breakfast with the girls' help."

While Mary and Laura wiped the breakfast dishes, Caroline packed the coffee mill and the tin dredging boxes of flour, salt, and pepper into an open crate with the iron spider and bake oven. "Put these where we can reach them easily," she told Charles. "The skillets and other things may go anyplace you can fit them, but leave room for the dishpan."

Caroline emptied the dishpan into the snow, then lined it with a towel and collected one tin plate and cup at a time from Mary and Laura. Through the window, they heard the jostle and clang of Charles fitting the crates into the wagon. They finished just as he returned. "This is the last," Caroline said, untying her apron and folding it into the top of the dishpan. She held the door for him, then turned to face the naked room.

The bare hearth and table, the cooling cookstove—the bedstead, peeled of its mattress. They had not left, yet this place was no longer their own. Only the calico edging on the curtains and the coats and hoods on the line of pegs by the back door had the look of home about them. Without Charles's fiddle box or her mending basket close by, even the chairs looked as though they might belong to anyone. There was more comfort in going than staying, now.

In the middle of it, the girls stood looking at her. Mary hitched Nettie up close to her cheek. Laura seemed stranded, as though she were understanding for the first time all that "going west" meant. A tumble of sympathy rolled across Caroline's breast. Like her pa, all of Laura's visions of the West had begun with the journey, not the departure.

Piecing together a smile, Caroline held out her hands for both Mary and Laura. "Come along, girls," she said. "Pa and the horses will be waiting." Laura took hold of her arm with both hands. Mary ducked beneath Caroline's elbow and leaned her head into the cinnamon-colored folds of Caroline's skirt. She felt a smudge of tears on Mary's cheek, but did not scold. Her own eyes threatened to swim as she shepherded her girls past the empty cluster of chairs before the hearth.

Mary and Laura did not speak as they bundled each other into their coats and rabbit-skin hoods. Caroline's fingers stumbled over her shawl pin until a little berry of blood ripened on her fingertip, bright as the girls' red yarn mittens. She winced and licked it clean.

"I wish Nettie had a shawl, too, Ma," Mary said.

"I am sure there is something in the scrap bag that will do," Caroline said as she tucked Laura's coat collar under her hood. "When we are all settled into the wagon, you may see. Hold Nettie close for now and she will not feel the cold." Caroline herself would have liked to take both of the girls up and tuck them inside her wraps. The steadiness she held so firmly for the children's sake was forming a brittle shell around her, and Caroline wished to temper it with their softness. Instead, she stepped back and looked them over. "You look very nice," she said, and nodded toward the door.

The horses greeted Caroline and the girls with billowed breath as they rounded the corner of the cabin. Although her fingers knew each stitch of its skin and its ribs protected every portable scrap of their lives, the wagon did not beckon to Caroline as she had hoped. The sight of it, full and waiting, only made her sorry for the weight and space her own presence demanded—another burden added to the load. Immediately a ribbon of guilt ran down Caroline's back as she imagined that thought rubbing against the bundle of living freight she herself carried.

Before she could reassure herself of the absurdity of such a notion, Caroline stopped short. Her trunk stood on the ground below the tailgate. All her best things, huddled in the snow, and the wagon crammed to the bows. The finger she'd pricked with her shawl pin throbbed. She dropped Mary's and Laura's hands, afraid that they might feel the selfish rush of her pulse.

"Charles?" she called.

What would she say if there were no room for it? Nothing less necessary could stay behind in its place, yet he might as well leave her as that trunk.

His boots sounded across the planks until he stood hunched, palms braced on his thighs, at the lip of the wagon box. Caroline watched the brim of his hat dip as he looked from her face to the trunk.

"Didn't want to chance lifting it by myself," he explained, vaulting himself down into the snow. "It's the size, not the weight. If you can help me get it on board, I can slide it up the aisle all the way to the front, under the straw ticks." Caroline closed her eyes, unable to hide her relief in any other way. Charles paused. "You didn't think . . . ?"

A lie would have been simpler, but she could not make room for the weight of it. "I'm sorry, Charles," she admitted. "I wasn't thinking."

With a nod, she was forgiven. Caroline wished now

and again that he were not so quick at it; Charles's good nature hardly left her time enough to reap the satisfaction of repentance.

As they bent to grip the leather handles, a chain of sleighs came hissing across the north field from Henry's place. Spokes of light from their pierced tin lanterns sliced through the air. Mary and Laura clapped their mittens, prancing on tiptoe as they named one face after another: Grandpa and Grandma Ingalls with Aunt Ruby and Uncle George; Uncle Henry and Aunt Polly; Aunt Eliza and Uncle Peter, and every one of the cousins.

Caroline braced herself to greet them. She could not let them see how much she craved and dreaded this moment.

One by one, Charles's and Caroline's brothers and sisters lifted their little ones down into the snow. Caroline watched Peter hold his hands up for her sister Eliza, brimming with her fourth child, just as Charles always did for her. She loved to see the ways their families mirrored each other. With three marriages between them, the Ingallses and Quiners were interwoven close as tartan—first Caroline's brother Henry had married Charles's sister, and then Eliza had married one of his brothers. Their children were double cousins twice over.

"Morning," Charles said to the whole company of them.

No one answered; they had not come to say hello.

Apprehension feathered through Caroline's stomach to see all of them together, yet so tight with quiet. The wagonload of family that had come to tell her own ma of her father's drowning in Lake Michigan had been muffled by the same sort of silence.

"Here, Caroline," Henry said, taking hold of one handle of her trunk. "Let me." Peter and George both stepped forward to latch the wagon box after them, and suddenly all the men were inspecting lashings and harnesses.

The women stood before the wagon as if it were an open grave, their noses pink with cold and the labor of not crying. The children, made skittish by their parents' restraint, collected in shy clumps around their mothers.

Practicality coaxed Caroline's tongue loose. "Take anything you can use from the pantry and the attic," she told Eliza and Polly and Mother Ingalls.

Polly thrust out a handful of brown paper packets tied with black thread. "Seeds," she said. "The best of my pumpkins and tomatoes, and those good pickling cucumbers. And don't you try to say no, Caroline Ingalls."

Caroline nearly smiled. Thank goodness Polly was always Polly. She could not have stood it if her brusque sister-in-law were soft with her today. Caroline obeyed and tucked the packets into her pocket.

"Write," Eliza asked. "We can't send the circulator until we hear where you've settled."

"Charles has a handbill from the land office in Montgomery County. He's told Gustafson to send the next payment there . . . ," Caroline trailed off.

Mother Ingalls handed Caroline a jug of maple syrup. "You won't find this in Kansas for anything like a reasonable price. Eat it or trade it—whichever brings you the most sweetness," she said with a wink.

"Thank you," Caroline said. "I wish there was room in your sleigh for my rocker," she told Eliza.

"Hasn't Gustafson bought your furniture?"

Caroline leaned across the press of Eliza's belly to kiss her sister's cheek. "I'd rather keep it in the family," she whispered. "Promise me you'll take it if Peter can contrive a way to get it home."

"Of course." Horses' hooves crunching across the snow interrupted her. "Oh my land," Eliza said.

Caroline turned, and there was Charley Carpenter's sleigh coming over the hill, with her sister Martha beside him. Martha's oldest boy, Willie, jumped out to help his mother climb down over the runner so Charley could lower a bushel basket swaddled in woolen veils into his wife's arms.

"Martha," Caroline gasped. "Oh, Martha, you shouldn't have, not so soon."

"I know it," Martha said, trying to laugh, "but that can't be helped." Her voice knotted. "I had to see you, sister, and you had to see our Millie."

"Martha Jane Carpenter, you don't mean to say you brought the baby?" Mother Ingalls said.

"Oh, pshaw. She's snug as a dumpling. My Charley made a nest of buffalo robes down between our feet for the basket, and I put two hot flatirons under her pillow. Look and see, Caroline."

Caroline pared back the layers of veils. Wreathed in flannels and goose down lay her niece, a wren-faced little thing, still ruddy with newness. The warmth of the baby's breath moistened the air around her. "Three weeks old yesterday," Martha said.

"I'm glad you came," Caroline said, though they'd only made it harder. The longer she looked at the child, the more the membrane holding back her tears thinned.

"You'll come to our place and warm up those flatirons before you go," Polly told Martha. "You'll all come."

The image of all of them crowded into Henry's cabin burned Caroline's throat like hot maple sugar. All at once, there was no more to be said but goodbye.

The men embraced briefly, a mittened clap on the back signaling the moment to break away. Caroline hugged her sisters and Charles's as long as she dared, tightening her clasp as she felt the flutter of emotion rising and then thrusting herself apart with a kiss. Eliza clung to her a moment too long. "Write," she said again. Caroline forced herself to nod. Something like a wad of wool had lodged behind her tongue.

Mother Ingalls saw her struggling and said not a word, simply took her by the shoulders for a good, bracing squeeze as they pressed their cold cheeks together. The older woman's firm smile tightened Caroline at the seams, so that when she reached the men Caroline found herself able to do for them what Mother Ingalls had done for her. She would not have them shame themselves with tears on her account.

"Look in on Ma and Papa Frederick when you can," she asked her brother. "I wrote to tell them." Henry nodded. A flash of heat stung the rims of her eyes and nose. She had not written of the coming child, had not told them that if it were a boy, he would be called Charles Frederick, for her husband and her stepfather. "There hasn't been an answer. I never expected them to come, not with the way driving pains Papa Frederick, but I had hopes for a letter," she confessed.

"There could be one waiting by now. If there isn't,

I'll send Ma's reply on to you when it comes," Henry promised. "You know they would be here if they could."

"Kiss your cousins," Polly commanded her brood. "You might not ever see them again." So the children solemnly kissed and hugged Mary and Laura, like little ladies and gentlemen performing a soundless square dance.

"You first, Caroline," Charles said into the long pause that followed. "I'll hand the girls up after."

With Charles at one elbow and Henry bracing the other, Caroline stepped up onto the doubletree and turned to perch on the edge of the sideboard. She grasped a bow and swung her legs over the wagon box. Inside it smelled of hemp, pine pitch, and linseed oil.

"Upsy-daisy," Charley Carpenter said as he scooped Mary up by the underarms. Her feet scrabbled in the air until her toes found the sideboard. Caroline steadied her with a smile and a pair of firm hands around Mary's waist.

Before Mary's shoes were on the floor, Laura was climbing between the spokes and the singletree. "I want to do it myself, like Ma did," she insisted.

"You're not tall enough to reach over the sideboards, little Half-Pint," Charles said. Only the tips of her mittens peeped stubbornly over the edge of the box. Caroline could hear her shoes scraping at the boards for a place to grip. "Maybe by the time we get to Kansas you'll be big enough," Charles teased, hoisting her up.

Caroline settled the girls onto the straw tick with the old gray blanket as Charles shook his father's hand and clambered in over the jockey box. With a lurch, he dropped down onto the spring seat beside her. Father Ingalls handed up the reins.

Charles cleared his throat. "All ready?" he called over his shoulder.

"Yes, Charles," Caroline answered softly.

Father Ingalls tipped his hat and stepped from sight. Caroline craned forward, but the wagon's canvas bonnet beveled out overhead, blocking her view. They had already said goodbye, Caroline reminded herself as she straightened her shawl and folded her hands into her lap. They were her mother's hands, nearly as broad as a man's. Like her mother, she kept them always folded, the long fingers tucked neatly into her palms.

Charles released the brake lever and the wheels hitched forward. The snap of movement loosed Caroline's grip on herself. A sob juddered halfway up her throat before she could clasp it back.

Charles looked at her, the tears in his eyes only add-ing a luster to his excitement. Caroline tightened her cheeks to echo his smile as best she could.

Those she could not bear to leave sat close around her, yet as she looked backward through the keyhole of canvas at the blur of waving hands, Caroline could not help but wonder whether Charles and the girls would be enough.

Four

The town was muted with snow. A steamy chill hung in the air, as though the drifts were exhaling. Charles drove past McInerney's and the Prussian dry-goods shops to the Richardses's storefront. "Always one of them willing to strike a bargain," Charles said. Caroline did not answer. Her back was striped with aches. The wagon rolled to a stop, and her body swayed with it. All the seven miles down into town she had held herself taut against the slope of the land. Now the leveling of the road left her unmoored, as though the steadying pull of the little cabin could no longer reach her.

Caroline held Laura on her hip and Mary by the hand as Charles and the two younger Richards brothers piled provisions onto the counter. To the food Charles added painted canvas tarpaulins, a ten-gallon water keg, and a pair of collapsible gutta-percha buckets. "Need more powder and caps, and lead for shot, too," he said.

"What kind of firearms you carrying?" Horace Richards asked.

"Rifle," Charles answered.

"That old single-shot muzzle-loader?" Linus Richards said.

Charles bristled. "One shot's always been plenty for me."

Linus Richards chuckled and put up his hands. "I'll be the last one to impugn your aim, Ingalls. Nobody trades more bear pelts here than you do." He glanced at Caroline and the children and dropped his voice only low enough to make her cock her ear toward the men. "Stalking a wild animal's one thing—a mounted brave with a full quiver and tomahawk besides is quite another. All I'm saying is, I wouldn't take my little ones into the Indian Territory without a decent pistol to level the field."

Caroline felt Mary's grip tighten as Horace Richards pulled two snub-nosed guns from under the counter. "We've got Colt army-model percussion revolvers and one brand-new Smith and Wesson Model Three top-break cartridge revolver."

Dry at the mouth, Caroline put Laura down and guided both girls toward the row of candy jars. "You may each choose a penny's worth," she said. The girls looked up at her, their astonished eyes like blue china buttons. "Go ahead. You're big enough to choose for yourselves. Any one you like."

From a neighboring shelf, Caroline gathered castor oil, ipecac, paregoric, rhubarb, and magnesia while the men haggled and the girls pored over the sweets. "Let's get two different flavors," she heard Mary tell Laura. "I'll give you half of my stick, and you give me half of yours. Then we'll both have two kinds of candy."

Caroline smiled. "That's my smart girl," she said.

Elisha Richards stood at the till with his thumbs hooked into the pockets of his vest and his nails scratching beneath them as though he were tallying the Ingallses's account against his flanks. With every un-dulation of his fingers, the sum mounted in Caroline's mind, until her head seemed to teeter on her neck. The expense was well within their reach, yet she could not keep hold of the numbers any more than she could take her eyes from the storekeeper's vest. It was cut from a rust-colored paisley that swirled her senses in a way she could not describe. Charles began to count one bill after another into Elisha Richards's palm, peeling the wedge of cash like an onion, and the movement of gray-green against the paisley field made the room roll around her.

It struck her that her body was behaving as though she could taste that vest and feel the pattern augering into her stomach. Caroline balked at the senselessness of it; she would not let such a thing as a swath of cloth take command of her. She set her jaw, refusing to acknowledge the saliva pooling under her tongue, but the queasiness that had overcome her before the stove was already at her throat. Senseless or not, she must put something between her eyes and her stomach.

"Mary, Laura, it's time for dinner." They half turned, reluctant to obey. She knew they wanted to stand at the counter to see their two sticks of candy paid for, but that could not be helped. It did not matter now what she looked at. Another minute and she would be sick where she stood. She swept forward and took them by the wrists. "Come, girls. Pa will bring your sweets."

Out in the wagon, she unwrapped the bundle of bread and plunged her teeth into a slice as the girls gawked at her. The first bite worked quick as a sponge. Her stomach grumbled for more. It was not garish smells or sights that set her senses raving, Caroline realized as she parceled out portions of bread and mo-

lasses to Mary and Laura, but hunger. She would have
to guard against that on the road.

Cold stiffened the molasses so that it clung to their
teeth in thin strands. Laura slipped a fingernail underneath a brown festoon and tried to pry it loose from her
slice.

"Laura," Mary said with a shake of her head.

"It looks like lace," Laura protested. "It's too pretty
to eat."

Laura's scolding melted on Caroline's tongue. They
had never noticed before the care she took drizzling
the molasses. Perhaps for a treat she would try spell-
ing out their names. She imagined her wrist guiding
the graceful flow of the syrup, the smiles of her daughters as they watched their names drawn out in curls of
sweetness. It was the kind of frivolity her own mother
could never spare time nor money for, yet practical,
too—it was high time both of them began learning
their letters.

"Ma," Mary insisted, pointing at Laura. "Look."

Caroline's hand blanketed Mary's. "It's very rude to
point," she reminded. "Now finish your dinner nicely,
girls, so you may have your candy," she said.

The back of the wagon jolted under a hundredweight
of flour. "All stocked up and cash to spare," Charles an-

nounced. "Where are all those empty sacks, Caroline?" he asked, shifting through the crates and bundles.

"Leave that to me, Charles," Caroline said. "You must have something to eat before loading all those provisions."

Too eager to sit, Charles leaned over the front of the wagon box, joking with the girls while Caroline unrolled the sacks and threaded her stoutest needle. She slit open the unbolted flour, cornmeal, beans, and brown sugar and filled a ten pound sack from each to round out her crate of daily supplies.

When the corners were sewn shut again she held the canvas mouths of the biggest sacks wide for Charles to lower the dry goods in, then quickly folded the edges together and basted each one shut. Mary and Laura knelt backward on the spring seat, watching as they sucked their sticks of candy. Their curled fists were like bright berries in their red yarn mittens.

"Did you get the pepper and saleratus?" Caroline asked.

"In my pockets," Charles said. "Bought myself a gutta-percha poncho," he added as he heaved one hundredweight and then another of cornmeal. "There's bound to be rain somewhere between here and Kansas." Caroline nodded. "And the Colt revolver."

Her mind veered around this news, as though she

might avoid the logical progression of thoughts: *The pistol could not have cost under fifteen dollars. Charles would not have spent such a sum without a reason.*

"Caroline?"

"Whatever you think is necessary, Charles."

Charles cinched the wagon cover down in back, leaving only a peephole against the cold.

"Have all you need, Ingalls?" Elisha Richards asked, stepping out to the hitching post to help unbuckle the horses' nose bags.

"And some to spare," Charles answered. "Anything else, Caroline?" She shook her head. The wagon box was packed tight as brown sugar. Anything else would have to ride in their laps.

"Good luck to you, then. It's been my pleasure trading with you." Caroline ventured a glance at the storekeeper's vest as the two men shook hands. Her eyes still had no appetite for it, but the garment claimed no sway over the rest of her. Richards nodded at Caroline as Charles swung himself up over the wheel. "Take care of yourselves and those fine girls."

The compliment touched Caroline squarely at the base of her throat. A small rush of pride ironed out her shoulders and trickled down her core. She bowled her hands together in her lap, as though they might catch the runoff. Behind them, a whorl of warmth embraced her womb—not the child, but the space it occupied suddenly making itself known. It was enough to remind her that she was more than a passenger.

"Thank you, Mr. Richards," she said.

The road ran straight out onto the lake, narrowing between a pair of slump-shouldered snowdrifts. Away from the plowed track, the ice looked tired, blotched here and there with a sweaty sheen where snow had melted.

"Charles?" Caroline asked, laying a hand on his wrist.

He stayed the team. "Pay no mind to the snowmelt," he said. "Ice'll be at its thickest here, where the snow's been plowed, so long as they've kept it bare all winter." Charles stood up to survey the track. The hills two miles distant seemed no more than waist high. "Looks clear as far as I can see." He gave the reins a gentle slap, and the wagon dipped from the creaking snow.

The horses' shoes struck the ice road as though it were the skin of a drum, and their ears pricked at the sudden sharpness. Through the plank of the spring seat, Caroline felt the wheels grind like sugar under a rolling pin. The sound made her shoulder blades twitch. She turned her attention to the rhythm of the team's gait. They had not sped up, but they raised their feet more quickly, as though they too mistrusted the sensation of metal meeting ice.

The flash of their shoes lifted a memory in Caroline's mind of the circus that had once passed along the road by the Quiners' door back home in Concord. Caroline smiled to think how she and her sister Martha had laughed at the great gray elephant delicately putting one foot and then another on the first log of the corduroy bridge spanning the marsh.

For all its bulk, that timid elephant must have been on firmer footing than this wagon and the supplies newly added, Caroline realized: hundredweights of cornmeal, unbolted flour, salt pork, bacon, beans, and brown sugar; fifty pounds of white flour; ten of salt; fifteen pounds of coffee and five of tea; the feed-box brimming with corn. Better than three thousand pounds of horseflesh pulling it all. Surely that corduroy bridge had been thicker than a plate of ice nearing the edge of spring.

Suddenly Caroline did not want her girls boxed in like cargo behind her. "Mary, Laura, come here and see the lake," she said, beckoning them over the spring seat. Mary settled onto Caroline's lap, big girl though she was, while Laura stood solemnly at her pa's elbow.

Charles halted the team. The lake lay like a mile

of muslin, seamed by the ice road with the sheared hilltops of the Minnesota shore binding the distance. Sounds from Pepin's banks seemed to bob in the air alongside them, small and clear as a music box.

"See that, Half-Pint?" Charles asked. "That's Minnesota."

"All of it?" Laura asked, poking her mitten toward the opposing shore.

"All of it," he answered. "Wisconsin's already a mile behind us now."

Mary huffed at Laura's pointing, but Caroline had no voice to settle her. It was too much to hold in her mind all that was behind them, beneath them, and before them. A lump thin as a sparrow's egg blocked her throat; if she so much as swallowed, its shell would shatter.

The waiting horses fidgeted. Their scraping hooves sent unwelcome tingles through Caroline's underbelly and the backs of her thighs as though she were poised at the edge of a precipice. Her breath was coming too quickly, as it had at her parting from Eliza. If they did not move forward, the surge of emotions would overtake her from all sides.

Caroline turned her cheek to her daughter's fur hood. Mary's candied breath pricked her nose with sharp, sweet notes. It was a summer scent, thick as the last sip from a pitcher of lemonade. First her mouth and then her eyes watered with the memory of that taste.

If Charles saw her striving to keep hold of herself, she did not know it. She only heard him chirrup to the team and felt the horses leaning into the harnesses.

The wheels grated, then skidded in place. Caroline jerked her head up in time to see Laura grab hold of Charles's shoulder to keep from pitching to the floor.

"Sit down, Laura," Charles said, and snapped the reins. The traces went rigid, but the horses' energy seemed to reach no further than the wagon tongue.

"Calkins must not be sharp enough," he muttered as their hooves licked at the ice. "Didn't expect we'd need to stud their shoes for one crossing."

Mary twisted around. "Nettie's all alone."

Caroline held her fast. "Nettie is as safe as we are," she said, but she heard no comfort in her words. Loosening her grip, Caroline shifted Mary across her lap and motioned Laura in. She wanted them near, but not so close against her that her own unease would touch them. She threaded her arms loosely around their waists, ready to snatch them close if need be, and let her nervous hands smooth their wraps. "Now let's all be still so Pa can drive."

Charles's mouth was folded so deeply with consternation that the whiskers beneath his lower lip bristled

outward. He slackened the horses' lines so that all
their effort would travel straight into the singletree.
The strain stood out on the animals' necks as their legs
slanted under them. Watching them, Caroline felt her
own sides clench.

"What's wrong with the horses?" Laura asked. "Is
the wagon too full?"

"Ben and Beth are strong enough to pull us across,"
Caroline assured her, "once they find their footing." It
was the strength of the ice that worried her, with the
two horses prying forward like great muscled levers.
Beth snorted and stamped a hoof. Caroline winced at
the impact. They were a mile from either shore.

No matter how strong the road might be, the ice
would be at its thinnest here in the middle of the lake. It
was one thing to pass steadily across the surface—quite
another to linger prodding at this frailest point. Could
not a deft stroke, like the blows she delivered to the
rain barrel's thick winter skin, open a split down the
center?

Caroline looked over the girls in their hoods and
mittens and flannels. Together they were lighter than a
single sack of flour, but the drag of so much sodden
clothing would carry them straight under if the wagon
broke through. Her eyes traced the cinched canvas

brow overhead. They were hardly better off than kittens in a gunny sack.

If the wagon did not budge in the time it took to pray Psalm 121, Caroline decided, she would lift the girls down and lead them across on foot. Even if she had to carry Laura, the three of them could slip over the mile of ice light as mayflies, leaving the team's burden nearly two hundred pounds the lighter.

Caroline prayed, and still the wheels had not moved. Nor could she. The psalm had given her imagination time to extend beyond the relief of reaching solid ground—to turning, safely hand in hand, to face Charles stranded on the lake behind them. What could she do for him or their daughters, clutching their small mittens on the opposite bank of the Mississippi, if the wagon rolled forward and the ice opened—

With a rasp, one metal horseshoe bit into the surface. Caroline held her breath for the collapse. Instead, a muscled jolt inched the wagon ahead. She felt herself leaning toward the team, as if her own scant momentum could coax them forward.

Once more the iron tires crackled over the ice, this time the sound as welcome as the snap of a tinderbox. Laura clapped her hands and cheered the horses until the wagon slanted up onto the Minnesota bank. Mary slipped out of Caroline's lap and burrowed under the spring seat to scoop up Nettie. "I won't leave you alone again," Caroline heard her promise the doll.

"Those horseshoes make pretty good ice skates," Charles proclaimed, "but I don't believe I'd like to have a pair nailed to my feet." Mary and Laura giggled. They could not hear the chagrin behind the boom in his voice. He would not say it had been his fault for stopping the wagon, but Caroline knew he would not be dousing such a situation with a joke unless he'd felt a scorch of responsibility.

"Go on with Mary," Caroline said, nudging Laura over the seat. Cold air rushed silently in and out of her chest. She was shaking, now that it was over. Relief saturated her, yet there was no lightness in it. Instead she was salted down with regret that she should be so thankful to put Wisconsin behind them.

"Good thing Ben and Beth pulled through," Charles said, cheerful again. Caroline had not gained enough control over her breath to groan at his pun. "Would have been a job to portage all this equipment across on foot."

Something in his voice slipped between her tremors and turned her head. "Charles?" she asked.

He cocked a smile at her, mouth half–turned up.

One look at him and Caroline did not need to ask

whether he'd thought about the ice. Not a wisp of fear so much as brushed his whiskers.

Perhaps the threat she'd felt had only been another queer spell, like she'd had in the store. It was as though a single droplet of any one sensation had the power to soak her through. The notion left her lightheaded, as if she had no traction on the world. Caroline pulled her shawl across the points of her shoulders and elbows, wishing for a sturdier veneer.

Charles's brow had begun to furrow. He was still waiting for her to speak. "We should make camp soon," she said, "if supper is to be ready before dark."

"The Richardses said there'd be a place along the shore just north of the crossing," he said. "Little spot the lumber men use in season. It's out of the way a mile or so, but I figure you and the girls would rather spend our first night out under a roof instead of around a campfire."

A house. The very thought lifted Caroline's cheeks and smoothed her forehead. "Yes, Charles," she said. "In weather like this it will be a mercy to have one more night of shelter."

Five

It was a bunkhouse, with beds lining the walls like shelves. Dry kindling by the hearth, a stubbled broom. Nothing more.

"Looks like you won't have to cook out tonight, Caroline," Charles said.

Caroline's lips smiled, but her cheeks did not follow. Already she felt herself shrinking from the starkness confronting her. The wagon was cramped and chill, but compared to this empty room it was intensely their own.

Mary snugged Nettie into the fold of her elbow. "It isn't very nice inside," she ventured.

"It will keep us warm and dry," Caroline said, speaking as much to herself as to Mary, "and that is plenty to be thankful for." She eyed the narrow bunks.

"I'll bring the big straw tick in for you and the girls," Charles said. "Best if I sleep out with the wagon and team."

She could not allow herself to consider how it might feel to sleep in this place without him—not if she was to get supper before dark. Caroline swallowed twice to spread the muscles in her throat. "And the two crates of kitchen things, please, Charles."

First he brought her two pails of snow and an arm-load of weathered-looking firewood from the pile outside the door—mostly pine, with some maple mixed in. She set the hardwood aside and laid a modest cook-fire with the rest. The flames blazed up merrily, the warmth burnishing her cheeks.

"We will need more hardwood to bank the fire for the night," Caroline said when he came in with the crates. "The pine hasn't enough pitch left to burn through until morning." She hated to ask him after all he had done this day, but already the dry pine was burning too hot and fast to trust with a pan of cornbread. Charles only nodded and buttoned up his overcoat.

With her own things in her hands, Caroline warmed to her tasks. She melted a kettle full of snow to a simmer and dropped in as much salt as she could pinch between her thumb and the curl of her first finger. The evening had the thin sort of chill that made her hunger for a pot of bean soup. Instead, hasty pudding would have to do.

She had hardly pulled her wooden spoon from the crate before the girls came rushing to help. Caroline met Laura with the broom and set Mary to straightening up the straw tick. Before long they were whinnying in circles around the bed, the broom held between them as though they were a team of ponies. Caroline let them run—they were restive from travel, and hasty pudding would demand more attention than she could share out if she were not to burn their supper.

The bag of cornmeal was chilled to the core. After the texture of the road, Caroline welcomed the even grit sifting through her fingers. Her hands moved in tandem, one sprinkling, one stirring. As the grains melded with the salted water, a sweet, starchy scent reached upward. Sometimes she crouched and sometimes she bent over the kettle, easing the long sinews in her back and calves by turns while the spoon droned its low swirling song against the iron kettle. Slowly the room behind her began to warm, as slowly Mary and Laura's play wound down into the rhythm of her stirring.

Caroline's hands were thankful for the movement, and her mind content with the stillness of hovering over the bubbling pot. If a thought began to stray back across Lake Pepin or ahead to the night to come, her tempo faltered and the hasty pudding bubbled and whined, calling her mind to attention.

By the time Charles came in with the carpetbag and another pail of snow, she had lost her misgivings to the kettle's eddies. The chamber pail was clamped under his arm. He set everything on the hearth to warm and squatted alongside her, tilting his palms to the fire. "Smells fine," he said.

Caroline smiled. "It's nearly ready."

"Ma?" Mary asked. "There's no table."

"That's because we're camping now," Charles said. "Come and get your plates, girls, and I'll show you how it's done." Charles paused, hooked his finger through the loop of Mother Ingalls's jug and lifted it from the box of tin dishes. "What's this?"

"Maple syrup," Caroline said. "Your mother brought it. To eat or trade, she said . . ." She trailed off. His palm was circling the jug's belly.

"Isn't that just like Ma," Charles mused. His whiskers met over his crimped lips, and Caroline saw the clutch of his throat. He opened his mouth and drew a breath, holding it for a moment. "Nothing like maple syrup on hot hasty pudding," he said to Mary and Laura, and pried the cork loose. It was foolish with the sugar maples of Wisconsin still nearly in sight, but the day had been sharp in so many ways that Caroline could not refuse the sweetness.

They ate from their laps, hunched along the edges of two bunks. Caroline savored the feel of the hasty pudding tracing a soothing line down her center. Its warmth gathered steadily in her belly, then seeped outward to press the chill from her skin.

They did not talk, tired as they were and spread along the wall with nothing but the empty room before them. Caroline tried to imagine how it would look with a man sleeping on every shelf. The place would be little better than a pantry stocked with lumberjacks.

Darkness sank down around them before they finished. Laura waited without a fuss for her turn for a drink, only to open her mouth and yawn mightily into the tin cup when Mary passed it to her.

"It's bedtime for little girls," Caroline said. Her own eyelids were thick at the rims, her shoulders grainy with fatigue.

Their nightgowns were still cold red bundles in the carpetbag. Caroline draped them over the broomstick handle and propped it before the fire like a fishing pole. She had Laura's shoes off and her dress half unbuttoned before Mary said, "I need the necessary,

Ma." Caroline nodded toward the chamber pail at the edge of the hearth. Mary shook her head. "The necessary."

Caroline pinched off a breath. A ring of exasperation burned below it, but it was her own fault. She had not thought to ask before undressing them. "Go and get your wraps, then, and Laura's," she said, walking her fingers back up the row of buttons.

Charles pocketed a pair of matches and put on his overcoat. "I'll light a lantern in front of the outhouse door," he said, and left them to bundle into their mittens and hoods.

Caroline went down on her knees to help Laura thread her toes into her shoes. "Ma," Mary said again, this time with a keener edge. Caroline looked up, primed to urge patience, and saw the grimace on her face.

"All right, Mary," Caroline said. She hoisted Laura to her hip stocking-footed and slung her shawl across the both of them while Mary scurried to open the door.

The necessary was a four-holer, clean enough, but scaled for grown men. Laura and Mary both sat leaning forward with their palms braced against the plank seat, as though they were afraid they might tumble down the latrine pit if they let go. Neither could they reach the strips of newsprint dangling from a quartet of bent sixtypenny nails on the facing wall. They waited for Caroline to finish her own business and hand them their paper.

Laura melted like a rag doll into Caroline's chest as Caroline fastened Laura's drawers and lifted her from the wooden bench. She blanketed Laura with the shawl and rested her cheek against Laura's forehead.

Outside, the glow of the two bunkhouse windows pointed their way back down the path. The little room had warmed since they first walked through the door, and Caroline found that she had warmed toward it as well. There were the girls' nightgowns toasting nicely by the fire and the smell of hasty pudding to welcome them. Caroline hummed a low-swaying air as she helped Mary and Laura into their nightclothes, for she did not trust her lips with the words:

Wi' mony a vow and lock'd embrace,
Our parting was fu' tender,
And pledging aft to meet again,
We tore oursels asunder.

She had just settled them under the covers when Charles brought in the fiddle box. Laura's drowsy eyes sparkled awake at the sight of it.

"Not tonight, Half-Pint," Charles said. "I'm tuckered out. But you and Mary can keep the fiddle warm for me all night, can't you?" he asked as he snugged the case under the corner of the straw tick at their feet.

"Yes, Pa," they said solemnly. Charles glanced up at Caroline. She needed no explanation. It was not the fiddle he wanted shelter for, but the box itself. She had seen him tuck the remainder of their cash—just over $138 by her figures—beneath its green felt lining.

"Don't you be plucking the strings with your toes," he teased, and ruffled their hair goodnight.

While the girls cuddled down to sleep, Caroline smoothed the leftover hasty pudding into a bread pan and covered it with a dishcloth to set up overnight. For breakfast there would be the fried mush, and bacon; the rest of the cold white bread and molasses would serve for next day's dinner.

Crouching by the hearth, she heated water in the dishpan and wiped the dishes clean. Into the kettle she quietly ladled a half dozen scoops of dry beans, then covered them with snowmelt and put the mixture to the back of the fireplace to soak.

She was unpinning her hair when Charles came in to pocket the two flatirons she had laid on the hearth to warm for him. "Asleep already?" he whispered, pointing with his whiskers toward the girls.

Caroline nodded.

"Good. Come on outside. I want you to learn how to load that Colt."

A wrinkle traveled up her spine. Caroline gave herself a moment to mute the sensation against her shawl, then followed him out.

The wooden box lay open beside a lantern on the wagon tongue. Compartments lined with red felt surrounded the revolver and its accoutrements. "It's an 1860 army issue—the same as your brother Joseph would have carried at Shiloh," Charles told her, as though she might be afraid of it. She was not frightened of the thing itself; she was only afraid of needing it.

"It's not so much different from the rifle. Tip the powder flask to measure out a charge, then pour the powder into the open chamber on the right. Drop a bullet in on top. No patch cloth. Last comes the cap." He pinched a bit of brass shaped like a tiny dented button from a tin with a green paper label. "This fits over the percussion nipple at the back of the chamber. Now watch." Charles pulled the hammer to half cock and twisted the cylinder so that the loaded chamber rested above the trigger. Then as if husking an ear of corn, he pried a lever loose from the underside of the barrel and bent it back until it clicked. "This tamps down the loaded charge in place of a ramrod," he said. "And that's all there is to it."

Charles let the hammer down softly before handing her the pistol. Caroline stripped off her mittens and tucked them under one arm. The revolver was cold in the places he had not touched, and heavy as the family Bible. "Go ahead," Charles said.

She could not push the latch of the loading lever straight down as Charles had done; it bit into the tips of her fingers until she rotated her grip and pulled it free of the catch from below. "That's fine," Charles said when she finished. "You'll need two hands to fire it—hold your arms out straight ahead and lace your fingers around the stock, the way you do to pray." Caroline's tongue rose to object to the juxtaposition, then halted. If ever she had cause to fire this gun, there would indeed be a prayer behind it.

"That's right," Charles said, "steady and even, just like that. We'll only keep five of the chambers loaded with caps while we're traveling. Safer that way. Just remember to twist a loaded chamber up to the barrel as you cock it."

Caroline cupped her elbows beneath her shawl as he packed the pistol away again and climbed up over the sideboards. "It'll ride up here, under the seat," Charles said. "I'll still use the rifle for hunting. With any luck that's the last time we'll need to open the box." He sat facing her with his hands laced between his knees.

She handed him the lantern. In the instant before he blew it out, the glow framed him in a halo of canvas. Firelight from the bunkhouse windows dusted over them. "Will you be warm enough?" she asked.

He patted his coat pockets. "Be snug as a tent in here with the canvas cinched down at both ends and these flatirons all to myself." His eyes slid down the curving length of her braid. Caroline felt the pinking of her cheeks and lifted her shawl over her head. She could not let him put his hands to her hair. There was neither time nor place for what would surely follow.

"The bundle of extra quilts is at the foot of the small straw tick," she told him. Still his eyes rested on her, asking her to do no more than fill his gaze. He could make her feel full as the moon, looking at her that way, and she was too tired to allow herself to melt into it. Filaments of heat were already drifting along her edges.

Caroline rustled her voice softly between them. "Charles."

"Hmm?"

"Will you reach the scrap bag for me, please?" she asked, snipping the moment short.

He got to his knees on the spring seat, leaning so far to reach the bag on its peg that he ought to have pitched over. It was thick through the middle and nearly as tall as Laura. Caroline shifted the bundle to her hip and reached one hand up to the lip of the wagon box. He took her hand in his, kneading her palm with his thumb. "Call if you or the girls need for anything," he said. "I'll be sleeping with one ear open."

Her smile crept into the dark. "Rest yourself, Charles." She felt the brush of his whiskers against her fingertips before he floated her hand back down to her. The wisp of movement carried her back to the bunkhouse without another murmur.

The girls did not stir at the clack of the latch. Mary lay with her rag doll up under her chin, her arms folded close as hens' wings around her calico darling. Caroline let her shawl back down to her shoulders and carried the scrap bag to the bunk nearest the hearth. Loosening the drawstring, she unfurled the bag into her lap. It was not a sack, but rather a circle of denim that would spread itself flat with the cord fully unlaced. Seven deep pockets, each holding one color, pinwheeled from a center humped with plain cuttings of flannel, buckram, and the like. Caroline chose two remnants of muslin to veil the windows, then felt her way into the pocket of browns until she found a swatch of felt, small and nearly triangular. A few nips with the scissors would turn it into a shawl for Nettie. She laid it on a bunk with their wraps, then bolstered the fire with slim maple logs before finally undressing.

She found herself standing before the hearth in the place where her rocking chair would be, were this their own fireplace. Without it she was not sure how to settle the day's many layers into herself. She turned to the straw tick, hunkered on the floor like a patchwork raft. The coverlet puffed softly up and down over Mary and Laura. Caroline watched them as she had that morning. Their tempo was so like a hymn, a strand of scripture encircled her.

> Cast me not away from thy presence; and take not
>   thy Holy Spirit from me.

With all that the day's travel had wrought, and all that the days still to come would bring, she had never felt so keenly beholden to the Lord's mercy. Caroline knelt where she stood. Her chin tipped down to meet her folded hands.

No prayer came to her. Eyes closed, she wavered like a solitary taper until in place of her own words of praise or supplication, a fragment of the 24th Psalm rose through her voice.

Who shall ascend into the hill of the Lord? Or
  who shall stand in his holy place?
He that hath clean hands, and a pure heart; who
  hath not lifted up his soul unto vanity, nor
  sworn deceitfully.
He shall receive the blessing from the Lord . . .

Caroline's brow furrowed and her heart pressed forward as she pledged the words into her clasped hands. It had not the usual shape of a prayer, but it was no less binding; she would do all that she could to keep her family within the sight of Providence.

The straw tick whispered around her as it always did, raising tufts of fragrance as she shifted into place beside Mary and Laura. In the anonymous room, the bedding smelled more of home than the cabin itself had. Traces of kerosene and rosemary mingled with something so familiar Caroline could not name it. Caroline wondered if it was the girls themselves. She had not slept alongside either of her daughters since Laura was weaned, yet their nearness saturated her with comfort.

Her hands slipped under the covers and met at the low mound of her navel. Soft creaks and burbles turned beneath them, as though her supper still simmered there. No swish or flutter. Perhaps, if she could not yet feel the small creature inside, she need not worry over whether it was sensible to the jostling wagon or the flood tides of her emotions. Within its cushion of waters, perhaps it felt nothing at all. Caroline shut her eyes and imagined herself enveloped in such a warm and fluid cradle—every sound and movement diluted, graceful. If she could not shelter herself from this journey's vagaries, there was some satisfaction at least in knowing she was a shield for the budding child. Beside her, the rise and fall of her daughters' breaths led her gently toward sleep.

A sound like the crack of gunfire shot through Caroline's consciousness. Motionless in the vibrating air, Caroline groped with her senses for her bearings. Nothing fit. The ceiling above her was peaked rather than flat, the bed too near the floor.

The tiny muscles along her ears strained into the silence. Only the dwindling embers whispered to themselves. No voices. Not a whicker from the horses; no movement behind her makeshift curtains.

Another shot brought her to her elbows. The sound seemed to cleave the air. It stretched too long and deep for the pop of a bullet, yet she could make room in her mind for nothing else. Caroline sat up and patted her hands across the straw tick, searching for the fiddle box.

"Charles?" she called in a whisper. Beside her, Laura stirred.

The latch rattled. Caroline froze. Bolts of alarm unrolled into her thighs and down the backs of her arms.

The door seemed to peel open. "It's the ice cracking on the lake," Charles's voice said. Thankfulness loosened her so thoroughly, she could do nothing but spread herself back over the mattress. Charles came to the hearth and nudged another length of hardwood into the fire behind her.

"Are you warm enough?" she asked.

With a creak of leather, he squatted down and leaned over to kiss her, whiskers softly caressing her skin. "That'll help," he said. He stood and went out, easing the door shut behind him.

Caroline laid her forearms across her ribs. Each crack of the ice scored a cold line across the hollow places in her body, like a blade that would not cut. The sharpness of the sound almost tickled down in her depths.

At the next report, Laura gasped. Caroline rolled to her shoulder. Laura's eyes were casting about the room, desperate to light on something she recognized. Caroline leaned into her view. Their gazes met, and Caroline saw her daughter's face curve with comfort. A pool of warmth opened behind Caroline's heart as she watched. She glided her fingertips over the peak of Laura's cheek. The baby roundness that had faded from Mary's face still lingered in Laura's.

"Go to sleep," Caroline soothed. "It's only the ice breaking up." Laura held fast to Caroline's gaze until another crack snapped her eyes shut. Caroline cupped her palm over Laura's ear, stroking the little girl's temple with her thumb. Laura smiled drowsily.

There is a happy land, far, far away, Caroline hummed. Her teeth clenched with the effort of holding back a quiver from her chin. They had traveled hardly ten miles from home, but in a heartbeat the breaking of the ice had driven a wedge a week wide into the distance back to their own little cabin.

Under her fingers, Laura's pulse had slowly quieted into a beat of feathery kisses. Caroline drew up her knees, making a nest of herself. Laura was too big now to fit inside it as she once had, but her breath, still tinted with maple sugar, filled the small spaces between them.

Six

By morning, Caroline's hip and shoulder could feel the floor through the straw tick. Soreness warmed the backs of her thighs when she rose. She rubbed the heels of her hands down the muscles along her backbone and winced. There was only so much she could blame on the spring seat. The rest was her body retaliating for being kept so tightly clenched the day before. Caroline closed her eyes and released as much of the lingering tension as she was able. Today there would be no more goodbyes, she reminded herself, no reason to hold herself so rigid. Today they could go cleanly forward.

To her hands, the morning was hardly distinguishable from any other. Caroline dressed and washed, laid the girls' clothes to warm before the fire, put fresh water over the beans, and swung the kettle into the heart of the fire. She fried up a dozen strips of bacon, then laid four thick slices of chilled mush into the drippings. The edges crisped like cracklings in the grease.

Charles came whistling in to his breakfast, as he so often did. His tune tickled her. A perfect match to the day, as usual. "Wait for the wagon! Wait for the wagon! Wait for the wagon and we'll all take a ride!" he sang for Mary and Laura.

His cheeks gleamed from the cold, and their eyes were bright with excitement. In the pan the fat popped and sizzled merrily around their breakfast. The whole morning was beginning to shine.

"Wouldn't wonder if the ice broke up today," Charles said to Caroline. He doused his mush with syrup. "We made a late crossing. Lucky it didn't start breaking up while we were out in the middle of it."

Caroline opened her mouth and then closed it. Had it truly come to him only now? She could not help herself. "I thought about that yesterday, Charles," she said quietly.

He looked at her as though he had spotted her lathering her chin with his shaving brush. Not angry, only puzzled by what earthly use she might have for such an idea.

Laura's fork had stopped moving. A long bead of

syrup trickled down her chin and onto her plate. Caroline could see the terrible picture widening behind her eyes as Charles's words sank in. "You're frightening somebody, Charles," she murmured.

He hugged Laura up against his side. "We're across the Mississippi!" he sang out as though they had just now stepped from the ice. "How do you like that, little half-pint of sweet cider half drunk up? Do you like going out west where Indians live?"

Caroline winced. Why must he stoke Laura's eagerness so? The child would be smoking with curiosity by the time they reached the Territory. If the western tribes were as bold as Concord's Potawatomis, such eagerness would not bode well. A brush or two with the Chippewas might have nipped Laura's appetite in the bud, but their cabin had been mercifully free of Indian intruders.

"Yes, Pa!" Laura chimed. "Are we in Indian country now?"

Caroline steered the conversation with a low, steady voice. "'Indian country' is a long, long way off. We must drive across Minnesota, and Iowa, and Missouri first," she said, making the names sound long and foreign. "It will be spring before we see the Kansas line."

"Oh." Laura ducked her head and poked at her

mush. She looked embarrassed, as though she had done something wrong but did not understand what. Caroline's appetite faltered. She had not meant to subdue Laura quite so thoroughly. Caroline dismissed her schoolmarm tone and tried again. "The sooner we all finish our breakfast," she coaxed, "the sooner we will be in Kansas."

Caroline checked over the room one last time. Nothing showed that they had been there except for the neatly swept floorboards and a few lengths of leftover maple added to the kindling pile. She opened the door to go.

Outside, the air was poised on the edge of freezing— moist, as though the lake had spent the night exhaling through the cracked ice. Charles's voice boomed out to greet them:

> *Where the river runs like silver, and the birds they*
> * sing so sweet,*
> *I have a cabin, Phyllis, and something good to eat.*
> *Come listen to my story, it will relieve my heart.*
> *So jump into the wagon, and off we will start.*

Laura let go of Caroline's hand and ran ahead to be swung up into the wagon box. Mary waited while Caroline carefully latched the bunkhouse door.

"I don't like riding in the wagon very much, Ma," she said. "Can't we stay and make this house pretty?"

Caroline held out her hand. "Pa will build us a pretty new house in Kansas."

Mary lingered. She seemed anxious, as though she did not like the feel of disobeying yet could not bring herself to move. Caroline reached into her pocket for the little triangle of brown felt. "See what I've found for Nettie to wear? A traveling shawl."

Caroline helped Mary wrap the fabric over the doll's shoulders and lap its ends together. "Nettie says thank you," Mary said. A flush framed her polite smile, as though she were suddenly feverish. "Ma?"

Caroline squatted down and touched her forehead. No warmer than a blush, but Caroline knew something was wrong. Mary had not resisted like this in leaving their own cabin behind. "What is it, Mary?"

Mary did not look at her. Her whisper steamed out in a hot, high-pitched little wail. "Nettie doesn't like crossing lakes."

What a splash of relief. Caroline smiled. "You tell Nettie she has nothing to worry about. There are no more lakes to cross." Mary took her hand and squeezed. A soft little squeeze, yet the depth of reassurance it contained watered Caroline's eyes. Caroline gave a gentle press back and together they walked to the wagon.

"See Nettie's new traveling shawl, Pa?" Mary said. "Ma made it."

"Finest traveling shawl I ever saw," Charles said, and hoisted Mary over the sideboards. *Traveling shawl?* he mouthed to Caroline.

She felt her cheeks dimple and put a mittened finger to her lips.

Four o'clock? Or maybe half past, Caroline guessed by the thinning of the light between the evergreens. The way her breasts throbbed made her wish it were later. They were always tender at this stage, but this feeling was something altogether different.

This morning she had left the top two hooks of her busk unfastened, as she sometimes did at home, to spare her breasts the pressure. By midday Caroline had promised herself she would not make that mistake again. Each frozen rut, each icy mudhole that shattered under the wagon's weight sent an unwelcome burst of heat juddering through them. The daylong embrace of her corset would have been so much the better. For the last hour or more she had sat with her arms folded tight beneath her breasts, bracing against the jolts.

"How far have we come today?" she asked.

"Oh, fifteen, sixteen miles," Charles said.

It did not seem far enough, when the day before they

had managed ten and all that time at the store besides. But Caroline was tired and sore, and with supper yet to fix. Her stomach was just beginning to scratch at itself. "It will take better than an hour to lay a fire and finish the beans," she said.

"Whoa there," Charles called to the team.

The wagon jerked to a halt. Caroline winced. Everything was instantly quiet. Behind her the girls' heads popped up like two rabbits peeking from their burrow.

"In that case, we'll camp right this minute." Charles scanned the roadside and shrugged. "It's as likely a place as any. There's enough snow, we won't want for water no matter where we stop." He turned to Mary and Laura. Their mittens made a dotted line across the back of the spring seat. "Unless you girls think we should keep on?"

"No, Pa!"

Every step across the board floor made Caroline's numbed toes feel bigger than her shoes. Corners of crates and boxes poked into the aisle, catching at her skirts as she brushed past. Most all of her neat stacks had jiggled into raggedy looking piles.

Caroline did not stop to set them right. She went straight for the kitchen crates and fished out one spongy wedge of dried apple from the sack. The water in her mouth began devouring it before her teeth had bitten it through.

Outside, Charles cleared a place for the fire and hammered the irons into the ground on either side. While he laid the sticks Mary and Laura brought him, Caroline strung the crosspiece and chain for the kettle.

It was an unruly little fire that flashed hot as sunburn on her face and hands, and no further. Her apron was warm to the touch when she tucked her skirt between her knees to stir the beans, but the heat did not penetrate. Everything from her earlobes back was left chill and clammy.

Caroline circled her spoon through the mass of warming beans. The way some of them struck the wood made her wonder if she had waited too long to stop for supper. They had soaked all night and all day, with a parboiling at breakfast and another at noon, and still they were not soft. Some had not even split their skins. Caroline reached for another stick of wood, then changed her mind. The flames already stroked the bottom of the kettle. It was not the fire's fault, then—it was her own. She had not accounted for how much heat the open air would steal away.

Caroline listened to the bite of Charles's shovel as he dug the latrine pit and pinched her lip between her teeth. He would be hungry after so much hacking at the half-frozen earth, and there was nothing she could do to hurry the beans without burning them.

Charles stowed his shovel in the wagon, lifted the spring seat loose, and set it down before the fire. It stood no higher than a step stool. Caroline made a little show of scraping the edges of the pot rather than sitting. The last thing she wanted were those boards across her back and thighs again.

Charles sat down with a little bounce. His knees sloped up higher than his hips, so he stretched out his legs and propped the heels of his boots—one, two—in the snow. He inhaled deeply and smiled. He would not rush her with words, but she knew he was hungry and waiting. Her own stomach had worn through the apple slice.

She spooned up three beans and tasted them. None were quite done. One, the largest, was firm in the center like a fresh pea. She glanced up over the edge of the spoon. They were watching her, eager for a verdict.

Caroline wavered. In the oven or on the hearth a bean like that might give up its bone in half an hour. Out in the open with unseasoned pitch pine, there was no telling how much longer. It was either tantalize them with guesses or serve almost-done beans now. Neither prospect suited her, but eating now would be less a hardship than waiting for a meal that might not improve with time. She swirled a drizzle of molasses into the pot, then dished up four platefuls.

They ate with thoughtful-looking faces, trying to keep their chewing inconspicuous. Charles handed over his plate without asking for a second helping. "That was a good hot supper," he said.

Caroline flushed. He meant it—Charles always meant exactly what he said—but if she parsed that sentence on a blackboard, *good* would connect to *hot* and no further. It was not quite a bad meal, but they ought to have had better—a meal with more virtues than its temperature. She would rather do without any praise at all than be complimented for not failing completely.

She scrubbed the dishes clean with hard fistfuls of snow, thinking of her stove. Her stove, with its four round lids and good steady oven. Beside it, the neat stack of dry seasoned stove lengths. Every bean she baked in it came out a soft nugget of velvet. Caroline smiled a little at herself. It felt good to miss that stove, good as a long hard stretch. That was one thing she could let herself miss. It did not sting like other, dearer things.

Charles closed down both ends of the canvas tight as knotholes.

The wagon had a new odor with all of them sealed inside it: the moist, vinegary musk of skin encased all day long in woolen wrappings, their sweat chilled and thawed and now chilling again. And Charles had hung the new poncho up on a hook alongside his rifle. It added a dry, rubbery tang.

Mary and Laura watched Charles roll up the small straw tick from the pile of bedding and push it onto the floor at the front of the wagon.

"Where do we sleep, Ma?" Laura asked.

"Right down here," Charles said, "where the spring seat was. Just like the trundle bed."

The space was narrow, even for the small tick. Its edges curled against the sides of the wagon box and made a little nest of it. Their two pillows bunched together where the sides met in the center.

Caroline nestled one hot flatiron in each corner to warm the foot of the small bed while the girls stood on the big straw tick to be undressed. She worked their red flannel nightgowns quickly down over their red flannel underthings and tied their nightcaps fast under their chins.

First Mary, then Laura hopped down into the nest of straw. Both of them grinned through chattering teeth at the novelty.

"Snuggle up close, now." They scooted together. Caroline laid two quilts over them. The third she tucked down in between the sideboards and the ticking, crimping the edges tight as a pie crust around her daughters.

Mary and Laura shivered gratefully under the stack of chilled blankets. Caroline watched them, so tired yet so clenched with cold that they fought to rest. She remembered how easily they had all settled down to sleep, warm and drowsy in the light of the cozy little bunkhouse fire the night before, and her breath hitched.

Suddenly it was not safe to look even that far back. Only forward. On the spring seat it had been simple. All day long she sat with the road reaching ahead and thought herself steadily forward. Toward the vague, bright notions of spring, the new land, the new house, the new child. Now there was nothing but the long still night before her, nothing to cast her thoughts onto but a blank wall of canvas as near as her toes.

No, it would be closer yet than that, Caroline saw as she and Charles undressed. Their own straw tick was longer than the wagon box was wide. A foot or more of it was folded under itself at one end. Unless he lay diagonally across the middle of the mattress, Charles must sleep with his knees kinked. Caroline was not sure she could stretch herself full.

She crawled across to the side nearest the girls and tried to crimp herself into something like a triangle to leave all the room she could for Charles. Mercy, it was cold. Cold filled every hollow straw beneath her. Her feet wanted to reach down for the hot flatiron she knew was somewhere beyond the icy stretch of muslin, but her body resisted and pulled her limbs in close to guard its own warmth. She would have liked to burrow into Mary and Laura's little den, with her knees drawn up and the sides hugging her all around.

Charles lifted the quilts and a fresh rush of cold slipped in with him. He climbed quickly in beside her, closing the seam between them—his knees pointing into hers, her seat in his lap, his chin peaking at the crown of her head. The cold from his nightshirt rattled a shiver through her back. He slipped his arm under hers, settling his fist over her heart.

The gentle pressure of his hand melted her as though she were made of wax. One tear and then another burned across the bridge of her nose. She had kept her sadness so carefully lidded these last two days that it had thickened into a stock so rich she could smell the salt before she tasted it. Caroline's throat narrowed so she could scarcely draw breath. Only a long thin note, too high to hear, seeped steadily through to warm the roof of her mouth.

———————

In the morning, a thin frost rimmed the underside of the wagon cover—their breath, adhered to the canvas.

Caroline's nightdress had climbed past her stockings, leaving her kneecaps bald to the chill even under the quilts. Charles's space beside her was empty; she could hear kindling just beginning to snap to life outside. She leaned to peek at Mary and Laura, trying not to stray outside the warm outline her body had made in the straw. Only the white crowns of their nightcaps were visible.

Caroline's breath hissed out in a pale cloud as she laced her corset. It was likely only her imagination, but it seemed she could feel the frigid lines of the steels through the heavy cotton drill. Her body warmed her dress, and not the other way around—that she did not imagine. She gathered Mary's and Laura's clothes and put them under her quilts. Perhaps the little heat she had left behind would warm them.

A rind of ice topped the water in the washbasin. Caroline broke it with the handle of her toothbrush. Charles came in just then with a pail of water steaming softly in his hand.

"Morning," he said, and, "here," as he poured the warm water into the basin. Caroline stood over it, not moving. The moist steam on her cheeks was heavenly.

"Are you all right?" Charles asked.

Caroline's toothbrush quivered with one last shiver as she nodded.

"Are you sure?"

Her reflection in the water showed a nose already pinking from the chill—as though she'd been crying. Caroline smiled and dabbed it with her handkerchief. "It's only the cold."

He did not believe it was only the cold when she fled from the pan full of bacon to retch into the snow. But it was. Nearly. If she had not been so hungry for warmth, she might have realized the fire was too hot, that their breakfast was indeed burning. Never mind that she had been too—what? Stubborn? Proud?—to heed the better judgment of her own body.

Her nose had caught the first whiff of something barely beginning to scorch, and quicker than quick she flipped the meat. Every strip turned up pink as Laura's hair ribbons against the black iron. Caroline stood over the pan with the fork in her hand, scoffing at her over-active senses. Why it was that a child in the belly turned a woman's nose into a veritable magnifying glass, she would never understand. *They that dance must pay the fiddler,* she reminded herself.

That was all the time it took for the drippings beneath a twist of bacon to singe in earnest. Caroline's nostrils flared in warning at the rising scent, but it was too late. All at once her gut rippled and her jaw watered, and still she held her ground. She would not be sick, she insisted to herself, any more than she would serve Charles and the girls two poor meals in succession. Caroline thrust the bacon to the edges of the iron spider and tried to whisk the burnt drippings apart with the tines of the fork until a wave of heaves bent her double. By the time she finished, the pan was smoking.

"It was the cold," she made excuse before Charles could ask. "I might have noticed in time if not for the cold."

Even through her watery eyes she could see the dubious cast of his face, but Charles did not argue. He handed her his handkerchief and leafed backward through his weather journal. "Another week or two at most and these temperatures'll be behind us," he promised.

Seven

A week, Caroline soon concluded, is too cumbersome a thing to count—or to be counted on. Even an hour was a deceitful measure. An hour might thin itself over three or four miles of level roads or be filled to bulging by one scant mile of sandy incline. An elusive ford or a single mudhole placed just so could swallow a whole string of hours right from the middle of a day. Time, Caroline decided, could be trusted to measure the distance between meals, and nothing else. But a mile was always a mile, no matter how long it took to traverse. Days spent on the road were best measured in miles.

Eighteen one day, just over twenty the next. Now and then a good long stretch of twenty-four, twenty-five miles. On the road a week became plain arithmetic:

a hundred and ten, a hundred and twenty miles, or maybe only ninety-five.

No cycle of washing, mending, and baking marked one day out as distinct from another. Each day formed the same narrow circle; six of them stacked together earned a Sunday. Only the Sabbath, immune to the tally of miles, managed to keep its identity.

Three things governed their moods: the quality of the road, the disposition of the weather, and the supply of fuel and water. Any one out of balance, whether leaning toward good or ill, left a mark in her memory.

First was the morning when the washbasin did not freeze. Her mind preserved other, earlier days, but that morning always stood out of its proper order. The water had been cold enough to sting her teeth, but it was not frozen. Close beside it was the night the knot in the wagon cover came loose, when the girls woke to find their noses and eyelashes sugared with snow.

Most of the meals she made were not worth the space it took to recall them: salt pork in the spider, cornbread in the bake oven. Now and then bacon, a bit of game. Ordinary mainstays that ought to have been simple to prepare. More often, cooking became a standoff between herself and the fire.

One could learn the temperament of a stove or a chimney, with patience and diligence master their most

fractious moods. In the open, each new cookfire announced itself a stranger, and it was a rare one that did
not require cajoling or pampering. Rain meant rigging up tarps and the delay of searching for wood dry
enough to burn. High winds necessitated laying the fire
in a hole and hunching over the pans. When there was
nothing better to burn than weeds, she surrendered the
fight and poured a quick batch of pancakes into the iron
spider, hiding her frustration under a layer of Mother
Ingalls's maple syrup.

Her triumphs were lackluster; nothing, down to
the coffee and tea, tasted quite like her own cooking.
The water in each new place imposed its own flavors:
swampy, sudsy, sulphured, greasy. Anything that did
not fall from the sky carried the faint too-clean tinge of
the powdered alum she used to clarify each day's supply of drinking water. Some bucketfuls held stubbornly
to their dust no matter how carefully she skimmed
the sediment. Dusty water did not matter so much to
the cornbread, but parboiling the salt pork from such
a bucket left a fine dredging of grit behind to grind
between their teeth. More than once Caroline thought
it would be worth backtrailing to Minnesota's frozen
woodlands to fill the ten-gallon keg with pure clean
snow, but even that would be seasoned with brass and
rubber by the time it found its way out of the spigot. At

least—the very least—she did not have to trifle with stove black or empty an ashpan on top of her other struggles.

Every day, while the spring seat squeaked against the wagon bows and Charles fidgeted and whistled beside her, Caroline wrote letters in her mind.

To Henry and Polly she described the lay of the land, its prospects for crops and husbandry, and its yield of game, as though her words might lay a path for them to follow. She wished she could put to paper the queer thrill of driving headlong into spring instead of waiting by the fireside for winter to melt and trickle away from them. The weeks seemed to warp and ripple beneath the wagon wheels. It made for such a pleasant sort of bewilderment.

For Ma and Papa Frederick she saved the news of their smaller travails, for her mother would neither believe nor enjoy a letter without some trouble in it. Things like the pheasant that somehow eluded Charles's good aim, the quick spattering of hail that woke them their first night inside the Iowa line. She left out the occasional roadside grave markers, only hinting at them by mention of the picked-over piles of iron hardware showing the places where abandoned wagons had rotted down to metal skeletons. They passed by enough ox bones leftover from the gold rush days, she mused, to fashion a bushel basket full of crochet hooks, buttons, and the like.

The truest of them went to Eliza. To Eliza she could confess how keenly she felt the want of walls and doors—something solid to partition themselves from the space around them. The arc of canvas left her always penetrable, never fully sheltered from wind, or sun, or temperature. Caroline did not know whether Eliza would understand that, but there was no one else she wanted to try to explain it to. Perhaps Eliza would not even fully understand the elation she had felt over the first good dinner she had fixed. Caroline doubted she could adequately convey it without sounding like a hedonist.

They had camped late that Saturday night along a riverbed, in the shelter of a clump of shagbark hickory. The campsite alone was enough to make her half-giddy: good hardwood and good water in plenty, both within easy reach.

When Caroline went to start breakfast Sunday morning, there was a string of small catfish dangling from the tailgate, and Charles, grinning by the fire. They were lovely little fish, with spotless white bellies, and their pewter backs lustrous in the sunlight. Caroline traced her finger along one smooth whisker.

"Went out before daybreak," Charles said. "I know I shouldn't have, not on the Sabbath, but I tell you Caroline, it didn't feel a bit like work."

Caroline laughed out loud. She could not help it, had not even felt it coming. It was the way those eyes of his twinkled. He looked as though catching those fish had already done him as much good as a full day's rest. They gleamed brighter yet at the quick chime of her laughter. "Sounds like we've both got something to repent for now," he teased.

A blush rouged her cheeks. She felt a girlish impulse to bat playfully at his arm, but they had played too much already. There would be even more to answer for if Mary and Laura caught them behaving this way on a Sunday morning. "Charles Ingalls, you'll be the death of me," she whispered. She lowered her eyes before he could give her that look again, for the one that followed it—the one where his smile crinkled into his whiskers—she never could resist.

At noontime the good hickory coals glowed bright and steady. Outside the campfire ring the temperature hovered on the fringes of fifty degrees. Now and then a bit of breeze, but nothing strong enough to tussle with the fire. Caroline dredged the dozen delicate fillets with white flour and fried them up crisp and golden brown. In a little kettle beside the skillet she stewed some dried apples with brown sugar and cinnamon. The familiar way the fish snapped in the hot lard while the apples bubbled made it nearly like cooking at her own stove again.

No milk or butter, no light bread, pickles, or preserves, and yet the meal had the flavor of a true Sunday dinner. The fish's thin skin crackled and its moist white flesh flaked apart on her tongue. Caroline ate until her belly was more than filled, and still her mouth wanted to keep hold of that fish. *Sinfully good,* Charles had said with a wink.

If she wrote it all down and sealed it in an envelope, Caroline wondered, would the humor keep fresh long enough to reach her sister? She liked to think their heartstrings were so closely interwoven that they might still share such moments in spite of the distance. And yet she could not blot out the worry that the months between the happening and the reading would only stale the story and leave Eliza too shocked to laugh.

How many miles had they come? Less than halfway, and already Caroline had the sense that a separation such as this could put more than miles between folks, could right this minute be working changes she might not be entirely conscious of and might never realize at all unless she and Eliza saw each other again.

Caroline gave her chin a little shake and smoothed

her hands into her lap. Such far-off things did not bear worrying about. Not when there was one fact this journey did not change, one fact that did deserve more than idle concern. But those uneasy thoughts Caroline could imagine committing to paper for no one, not even herself.

When she tried to think of the coming baby, the pictures formed in the back of her mind instead of stretching out before her. She could see herself only in the rocker where she had nursed Mary and Laura, with a hazy-faced bundle in her arms and Black Susan purring at her feet. Out on this widening land there was no frame to hold new scenes of rocking and feeding. Was that the reason the child had still not quickened—because her mind had not made it properly welcome? Or had her body already communicated to her brain that there was no need to imagine such things for this baby? If there were no life in it, Caroline tried to reassure herself, her body would have expelled it by now. Wouldn't it? That was such cold comfort, it made her shudder. The days were so full of jostles and bumps, she told herself, how could anything so small possibly make itself felt? But she had felt both Mary and Laura when they were smaller yet.

Only a little more pressing was the matter of who would help her when it came time to bear this child.

Even a stillborn babe must have hands to catch it. At home she never needed to explain. She had only to ask Charles to run for Polly, and he understood.

Always it had been Polly at the foot of the bed, Polly, with her face so stolid that Caroline could hardly consider quailing at the pain. That was the one thing she could not bring herself to try imagining: a different face looking up from between her knees, different hands reaching where none but Polly's had reached before. Worse yet was the thought of no one at all.

Caroline knew what Charles would look for in land: good running water, timber, and plenty of game. Not one of those daily necessities could be sacrificed for the momentary need of a claim alongside a neighbor with a wife, and so she kept these thoughts to herself as each day made another small stitch in the long gap between them and Kansas.

Nights, she and Charles took to sitting before the fire, talking. Or rather, Charles talked while Caroline concentrated herself on the mending.

"What's that?" Charles asked.

Caroline held a yard of the fabric up before her. Some days before a set of threadbare pillowcases had caught her eye in the scrap bag. In spare moments she had split their side seams and joined them into one long stretch. "A curtain," she answered. "To go under the loft."

"Looks fine. I'll help you hang it in the morning."

Caroline smoothed it thoughtfully across her knees. "I thought I'd blanket stitch the hem in red first."

Charles smiled and gave his head half a shake. "Here," he said. He handed her his mittens. The tops of them hinged backward to uncover a row of finger gussets; when she put them on, only the tips of her fingers were left exposed. He watched her adorn a few inches, then said, "Wherever we are, you'll always contrive to make it look like home."

Caroline's breath caught. For a moment she thought the baby had given a little flutter, but it was only a quick beat of delight at his compliment.

"Thank you, Charles," she said.

He balled his fists into his pockets and tipped his head back to look at the sky. "If I could build a roof so fine and high as that, I'd never want to move again."

Caroline watched the firelight stroke his whiskers. He was a man in love with space. Every mile they traveled seemed to loosen him. How, she wondered, could she learn to find such ease in being wholly untethered?

"Charles, tell me how it will be in Kansas." Like a child asking for a bedtime story. "Not the giant jackrabbits and horizons. Tell me how we'll live this first year."

"Well, I figure we ought to save all the money we can toward preempting our claim. For a quarter section at $1.25 an acre we'll need $200 plus filing fees, and the land office won't take pay in pelts. So I'll hunt and trap this winter and trade furs for a plow and supplies enough to last until Gustafson's payments arrive. Should be plenty of game to see us through until spring. Then I'll plow up a plot for sod potatoes and another for corn. Land won't raise more than that the first season. The next year we'll sow fields of wheat and oats and anything else we want."

"I've brought seeds from our garden," Caroline said, "and Polly's. She sent me with the best from her pickling cucumbers." Those cucumbers would be like a little taste of Polly herself—crisp and sharp with vinegar.

What, Caroline wondered, would make the home folks think of her? When they wanted for music, even the music of laughter, they would pine for Charles, of course. What taste, what sound might make their hearts whisper: "Caroline?" Perhaps no more than a fragment of red cloth in their scrap bags.

Caroline swallowed hard. *Forward,* she coaxed herself. *Not back.* "And the house?"

"The turf's so thick out there, some of the emigrants carve up the sod and use it for bricks. Makes walls a foot thick, easy. Keeps them cool in the summer and warm in the winter, and there's no end of supply."

"Oh, Charles! Not a soddie?" A house of dirt, the walls crumbly and hairy with roots. She shuddered as though one of them had reached out to brush her back.

A glint of consternation, then, "I'll build anything you say."

Caroline regretted the sound of her words as soon as she'd heard them. She gave a half-wincing smile and spoke more carefully this time. "I hadn't thought of anything but good clean wood."

"Then that's what we'll have," he said, good-naturedly as ever. "I expect the timber won't be so big as we're used to, so it'll have to start small." She could see his mind pacing the place out in the space beyond the campfire. "One room, say twelve by fourteen, with a fireplace at one end, and windows east and west. Puncheon floor. A good slab roof will do as well as tar paper and shingles, and cheaper, too." His voice slowed to a leisurely sway as he plotted out the details. Caroline's needle stilled to listen to him. "Dunno if there'll be enough fieldstone for a chimney in those parts. I halfway hope there isn't—I'd rather patch a stick and daub chimney now and then than spend the next thirty years plowing stones out of my fields."

His eyes had focused on a spot just outside the firelight. The depth of his concentration made it seem as though the darkness were no more than a doorway into something real and solid. Caroline fancied she could reach through it and touch her hand to the latch string. She joined her gaze to that spot, testing the feel of it. Her heartbeat quickened. Suddenly she craved a destination as much as she craved the taste of Polly's pickles. Kansas was too vast a thing to pin herself to, and Montgomery County only an empty square on Charles's map, without a single dot of a town. Caroline could not conceive of the infinitely smaller speck she herself would make on that map.

Real or imagined, she needed some mark to aim toward, and what better place than a house? A home. She wanted to be able to see it in her mind, to picture herself inside it as she had not dared to do since Charles informed her they would be leaving the furniture behind. If she could do that, Charles might stop the wagon anywhere he pleased, and she could pin that vision of home to the map.

Caroline's hands toyed with her thread as though it were a latch string. It was risky, fashioning another such reverie with no firm promise that the reality would match. She looked again to Charles. The image he'd built was still before him, solid as though he'd made it out of boards. Perhaps yoking her vision to his would secure it somehow. Caroline gripped the leather latch string in her mind, and pulled.

The room that opened before her was so new she could smell the freshly hewn logs, yet immediately familiar: a straw tick snugged into each of the corners beside the hearth, her trunk beneath one window, the red-checked cloth on the table and the bright quilts on the beds. Without looking she knew Charles's rifle hung over the door. Even the curtains she recognized—their calico trim from a little blue and yellow dress of Mary's that Caroline had loved too much to tear into rags.

The whole house might as well have been standing there finished.

"Will that suit you?" Charles asked. His voice was so near, it was as though he were standing beside her in the imagined doorway.

Caroline whispered, "Yes, Charles."

Eight

C aroline held the vision before her all the way to the very rim of Kansas—the Missouri River.

It bore little resemblance to the map. On paper it was a thick line squiggling between Missouri and Kansas as though it were caught in a crimping iron. Creeks and streams veined the map with blue.

This river was less than half a mile across and so yellowed with mud, it looked as though it had been dredged with mustard powder. The opaque water did not seem to flow, but to roll. It carved steadily at its own banks, paring away great slices of earth that crumbled, brown sugar–like, into the water.

They waited almost three hours to cross at Boston Ferry and gave up four dollars from the fiddle box for the privilege. Ferries farther downstream in St. Joseph were apt to charge as much or more, Mrs. Boston said, and their lines were sure to be longer. "Why, by the time you get there you might not even cross today, and those that run their boats on the Sabbath aren't the sort I'd trust with all my worldly goods."

That settled that. Charles could not keep himself confined to the wagon long enough for dinner much less another full day, not with Kansas in plain sight. He stood poised along the bank, hardly remembering to eat the wedge of cornbread and molasses Caroline put in his hand. Caroline considered the opposite shore. No pattern, texture, or color marked the Kansas side as distinct from Missouri. Yet there Charles stood, looking as though he were about to step from burlap to brocade. That land called to him, and he could scarcely wait to answer.

Mary did not like it, not from the moment she spotted the ferryman opening up a hatch to shovel water from the hull. She spent the last half hour before their turn to cross scooted in close to Caroline, with Nettie clamped under one arm and her fingers woven into Caroline's shawl, while Laura asked Charles a dozen questions. *What's this do, Pa?* and *What's that? What makes it go, Pa?* and *Why does it go sideways?* Charles named the stob and pulleys and cables for her, and tried to explain how the ferryman slanted the oar board against the current to trick the water into pushing the raft across instead of downstream, but it was more than either of the girls could grasp. For Laura it was enough that her pa understood how it worked. Mary was not comforted.

Caroline ran her hand over Mary's hair as Mary struggled to make sense of it. Barbs of chapped skin snagged the fine golden strands. On either side of the part, Caroline could see the lines the comb had scored that morning. All of them needed a good soak in the washtub. At home their hair would have been glossy by week's end. Now it was only dusty and lusterless, the part faintly gray instead of white.

The wagon gave a little jolt and Mary startled. The ferryman was signaling Charles onto the raft. "I don't want to see anymore," Mary said. "I want to go back on the straw tick."

Caroline put her hand to Mary's knee. "Stay here where I can reach you until we reach the other side."

"I don't want to." She was beginning to flutter with panic as the raft loomed nearer. Caroline pressed more firmly. "Ma? I don't want to."

Charles heard and slowed the team. The ferryman waved again. "Move ahead!" he called out.

The wagon stayed in place. Caroline could feel both Charles and the ferryman turn toward her. She must appease the child or scold her, and fast. The quickest would be to let Mary go and burrow under the gray blanket. But this was no two-mile ice crossing. The child had watched the ferry shuttle more than half a dozen wagons safely from shore to shore. She could not let Mary's fear keep cutting itself larger and larger patterns.

Caroline spoke low and swift. "Mary, we must all learn to do things we don't want to do. You may be afraid, but you may not let your fear chase you away from what must be done. This is a good sturdy raft, and it will see us to the other side if we all sit still and let the ferryman do his job. Be a brave girl, now, and don't keep the ferryman waiting." She gave Mary her handkerchief and faced herself forward.

"All ready?"

Hands folded, she nodded pertly to Charles and ahead they rolled. Mary hiccoughed silently beside her. Each little spasm jabbed at Caroline's conscience. She had been sure of herself when she spoke, but how could it be the right thing if it left the both of them stinging? Caroline gave her head the tiniest shake. She could not ask herself such things. A question like that had no serviceable answer. If she did not block its path, it would circle her mind, searching for one. So she began to sing:

We are waiting by the river,
We are watching on the shore,
Only waiting for the boatman,
Soon he'll come to bear us o'er.

All of them perked up at that, even the impatient ferryman, and it cheered Caroline to see it. She matched her tempo to the sharp ringing of the horses' hooves on the boards, and so she could not help slowing nearly to a stop as the ferryman motioned Charles to drive closer, closer, closer yet to the front of the raft. As the wagon began to tilt toward the center of the river Mary closed her eyes so tight the lashes all but disappeared.

Caroline resisted the urge to pull Mary onto her lap. She had promised the child she was safe where she sat and must not do anything to contradict that. Caroline made herself as still as she had told Mary to be, except for her toes, which slid forward to brace against the wagon box. Laura leaned back and gripped the edge of the spring seat and asked, "Why, Pa?"

"The logs at the ends of the ferry boat are cut at a slant like the blade of my ax," Charles said. "That makes them fit snug to the riverbank's slope under the water. The ferryman can't move us unless we help tip the logs off the bank. Watch him, now."

Behind them the young man—Mrs. Boston's son,

judging by the look of him—unfastened the mooring rope and sank a pole into the water between the raft and the bank. He pried upward against the hull until with a sandy scrape the ferry came loose. Then with a leisurely swoop he leapt aboard.

"Center them up now," he instructed Charles.

Ben and Beth found level, and Caroline felt herself lift as though the water had unhitched her from her own weight. "Oh!" she said. Mary and Laura and Charles all looked at her. "It's so light." She did not know how else to explain. Her own bed was not half so yielding as this river. There on the hard spring seat her whole body felt as though it were suspended in that soft space between wakefulness and sleep. She leaned back and let the swaying, swishing current rise up through the logs, the wheels, and the boards to rock her.

This was altogether different from tiptoeing across the brittle Mississippi. This river was a living road. It opened itself for them, made room for them to settle into its waters, beckoned them with the tug of its current. This river would not crack behind them.

Just over halfway across the ferryman cranked the windlass and the ferry's nose swung around to angle downstream. "Back them up a couple of yards now, if you please," he said to Charles.

With his hand on the brake Charles persuaded the

team backward. One step at a time the front of the raft began to edge out of the water. Mary's breath hissed in and no further. She did not breathe, but she sat there with her hands folded just like Caroline's, a perfect little statue of obedience and bravery. Pride buoyed Caroline up so light, she was still floating as the ferry docked and the wagon pulled off down the road.

Charles was jubilant. "Kansas!" he said, and that was all for nearly a mile, he was so lost in his own satisfaction. Then his toes began to bounce. Next thing Caroline knew he was whistling "The Campbells Are Coming," and then he was grinning too broadly to whistle. He slapped his knee and chortled instead.

"Charles?" Caroline said. Her own voice curled toward laughter.

His eyes did not twinkle—they shone. Charles bellowed out:

The Ingalls are coming, hurrah, hurrah!
The Ingalls are coming, hurrah, hurrah!
The Ingalls are coming to Indian Territ'ry,
All the way 'cross the Missouri!

All the way 'cross the Missouri. Caroline traced the map in her mind as she figured the sum. Some four hundred twenty-five miles they had come. Four hundred twenty-five miles. With still two hundred more down into Montgomery County—Indian Territory. She did not like to call it that, but that is what it would be until the Indians moved on. It made her sort of flutter inside to imagine what this land might be holding in store for them. Caroline shivered a delicious little shiver. She had felt this eager, frightened tremor only twice before: stepping up to the justice of the peace with Charles on their wedding day and again five years later with the first tentative pangs of Mary's birthing. Crossing the river Missouri was the same sort of threshold, Caroline realized. Like the other times she must go ahead, uncertain of whether the world was about to open or close around her.

Nine

"What would you say to stopping early, Caroline?" Charles asked.

"Now?" She did not know what else to say. It was only midafternoon; they were not ten miles inside the Kansas line.

Charles nodded. "I don't like the look of that sky."

Caroline turned westward. The horizon was like a pan of dishwater. A rumble, faint as a cat's purr, ruffled the air. "Well, I'd be thankful for rain enough to fill the washtub and the time to use it before Sunday," she said.

Charles's mouth hooked into half a smile as he unfolded his map. The points where the creases met were wearing thin as the elbows of his red flannel shirt. "I'd stop right here if the ground were higher."

Caroline scanned the landscape. They stood in a

gentle hollow, broad and shallow as the center of a plat-
ter. The slope was so gradual she had not felt it.

"We can't be but a few miles from the Saint Joseph and Western line as the crow flies," Charles
said. "Ought to be some good level stretches along
the railroad bed. First likely place I see, we'll make
camp." With that, he eased Ben and Beth due south.
The edge of the wind angled across Caroline's face as
they turned off the road, flapping her bonnet brim
eastward. The wagon cover gave a shiver as the same
stiff breeze strummed its ribs.

Caroline let her core ease as the wheels sighed into
the spring-softened earth. Already the smell of rain
dampened the air. Caroline smiled to herself. Even a
fleeting thundershower might grant her enough rainwater to rinse out their stockings and drawers. Perhaps
even soap the crust of molasses from Laura's cuff.

Alongside the wagon Caroline watched the breeze
carve shapes through the grass. The long blades whispered, then hissed, too bent by the wind to stroke the
wagon's belly.

They had not gone a half mile before the storm
struck them like a roundhouse.

Rain stabbed down as though it were intent on piercing the wagon cover, while the wind gusted it against
the canvas with a sound like scattershot.

"Jerusalem crickets!" Charles thundered into the weather. "I never saw a storm come on so fast."

Ben and Beth tucked their chins to their collars, turning their faces from the sally. Charles stood to grab the gutta-percha poncho from its peg and began hitching it toward his shoulder, searching for the neck. He had not stayed the team.

"Charles? Shouldn't we stop?"

"Ground's too soft. If we don't keep on, we'll be mired in half a minute. Best we can do is try to walk it out. Here," he said, handing her the reins. "Hold them while I find my way into this thing." With the lines in her hands Caroline could feel the forward slide of the horses' hooves that preceded each step. "Go on back with the girls and keep as dry as you can."

Caroline clambered over the spring seat and straw tick into the aisle. Standing on solid ground, she had only begun to feel the child's downward pull on her balance, but in the moving wagon, tension ricocheted between her heels and the balls of her feet as she fought to keep upright. Staggering, she made her way to the tailgate and cinched down the ropes, closing the back into a keyhole. Still the wet canvas shuddered and snapped between the wagon bows.

She turned, barking her shin against the provisions crate. Its edges were damp with spray. She tugged, but the crate would not move—pinched by the boxes of kitchenwares crowded around it. Caroline snatched up the dish towels and blanketed the bags of flour and meal.

With a sound like a spank, the wind broadsided the wagon. "Ma!" Mary and Laura wailed.

Behind her, rain was hissing up over the sideboards to spit at the girls.

They had left too much slack between the bows; the row of knots along the wagon's sides were not drawn fast enough against the weather.

Two solid feet of boxes and bundles stood between Caroline and the sideboards. She hinged at the waist, putting her hands out to catch the wooden lip.

From either side of the bows, the wagon cover bellied toward her. Caroline tucked her cheek to her shoulder and thrust one hand down between the wagon box and the cover, searching for the rope. A whiskery wet knob of jute met her fingers. The knot was already so fisted with water and wind, she could not feel its loops and strands, let alone part them. Every crack of the canvas kicked a spray of rain into her face. Defeated, Caroline shifted her weight to the heels of her hands and vaulted herself backward.

She stood panting a moment in the center of the wagon, mopping her face in the crook of her arm while lightning flared and Charles shouted calm to the horses.

Then without a word to the girls she stripped the gray blanket from their knees and began bunching it into the gaps as best she could.

With every ram of the blanket she upbraided herself for being so ill prepared. She had known it must rain. Of course it would. On the trek she and Charles had made from Jefferson County to Pepin it had rained every afternoon for a solid week. As she sewed and oiled this wagon's cover she had thought of little but the wind and rain and sun that would strike it.

But she had not considered all the ways in which a storm such as this could reach beneath it. Thunder vibrated the boards at her feet. Lightning backlit the canvas as though it were the wick of a kerosene lamp.

In the midst of it all, the girls cowered at the far end of the straw tick like two doused kittens. Mary clutched Laura, too frightened herself to be any comfort to her sister.

Looking at them, Caroline felt meager as the wagon cover. No matter how she tried to put herself between her girls and the storm, she would not be able keep its rage from touching them. She wished she could cocoon them both close against her breastbone, as she had when they were babies. The soft thunder of her heart had been enough to soothe them then, but she could not gather them near enough to hear it now.

Nor did she know which of them to reach for first. She had not arms enough to shelter them both at once. Laura was still so little, but Mary was plainly smothering in her own fear. It did not seem fair that each could have only half of her, nor that her heart should favor one side of her chest. Not since Laura was newly born had Caroline felt so keenly that she might not be mother enough for two. And soon there would be a third. The thought made her want to cry out for her own ma.

Aside from the vanity of new hair ribbons, Caroline realized, she had given hardly a thought to Mary and Laura when she agreed to go west. She had bundled them into the wagon like the blankets and sheets. Now she must answer for it.

Doubtful though she was, Caroline could stand apart from them no longer. Their faces were unthreading her chest. Whatever thin comfort she could offer belonged to them, and nothing but the press of her daughters could assure her she was equal to her task.

Caroline kneed her way onto the mattress and put her back to the spring seat. "Come here my girls," she urged. They broke loose from each other and came skittering toward her with an eagerness that spread the edges of her heart.

Mary and Laura huddled so close against her sides,

the tips of her steels dug at the soft flesh under her arms. At once Caroline saw that it did not matter what she did, so long as she was there for them to cling to. Their trust in her was built of thousands upon thousands of moments already past. She was *Ma,* and that in itself was enough. Just pressing against her seemed to sand away the edges of their fear, and Caroline's own flesh yielded to welcome them.

Thoroughly bolstered, Caroline swaddled her shawl around their shoulders and shielded their laps with a quilt. With long circles, she passed her hands slowly up and down their backs, kneading their taut spines with her knuckles. Cold needles of rain struck the back of her neck as she stroked. Caroline let them melt into her collar; she would not break her rhythm to slap them away.

Lightning slashed through a clap of thunder, and Mary's body recoiled from the sound.

"There is nothing to be frightened of," Caroline soothed. "It is only light and air bumping together."

But the next crack sounded so near, it tingled the pit of her stomach. Reverberations cored through her arms and legs. Caroline cupped her palms over Mary's and Laura's ears and rocked the girls from side to side, tucking her chin close to their heads as she began to sing:

Wildly the storm sweeps us on as it roars,
We're homeward bound, homeward bound;
Look! yonder lie the bright heavenly shores:
We're homeward bound, homeward bound;
Steady, O pilot! stand firm at the wheel;
Steady! we soon shall outweather the gale;
Oh, how we fly 'neath the loud creaking sail!
We're homeward bound, homeward bound.

"I want to go home, Ma," Laura said. "Can't we go home?"

All Caroline's self-assurance washed straight down her throat. Lightning cut through the sky again before she could speak. "Our house belongs to Mr. Gustafson now. We had storms in the Big Woods, Laura. This one is no different." If she pulled the truth any thinner, it would tear. There had been storms—storms that struck a roof and walls made of logs as big through the middle as Laura herself. All around the cabin the trees had sifted the raindrops and combed the wind into narrow strands. Here, they were neither out nor in, their roof no thicker than a hat.

"Is Mary crying?"

Caroline nodded and pushed her lips into a silent *shhh.* This once she would not scold Mary for her tears. The child was already as ashamed as she was afraid; Caroline could feel Mary's hot face boring into her side.

Laura reached across to pet her sister's arm. Mary sniffled and ventured to show half her face.

"I'm scared, too," Laura said.

Caroline watched Mary wipe her cheeks and offer Laura her hand. Their fingers laced fast as corset strings over Caroline's belly. Lightning scratched across the sky and both girls ducked, then peeped up to smile sheepishly at each other before chancing a glance up at Caroline.

In that moment Caroline's love for them danced over the surface of her skin. If the child inside could not feel the warm ribbon of its sisters' arms stretching overhead, she hoped these waves of affection might embrace it.

The wagon itself seemed to float with her, then the southeast corner pitched sideways. The slant was not more than a few inches, but her body tipped like a bowl of water with all her muscles pulling toward level.

"Charles?"

He was shouting to the team. The wagon hiccoughed forward, then dropped back. The reins snapped like thunder, and again the wagon leaned and slumped, less sharply this time. Caroline felt the catch of the horses' next pull, the strain so strong her shoulders crept up alongside her ears. Then the release. They had not moved an inch.

"Charles," she called again.

"That's it," he barked over his shoulder. "We're stuck."

She heard the reins strike the floorboards before the spring seat bounced up, knocking the top rungs of her spine. Charles was on his feet, cinching down the ropes at the wagon's mouth. It was dim as the inside of a flour sack.

"I've got to unhitch the team, chain them to the leeward side of the wagon," Charles said. He stood mopping his face and whiskers in the crook of his elbow. "Caroline, I need your help managing the canvas so I can get the harnesses under cover." The girls' heads tilted up at him, their bodies furrowing against this news. "You girls will have to sit tight," he told them.

"Are the horses scared, Pa?" Laura asked.

"No, Half-Pint, but they're colder and wetter than they've ever been before. I haven't got a chance of rigging a tarpaulin up in this gale," he said to Caroline. "The best I can think to do is get them out of the wind. I need you to stand inside and hold the canvas closed while I unbuckle the lines. I'll shout for you to open up when I'm ready to hand the harnesses in."

"All right, Charles." Caroline unwedged herself from the girls and unwound her shawl. She folded it into a neat triangle and laid it between them. "Mary, Laura, will you please keep this warm and dry for me?"

They nodded, hunkering protectively over her shawl, still crouched with fear, yet unwilling to cave to it.

"That's my brave girls," she said, and it starched them up some to be called so.

Caroline eased herself over the spring seat, where Charles stood waiting, and tucked her skirts back between her calves.

"All ready?" Charles asked.

She nodded and reached for the ties.

"Not yet," Charles said. "I'll cinch them up behind me from the outside and hand them in." He turned up his collar, screwed his hat nearly to his eyebrows, and tipped himself out into the storm. The opening shrunk like a knothole behind him. Then his fist full of ropes punched down between the canvas and the wagon box.

Caroline crouched down and took the ties from him. Each gust rattled her shoulders as the wind tried to fillet the canvas from the wagon's back. For forty beats the storm lashed its rhythm through her body before she heard Charles's call, muffled through the wet canvas. The ropes burned across her palms as she loosened her grip, and a snarl of straps and traces came at her. She bailed them in one-handed, kneeing them into the corner, all while groping for the rope she had lost hold of. Rain planed across her face and into her ear. Then came Beth's collar, a leather doughnut heavy with rainwater.

"Close up," Charles shouted.

She had not the muscle to pull the canvas tight again, so she coiled each rope twice around her fists and braced her heels. "Mary, Laura, get back," she called.

"Why, Ma?" Mary asked.

"Get *back*," she said again, her voice cocked and loaded, and threw herself backward into the spring seat. The twists of jute crimped the skin on the back of her hands as the wagon clamped its mouth shut.

It was like driving a team of runaways, holding those ropes. They pulled so insistently, the joints at the base of her fingers scraped against one another. Before she could rearrange her grip, she felt the yoke strike the ground and Charles bellowed again. She stood and threw her arms wide, opening the wagon's throat as Ben's half of the tack spilled inward.

"I'll be in soon as I've got them chained to the feed-box," Charles shouted. "Can you hold a little longer?"

Caroline's pulse thumped cold in the pads of her thumbs. She mustered up a shout and flung it out to him. "Yes, Charles." Again she hurtled herself backward, and the canvas shrank shut.

In a moment the girls jolted at the sound of the chains rattling out of the jockey box and through the iron ring. Then Caroline felt the wagon jounce and knew Charles had climbed to the doubletree. His boot heels knocked against the falling tongue, and then his hands were parting the canvas.

"Give me some slack," he called, and Caroline let loose the ropes. With a gust of wind the wagon cover seemed to inhale, raising Charles to his toes. "Great fishhooks," he cried.

Caroline grabbed for the canvas flapping below his fists, and together they tugged it back down.

"Reel one end of the rope in taut and stand on it," Charles yelled to her. "Clamp it under your heels."

As soon as Caroline had done as he instructed, Charles tumbled in with the other end. He crouched on the floor and knotted his length around hers. Then he hooked the pair of horse collars onto his elbow and heaved them over. "Step back," he said, and wound both ends of the rope through the collars until they were secure. When he let go, the wind pulled the knot tight against the weight of the collars.

Charles sank down into the bramble of wet tack. "Caroline, how did you ever hold against that wind?"

"I don't know, Charles," she admitted. She looked at him, and the girls. "I only knew that I had to." She was so rigid with tension, she could not even shiver. "Girls, my shawl, please, quick."

The fabric was warm as they were. Caroline swathed it close around herself and stroked the rain from her face with its ends. Wet streaks of hair channeled rainwater down her temples and neck. With her fingers she pried the strands from her skin and combed them into place.

"I tell you, that rain is falling every which way but down," Charles said. He took hold of his whiskers as though he were about to milk his chin. With a twist, he wrung a fistful of water onto the floor.

Laura giggled first, then Mary.

"Think that's funny, do you?" He did not quite snap at them, but all the expression seemed to have vacated his voice. The girls pinned their lips together.

Caroline could not cipher his tone, so she frothed up her own voice with cheerfulness. "Charles, let me take those wet things," she said, hoping a layer of his frustration might peel away with them. "Mary, Laura, find Pa some dry clothes in the carpetbag and make room for him on the straw tick while I see to supper."

Caroline spread the poncho across the spring seat before making her way to the back of the wagon. There, she unswathed the crate and picked over the provisions. There was the bake oven half-full of cornbread, but that she would hold until breakfast, to warm over a fire. If they must have a cold supper, Caroline decided, she would make a treat of it—crackers and cheese and dried apples—though what she wanted most just then was a mug of tea and a baking of light bread hot enough to melt butter.

To distract herself from useless wanting, Caroline fanned a handful of apple quarters like a flower on Mary's and Laura's plates. She planed long yellow strips from the wheel of cheese and layered them in between the apple petals. A few crumbles of cheese brightened the center of each plate, and a white ring of crackers framed it all. For Charles she made no such dainties, only neat stacks of apples and crackers, with a cut of cheese thick enough to make her wince as the knife's handle pressed into her rope-roughened palms.

"What happened to your hands?" Charles said as she passed him his plate and a mug of water. He was hoarse from shouting.

Pink welts striped them from side to side. "Only a bit of rope burn," she said. "Nothing that won't mend."

Charles put down his supper and reached for her wrist. "Let me see."

He would blame himself if he saw them—no matter

that he was not the one who had coiled the ties around her hands. "It's all right, Charles," she insisted. "I can manage."

A sigh hissed between his teeth.

"Your cornbread won't be any less sweet for it," she ventured to tease. *I never ask any other sweetening,* he'd said since that first supper in Pepin, *when you put the prints of your hands on the loaves.*

A short snuffle—almost a laugh—escaped his nostrils. "All right, Caroline," he said.

She saw from the way his movements loosened when he bowed his head to pray that it had been levity enough to oil his hinges. He cleared his throat for the blessing and winced.

"Rest your voice, Charles," Caroline said. "I think Mary is old enough to say grace for us. 'For what we are about to receive,'" she prompted.

Mary straightened up and refolded her hands primly. "For what we are about to receive," she repeated and then took a careful breath, ". . . may the Lord make us . . . ," another breath, ". . . truly thankful." Her eyes popped open, looking to see if she had done right.

"Very nice," Caroline praised her. Mary puffed up like a vanity cake, muddling Caroline's pride. Had she sown the wrong kind of modesty in that child? From the day Mary was born, Caroline had known that warding off vanity promised to be the greatest task in raising her. She had felt it welling in herself as she gazed on those delicate blue eyes and stroked the first golden wisps of Mary's hair. How, she wondered then and ever after, had she made anything so beautiful?

Laura sat in awe of her sister. Caroline watched her fork a crumb of cheese from the center of her plate and taste it carefully, as though the food might be sauced with a new flavor after being blessed by Mary's voice. Caroline sat down beside Laura and smoothed her little brown braids. They were so waxed with the week's dust and oil, they would likely hold their shape without ribbons.

Once again there would be no Saturday bath, Caroline realized, just as there were no fresh loaves of light bread. At this hour the inside of their cabin would be fleecy with yeast and the breath of bathwater—unless Mrs. Gustafson, being a Swede, did her baking and bathing by a different timetable. Caroline scanned the dim expanse of the wagon. She thought of how the girls' small white backs glistened in the yellow firelight as she poured warm snowmelt over them, and the feathery feel of their clean toweled hair. Buttoned into fresh flannel nightgowns, they would stand at her knees to have their hair braided tight and damp to make it wavy for Sunday. The little house glowed orange in Caroline's memory.

She nibbled steadily at her dinner while the thunder numbed their ears, determined to enjoy the fruit and cheese before her rather than pine for what was behind her. But Caroline could not keep her thoughts confined within the wagon. Often Saturday nights she found time to read or crochet by the fire while her own bathwater heated in pots and kettles on the stove, easing herself into Sunday with the sound of Charles's fiddle or his whittling knife. Tonight there was little to do but wipe the dishes and go to bed, and she said as much as she collected their plates.

Mary tugged at Caroline's cuff. "Where are we going to sleep?" she whispered. Caroline looked over Mary's head. The spring seat and harnesses filled the girls' bed space.

"I can double up the small tick, sleep in the aisle," Charles rasped.

"I wish I could make you a mug of tea for that throat," she said.

Charles waved a hand. "It'll pass."

Caroline brushed the crumbs from the plates with a damp dishcloth and fitted them back into the crate while the girls squatted in the aisle with the chamber pail. They brought Caroline their soiled rags and she rinsed them over a bucket with water from the keg. It seemed foolish, spending drinking water on such things with the heavens spilling down on them, but she dared not tussle with the wagon cover again until the wind calmed.

Charles walked the chamber pail back to the tailgate and sat down on the molasses keg while Caroline readied the girls for bed. She laid the pillows so the lean of the wagon would tug at their ankles rather than their ears, and tied their nightcaps close under their chins.

Perched on the edge of the tick, they watched Charles unfold a tarpaulin the length of the aisle and lace a slender rope through the line of metal rings that bordered its edge.

"What are you doing, Pa?" Laura asked.

"Got to be ready—" He cleared his throat and shook his head.

"Pa is preparing a shelter for Ben and Beth in case the rain doesn't stop," Caroline explained as she folded the girls' dresses and petticoats and tucked them into the carpetbag.

"Oh, Pa, do you have to go out in the rain again?" Mary asked.

"The horses must stand in the weather until Pa can cover them," Caroline said. "Ben and Beth have brought us this far, and we must take care of them." She paused with Mary's blue wool half-folded against her chest, thinking what it would mean if either of the horses took sick. "Now let Pa work so he can rest."

When he was done Charles rolled the tarpaulin up like a rug and doubled it in the middle. He carried the bundle to the tailgate and propped it alongside the kitchen crates.

"It's time little girls were asleep," Caroline said when he lifted the lid from the chamber pail and began to unbutton. "Let me hear your prayers."

Mary and Laura got to their knees at the head of the aisle and latched their folded hands under their chins. Their two voices chorused *Now I lay me,* drawing the day closed like two ends of ribbon weaving a bow.

"And God bless Ben and Beth," Laura added as a little flourish. Caroline smiled. All finished, they scuttled under the quilts and reconciled themselves to sleep. Caroline salved her sore hands with the softness of their hair and kissed them both goodnight.

Charles did not undress. He laid the small tick down in the aisle and wedged himself into the narrow trough it made. His shoulders were straightjacketed by the sides of the ticking, and his calves extended beyond its edge.

"I should wake you if I hear the wind calm?" Caroline asked.

Charles nodded. She handed him a pair of quilts, and he closed his eyes without another word between them.

An unexpected sense of solitude descended around Caroline as she undressed herself and unpinned her hair. She sat in her shawl and nightdress at Mary's and Laura's feet, reluctant, somehow, to join them under the covers in spite of the mounting chill. The wind and rain had melded into a curtain of sound, and there was nothing she need do—indeed nothing she could do—without waking Charles and the girls. She had not found a moment such as this for herself since Wisconsin. The stillness within the wagon cocooned her thoughts from the weather and its consequences, and Caroline settled into the quiet space within her mind. Tomorrow would be the Sabbath, and they would not move, no matter the weather. The storm had granted her a complete respite, as though she'd been unharnessed after a month's worth of relentless forward momentum. The feeling was akin to the exhale that accompanied the unfastening of her corset each night. And why, she wondered idly, was she always inclined first to empty her lungs in the moment her body was freest to expand? Tomorrow she would only be still, like the psalm said, Caroline thought as she edged in alongside Mary—*Be still and know that I am God.*

"Caroline?"

Caroline felt her eyelids rise, but not a particle of light met them. She rose up on an elbow. "What is it?"

"The wind's died down enough, I think I can rig something like an awning to shelter Ben and Beth," Charles said. Caroline broadened her attention to the sounds outside the wagon. The sky still wrung itself overhead, but she could hear a difference in the way the rain struck the canvas. The drops fell freely now, no longer flung sidelong against the wagon's western flank. "Is the poncho dry?" Charles asked.

She sat up and leaned across Mary and Laura to pat her hand over it. "Nearly."

He beckoned for it, and his boots. She lifted the garments gingerly over the girls. Dirt crusted the soles of the boots. "Do you need help?" she asked, reaching for her shawl.

Charles shook his head. "You stay in with the girls. The noise is likely to wake them." He shouldered the rolled-up tarpaulin. A rope dangled from either end.

Caroline followed him down the cockeyed aisle, hearing more than seeing him secure one of the ropes to the tailgate latch, then loosen the cover and lean out to boost the rolled-up tarpaulin onto the roof. It landed with a thump, sagging the canvas and jostling the hickory bows. He hesitated. "I may need you to open the front of the wagon cover so I can tie a rope inside."

Caroline tested her fists. The palms were tender yet, but so long as the wind did not wrestle with her as it had before she would manage.

"All right, Charles."

The girls stirred as Charles threaded himself through the opening and into the rain. All Caroline could see of him were the toes of his boots as he strained to push the tarpaulin farther across the roof. In a moment a whiplike *crack* snapped overhead—the other end of the rope, landing halfway across the roof. Then it hissed against the canvas as Charles reeled it back for another throw.

Mary bolted up on her hands and knees before Caroline knew she was awake. "Ma?"

Caroline waded back through Charles's bedding to reach her. "It's only Pa, making a tent for the horses."

Mary crawled into her lap and augered herself close against the soft new curve of Caroline's belly. "I don't like it here," she said in a pouting tone Caroline would have corrected under any other circumstances. "Where are we?"

"We are in Kansas," Caroline said.

"I don't like Kansas," Mary declared.

Again the *crack* came, this time farther toward the front of the roof. There was a little lift of the wagon as Charles jumped to the ground. A few heartbeats passed, then the front of the wagon dipped with his footsteps as he mounted the falling tongue then passed from singletree to doubletree to sideboard.

"That's Pa again, pulling the tarpaulin across the roof," Caroline said. It blundered up the wagon's spine, bumping its way from one bow to the next.

"Lie back down with Laura," Caroline told Mary when the tarpaulin flattened the canvas above them. "Be a good big sister and settle her if she wakes. Pa needs my help now."

Once again Caroline climbed over the spring seat, the boards damp against her stockings where the poncho had lain. She had lost count of how many times she had hoisted her legs over that hateful backboard this day.

Caroline found the horse collars and crouched to untwist the ropes that held the mouth of the wagon cover shut. Without the wind driving them, they were staid as apron strings. Charles pulled the tarpaulin line taut and leaned in to secure it to the nearest bow.

"There," he said. "Close up the cover and go on back to bed, Caroline. I can manage from here."

Back Caroline went, over the spring seat and under the quilts, where she was informed that Laura did not like Kansas, either.

"Hush now," she said. "We should all be asleep." They heard nothing at all over the rain, and felt no movement for long enough that the stillness became conspicuous. The girls did not speak, but Caroline sensed their rising apprehension as the silence lengthened. No harm could have come to Charles, but surely something should have happened by now. It was as though he were standing stock-still in the rain. The raindrops ticked against the canvas like a clock until it seemed something must be wrong. His name sat waiting in her mouth, but she did not know whether she might alarm the girls more by calling out to him or by leaving the silence to deepen. And then Charles's voice pricked the sidewall, so near to her pillow that Caroline's shoulders flinched at the sound.

"Caroline?"

She closed her eyes. "Yes, Charles."

"Lean up close to the sideboards and talk to the team," he said. "I'm afraid it's going to startle them something awful when I unroll the tarpaulin."

Once more Caroline peeled herself from her covers to creep down the small hill of the straw tick, clucking her tongue. "Here, Ben; here, Beth," she crooned, "poor wet things. Steady now. Easy." Mary and Laura inched up on their bellies to whisper sweetly to the team. There was a snuffle and a nudge at the canvas. Laura flattened her palm against it.

"Ben's nose," she said. "I can feel him breathing."

"How can you tell it's Ben?" Mary whispered.

With a flap like a clothesline full of sheets, the tarpaulin unfurled down the side of the wagon. The horses' chains hummed tight, jerking the wagon bed upward as Ben and Beth tried to rear back from the crashing canvas. Laura snatched her hand away, tumbling backward in her surprise.

Caroline listened to the chain links clinking, the horses' heavy breath steaming from their nostrils. "Steady," said Charles's voice, "steady now," and Caroline felt her own breath slowing at his words, whooshing softly over her upper lip.

Charles reached in over the tailgate and clattered through his toolbox. Caroline heard him lever out the iron stakes that held her pots over the campfire, and then he was gone. In a moment the clang of his hammer rang out shrill in the dark as he pounded the stakes into the ground.

As she settled Mary and Laura back to bed, Charles tugged the tarpaulin's corners down to the stakes, gently rocking the wagon. The girls were asleep again by the time he came in over the tailgate and stood, arms half lifted to hold the drenched wings of his poncho away from his body.

"They'll stand the weather all right for now," he said.

Caroline nodded. Like a piece of dough laid into a pan, Charles always seemed to expand to fit whatever shape a task demanded of him. There was no need to thank him for such a thing, yet she felt so rounded with thankfulness that she did not move until a shiver shook him by the scruff of his neck.

Caroline handed him his nightshirt and a towel. "Drape your wet things over the crates," she whispered. "I'll see to them in the morning."

She did not mean to watch. From her bed there was only his outline as he stripped off his rain gear and then his clothes, threads of glimpses like a spiderweb in sunlight. Charles pared off his shirt, and the movement silvered his wet shoulders and glinted along his spine. As he stepped from his trousers the loosed metal tongue of his belt buckle tinked a bright note in the darkness and Charles paused, turning half-toward the front of the wagon.

Could he see her, running her fingers down her braid the way he did when he was hungry for her? That was not what she wanted now, and so Caroline muted her palms against the straw tick. She wanted only to admire him as he stood, so bare and capable in the faint dusting of light.

Why a man of such breadth had chosen her, why he seemed to delight in her very narrowness, Caroline could not fathom. When she had consented to be his wife, his first indulgence had not been a kiss. He had instead reached out to place one hand and then another around her waist. His thumbs met at her navel, and Caroline watched the pleasure spread across his face. "A perfect fit," he'd said as the warmth of his palms breached her skin and trickled through the deepest recesses of her body. Even now she wondered when he might have decided to kiss her, had she not risen up on tiptoe and offered her lips to him.

Now Charles straightened his back, his elbows windmilling upward, and Caroline heard the sound of his fingernails combing through his scalp. She smiled to herself. The one thing Charles could never do was tame that hair of his. With a shrug, his nightshirt snuffed out his nakedness and Caroline closed her eyes, penciling the shape of him onto her dreams.

She woke with Mary's cold toes knuckled into the crook of her knees. On her other side Laura had screwed herself into a little knot.

Caroline sniffed the air. A dull, almost meaty smell tinged the wagon—the pile of damp harnesses. The storm's temper had eased overnight, but the rain had not abated. Streams of it sluiced off the canvas, striking puddles in a way that made her bladder tingle. She had not emptied herself all night. Caroline looked toward the rear of the wagon. Charles and his narrow bed filled the path to the chamber pail.

Gripping against the downward press of her water, Caroline deliberately rustled the carpetbag as she dressed. The damp had reached into everything. Her dress and drawers were clammy and seemed to have thickened, like drippings in a cooled skillet. Even the good stockings she saved back for Sundays still held the shape of her feet. Nevertheless, the left one hugged her shin too tightly where the beginning of a bruise shined her skin. She put on her second-best navy wool with the black braid, never mind that there was no call for it. It would be at least as warm as her everyday, and she wanted to feel a touch of fineness.

The wagon's pitch tugged insistently at her bladder, forcing her to draw her belly upward until she felt as though she stood on tiptoe. Caroline nudged a toe under Charles's pillow and whispered his name. He opened one eye at a time and looked up at her. She nodded toward the tailgate.

Charles stood and they minced a half pirouette in the straw tick so that she could pass.

The rear of the wagon was in disarray—Charles's poncho drooping over the churn dash, his shirt and trousers splayed nearby. Beside the chamber pail was the drying puddle where he had come in from the rain, its edges curling into brown scales. Caroline lifted his boots aside. A skin of mud ridged the floor where they had stood.

All of those things must wait until tomorrow.

She need attend only to herself and her little brood, Caroline thought as she held the washbasin out into the deluge. Runoff licked its way past her cuffs and into the crease of her elbows before she pulled her hands back under the canvas.

Behind her, Charles rolled up his bed and dressed in his second best—more because the clothes were dry than for Sunday's sake, Caroline supposed—then went out over the tailgate with his shovel. The feedbox flapped open and the girls were awake. Almost immediately their tempers began to snarl. They quibbled over who had first rights to the chamber pail and then who should button up whom first, their voices sharpening so fast they nicked Caroline's patience.

"Girls, please," she said. It was more a request than a warning.

"I only have one button I can't reach," Mary said. "Laura always does mine first."

"Mine's all open and it's too cold to wait," Laura protested.

Caroline hesitated, the words poised at the tip of her tongue. She did not want to soil the air further with the sound of her own scolding, yet this time they must be told, not asked. She closed her mouth and leveled a silent eyebrow at them. Mary swiveled Laura by the shoulders and buttoned her up the back.

"The water's cold, Ma," Laura protested again as Caroline scoured behind her ears.

"It is the best we have," Caroline said, "and we can be thankful it is not frozen." Laura's shoulders turtled up to her earlobes.

Mary joined in, "We're all cold, even Ben and Beth, so you must not complain." She fairly sizzled with superiority.

Mary turned to Caroline expectantly. Caroline did not praise her. Mary had said nothing wrong—Caroline could not help but recognize her own sentiments dressed in a smaller size—but it troubled her that Mary took such care to polish her tone to a gleaming point. Vanity again, buttered with virtue. *Virtue is the purest kind of beauty.* Hadn't she always impressed that upon her daughters? Only just now, watching Mary, it did not feel true.

"Forty-three degrees," Charles said as he came in, noting it in his weather journal. "And I'll bet it's not much warmer in here."

Caroline wished he had not announced it. She herself was not cold enough to shiver, but the chill was so embedded in her clothes that her skin resisted touching the fabric. Pinning a number to the cold only made her more sensible of it.

"Everybody taken their turn?" Charles asked, hefting the chamber pail by the handle. He opened the rear of the wagon cover and flung the contents out into the rain. "Tried to dig a latrine pit under the tarpaulin but it'll likely be full of water by the time anyone needs it," he said as he swirled the pail full of rinse water and cast the swill out again. "It's like digging at the bottom of a well out there. I left a bucket hanging below the feed-box to bail it out."

Charles sat down on a crate and scrubbed his sides with his fists. "Sore," he said. "Had to lean backward stiff as a rafter to hoist the tarpaulin onto the roof."

"We'll all rest ourselves today," Caroline said, tying on her apron.

"Is it Sunday again, Ma?" Laura asked.

"It is," Caroline answered. Laura knew better than to scowl, but the news swept down her face like a sad-iron.

"Are you too tired to drive, Pa?"

"I am, Half-Pint," Charles said, patting his knee for Laura to climb aboard. "And it's a good thing, because Ben and Beth are too tired to pull."

Laura wilted onto Charles's shoulder and buckled her lips over a sigh. "Why doesn't Sunday ever wait until *I'm* tired?" she lamented.

Caroline's cheeks twitched with a laugh she could not spill. A still and rainy Sunday might test any three-year-old's forbearance, but none so sorely as Laura's with the way she took after her pa.

Laura sat up again. "You aren't too tired to make breakfast, are you, Ma?"

This time Charles could not bite back a chuckle. "By golly, Caroline, she's found the only thing that's allowed to grumble on Sunday—a stomach," he teased. His rumbling laugh warmed the air.

Charles leafed idly through his weather journal as Caroline scraped the cold beads of molasses from their breakfast plates. "Hasn't been a rain like this in years," he said. "Not in our parts, anyway."

She folded her apron into the kitchen crate and took in the length of the wagon. Disarray crowded every edge of her vision, most of all the big straw tick, its quilts splayed back and the sheets rumpling beneath Mary and Laura. Sunday or not, the bed must be straightened if the four of them were to have anywhere to sit. Caroline shooed the girls into the aisle. As she pulled the top sheet from the mattress a flare of aches lit the backs of her arms.

"Mary, please climb up on the bed and help me fold the sheets." She handed Mary one end and began backing down the aisle with the other.

"I want to help, too!" Laura insisted, grazing Caroline's bruised shin to reach for the hem.

Soreness blurted past Caroline's elbows as she hoisted the bundle away from Laura's fingertips. "Climb up beside Mary and take one of her corners," Caroline told her. "There isn't room for both of us here."

Caroline's breath began to heat the back of her throat as she stood idle, waiting for the girls to negotiate who should take which side. She would have done better to fold it herself in spite of her aches than let this sort of peevishness stain her morning.

"Mine's wet, Ma," Laura said.

"Mine, too."

Caroline's elbows went slack. Her end of the sheet brushed the aisle. "The weather makes everything feel damp today, girls. It can't be helped. Now please, help me fold this sheet up nicely."

"No, Ma," Mary said.

The contradiction came within a hair's breadth of lighting Caroline's temper by the wick. She opened her mouth and found she had no words to parry such bald-faced disobedience—especially from Mary.

Mary climbed down and held up her corner. "It's wet. See?" It was. Not clammy with cold, but more sodden than freshly sprinkled laundry.

"Is the bottom sheet wet, Laura?"

Laura tugged it up into her lap. "Yes, Ma."

Caroline stifled a groan. She skimmed her hands across the mattress. All along the west end, the cover was heavy with moisture. Practically wincing with reluctance, she unbuttoned one corner and fished out a handful of damp straw.

Baffled, she touched the canvas wall above it. Dry.

"How in the world?" she wondered aloud, and then she saw. A tongue of the gray blanket had lapped out into the rain. Caroline pulled it, black and drooling, back under cover. In the places where the two abutted, the ticking had spent the night supping rainwater into itself silently as a cat at a saucer.

Caroline's sigh formed a small gray cloud as her whole morning deflated under the weight of one soaked blanket.

With Charles's help she spread the sheets, one over each side of the aisle, to dry as best they could. The gray blanket Charles strung from the front bows with its wet hem drooping, frown-like, toward the floor. The entire wagon dimmed. Caroline pulled the end of the straw tick across her lap and resigned herself to plunge her arms in to the elbows. At least it was soaked only at the foot, where she could sift out the wet straw without emptying the entire mattress. For that small mercy she managed a pinch of thankfulness.

It did not last long. Each stiff fistful of straw stabbed at her sore palms. Cold and pain numbed her hands until they became insensible to the task—her fingers could no more feel the difference between wet and dry than between nutmeg and pepper.

Caroline sat back and balled her fists beneath her arms. Two pillowcases full of straw slumped beside her, and more yet to come. "I declare, I don't know what to do with all this." In such weather it would sooner mildew their pillowcases than it would dry. Yet she could not bring herself to simply toss it out into the rain. *Waste not, want not,* her mother's voice chimed, but what earthly use could there be for wet straw?

She might as well empty it out onto the boards before the spring seat to catch the muck from their shoes when they came in from their necessaries. And then how long before the wagon began to smell of a barnyard?

A thought cocked her head. "Charles, would it do any good to spread this under the tarpaulin for Ben and Beth?"

The question brought him to his feet like a slap of reins. "Wouldn't do any harm." He chucked her chin on his way past. "Leave it to a Scotchwoman," he said.

Boredom saturated all four of them by noontime. They sat clumped in the utmost center of the gutted mattress, hitching themselves inward from its edges—edges Caroline knew would not dry before nightfall.

The girls were sullen and peckish. They did not complain, but Caroline could sense their moods fermenting. The slightest provocation and up they would foam. Charles was no help, twiddling with his compass and twitching as though every spat of rain were a backward footstep. She had never known a man so prone to rusting the moment his momentum was stilled. He had positioned himself, she noticed, on the west side of the wagon, as though cringing from the eastward pull of the sunken wheel.

Caroline drew her shawl to her earlobes and exhaled down into her collar, warming her neck and the underside of her chin with the feeble cloud of warmth. Cold limned her nostrils and fingertips. All the heat she could muster had settled at the back of her throat—two little burrs of it—and these she tried to smother. What glowed inside them did not belong to the Sabbath.

This was not the sort of stillness she had craved, with every inch of her laboring to rest. The energy her body needed to resist the cold tightened her muscles until they begged to be moved. Her mind itched just as badly, piling up a stack of undone tasks: the balding fabric at Charles's elbow, the molasses piping on Laura's sleeve, the thinning heel of her own stocking. A little droplet glimmered at the tip of Laura's nose, winking in and out. The hot pinpricks in Caroline's throat gleamed brighter with every breath Laura took. How long could the child leave it dangling there? As Caroline reached for her handkerchief, Laura's mitten swiped the dribble free.

Caroline's temper tried to rear, but there was not spark enough in it to burn past the chill. "Laura, please. Use a handkerchief," she said, blotting the soiled wool.

"We don't know how long it will be before I can wash these mittens again."

The scratch and hiss of a match interrupted her. Caroline and Laura both looked up. A tiny flame cored with blue lit Charles's face, then dipped into the bowl of his pipe. He puffed, then exhaled a soft column of smoke. Caroline did not protest. Behind the blaze of sulfur, the pipe's sweet smell ached of home. Charles lay back on an elbow and blew a languid ring for the girls. Laura reached up and tickled it into wisps.

"Don't, Laura," Mary said.

Charles blew one afresh, and then another. "There's one for each of you to do as you like with." Mary's floated over Caroline's head. She imagined drawing her number fourteen crochet hook through it, whisking its rims into latticed garlands—like the scalloped wrist, lying half-finished in her work basket. Its curves and lattices looped through her thoughts. She closed her eyes and let her threadless fingers work the pattern.

"I can't sit here like this any longer," Charles said. "I'm going out to see the lay of the land."

Caroline straightened up. "In this weather?" He did not answer, only leaned to tug on his drooping socks. She tried again. "Charles, why not stay in and play us a hymn on the fiddle?"

"This kind of weather's worse for the fiddle than it is for me. Best keep it warm and dry in the case. Won't hold its tune anyway. How would you like to fetch me my poncho, Half-Pint?"

"Yes, Pa!"

Caroline sat helpless at Charles's artfulness as Laura scrambled down past her. He knew Laura would not refuse, just as he knew Caroline herself would not contradict him and tell Laura to stay put.

"Here, Pa," Laura said. Caroline was nearer. She thanked Laura and lifted the poncho from her outstretched arms. Moisture still clung like sweat to its shoulders.

"It's wet yet from last night," she told Charles.

Charles took the poncho from her. "I've got enough impatience flaming in me to dry it from the inside out," he said as he threaded his head through.

Impatience—the very idea! They had not lost a minute of travel. Mired or not, they would have halted early and spent this day stilled for the Sabbath. Yet he would take himself out into the weather—in clothes soggy as day-old dumplings—as though they had not put some four hundred miles behind them in less than two months' time.

"It's Sunday, Charles," she reminded him.

"It's not work, Caroline." He snapped his collar up

to meet the brim of his hat. "Taking a walk doesn't break the fourth commandment."

Caroline's lips fluted downward. A tart *Whatever you think is best* might give him pause if she slanted her words just so. But there was not room in the wagon for them to pry at each other this way. Not on Sunday, and with the girls underfoot. Better to have him doused and satisfied than dry and sullen in such small quarters. Caroline balled her fists inside her pockets and said only, "Be careful."

He took his gun from the hook and ducked around the gray blanket. The wagon jerked like a slammed door as he jumped to the ground.

Caroline followed to tie the cover down behind him, then paused a moment behind the blanket-curtain. The muscles lining her backbone and the spaces between her ribs were weary of bracing against the tilt. Lately when she tired it was a bubbling sort of exhaustion, as though her muscles and joints were stewing in ammonia. She arched her back and spread her arms wide. The fringe of her shawl brushed the sidewalls. Caroline yanked her hands right back. Not even the canvas could leave her be.

Caroline unlocked her jaw and rolled it from side to side so that her ears crackled. One long inhale, then another, chilled her mouth before she went back around the blanket and over the spring seat to the girls.

Their faces as she settled down beside them plainly said, *Well?*

Caroline's jaw bulged anew. Why must they always *do* and never simply *be*? Charles might have his solitary tramp, but there would be no respite for her. The children were like little tops that must be kept spinning, always spinning. And on Sunday they must spin slowly, quietly, without tipping.

"Why won't the thunder stop?" Mary asked. "It makes my ears tired."

"You must not complain," Caroline retorted. Vinegar flavored her voice, and she knew by Mary's sour look that she had tasted it, too. Caroline pulled another cooling breath across her tongue. If she were going to let her vexation flare outward, she would have done better to put her foot down with Charles than singe the girls. Then at least it would have served some purpose. Nor could she simply swallow her ire and leave the child beneath her apron to pickle in such brine. She had charge over their moods, and she would not squander it.

Caroline tuned herself to the rumble of sounds from outside and began to understand why Charles had been so insistent on examining the landscape.

"That is not thunder," she explained. "There is likely a creek nearby. I shouldn't wonder if the rain has flooded it."

Indifferent to this news, they lay down with their heads propped at her hips. Mary picked at the row of jet buttons running down Caroline's basque while she told them the story of Noah's ark.

"Two by two by two," Laura droned. "Pa and Ma, and Ben and Beth, and Mary and me."

"One of us ought to be a boy, to make it right."

"You," Laura said.

Mary lifted her head and glared at Laura. "I don't want to be the boy."

"You came first, like Adam, so you have to."

Mary sulked.

Caroline closed her eyes. Everything pressed on her—the wet canvas overhead, the girls leaning on either side, and the ripening child motionless as a stone in her belly. If she did not get out from under it, even for a moment, she would vanish under the weight of it all.

"I am going outside for my necessaries," she said, drawing her shawl over her head. She paused reluctantly before going over the spring seat. It would be foolish not to ask. "Do either of you need to come?"

Laura shook her head. Mary seemed to consider. *Please, no,* Caroline silently implored. "Mary?"

"Not now, Ma," Mary decided.

"Very well then. Sit nicely here until I come in."

Caroline fetched her rag from the handle of the chamber pail and hunched out into the weather. The rain fell straight as threads from the sky. Crouched on the falling tongue, she lowered one foot as though she were testing a tub of bathwater. The mud enveloped it like a stocking. Step by step, she toed her way through the ooze and ducked under the tarpaulin.

The latrine was a round depression, less than knee deep. With her skirts clutched in one fist, she bailed a bucketful of rainwater from it, then straddled the hole.

Ben and Beth eyed her. Their fetlocks were curled and pointed with mud. She was near enough to Ben to touch the steam from his nostrils. It did not seem fair that she should foul the horses' ground, but that could not be helped. Caroline turned her head and let go her water. It made no sound over the unfaltering beat of rain.

The moment she sat down on the spring seat the girls peeped around the gray blanket and watched her peel off her shoes. Her stockings had kept dry, but her shoelaces were so caked they must be put to soak before they stiffened into twigs. There was nothing to do for the shoes themselves but wait for them to dry enough to scrape clean.

"Your shawl's dripping, Ma," Mary said.

"I shouldn't wonder," Caroline answered. She swung

herself out from under it. An arc of brown droplets struck the floor. More mud. At least she had kept her second-best skirt clean, Caroline thought as she flopped the muddied fringe out into the rain to rinse, then strung the shawl across Charles's gun hooks to drip dry.

Colder now than she had been before, Caroline sat down on the straw tick and pulled a quilt over her shoulders. Again the girls served her those expectant looks. This time Caroline refused to meet their gaze, looking instead to the diamond-patterned mesh of the shawl hanging behind their heads.

It shamed her to realize that the rain had not put out that spark of selfish ire. In her own way she was no less impatient than Charles—only better able to hold herself outwardly still. How childish, to think herself above him rather than admit her envy that he could escape. Caroline let her eyes rest on Mary and Laura. Of the four of them, only the girls had acted their age, bearing the day's trials with as much grace as could be expected from such young children. They deserved something of a treat.

Caroline reached for the work basket and cut a length of red worsted. She tied its ends together and strung the yarn over her hands.

"Oh, Ma!" Laura clapped. "Can we play cat's cradle on Sunday?"

"*May we,* Laura. And no, you may not. But watch, girls, and listen." Her fingers dipped in and out of the loops, playing over the strings like a silent fiddle. It had been years since she made the figure, but the pattern was familiar as a childhood tune.

As she wove the string, she told them the story of Jacob, who slept with a rock for his pillow, and dreamed of a ladder filled with angels ascending and descending from heaven.

"Cat's whiskers," Mary said when Caroline reached the middle of the yarn sequence.

"You must not interrupt, Mary."

With a flourish Caroline twisted her wrists and Jacob's ladder appeared in a mosaic of red triangles between her hands. The girls' mouths popped open in delight.

Into their moment of wonder Caroline recited, "'And, behold, I am with thee, and will keep thee in all places whither thou goest, and will bring thee again into this land; for I will not leave thee, until I have done that which I have spoken to thee of.' And Jacob awaked out of his sleep, and he said, 'Surely the Lord is in this place; and I knew it not.'" Her heart beat faster as she said the words. *Surely.*

Caroline felt her gaze lift to the arch of the wagon bows framing her daughters' heads. The rain still fell and somewhere beyond a creek still roared, but a warm shiver fanned across her back and down her arms.

"Do it again, Ma, please," Laura begged.

Caroline blinked. Had the girls felt it, too? But Laura was looking only at the yarn. Caroline smiled and shook her head. To do it again would turn it into play. "But if you can tell me what is special about a manger," she conceded, "I will show you how to make one from the cat's cradle."

"Bible-Mary laid her baby in the manger," Mary piped.

"That's my smart girl," Caroline said.

They were taking turns with the yarn when Charles climbed inside and stood dripping in the space before the spring seat as though it were a porch. Water rained from his hem into a ring on the floor.

"Creek's about half a mile from here," he said. He took his hat by the crown and flapped it. An arc of droplets spattered the canvas wall. "Flooded so high I can't even tell where the blasted banks ought to be."

"Charles, please," Caroline said, her hand at his elbow. She could not have his oath fraying the peace she had somehow spun out of this day.

"I know it. And I'm sorry, Caroline." He dropped

his hat onto the spring seat and flopped down beside it. "But we're stuck here and that creek is only the half of it. There isn't but a hand's breadth of daylight between the mud and the front axle." Great clods of mud rolled from his boots as he shucked them off. "Ben and Beth can't hardly lift their own feet, much less pull. This ground'll rust their shoes and rot their hooves if we leave them standing, even if we empty the whole straw tick under them."

She looked at the limp socks slouching past the ends of his toes. "Are your feet dry?"

"I haven't the foggiest. I'm too wet everywhere else to know the difference." Beneath the poncho's seams his shirt and pants were dyed dark with streaks of wet.

She pulled a pair of his winter socks from the carpet-bag. "Here. They're not clean, but they're dry. For now, at least." Charles took them without a word.

Though his mood was no brighter, all the sharpness had gone from it. He was only cold and wet and disappointed. Caroline watched him pull the socks from his wrinkled white toes, and all her sympathy reached for him. If her shawl were dry, she would have liked to drape it around his shoulders. The quilts would do just as well for warmth, but they would not enfold him in the same way. Instead she finger-combed the fringe of damp whiskers away from his neck.

"You were right, Caroline," he said, shaking off a shiver. "I shouldn't have gone out."

"Just so you're here, Charles," she soothed, blotting his collar with a towel. "I only wish I could contrive a hot meal for you." She gave a fleeting thought to heating a mug over the lantern for tea.

"I'll warm soon enough, now that the rain can't reach me." He looked at the girls stringing yarn over their fingers and cocked an eyebrow at Caroline. She only smiled and nodded toward them. "Tell Pa what you learned from that yarn today."

While Mary and Laura told Charles about the manger and the ladder, Caroline considered the provisions. Until the cornbread ran out it had not occurred to her that nearly every bit of food they carried, from the salt pork to the flour, was raw. Even with sixty-odd dollars lining the fiddle box, they could not afford to keep making whole meals of crackers, cheese, and dried apples. She had enough flour to fill a washbasin and more water than she could ask for, yet she could not bake so much as a crumb. As a child, she could not have imagined such a conundrum. There had been want back home—during the spare times in Concord there was many a day without anything better than breadcrumbs in maple sugar water—but never in her life had she gone without for need of a cookfire.

Caroline tied on her apron and waited as though the garment itself would tell her what to do. If such a thing could speak, it would surely be in her mother's voice. She knew what her ma would think to see her standing stock-still among sacks of food and thinking she had nothing to eat. Ma, who had fed a whole litter of children, sometimes down to the last pinch of dust from the flour barrel. Her mother would have wept for joy to see crates half-filled with salt pork and bacon, and only four mouths to fill—just as she had wept at the stranger who gave her a barrel of flour on credit. Caroline no longer recollected his face, but that barrel stood like an altar in her memory. All of them had knelt down on the spot to thank Providence for it; she could still feel the kitchen floorboards under her knees.

Caroline grasped the knife and carved the cheese into chunks large enough to fill their hands. They would eat it in spite of the expense, and give thanks for their plenty.

The girls nudged closer as she lay down beside them, seeking her warmth. Their teeth had clinked like china as they shrugged out of their coats and hoods and into their cold nightgowns. The best she could say for the sheets was that they were no wetter than anything else by the time she tucked them back over the limp ticking.

Now Caroline felt a thin layer of herself rising through the quilts to shelter her girls, as she always did when they were so near. Even when they were not seeking protection, Caroline could not help making a shield of herself between them and the world.

Their warmth was welcome, yet Caroline wished Mary and Laura could sleep in their own place, that it could be Charles alongside her instead. With Charles she could release that motherly hovering and settle fully into herself—and into him. To lie fitted side by side, bolstering one another without a word. That was all she wanted. Even after ten years of wedlock, Charles treated her touch, her very presence, as something he must earn. When she could give to him unasked, his deference became a gift to both of them. It would do them both a world of good after such a day as this had been. A man so chilled and stymied should not have to huddle alone on the floor. Yet tonight they must be *Pa* and *Ma,* not *Mr. and Mrs. Ingalls.*

Ten

"Pack up a few pounds of provisions, Caroline," Charles called in through the canvas. "I've found a place to camp. Little rise just to the south."

Caroline leaned out over the tailgate. Sometime in the night the rain had stopped. It was brighter, too, with the sun beginning to press against the clouds, yet cold enough still that she kept her shawl pinned at her collarbone.

"Charles?" she asked. "You don't mean to leave the wagon?"

"I can't see any way around it. Guess I'll have to sleep here. Won't be any worse for me than the last couple nights. Just give me time to lash together a shelter," he said as he untied the ropes that held the team's awning. "Hand me my ax?" he asked.

"Come in and have some breakfast first," she insisted. With a grin, he hoisted himself up to steal a kiss good morning from her parted lips.

Caroline scooped a helping of dry oats into each bowl, then sprinkled them with brown sugar.

"Like the horses eat?" Mary asked.

"Eat that up and you'll be strong enough to pull the wagon," Charles said. His own bowl was empty before Caroline sat down. "I'll be back soon as I've got a framework up," he said. He pulled a length of twine from his pocket. "Roll up the bedding in the big straw tick. I'll need the loft boards to make a floor."

The roar of the creek scrubbed Caroline's ears as she winnowed the kitchen crate down to bare essentials. Thankfully the sound did not prod at her a thousand times over as the storm had. Without the rain-beat constantly delineating the canvas's perimeter, she noticed, it seemed as if the wagon had expanded overnight. She paused to consider the space around her. Cramped as it had felt the day before, the wagon would likely dwarf whatever shelter Charles was "lashing together" out in the open. Caroline's next thought pinched at her: Kansas promised Charles a boundless horizon, yet they were hardly inside the border and already her own meager territory was shrinking.

It would not be forever, she reminded herself. Only

until the creek went down. In the meantime they all must have hot food and flatirons to warm their bellies and their beds.

Caroline licked her lips and released the bitter little cloud. "Selfish," she murmured, and shook her head. Always, it was selfishness that blighted her. What business did she have brooding over elbow room—as though Charles would do any less than his utmost to shelter them? As though he had ever done anything other than his level best for them.

Caroline pulled her mixing bowl and cutting board back out of the crate. She must do no less to keep them nourished in both body and spirit. If she sliced the bacon and measured out the beginnings of corn dodgers right here, dinner would be ready for the fire the moment she arrived at the camp.

In her vigor, Caroline knocked the floor through the bottom of the cornmeal sack with her enamel mug. The sound startled the girls. They came running up the aisle to peer down into it.

"Is that all we've got left?" Mary asked.

"There is another great big sack under the loft," Caroline said. That was so, but it was not full. By now it had likely thinned worse than the straw tick. Before they moved on she would have to gauge Charles's map against what remained.

Caroline tipped her bowl and brushed the meal back into the sack. She reached for Mary and Laura's tin cup and began again. Until she knew how much time the delay would consume, she must measure with the smaller cup no matter how much distance the map showed yet to traverse.

Salt, lard, and saleratus went into the bowl, then Caroline covered it with a towel and took stock of the rest of the foodstuffs in her kitchen crates.

Both her dredging box and the flour sack were better than half-full. That would see them through when the meal sack gave out. And there were the beans. The time they must sit stranded would let her make good use of the beans at last. The brown sugar and molasses had not fared so well, but that deprived only their tongues. At least in this weather she did not have to worry about the sugar seizing up.

The meat was another matter. She had not thought to scrape the bacon since before the rain, and in the damp the usual stubble of mold had grown thick and mossy. Caroline upended the slab and shaved the green free. The salt pork had long ago gone from pale pink to a soapy shade partway between yellow and gray. That was no matter. Salt pork paled just as soon in a pantry as in a wagon.

Aside from the cornmeal, Caroline reckoned she

could make do until the end of the week without pulling from the stock beneath the loft. She topped the crate with her apron then shooed the girls from the straw tick to roll it up, pillows and all.

Caroline did not count how many trips it took Charles to ferry the necessary materials and supplies to the campsite on horseback. Each load loosened the space inside the wagon so agreeably, she hated even more to think of leaving it. Then he came for the planks that formed the sleeping loft.

One by one Charles levered them up and carried them out while Caroline kept back, silently folding her pillowcase curtain. That small stretch of planks had let her mind divide the wagon box into three room-like sections—one for traveling, one for sleeping, and one for everything else.

Until now, they had been only paused. But with their living space dismantled and their things strewn between the wagon and the campsite, the sense that they were stranded rushed in to fill the empty places.

Only one thing appeared unmoved—her trunk, standing off to one side. The moment her gaze fell across it Caroline steadied. She had not seen it in weeks.

Caroline waded through the sacks to spread a hand over the peak of its belly. A picture of what lay inside built itself layer by layer in her memory. Everything rich and fine and delicate, all of it sleeping beneath her palm—untouched since Wisconsin.

"Mary, hand me my work basket, please." With one hand still on the lid, Caroline fished into the compartment that held her steel crochet hooks and pulled out the key to her trunk. There was no reason to open it, except that she wanted to. Caroline turned the key and lifted the lid no wider than a slice of bread. The smell of newsprint, dry and crackling, met her nose. Caroline inhaled softly. That reassuring scent and all the others behind it unfurled into her lungs. It was like stepping back across her own threshold—*home*, packed tight and snug and waiting.

There was no more she needed to take from the trunk than that. Caroline latched the lid and slipped the key into her pocket.

"Aren't you going to put the curtain in?" Mary asked.

"It would not fit," Caroline said.

"You didn't try," Laura said.

"You must not contradict, Laura," Caroline said as she lifted the girls onto the lid. She stood by a moment, held by their upturned faces. It made such a pretty picture—all the precious little things she loved best in the world, stacked together.

———

"It's not far, but the first half mile isn't fit for you and the girls to walk," Charles explained. "Ground down here's so waterlogged it'll swallow you to the knees if you step in the wrong places." He lifted one heel to show the slick of brown streaking his calf. "Ben and Beth have been back and forth enough they've got the shallowest route pretty well figured. If you ride with Mary, I can lead both horses and still carry Laura on my arm."

"Aw, Pa," Laura cried. "I don't wanna be carried."

"Laura, be still," Caroline said. She did not care for Charles's plan any more than Laura did. Or Mary, for that matter, who silently telegraphed her reluctance through the clutch of her mitten. Caroline squeezed back, disguising her own jitters as reassurance.

There was no other way. They owned but one saddle, and so she must ride Beth astride while somehow keeping hold of both Mary and the saddle horn. She lifted her chest and leveled her chin. If this is the way it must be done, then she would do it.

Caroline let go of Mary's hand and kilted up the front of her skirts. Holding to a wagon bow she felt with her right foot for the stirrup. When her heel snugged tight against the loop she eased her left over Beth's back. The horse's girth opened a wide wedge of space between her knees. Caroline's hamstrings twanged.

"All right?" Charles asked.

Caroline nodded, and Charles lifted Mary into her lap. Her daughter's knuckles turned pale as they clenched the saddle horn.

Caroline put her arm around Mary's waist. Her other hand reached for the saddle horn. With her calves she hugged Beth's flanks, gripping her thighs against Mary's.

"Beth's not going to have sure footing," Charles warned both of them. "She may lurch and sway, but she won't fall." He caught Caroline's eye. "I wouldn't put either one of you up there if I didn't trust her." Of course not. She knew him well enough to know that. Still, hearing him say it eased her mind even if it did not loosen her grip. "You be a big girl and hold fast," he said to Mary.

Mary nodded, huddling closer yet over her handhold.

Charles crooked his arm into a seat for Laura. "Climb on, Half-Pint."

"Please, Pa?" Laura asked, looking longingly at Beth. "I won't be scared."

"Makes no nevermind who's scared and who isn't. I can't lead Ben and Beth and carry more than a little half-pint of sweet cider half drunk up."

Laura obliged. Charles shouldered the tailgate back into place and cinched down the canvas one-handed before clucking the horses forward. Beth began to walk, her careful gait rocking Caroline from the hips.

Behind them the wagon stood beached like a small ark. Caroline wished she could have sewn a keyhole or a latch string into its cover. Anyone who happened by might untie the ropes and see plain as plain what they carried. All that remained of their provisions, her trunk, the fiddle. *Good heavens,* Caroline thought— the fiddle box and its secret lining of greenbacks. If anyone helped themselves to that it would leave them doubly bereft.

"Charles," Caroline called, her voice pitched high enough to stop him midstep. "The fiddle box?"

He patted his breast pocket. Caroline nodded, only partially eased. Her shawl slipped with the movement. Every step tugged it a little lower. It was not pinned high enough, but she could not let go of Mary to adjust it.

"Wait, Charles."

Caroline let go of the saddle horn to unpin her shawl, opening it wide. "Lean back into me, Mary," she said. Mary hunched her spine backward, still clinging to the saddle. Caroline put her palm to Mary's chest and hugged her gently in. "Let go now," she coaxed. "Hold on to me instead." Mary uncrimped one fist and latched it to Caroline's arm. Then the other.

Quickly Caroline swathed the long ends of the shawl around her, bundling Mary close. She anchored the knot with the pin and said, "All right, Charles."

Again her hips rolled with Beth's steps. Secured against her ma, the tension left Mary's body, and as the terrain began to steepen she and Mary buttressed each other like a pair of hands pressed together in prayer.

How long had it been since she last held Mary swaddled like this? The shawl, the rocking, the small body finding ease against hers—all of it carried her back to that first winter with Mary.

Those early January days before the fire, her shawl had become a doubled embrace, its arms cradling her and the baby both. Seeing the familiar work of her hands wrapped around the child who was still too new to be believed, Caroline had begun to be able to think of Mary as hers, and of herself as *Ma*.

She looked down at Mary now. Such a big girl, yet still small enough to take refuge in that same nest of red worsted. *Whatsoever ye shall bind on earth shall be bound in heaven.* She leaned down to brush her cheek over the top of Mary's head, wishing it were her daughter's hair meeting her skin instead of the rabbit-fur hood. When the new child came, Caroline vowed to herself, she would bind it to her with these same threads.

Somewhere in its cushion of salt water that child floated and rolled. The farther Beth's feet sunk, the deeper the saddle rocked. Mightn't it be enough to encourage the small being within to brush against her, to give some assurance of its vitality? Caroline pulled her awareness from the touch of the saddle and stirrups, the horse's flanks, and Mary's back as best she could. She could sense her womb's shape and weight, a smooth sheath of muscle poised above her hips. Nothing more.

Caroline exhaled her disappointment. Mary settled back into the space it made, surprising Caroline with the solidity of her presence. Not even quickening yet, and already the child to come could deprive its sisters of her attention, and with Mary right there in her arms. Caroline considered Mary, how she had calmed, and could not help absorbing that same calm herself. Their comfort spiraled one into the other, as it always had. From the very first, she found she could not suckle her baby girl without feeling nourished herself.

It was a kind of sorcery: What her girls believed of her, they made real, and in so doing fed back to her. Every day it happened, though never with the magnitude as it had during the storm. Their faces cried out for a refuge, steady and serene, and that is what she had become, lifted from her own doubts by the sheer force of their need.

Caroline closed her fist over Mary's bare fingers. The palpable warmth she passed into those cold little hands left her wondering: How much of what they loved in her was real, and how much was fashioned from what they envisioned her to be?

At the lip of a small rise, a stand of trees cupped a plot of open ground. There Charles had fashioned an open-ended lean-to of branches and canvas. Two forked boughs stood on either side of the entrance with a third strung between them—very like the stakes and spit that held her pots over the campfire. Two more slender poles angled backward from the forks, forming supports. A tarpaulin made the roof.

Beneath it, Charles had laid the boards from the wagon loft over a crisscross of limbs to raise a floor a few inches above the spongy ground. The platform was just larger than the big straw tick.

It was as she had expected: small, sturdy, and adequate. With the time and means available, he could have built nothing more elaborate.

Charles halted the horses and looked back for her approval. His face pained her. He so wanted to please her, and this was all he had to offer.

Caroline did not have so large a thing as a smile to give in return, but she would not let him be disappointed. There was something smaller and truer she could offer.

"You've done well, Charles," she acknowledged. Saying the words broke a little path through her resignation. Again that ray of thankfulness shone out for a man who so rarely failed to furnish their needs. Still, she did not relish the thought of using such a bleak little thing. Well then, that was all she would do—use it. They would not live in it.

Charles plopped Laura inside the shelter and reached up for Mary. "I'll dig a latrine pit and a trench for runoff in case the rain comes again. We're nearer the creek than the wagon, so at least we won't want for water."

That was a fact. Caroline could hear the creek churning louder yet than before. By the sounds of it she must not only clarify every bucket with alum but boil the filtered water before it would be fit for drinking or cooking. Caroline put that task to one side of her mind. The tea must be boiled anyhow, and she needed no water to fry bacon and corn dodgers.

Charles built the fire so high, the sound of its burning was like horses galloping. "Tore a few pages from the back of my weather journal for tinder," he admitted. The flames roasted Caroline's cheeks deliciously until she felt crisp as a potato skin. How she would relish a potato! First her teeth snipping through the skin, then sinking into the powdery white inside, hot as steam turned solid. Nothing in the world filled a cold belly like a potato. She could feast all day on roasted potatoes—potatoes and thick slices of white bread quilted with butter. Perhaps even a mug of sweet milk, hot from the udder. Such a meal would be velvet on her tongue after all these weeks of salt meat and cornmeal.

Caroline's stomach grumbled at her, and she set to work. She fried bacon, quick and sizzling. Hot pinpricks of fat spat onto her hands, and she did not flinch from them. The iron spider hissed as she spooned corn dodgers into the drippings. Her mouth watered. Much as she craved the fleecy white meal in her mind, she could not keep hold of her imagined feast with those smells and sounds before her.

In between turning the food she steeped two great mugs of tea for herself and Charles. Each golden swallow ringed her throat with its warmth. For Mary and Laura there was nothing but plain hot water. Filled straight from the kettle their tin cup would blister their hands as well as their mouths, so they squatted patiently beside it and took turns blowing ripples across the steaming surface. Such good girls. Caroline wished again for milk, to cool their cup and treat them to cambric tea.

It did no good to warn them of the bacon, nor Charles.

Sparkling hot, the strips of meat branded their mouths and salved their chapped lips with fat. Mary and Laura grinned at each other as their tongues juggled the hot meat. Caroline felt her own smile glistening as she watched. What potato, what bread could fill her as much as the sight of them all warm and dry at last? Caroline set her plate aside and stretched out her legs to toast the soles of her shoes.

"I'm leaving the Colt with you and the girls," Charles told her. "Under the carpetbag. You remember how to fire it?"

Caroline nodded.

"Good. If you need me for anything in the night, fire a shot," he continued. "But don't worry if you hear the rifle before daybreak. Going to see if I can find us some fresh game."

Caroline raked the last flatiron from the coals and wrapped it in flannel for him. He pocketed the hot bundle.

"Good night," he said.

She did not reply.

Charles took her softly by the shoulders. "Caroline?"

Her eyes flickered away from his face. What might he ask that she could answer? If it were all right for him to leave them without door or walls? If she were frightened? True or false, she could not answer him. She could barely smooth the trembling from her lips. There were tears gathering uninvited, tears she could not press back alone. Before she shamed herself Caroline looped her arms under Charles's, laying her palms over his shoulder blades, and pulled herself into his chest.

His hands slid down her sides. Those broad firm hands that had once spanned her waist. Could they feel the laces at the base of her maternity corset now? As if his touch melted through the knots, her body gave a great shiver, then slackened. Caroline pulled in a breath. Nothing hampered its way. Her chest felt spongy as though from crying, but the trembling had gone.

Not a word passed between them as she stood with the crown of her head notched under his chin. Only breath. Her chest rode his inhales, then carried back his exhales.

Charles moved one hand up her back, to the nape of her neck. Caroline felt his heartbeat deepen as his knuckles brushed her chignon.

"Charles," she whispered. She tilted her head to meet his gaze and the whole coil of her hair tipped into his palm. He kissed her then, chastely, in the space between her brows. The warm print lingered after his lips had left her skin, a seal against whatever fears might reach for her in the night.

Caroline brought her palms to his chest and gently eased herself from him. "Good night," she said.

She lifted the blanket flap and went in. Mary and Laura lay at her feet with the quilt's red binding pulled up over their noses. She knelt to kiss each of them as Charles had kissed her, then undressed, said her prayers, and lay down beside them.

The rifle shot woke her. By the time Charles came over the rise with a white bird dangling from his belt, she had smoothed her hair and put the coffee pot on.

"Snow goose," Charles said. "Must be a straggler, it's so late in the season. Or maybe it got caught in the storm. Should I fetch the tin kitchen from the wagon?"

"No thank you, Charles. I'll fry it in the spider for breakfast."

It was better still than the hot bacon the day before, rich and fresh and running with juice. A hint of salt and pepper made the savory flavor bloom in her mouth.

Laura lifted her drumstick to nibble the last shreds from the bone and said, "Look, Pa."

Caroline looked up as well, ready to address Laura's manners. Little though she was, Laura never would have flaunted her table scraps that way at home. But Charles and Laura's attention was not where Caroline expected to find it. She looked beyond the bone in Laura's fist and saw a man on a black pony emerging from the trees. Charles rose, plate in hand, as the rider approached.

Caroline sat still as a rabbit poised to run, watching. The stranger was strung together like a ladder—perfectly straight up one side and down the other. His horse was lightly built, slender through the back and face. "That your wagon down there in the dale?" the man asked.

"Certainly is," Charles said. He handed Caroline his plate and propped his fists at his hips. "This your land?"

"Nearly."

Caroline blanched at the two plates in her hands. Not only had they set up camp on another man's stake, but their mouths were half-full of his game. Quietly she stacked the dishes onto her lap and swallowed.

"We're only passing through," Charles said. "Be on our way just as soon as I can dig out and ford that creek."

The man swiped a hand through the air. "You're welcome to camp as long as you need. I heard a shot this morning and thought I ought to make sure there wasn't any trouble. The name's Jacobs," he said to Charles, then "ma'am," with a nod to Caroline and a glance that traveled down to her lap.

Caroline could not tell whether it was the plates of purloined goose or her own form that drew his attention; she was rounded enough at the navel now that anyone who chanced to look might notice. Either way, his eyes did not linger.

Charles extended his hand to Jacobs. Caroline folded her fingers inside her palms to hide the lines of grime under her nails. "Ingalls," Charles said. "Headed down into Montgomery County."

"Looks like you've come a distance already."

Caroline would have liked to whisk a sheet over the camp at that. Anyone would think them vagabonds, with their hacked-limb shelter and soggy wraps slumped over the tarpaulin ropes. This man had a silky black beard trimmed so short and neat it lay flat as horsehair. For the first time she noticed how Charles's hair had grown. The back of her own neck itched to see how far it had strayed into his collar.

"Left Pepin County, Wisconsin, nearly five weeks ago."

"That so?" Jacobs asked, but his attention was on Ben and Beth. Caroline marked the way he studied them. If he had looked at her so intently, she would not have thought him a gentleman. "Fine, strong team you've got there," the man said.

"That they are."

Jacobs ventured further. "Fact is, I've been on the lookout for a good pair of draft horses. Got three and a half years in on a claim the next section east of here, and a preemption filed on this one. It's a railroad section, $5.50 an acre."

Charles gave a low whistle at the price—better than four times what they hoped to pay.

Jacobs nodded. "Don't I know it. One fine crop would put me within arm's reach of paying it off—that is, if I can clear enough acreage to sow in time. I wonder if you'd consider a trade?"

Charles glanced at Caroline. She said nothing. "That would depend on your offer."

Jacobs looked down at his horse, then back to Charles, weighing him in a different way than he had measured Ben and Beth. If he looked much longer, Caroline thought, she would be compelled to rise and stand beside her husband. "I'll offer my matched pair of mustangs," Jacobs said at last. "This one and her twin sister."

Caroline considered the pony. Where Ben's and Beth's muscles bowed outward, this creature was small and sleek. Not much more than fourteen hands high, but with a spry stance that belied her stature. And a coat so bright and black, just looking at her gave Caroline pleasure.

"The other mare's set to foal this summer, so there's a mule colt in the bargain," Jacobs went on. "I've had a look over your wagon, and there's nothing in there the pair of them can't pull as far as the Territory."

Had he inspected the wagon with the same intensity that he scrutinized everything else? Caroline did not like to think so.

"Guess there's no harm in going for a look," Charles said.

"When will we have dinner, Ma?" Laura wondered again. She had been promised dumplings and gravy, and though breakfast still filled her belly, her mind was already hungry with the thought.

"Not until after Pa comes back," Caroline answered. She laid her dish towel over the iron spider to keep the flies from the drippings. The plates were wiped and the camp tidied, and still he had not returned. A pot filled with the remains of the goose simmered at the edge of the fire.

Caroline brushed her hands on her apron. The calico was tacky with the week's grime. More than a week. Here it was already Tuesday—another washing day come and gone—and she could not leave the girls alone with the fire to haul water for laundry. And there would be no mending, for her work basket was down in the wagon. There was not a lick of work she could do until Charles returned. Yet she could not sit idle. If she did not busy her hands somehow, her thoughts would begin to chase in circles. Charles had not been gone long, not really, but he had already taken more than enough time to ride half a mile and see a horse.

Beth nickered and tugged at her picket pin. Caroline went to her and reached up to rub the long white blaze on her forehead. "Easy now, Beth," she said. "They'll come back. Your Ben and my Charles, they always come back." Beth shook her head, tinkling the iron ring on her picket pin. Caroline rubbed Beth's nose and scratched under her chin. She had not known Beth to be nervous before. She half wondered whether the animal could sense what Charles was contemplating on his errand.

"Laura, don't," Mary said behind her. Caroline turned. Laura had pulled a stick from the kindling pile to draw on the ground. "You'll get all dirty."

Caroline looked at Laura's muddy squiggles and zigzags and her thoughts lightened. "Mary and Laura," she asked, "how would you like to learn to write your names?"

Mary's nose gave a dubious little crinkle. "In the dirt?" she asked.

It was only a single bristle of irritation, and Caroline did not even feel entitled to that. Few would believe her if she said so, but such a fastidious child was not always a blessing. What did Mary expect? She had neither slate nor pencil. All their books and paper but for Charles's weather journal were buried at the bottom of her trunk. Still, there must be something she could contrive.

Caroline went to the kitchen crate and opened the sack of meal. Her eyes measured the scanty depth. It would not be waste if it fed their minds, she decided, and pulled out a fistful to sprinkle onto a clean tin plate.

"On a dish?" Laura asked.

"Come and see," Caroline said.

With the handle of the wooden spoon, she traced an L in the grit. "L is for Laura," she began.

Over ten years had passed since she had been anyone's teacher, yet the charge of excitement it gave her was as potent as ever. She had not been much more than a girl herself then, but Caroline remembered how it had felt to coax a pupil to the threshold of understanding. Then that breathless moment—waiting, watching, for the mind to reach forward and grasp. Oh, she had shown Mary how to sew a seam, and both of them were mastering a growing list of little household tasks, but this was different. This was real learning. And these were her own two girls.

Both of them were so quick to learn, Caroline's pride and pleasure whirled inside her. Each stroke held her poised for the next like their first wobbling steps forward.

Mary frowned at her work. "I want it to look like yours, Ma."

Caroline lavished them with her best praise. "You have both done very well."

"I mean when you write letters on paper. It's prettier, all long and fine."

"Like ribbons," Laura agreed.

"Our letters look like sticks," Mary said.

"This is called printing. Once you have learned to print each letter nicely, I will teach you how to write."

"Show us, now, Ma," Mary begged. "Please."

Caroline gave the plate a shake, then drummed the underside with her fingertips to even the surface of the meal. She eased a hairpin from its nest and began to trail it across the tin, taking extra care with the flourishes and gracefully knotting the cross of each *t*.

Dear Ma and Papa Frederick,
    The girls have asked me to write a few lines. Though these words will not reach you, I hope that

you are well and not worrying yourselves on our account.

Beth whinnied, and there was Charles coming up over the rise. A bulging flour sack rode on his back as though he were Santa Claus. Suddenly self-conscious of what she was doing, Caroline shook her letter from the plate and quickly threaded her hairpin back into place. "Well, Charles?" she asked before he had one foot out of the stirrups.

He swung down from the saddle and tossed the sack into the shelter. "Straw," he said. "Jacobs spared us some for the tick."

"Charles! You didn't ask him for such a thing?"

"Pshaw. You know me better than that. He offered. Said he'd seen the straw on the ground by the wagon and figured we'd have use for some fresh."

Caroline did not know how to greet this news. She could not fault the man's generosity, but there seemed to be nothing about them that escaped Jacobs's notice. If they must be so bared, she wished he would do the courtesy of leaving some things unremarked.

"Man's got a good piece of land up there," Charles went on, squatting down to peek inside the bake oven. "I can see why he wants to trade. There's a good many trees to clear, but none that'll leave stumps anything like I grubbed out of the Big Woods. Ben and Beth should have an easy time of it."

"And his team?" Caroline prodded softly.

"Oh, they're a fine-looking pair. You'd think their coats were woven out of black silk, the way he keeps them brushed. Jacobs is so eager to get Ben and Beth started on his acreage, he offered to stable both teams until the creek goes down."

Again that keen generosity. It was beginning to rub almost too close to charity. Something in her wanted to object, if only to give herself a moment to hold the decision in her own hands. "It sounds as though it's more than a fair proposal," she allowed. "But without Ben and Beth how will we plow our own claim?"

Charles pulled the fading Montgomery County handbill from his pocket and passed it to her. Its corners were rounded with wear. "'Wide Open Land: One Dollar and a Quarter an Acre,'" he quoted. "Where we're going I won't need draft horses to break ground. Anyhow, place like that'll be flooded with folks coming and going before long. Plenty of opportunity to trade for a bigger team if these two aren't up to the job. Meantime it'll save us a week's worth of feed and then some. Mustangs won't eat like draft horses. They'll need less land for grazing, and less timber for a barn. I can't think of any good reason to refuse."

"If he cheats us, Charles—"

"I don't see how he can. A thief has to be able to run if he wants to keep ahead of the law. Man's got a wife and four boys, not a one of them over eight years old. There's a spanking new cookstove and a pair of glass windows in the kitchen. That reminds me." He reached into his coat pocket and pulled out a bundle made of a blue-checked napkin. "Mrs. Jacobs sent a fresh baking of light biscuits."

They were warm yet. Caroline untied the corners of the cloth. A moist, yeasty cloud filled her nose. "My land," Caroline said. She sat slowly down on the spring seat and tapped the golden bottom of one biscuit with her fingernail. The light hollow sound set her mouth swimming.

"There's just something about them, Caroline," Charles continued. "I know Ben and Beth'll pull us anywhere I point them, but this pair seems to *want* to move. Their feet are as itchy as mine." The spark in his eyes told her the deal was as good as done, but still he looked at her, asking.

Caroline chalked out her thoughts one last time. Aside from bumping into her pride, Jacobs himself had done nothing to arouse ill ease. That alone was not ample reason to doubt him at his word. Yet it did not seem prudent to entrust their team to a perfect stranger with nothing to back his end of the trade. Caroline drew a breath to speak, and the scent of the warm bread in her lap beckoned to something beyond prudence.

"If you think it's best for all of us to trade, well then, we'll trade," she consented.

Charles slapped his knees and sprang up. "I'll take Ben and Beth over to Jacobs's place right this minute. Do them both a world of good to be under a solid roof for a while."

Laura trotted alongside Charles to Beth's picket pin. "Where are Ben and Beth going?" she asked.

"They're going to stay with Mr. Jacobs's horses in his stable."

"What about us?" Mary wanted to know.

"We're going to wait right here until the creek goes down and the mud dries up."

"I'd rather stay in a stable than any old hut."

Caroline's voice whipped out sharp. "Mary!"

Charles interrupted. "Jacobs did offer, Caroline." He spoke low and easy, the way he talked to the horses— the way she herself spoke when she wanted him to moderate his voice.

That was too much. She gentled her tone, not her sentiment. "We are not going to sleep in the hay like animals. Pa has made us a good shelter right here."

"Bible-Mary stayed in a stable," Mary pressed, "and her baby, too."

Caroline threw up her hands. "Mercy, child!"

Laura pulled at Charles's coattails. "Did you get to see his ladder, Pa?" she asked.

"What's that, Half-Pint?"

"Jacob's ladder."

Charles's great laugh rang out across the clearing. As quickly as she had snapped at Mary, Caroline put a hand to her lips. Try as she might to hold her mirth close, she felt her smile unrolling into her cheeks. It was as though Providence were winking at them.

"This Jacobs is a mister," Mary explained. "They didn't have misters in Bible times."

"Pa doesn't call him mister," Laura said to her shoes, and Charles laughed again.

Caroline shook her head. Oh, these children and their notions. What a pair they made—Mary, with her thoughts plain and straight as hems, and Laura's head a tangle of fancies. Between the two of them Caroline could scarcely find her footing.

Laura's chin brushed her collar. Caroline's hand slipped down to her throat and her smile turned over. Dear little thing. She looked forlorn as a little brown wren without a song.

"That's all right, Laura," Caroline soothed. "I'm

pleased to see you can remember your Bible stories as well as Mary."

Laura peeped up. Caroline nodded at her. *Yes, truly,* that nod said.

Back came Laura's smile, and Caroline marveled at the power these children granted her to render them happy or sad.

The creek needed only a few days to calm; the soggy ground lingered for a week. One solid week they were neither wet nor cold nor moving. Every day Charles dug at the mired wheels. Every evening Caroline soaked and scrubbed his mud-stiffened trouser legs in buckets by the fire. For a day or two Caroline reveled in the motionlessness, then the camp blurred like the road—all bean porridge, backache, and lye.

Not one thing in the camp, not the bed, the cookware, nor the spring seat, stood taller than knee high. The wagon's low cover had only made her imagine she was forever stooping. Out here, her body quickly informed her of the difference. Caroline did not allow herself to complain in words the girls might hear, but her hunched and crouching muscles cursed freely.

By the time Charles declared they would strike camp the following morning, Caroline was ready to welcome road and wagon both. Their drawers and socks were

clean, if dingy from the creek water, and she had gotten ahead of the mending. She had nothing else to show
for it.

Caroline climbed into the wagon behind Mary and
Laura. Beneath her steps the boards rang out solid and
even as she straightened the crates and squared the
sheets over the straw tick. The clean white walls spread
over her, smelling of sun-bleached cloth. Pleased, she
took her seat. Up off the ground she felt lofty as a ridgepole.

"Come here, girls," she said, patting the board beside her, "and let me tie on your sunbonnets. Then we
will be all ready to go when Pa comes with the horses."

Laura spotted Charles and Jacobs first, each leading
one black mare down into the hollow. A brindle bulldog trotted along behind. "It's Pa!" she said.

"Those aren't Ben and Beth," Mary said. "Are
they, Ma?"

"But that's Pa," Laura insisted.

"You are both right," Caroline answered. Neither
was satisfied, and they peered out across the grass.

"You have very nice ponies, Mr. Jacobs," Mary said
politely as the pair approached the falling tongue.

"I'm glad to hear it, Miss Ingalls," Jacobs said, leading one right up to the wagon box, "because they're yours now."

Mary blushed to be addressed so gallantly. Laura dropped from the spring seat and leaned out over the front of the wagon on tiptoe. "Look at our pretty ponies, Ma!" To Charles she said, "What's their names?" and the little horses tossed their heads and stamped their feet, preening. Charles was right—in the sun the mustangs' sleek black backs had the sheen of silk.

Caroline sat still, watching Jacobs as Mary and Laura were allowed to finger the velvet noses and rechristen the mustangs Pet and Patty. His wistful smile touched her, made her almost lonesome. Eager as he was to break his land, he had traded away something fine and beautiful to do it, and his face could not hide the loss.

The full measure of the trade did not sink into the girls until Charles and Jacobs began hitching the mustangs to the wagon. For that matter, it was not fully real to Caroline until she saw the men tightening up Ben's and Beth's belly bands and drop straps to fit the smaller animals.

"Where are Ben and Beth?" Mary asked.

"They're staying here to help Mr. Jacobs plow his fields," Charles said.

Laura whirled around. "Ma?" Her lips quavered.

Caroline set her face and nodded. Mary and Laura looked at each other, then just as quickly looked straight ahead. Caroline did the same. There was nothing she could say. Her throat had closed. She could not watch her daughters' faces ripple and clench. It stung more to see them so little and so brave than it would to watch them cry.

It was not just the girls that threatened her composure. Ben and Beth were only stock, but she and Charles had had those horses longer than they had had Mary and Laura. Acre after acre, mile upon mile they had been a good, steady team. Caroline was grateful to them in a way she did not know how to express, and now, she realized, she would not have the chance to try. To drive away without giving them so much as a pat goodbye was nearly like leaving home all over again.

Caroline's eyelids burned. Her hand darted into her pocket and clenched her handkerchief. There had been no tears leaving Pepin. How absurd to think of crying now, over horses. Everywhere she tried to pin her gaze made the burning worse. Then her eyes found the bulldog. He was already squinting up at her, and with some suspicion. His jaw was thrust out, the lower teeth denting into the upper lip like pinking shears poised to snip. The black folds of his nose quivered in Caroline's direction, then he snorted, twice. He seemed vexed, as though something clouded her smell and would not let him scent her properly. He sniffed instead at Charles's ankles, then circled the wagon once, twice, three times. On the third pass Caroline heard him wetting on one of the wheels. Then he trotted back to the mustangs' heels, plunked himself down, and licked his nose.

Jacobs buckled the last mud strap and ran his hand over the mare's flank before extending it to Charles across the wagon tongue. "Good luck to you," Jacobs said. He tipped his hat to Caroline and the girls.

"And the same to you," Charles said.

Jacobs took a single step back, as though trying out the feeling of turning his team over to Charles. Charles waited, respecting the man's last opportunity to change his mind. All the heavy straps and buckles that harnessed the animals to their wagon did not matter. For as long as Jacobs cared to linger, the mustangs still belonged to him. Slowly he put his hands into his pockets, and Caroline knew his mind had made the break. Only his gaze seemed unable to let the beautiful little creatures go.

Caroline said, "The light biscuits Mrs. Jacobs sent were a treat after so much travel. Please thank her for us."

Jacobs turned his face gratefully up to her. "I'll do

192 • SARAH MILLER

that, Mrs. Ingalls." He gave a nod, curt and final, then turned and walked quickly eastward.

The bulldog did not follow. He sat completely unperturbed, watching Jacobs go.

Charles climbed up onto the spring seat and still the dog did not budge. "Charles," Caroline said.

Charles called out, "You want to whistle for your dog?"

Jacobs half turned, still walking away as he spoke. "No sir. If he wants to follow me he's welcome. Otherwise, he's all yours. I couldn't lure that fella back with a side of beef. He's taken a shine to those mustangs like you've never seen in your life. I guess you could say the three of them were pups together. As far as he's concerned, those are his ponies. You and I just have the loan of them."

"That so?" Charles asked.

Jacobs slowed only enough to keep from shouting as the distance between them widened. "That's a fact. He'll let me take one pony at a time anywhere I please. But the minute I start hitching up the both of them, he's waiting under the wagon like a sentry. I promise you've never seen the like of it. You won't want for a better watchdog. Once he sees you're the one taking care of those mustangs, he'll guard every stitch you've got and treat your children like his own."

"What's his name?" Laura called.

"He answers to Jack, but I don't think he'll much care what you call him, so long as he's with his ponies. Good luck," Jacobs said again over his shoulder.

Charles shrugged and then chirruped to the mustangs. Pet and Patty thrust forward, their small muscled rumps rounding. With a great creak the wagon came unmoored and bumped up to level. Charles turned the horses sharply to keep the rear wheels from sinking into the hollow. Up bounded the bulldog and dodged between the wheels to follow.

"Well I declare," Caroline said.

For a little while the wagon rolled along flat and smooth in the soft earth, then began the long climb toward the road. Caroline craned into the slope, curious how these small horses would take the load. Where Ben and Beth had only to lean ever forward to make the wagon follow, this team strove ahead, truly pulling. Caroline could see the effort of it flowing under their hides with every step. At the lip of the road the mustangs touched noses, the gesture like a wink between them, as though they knew their labor made them even more beautiful.

Charles laughed.

Caroline blushed. Perhaps she had spoken the thought aloud. "What is it?"

"I don't know," Charles said. "I just feel like laughing. Maybe it's the horses."

"They are lovely to watch," she mused.

"It's something more than that. Feel them," he said, handing her the reins.

She took the lines firmly in her hands. In only a few steps the team's eager rhythm loosened her wrists, traveling past her elbows and into her shoulders. It was like dancing, with the leather straps a line of music running from the horses into her palms. Caroline's breath lifted, light and airy, into two soft notes of laughter.

Charles grinned. "Feel it?"

Caroline nodded.

"I don't know when I've run across a finer matched pair than these," Charles said. "Tell you the truth, I don't know how we'll tell them apart after the one foals."

Caroline studied the rounded sides of the mare in front of her—the one Mary named Pet. "She can carry that colt, and the wagon, too?" she asked.

He raised an eyebrow at her.

She flushed more deeply and gave him half a smile in return. "I'm not pulling the wagon, Charles."

He laughed again and took the reins.

Eleven

Kansas.

The land seemed to move, to breathe all around them.

It was not empty, not void of trees, as Caroline had assumed from the grand boasts of Charles's handbill. But the scattered stands of timber did not define the landscape as they did in Wisconsin and Minnesota. They did not even hem the edges of the roads and fields as they had throughout Iowa and Missouri. Here on the prairie they gathered modestly in low-lying areas along creek beds and riverbanks to mark the places where water flowed, fringing Caroline's view with hints of green.

Just gazing across the prairie made her eyes feel somehow larger, fuller. Caroline had not known they could hold so much space at once. Without trees acting as walls there was not even a ceiling, nothing to fool her eyes into halting at some arbitrary height. It was as though a lid had suddenly lifted from the world. Caroline knew she was not seeing more, not really, but the sensation of it was so very different from taking in a view made up of separate pieces all vying for her attention. Clearer, invigorating. The world ceased to be an assemblage and became one thing, one simple thing.

It sounded different, as well. Always the sounds of the wind had come from above, rustling the leaves and tousling the evergreens. Here it whispered beneath her, so that its voice seemed to rise up from the ground. She could hear great sweeps of it passing across the prairie, lifting and falling like living breath. Here the very shape of the wind was visible. The tall swaying grass made it so, and by looking closely Caroline saw that the wind was not composed of one single movement—it fanned with hundreds of fingers through the tall blades all at once, stroking ruffled, swirling patterns all over the prairie.

Charles was smitten. She had not seen his face so soft with wonder since the day Laura was born, had never in her life seen him so at ease. The constant rushes of motion around them worked a kind of magic on him, appeasing the restlessness he'd always battled. Caroline herself was not sure whether he was driving more lei-surely, or if the way the grass seemed to dash alongside the wagon had altered her own sense of speed.

They breasted a roll of prairie, spring green and golden. The sky was sudsy with clouds. Before them, the sun was sinking between the hills like a coin tucked into a pocket. Light melted into the hollows and dales. From where she sat high on the spring seat, Caroline fancied she could feel the very curve of the earth.

This was to be home, she told herself. This was where her child would be born. She hugged her folded hands around the small hill that was her belly. Her own roundness mirrored the abundant swells before her, making her welcome.

All her life she had been accustomed to making do with little if any to spare. *We must cut the coat to fit the cloth,* her mother had so often said, and by mimicking the careful movements of Ma's broad hands Caroline had learned well how to stretch every thin scrap of food or fabric or fuel she was given.

On this wide teeming land life could be different. She could smell it in the moist soil, feel it in the way the waving tufts of grass seemed to brush at her heart. Caroline looked again at Charles. He was aglow. Simply aglow. You could not sit beside him without feeling it. But it was in her, too. Seeing the spread of this country opened her somehow, broadened her so that it seemed her expectations stretched out not just before her, but all around her in a way she had never felt before nor could quite describe. Perhaps, she thought, this was what Charles had felt all the time back home, this boundless outward reaching. No wonder his fiddle so often sang of lively marches without horizons. The music was the only part of him that could not be constricted by walls and fences and trees.

Belated sympathy for him saturated Caroline's chest. So much of what she had fallen in love with—what she had taken for vibrancy and zest—had in truth been frustration. Ten years, and she'd only now begun to understand. Perhaps if she were a different kind of woman, one that looked outward more often than inward, she might have recognized it sooner. Were she not carrying this child, this fleck of him inside her, she wondered, would she have been able to grasp it at all? Caroline tucked her bonnet brim aside to study him. Charles was already a fine man, and this land could only change him for the better. Almost against her will, that thought rippled into another: Could he change so fully that she would no longer recognize him? No, she assured herself, that was not possible. This place would not alter him, but give him room to fully unfold himself. Suddenly it dazzled her to imagine how much more of a husband and father he might become, now that he would not always be butting up against the edges of his world like the honeybees that buzzed into their cabin only to be confounded into exhaustion by trying to fly back out through the windowpanes.

The further south they drove, the more the landscape opened, and the further it opened the more deeply Caroline pondered its possibilities. This was a place made for a man as versatile as Charles. Farmer, hunter, and trapper alike could make a living from the land alone. Carpenters would surely be in high demand before long. He could define himself any way he liked, or not at all, as he pleased. If he so chose he could devote himself to any business he had a mind for instead of cobbling together a livelihood piecemeal. Country like this lay as an invitation for Charles to reap as much as he could sow—whether from the land itself or from those who would settle it—with nothing to hamper his reach.

Charles knew it better than she, had likely reckoned it would be this way since before they crossed the Mississippi. He was so happy it was comical, very nearly indecent. Caroline had never seen him look at her so boldly—boldly enough to make her flush to the tips of her ears and turn her head so that her bonnet hid her face from him. Only the girls in the wagon box and the baby already in her womb kept his gleeful hands from straying from the reins to the delights of her body. After a mile she chanced a peek at him and noticed that whether he was looking at her or the prairie his expression did not change. Caroline sensed then that the two of them were curiously tied in his mind. He did not know how else to show his burgeoning love for Kansas, and so he wanted to do with her what he could not do with the land.

Caroline slid closer to him, so that their hips touched. She could give him that much, at least. Pleased, he shifted the reins to one hand and with a glance that said *May I?* laced an arm around her waist. His warm palm rested softly on her flank. Caroline laid a hand over his and wished again that the child would move, for both of them.

If she bore a son, she mused to herself, what a gift that would be to all of them in this vast place. A set of footsteps to follow Charles along any path he settled on, another pair of hands to share out the labor. And if it were a daughter, what then? Her mind flipped like a coin at that. It would be harder, without her brother Henry's help, for Charles to manage a full quarter section alone, no matter how amenable the land.

Caroline blinked. She was thinking of this child as if it were a tool, an instrument to help them stake their claim. What of the child itself, the person it could become? Beyond the near certainty of blue eyes, she still could not make her mind form a picture of this baby, nor the life it might lead. Caroline felt her thoughts taking that peculiar shift backward as though she were trying to remember the child rather than imagine it. Back to the Big Woods and the familiar image of herself in her rocker before the fire, Black Susan purring at her feet.

None of it was right. This baby would be born not in winter, but on the coattails of summer. Not in the woods, but on the open plain. There would be no cat, no blazing winter hearth, no rocking chair. Caroline gazed out over the long clean grass, trying to picture instead the little house Charles had conjured before the campfire, with its blue and yellow calico curtains. How would it be inside that one room, with not two, but three little girls to bring up?

That was a different view altogether. All in one great swoop, the same vastness that held so much promise for Charles revealed to Caroline how small the places that could belong to her and the girls were by comparison. The square corners of the imagined house, the neatly turned edges of the garden, seemed sharper, narrower. Their little house in the Big Woods had rarely felt cramped, but now, without the great dark trees partitioning her view, Caroline understood just how insignificant it had been.

She turned backward to look at Mary and Laura, flushed and dozing on the straw tick. There was no place, yet, for her daughters to find room to expand in country like this—no churches, no schools, no community at all to speak of. Not even the narrow congregation of kin.

One day, if enough women came, the land would open itself to the cultivation of such places, to crops that fed more than the body. Until then, Mary's and Laura's minds would be confined to a vista no wider than their own sunbonnets. Both of them needed more. Caroline had only to look at them to know it. Mary was already too bright, and Laura too spirited to flourish without that promise. For their sake she could not root herself to a place without it.

Caroline said aloud, "The girls must have an education."

"Hmm?" Charles said.

"The girls must have an education," she said again.

He nodded without looking away from the horizon. "That's so. Any time you judge them ready."

"Mary is nearly ready now. I hate to make her wait."

"Why wait?" And with a wink, "Seems to me you were a schoolteacher once."

It was the wink that did it. Caroline saw no room for teasing in this; the breadth of their daughters' learning could not ride on something so light as a wink. A wind rose up in her, strong enough to form a shout. For a moment Caroline could not think sensibly. It was all she could do to grip the rush of anger and rein it back. She would not let it go racing out at him. Her body went stock-still with the effort of speaking quietly. "Two terms, Charles. I taught just two terms and then I was married. That's been better than ten years ago. Mary and Laura will have more capable instruction than that."

She could hear the muscled quiver in her voice. It pulled Charles's eyes from the scenery and his arm from her waist. She felt the hard set of her face as his eyes met hers, saw it bewilder him so rapidly that he nearly looked hurt. "I've never known you to be incapable of anything," he said.

Caroline sat dumb. A compliment. Of course. He had no end of them—if not completely true then always sincere. Usually it was the sincerity that disarmed her.

Not this time. Yes, she could teach them all she knew, but her learning was a decade old. She would not let her own limits be imposed upon their daughters.

"Promise me, Charles," she said. "No matter where we settle, Mary and Laura will have a formal education."

He slowed the mustangs to study her. She watched the small muscles around his eyes contracting as he searched for something that would tell him what he had done to light such a flare between them. When he spoke the words were stripped bare. "Caroline, I swear to you—"

Caroline's breath hissed back from the word. Even this was not worth making an oath of. "Please, Charles. Don't swear it," she said. "Only promise me."

"I promise you. Our children will have proper schooling." He broke her gaze only long enough to sweep his eyes quickly over her belly. "All of them."

Caroline nodded. "All right," she said, and her voice was her own again.

He moved to touch her and changed his mind, as though afraid she might singe him again. The last thrash of her anger went limp at that, and she felt too much at once. Grateful. Relieved. Repentant. And proud.

Charles gave the lines a little flick and the wagon sped up. Caroline waited for the wheels to carry them ahead, away from that spot, then crooked her hand into the crease of his elbow, squeezing softly to steady herself, to thank him, to apologize. He pulled it in against his side, forgiven.

Next day he was bright as ever. Caroline had sobered, troubled that she had so quickly managed to find limits in a limitless landscape. A pale scar from the hungry years, she thought ruefully, the same one that left her always mindful of the bottom of the flour barrel even when it was full to brimming. Never mind that she was plump enough now to dimple at the elbows. She still could not look at anything, it seemed, without gauging the needs it could satisfy and for how long. Not like Charles, who enjoyed everything the world laid before him right until the very moment it ran out. That alone was enough to tell her that his growing up had not been marred by want.

She had no desire to begrudge him his cheer, but it got to be a little like sunburn, sitting there beside him with no way to shade herself as he radiated happiness. Beautiful as it was, the view no longer fed her in the same way it fed him, and the more he feasted on it, the more keenly Caroline felt the lack.

What she felt was nonsensical, she scolded herself. Nothing had been taken from her. Nothing tangible would be denied her. Yet it pinched ever so slightly to watch Charles unfurling like a beanstalk beside her, knowing that Kansas offered her no similar satisfaction, no chance to reach beyond what she had been for the last ten years: *Mrs. Ingalls, Ma.* She could stretch forever toward that horizon and grasp nothing new.

As if it had grown out of her thoughts, a dull ache

206 · SARAH MILLER

meandered across her right side and descended into her belly. Caroline followed it with the heel of her hand, but the narrow cord of pain was too deep to reach. The only part of her that could be counted on to expand in this place was her womb, she thought, and even that was half Charles's doing.

Caroline moved to fold her hands together again and found her left had formed a fist in her lap. She had fairly balled herself up with envy. Envy, of all things, when everything they shared was bound to increase. And after she had vowed in the bunkhouse that first night to do all she could to keep her family worthy of Providence's care. She wiped the damp palm across her skirt, uncrossed and recrossed her ankles. It helped some to break that selfish thought up and brush it away, but she did not know what to do with her hands, did not like the empty feel of them, or trust them not to clench up again. They needed something of their own to hold besides themselves, the way Charles had his reins and the girls their playthings. But what? She did not want to sit there with a wooden spoon or a skein of yarn in her lap. Her books and slate came first to mind, but they lay at the very bottom of her trunk, and anyway, she was not a teacher anymore and never would be again. Perhaps if she had never taught school, Caroline thought, never held an envelope filled with dollar bills she had earned herself, she would not feel so empty-handed now. Not even Mary or Laura would fill that space in the way she wanted.

Seeds. The little packets of seeds she had saved from the garden, and Polly's, too. Those belonged to her in a way that nothing else inside the wagon did. Only she could not very well go digging through the crates to find them now. There was no call for it, no way to explain why she wanted them. The best she could do was fan out the handful of neatly labeled envelopes in her mind and imagine how the seeds folded safely inside would feel through the paper. There were the winkled round beads that were turnips, cabbages, and peas; the cucumbers, tomatoes, and onions with their sharp pointed ends; the flat squash seeds broad as fingernails; the tiny bearded carrot seeds. They had reached up out of the Wisconsin ground, and come spring she would work them into the Kansas soil so they could take root. Those lacy tendrils, finer than her finest crochet thread, would bore down through the dirt until they found something to grasp and hold themselves firm. Seeds always reached down before reaching up and out.

There was comfort in that.

Twelve

The willows along the Verdigris River traced a soft green line over the prairie. Their trunks were slender, and their young leaves not thick enough yet to provide much shade. Through the haze of yellow-green, Caroline could make out the tops of a few dozen haystacks on the opposite bank. They seemed to stand in crooked rows and squares.

"Must be the outskirts of Independence," Charles said.

Town. Caroline's heart began to patter.

Laura pulled herself up by the back of the spring seat. "Where, Pa?"

Like Laura, Caroline wanted to stand up in her seat to see this town, this place so fresh it had not earned itself a spot of ink on the map. Caroline had only half believed it would be here at all. She took hold of the outermost wagon bow and stretched her tired back out long and tall, tipping her chin toward the horizon. The smell of the river skimmed past her nostrils, a clean, silvery scent.

Somewhere just beyond the river were people, supplies, news. Perhaps, Caroline thought breathlessly before she could help herself, perhaps a letter. There had been waysides and whistle stops all along the road, but all that had mattered about them was how much they charged for feed, or how many miles' travel they signified.

"This is the last town before the Indian Territory?" Caroline asked.

"So far as I can tell. Map's no help for that anymore. I expect it'll be the last town between us and the Territory, anyway," Charles said.

She had known the answer before asking. Today or tomorrow they would drive past the rim of the nation. No matter how far beyond Charles drove, this town would belong to them, and they to it, and so Caroline was anxious to learn what kind of a place it was, what kind of people inhabited it. She gave the wagon bow another gentle pull, craning as far as she could toward those haystacks without betraying her impatience. This once, she would not mind strange faces looking at her.

What would they see in her, she wondered, what would the people of Independence expect of a woman come to claim a quarter section with her husband? Perhaps she would surprise them. Perhaps she would surprise herself.

The Verdigris was high enough to lap at the underside of the wagon bed, but calm, and they forded the river easily. With a snort and a splash from Pet and Patty the wagon emerged from the screen of willows and the western bank came into view.

Had she been standing, Caroline would have sat right back down again. The haystacks *were* the town— little half-breed buildings, timber on the bottom, hay on top, no larger than sheds. Caroline felt the wagon bow slip through her hand as she sank into the shell of her corset. How could anyone properly call this place a town?

Charles pulled up before one of the hay shanties. A faded sign in front announced *Bred and Pize for Saile huar.* Caroline winced at the attempt. This place was not fresh, but raw.

Charles ducked through the low door and in a few minutes brought out a loaf wrapped in an old sheet of newsprint. "Here's a treat for you, Caroline. Light bread."

It felt a trifle heavy to go by the lofty name of light

bread, but it was warm and smelled of yeast, so she un-wrapped it and sliced it thickly.

"'Immigration still continues to pour in,'" Charles read from the paper as she waited for the molasses to find its way from the bottom of the jug. "'As many as twenty claims have been taken in this vicinity in one day. At that rate every quarter will have an occupant by spring.'" His face sobered some. "Sounds like we didn't get here any too soon. I'd better inquire at the land office for the best prospects."

He did not wait to eat his dinner, but drove with his bread in one hand and the reins in the other past the clusters of hay-topped sheds toward what Caroline had taken for a house and barn from the riverbank. They stopped between the two, and she saw that the pair of buildings comprised the whole of Independence's business district. A double-log structure, the hotel, proclaimed itself the Judson House. The store with its sawn-board walls and shingled roof looked like it might just fit inside their house in Wisconsin. Size not-withstanding, it was by far the neatest, most sturdily built place in town, and it bore its few months' weath-ering almost boastfully. The proud little building was already the matron of Main Street, Caroline mused, a grande dame in her graying boards and shining glass windows.

It was a fanciful idea, something like Laura might come up with, and Caroline felt it nudging her impressions of Independence into a more charitable light. The town was undeniably raw, but it did not intend to remain so. This was a place still becoming itself.

"Huh," Charles said, looking the street up and down. "Maybe the land office is sharing quarters with the store. Ought to stock up either way," he said. "I'm short of tobacco and I better get more powder and shot while I have the chance. What else do we need?"

Caroline weighed each dwindling sack in her mind. "We still have plenty of beans and dried apples. The cornmeal, flour, and sugar are all low, especially the meal. Coffee. Some fresh salt pork or bacon would be nice. Molasses. And maybe, if they have any—" she stopped. "No, never mind that." He had already treated her to the light bread.

"What? There can't be a thing in this town that's too good for you." His eyes twinkled, and Caroline felt the quick bloom of pleasure warm her face. She wished she were not so prone to blushing at his flattery. He could turn her ears halfway to red talking that way, and he knew it. "Tell me or I'll have to guess," he teased, and Caroline's earlobes tingled. The man had no mercy.

If she told him now it would sound silly. And if she did not, Caroline knew he would buy her something far too extravagant. Tins of oysters or a yard of fancy trim to make over her old apron. She looked up from her folded hands. "Pickles. Just a small jar of cucumber pickles."

"Pickles," Charles repeated. "That's it?" Caroline nodded, wanting very much to wriggle out from under the bemused slant of his smile. "Laura, hand me the fiddle box." He pocketed a twenty dollar note and went inside. Before Caroline could wipe the crumbs from Mary's and Laura's mouths, he was back again.

"Nobody there," he said.

"What do you mean, Charles?"

"Shelves are full of goods, but there's not a soul inside." He shrugged and walked across the street toward the hotel.

Caroline turned again to the brightly polished window panes. How could a store keep itself stocked and spotless with no one tending it?

A sort of grumble came up from under the wagon. Surprise lifted Caroline's brow as the unfamiliar sound registered. Jack, who had been every bit as docile with the children as Jacobs promised, was growling. She looked out the back of the wagon and saw what Jack saw: a man with a hay rake over his shoulder was nearing. The man leaned the rake against the door jamb of the store in a way that suggested to Caroline that he owned the place before approaching cautiously. "Hey there, fella," he said, and squatted down with his palm open for the dog to assess. "Take it easy, now." And then to Caroline when Jack dismissed him with a snort, "Looking to stock up, ma'am?"

"Yes, sir. My husband—" She did not want to shout or point with the girls looking on. "See him there, headed for the hotel?"

The man stood and hallooed.

Charles turned. "This your place?"

"That it is. I'm Wilson. Sorry to keep you waiting. Irwin and I—the two of us run the store—we got so busy raking hay we didn't see you pull up. It's a mite early for haymaking, but come winter there's no excuse to be short of fodder in this country."

"A sound investment," Charles said, so gravely that Caroline could hear a joke coming behind it. "Whatever your stock doesn't eat, you can likely sell as roofing."

Wilson laughed. "That's a fact. The Indians call it Hay House Town." Chuckling, the two men headed together through the doorway. Their boots were ringing on the board floor before Wilson turned and asked, "Will you come in, ma'am?"

There was nothing she wanted more just then than to go into that store. The reflection of the wagon cover had filled its windows so that from where she sat Caroline could only just see the shelf tops. Since the wagon stopped her mind had been fleshing them out with neat rows of provisions in their sacks and cans and jars, polished tools, bright bolts of cloth. Her eyes would be so grateful for such plenty—not only the quantity, but the color and variety. Even the crisp black words printed on the labels would be a treat. Most of all, she wanted to stand inside those square board walls with a straight, solid roof over her head. Caroline grasped the wagon bow, this time to offset the way her balance shifted now when she stood, and realized just in time.

It was no longer seemly for her to be in public. How many weeks had passed since any man but Charles had seen her? Three, and Mr. Jacobs had likely suspected even then. She glanced up and down the street. There was no other woman abroad, much less one in her condition. Sitting still up on the spring seat it was not so plain, but if she stepped from under the wagon's cover, the outline of her dress would make her instantly, doubly conspicuous.

Still, she hated to say no. There was a thin, wheedling feeling taking hold of her throat that would not let the word pass. It was such a rough place, she argued with herself, and men would not show their disapproval with the same sidelong glances as women. No, men would self-consciously look away, not knowing how to speak to her—or whether to speak to her at all—and that would be every bit as bad. Worse. Wilson himself might blush to the collar if she stood.

Caroline let go of the wagon bow and the spring seat gave a tiny sigh, as though disappointment had made her heavier. It was no business of hers to diminish whatever propriety this fledgling town had managed to accumulate by indulging herself, so she said, "Thank you, no. The children and I will wait in the wagon."

The only sounds that drifted out to her were footsteps, and the indistinct back-and-forth of two voices. Then Charles, louder and clearer: "A dollar a pound for white sugar? Haven't you heard, the war's over?"

Had she heard right? They had never seen the like of such prices in Wisconsin. Caroline held her breath for Wilson's response.

Wilson's voice rose slightly to meet Charles's, but his tone stayed level. "You'll find there's not tremendous call for white sugar out here, friend."

"Wouldn't think so at those rates," Charles said. "I'd rather preempt an acre of land than twenty ounces of sugar."

A dollar a pound. It staggered the mind to think of anyone in these hay shanties paying that kind of money for such a small luxury. President Grant himself would have to come calling before she would put white sugar on her table at that price. And what of the things they did need—the brown sugar, cornmeal, and flour? The arithmetic was numbing, the swelling figures painful as bruises to contemplate. If all Wilson's prices were so steep, by fall there would be nothing but green felt lining the fiddle box.

"A man can't expect Mississippi River prices on the Verdigris," Wilson's voice went on. A flare of anger blurred Caroline's mental arithmetic at that. Of course they had expected prices to rise as they approached the frontier, but three and four times more? That was something else altogether. From the way Wilson was talking now, Caroline could guess that Charles had reacted no better. The storekeeper's voice sounded as though it were backing away from what he had just said. She slid across the spring seat to listen more closely.

"It's not so much the goods as the hauling," Wilson explained. "Look, the southern branch of the Union Pacific line runs only as near as the other side of Labette County. I'm paying them top dollar to get it that far, plus another $2.25 per hundredweight on overland freight to Independence. I promise you, these are the fairest rates I can afford. If you want anything like back East prices, you're welcome to make the drive out to Oswego or Fontana yourself, and no hard feelings."

The names of the towns were not familiar to her. Perhaps they were not on the map. How far, then? Caroline wondered. And how much cash did they have, how long would it last? Always the same questions, since she was a child: *How much? How far? How long?* The stack of bills had seemed almost too much when they left Pepin—enough to stock the wagon and secure just over one hundred acres besides. Still, she had never expected all of it to last as far as Kansas, not with paying upward of forty cents a bushel to keep Ben and Beth warm and hale until the snow broke. That constant nibbling had taken a greater toll than the bridges and ferries, Caroline realized. If only she'd paid more attention, kept better count.

Her mouth was open now, the breath coming in spurts. Silently, Caroline brought her lips together. She pulled an unbroken stream of air through her nose and held it. One small crack and the old fears came tumbling in. Quickly, methodically, she sealed off her mind with calm thoughts. They had made it safely to Montgomery County. Right this minute there was food and money in the wagon. She could go and touch the crates and sacks if she wanted to, slip her fingers under the lid of the fiddle box and feel the crisp edges of the bills. She had her seeds, and Charles his gun. They did not owe a cent to a soul in all the world, and the government would not require payment on a preemption for nearly three years. And there was Gustafson, she remembered. That was enough to let her breath out smooth and warm. The Swede owed five hundred and six dollars. The fiddle box had only to hold out until Gustafson's next payment. There could be a letter waiting now.

Caroline half stood to peer through the doorway for any sign of a postal cabinet behind Wilson's counter. Beneath her, Jack rumbled again. Another man, this one with a scythe, was approaching the store. Caroline sat down again and moved back to her side of the spring seat for good measure. The fellow skirted the wagon, too preoccupied by Jack to truly notice her, tipping his hat on the way past.

Inside, the men's voices rose convivially in greeting and introduction. Caroline permitted herself the tiniest of sighs. Charles would be longer now, with men to talk to. For all that he loved to revel in the feel of open space around him, there was a part of him that came alive only in a crowd. As he cast about for land prospects, Caroline could make out that extra flourish of liveliness in his voice. She had not heard it once in all these weeks. It was good to hear.

"Is it true what the paper says about immigration? Twenty claims a day being filed?"

"Some days it sure feels like it," the new voice said. "Other days Wilson and I could mow an acre of hay without missing a customer."

"Figured I'd better check in at the land office, see where the most open country is. Which of these sheds is it?"

"There isn't one."

Charles's voice spluttered, "No land office? I've got a handbill right here says Montgomery County."

"That may be so, but there wasn't any printing press in this town until just over a month ago. Any advertising you've seen'll have come out of Oswego, same as any newspaper prior to March."

Before Caroline had time to absorb this, the bulldog stalked out from under the wagon, pointed his face south, and growled. She had never heard such a growl from a tame creature. It was a low, savage sound that prickled all down the back of her neck. Gingerly, she leaned out around the canvas to see what had provoked him. Across the street, a trio of Indians were eyeing the mustangs from their own ponies. Long black scalp locks striped their heads and brushed the shoulders of their ribbon work vests. Tufts of hair trimmed the seams of their leggings.

Caroline flattened her back against the spring seat. Her skin felt strangely light, as though every hair on her body were lifting to reach out, whisker-like, in anticipation of danger. Something about them frightened her, something deeper than Jack's ire. She did not want them to see her looking at them again, so she closed her eyes and waited for their image to flash against the darkness of her eyelids.

Three sleek black scalp locks glinted in her memory. That was all, and it was enough. She remembered now, and understood: in Wisconsin, the Potawatomis dressed their hair that way only in preparation for war.

"What's Jack growling at?" Laura asked. She was starting to climb over the seat.

"Stay back, Laura." There was no tone in her voice. Caroline did not hear how loudly or softly she spoke and did not care so long as Laura obeyed. Her ears had room only for her own racing thoughts.

How near to let them come before calling for Charles? If they meant no harm and she created a scene there would be trouble, worse trouble maybe than if they had some kind of malice in mind. It was broad daylight, in the center of town, such as it was. All they had done was turn their heads.

But those scalp locks. Everything in her told her not to ignore them as the sound of unshod hooves striking hard-packed dirt came steadily nearer.

Jack growled again, so long this time Caroline

thought he must be scraping his lungs raw with the sound. Then he snorted and strutted back under the wagon. Caroline sat quite still a moment, then leaned out from under the canvas. On one side, the Indians were riding away up the street, and on the other was Charles, heading out of the store with Wilson just behind him.

"I'd head into the southern or western townships if I were you," Wilson was advising. "There's still good land open in Rutland, Caney, and Fawn Creek. Just don't be surprised if the Osages come calling." He paused to give a wave to the departing Indians. Two of the three riders raised an arm in response. "They've got in the habit of collecting five dollars from each settler. Rent, as they see it."

Five dollars. Four acres' worth. "Do they always—" Caroline faltered, knowing how the question would sound coming from a woman fresh from the East. "Do they always dress their hair that way?"

Wilson gave her the wry glance she expected. "More often than not. They mostly save the horse hair roaches for special occasions."

Caroline did not concern herself with the tenor of the storekeeper's reply. The reaching, listening sensation had vanished from her skin, and her senses seemed to retreat back into her body. In its place there was a vague unease that came from knowing the signals she relied upon to interpret the woodlands tribes had no currency among the Osages.

Charles handed up twenty-five pound sacks of meal and brown sugar and unbolted flour while Wilson and Irwin brought out two bushels of oats and one of shelled corn for the feedbox. No meat.

"I couldn't do it," Charles said quietly, "not at these prices. I can hunt us plenty of game, but I can't shoot feed for Pet and Patty. Feed's sold by the pound here, not the bushel. Would have bought myself some nails, but I couldn't afford them and lead for shot. The heavier the goods are, the more they cost. That reminds me—I treated us to roasted coffee beans instead of green. With what they add on for freight, green coffee isn't any bargain here."

No great loss without some small gain, Caroline thought, though at times the gain was so trifling as to seem almost spiteful. That was not his fault, though, so Caroline raised her lips into the shape of a smile. "That will be nice." And then, tentatively, "No letters?"

Charles shook his head. "Not even any post office yet. Letters come in with riders from Oswego, one county over. Costs ten cents apiece to collect them." He unfolded the map and frowned. "Fontana's over a hundred miles northeast, up beyond Fort Scott. Oswego's not marked. But if it's the other side of the Union Pacific's south branch, it's got to be a good thirty miles east." He took up the reins and turned the mustangs westward.

His plans had not changed, then. Caroline folded her hands and pointed her bonnet brim straight ahead.

For the first time since Wisconsin, Caroline felt a pull from behind. Every mile that spread between them and Independence tugged at Caroline as though her corset strings were looped over the hitching posts. It was not so much the town itself calling to her, Caroline reckoned, but the notion of a town—a link to the society of others, however rudimentary it might be. The farther Charles drove, the more tenuous that join became.

So Caroline was not as startled as Charles when they found themselves suddenly at the edge of the wide cut in the earth. The feeling of an approaching rim had held her poised, leaning slightly backward these last ten miles. And now there was the very break she had sensed, inches from the mustangs' noses. Perhaps it was not the line between Kansas and the Territory—perhaps they had already passed that boundary—but this cleft in the prairie's flesh, with the slender vein of creek flowing through its bare red bluffs, spoke to her as the Missouri had spoken to Charles. Life on the opposing shore would be measurably different. How many more wagons must follow them across that creek, Caroline wondered as Charles frowned at his map, before the seam it embodied drew tight and disappeared?

Down into the bottomlands the mustangs went, not pulling now, but pushing to hold the wagon from skidding down the steep grade. Caroline held her spine rigid as the brake lever and angled herself backward, and still she could not fully resist the steady downward momentum. This land was uncanny, she thought as the wagon slid lower and lower, the way it managed to make her body enact the shapes of her emotions.

Between the hot red cliffs the bottomlands spread out still and smooth as the first page of Genesis. Across the creek grazing deer stood and wondered at them, utterly unconcerned by their presence. The place seemed a little world unto itself, unreached even by the wind. Not a breath of air rumpled the grass as Charles stopped the horses to drink. Caroline, too, felt suddenly untouched once the wagon leveled. Down here no unseen currents pulled or pushed at her. In this sheltered place there was nothing to feel but herself. She opened her hands and brought them to her sides, gauging herself from without and within.

The heat of her palms warmed the dusty blue calico and then slowly reached through corset and chemise to greet her skin. Across the gentle stretch of her belly the pulse of each fingertip drummed softly. Somewhere between them, Caroline hoped, the still and silent little creature inside could feel that same calm throbbing and know it signaled welcome. She did not know how much longer she could await the answering telegraph of elbows, knees, and heels before admitting something must be wrong.

Charles leaned toward her, drawing a small breath as if to speak, then closed his mouth and looked back to the creek. Caroline fitted her hands into their accustomed knot and waited. "Creek's pretty high," he said. "But I guess we can make it all right." He pointed out the old wheel ruts that marked a fording place—two deep grooves butting up neatly to the water's edge. "What do you say, Caroline?"

Her stomach gave off an unexpected shimmer of unease. Close behind, Caroline felt her awareness rising of its own accord, as it had at the sight of the Osages on the street.

Strange. Nothing before her had changed. She had not felt the least bit wary until he asked. Puzzled, she studied the creek up and down, searching for whatever it was that might have put her senses on guard. The water was high and deep, as Charles had said. But she had known that before he'd said so. The swath of darker silver streaking its middle was perfectly plain. She looked at the ruts Charles had pointed out. If they were unlike any of the other ruts she had seen in the last seven hundred miles, she could not say how.

Caroline closed her eyes as she had done on the street in Independence. This time nothing leapt out at her in warning. The creek flowed no differently, no more menacingly in her mind. She opened her eyes. Charles was looking at her, waiting. Still she did not speak. The cold liquid feeling remained lodged in her middle, though there was not one thing in the scene before her that she could blame for it. It was as placid a spot as could be, with the soft green willow boughs swaying lazily above the surface of the creek.

Caroline thought again of the Indians and their scalp locks. She had not been fully right about them, but neither had she been fully wrong. In Wisconsin the flutter of apprehension they had triggered might well have saved her life. Here it had only made her look foolish and fearful. She squirmed inside, remembering how Mr. Wilson had looked at her when she asked about the Indians' hair. The storekeeper could think her a silly woman if he liked, but Caroline could not abide the thought of her husband giving her that same look. She wished Charles had not asked.

There.

The little swell of recognition momentarily pushed her fear aside. That was it—not the creek at all, but the question itself. It was not like Charles to ask such a thing. Always he consulted her before deciding when and where to camp, but the roads with their forks and fords and bridges, those were his business. If the route confounded him somehow, he muttered only to himself over the map.

There was no mistaking his wariness now. It wafted from him like a scent. He was not just taking in the scenery as Pet and Patty drank, but scrutinizing it. Caroline watched him look at the horses, then at Jack, searching for a reaction to link with his own. Something, some tiny thing, must have whispered at him not to cross, so faintly he could not make it out.

Did you hear that, too? That was the question buried under what he had asked. She had not, and so she did not know what to say. She could not say yes and did not want to say no. All she could think to do was give him permission to do as he thought best.

Caroline spoke low and firm. The words alone would sound flippant if she were not careful. He must hear the trust embedded in them. "Whatever you say, Charles."

Such a long pause. Even Pet and Patty stopped drinking to listen. Caroline heard the water dripping from their noses, the lapping of Jack's tongue as it poked in and out of the creek.

"I'll tie down the wagon cover," Charles decided.

No. The word flashed through her whole body, bright and sizzling cold. Then, with a shudder, it flashed out again. Charles had jumped to the ground, leaving the spring seat jiggling back and forth behind him. He yanked at the canvas straps so harshly that Caroline could hardly keep hold of her thoughts with the wagon shuddering around her. He was only being careful, she told herself, by securing the cover so tightly. He had never in his life knowingly put them in danger. She must trust his intuition as she had trusted her own.

"They may have to swim, out there in the middle," he said as he sat down beside her again. "But we'll make it all right, Caroline."

Another pinprick of unease struck her, and her body recoiled ever so slightly from the wall of her corset. She had not asked for reassurance. It could only be himself Charles was reassuring, and it had not worked. Everything about him was pulled taut as the wagon cover—his mouth, the grimacing muscles around his eyes. He had the reins wrapped so firmly around his fist as to make the skin stand out in little bulges between the leather. Caroline looked again at the line of ruts. They pointed so clearly into the creek, there could be no questioning this as a ford.

As the wheels dropped into the ruts Laura piped up behind them, "I wish Jack could ride in the wagon, Pa."

If Laura took to the new baby half so quickly as she had taken to that secondhand bulldog, Caroline thought, she would count herself lucky. Charles did not answer. Had he even heard?

"Jack can swim, Laura," Caroline said. "He will be all right."

One by one the mustangs' legs cut into the flowing water, carving wide V shapes across its surface. Then came a little sideways tug as the creek began wending its way between the spokes of the wheels like a needle pulling a thread through cloth. Charles slapped the reins again and the team continued gamely forward.

Caroline watched the water lap gently at their bellies with a sympathetic shiver. It crept steadily up the horses' sides until their wet black backs shone patent leather smooth in the sun, then disappeared altogether. Beneath her, Caroline felt as much as heard the creek sloshing now and then at the underside of the floorboards.

They were already nearly halfway across. Charles leaned back a little and the rigid angle of his elbows eased. He smiled bashfully at her, a smile like that of a boy suddenly no longer frightened of the dark. Caroline unclenched herself and felt the gentle hug of her corset welcoming her back. Then the reins drooped. The mustangs had hesitated, their ears swiveling upstream.

There was no time to ask what or why. A gush of water came splashing at the sideboards. It hit with a jolt that jostled Caroline's jawbone, then pushed its way under and around the wagon box. The furrows around Pet's and Patty's necks melted away as the current scooped them up. The wagon gave a funny sort of dip and then they were floating, horses and all.

Instinctively Caroline scooted inward, lifting her feet from the floor, but no water breached the seams. Only the churning of the mustangs' hooves reverberated through the water and up the wagon's wooden tongue into the box. Caroline felt the faint echo of their chugging in her chest as though a steam locomotive were passing.

"Gee!" Charles called out, and Caroline's attention expanded outward. He was half standing, leaning with the reins, trying to steer the mustangs toward the right.

Upstream. It felt immediately wrong. They always forded crosswise so that the horses could work with the current, not against it. Caroline searched the opposite bank for her bearings. Nothing aligned. No opposing set of ruts, nothing. It might have been a different creek altogether. Even the willow trees lining the shore hunched closer overhead, as though they had shrunk. No, Caroline realized, not shrunk. It was the creek itself that had risen, enough to catch hold of the willows by their lowermost leaves and slant the boughs downstream.

Caroline looked out beyond the horses' heads. There was the ford, already some rods upstream from where it had been when they set out moments before. The surge had washed them past in a matter of seconds. Caroline watched with one hand over her mouth as the landing place began slipping out of sight altogether.

The wagon was a boat, with no rudder or oars but the two black ponies. Pet and Patty snorted and paddled mightily against the current, but it was all they could do to hold the wagon in place. Then for a moment they began to gain ground. The sound of the water striking the side of the wagon box stopped. Quiet opened up like a hole around them. Caroline did not like it. Her stomach plummeted just half an inch and stopped short.

They had fallen without falling, Caroline thought without fully understanding herself, plunged into a hollow whose depth she had no way of sounding. From under the surface came an almost imperceptible tremor, and Caroline knew her answer was on its way. The creek was marshaling itself. She felt it coming, a gathering rush from upstream.

Caroline spun in her seat. The water must not reach the girls. It would pull them downstream like the willow boughs. Mary was already crouched down on the straw tick, but Laura sat straight up, her blue eyes violet with excitement. Caroline's mouth went dry in one breath. There was next to nothing she could shield them with.

"Lie down, girls," she commanded. They dropped as though her voice had knocked them over. It was not enough. She whipped the gray blanket down over them. "Be still, just as you are. Don't move!"

The current came at the wagon in a great, muscular arm, caught hold of the back of it and swung it like a pendulum. The shore went swinging with it, out of sight until there was nothing but water before them. Caroline flattened herself backward against the spring seat. The whole of the creek was coming at her as though it would leap straight into her lap. It crashed and foamed against the boards, inches from her knees. Dark drops of spray shot up and dotted her skirt.

The water reared the mustangs backward, straining the pole straps that bound them to the neck yoke. They snorted and kicked and pulled, their noses inching nearer and nearer the narrow pole that joined them to the tongue. Then with a whinny the creek forced them up again. Caroline gasped and gripped the seat as the front of the wagon tipped upward, pried by the tongue.

The leather straps and steel rings would likely hold, but the wooden yoke? Caroline flinched at the thought. With the weight of two horses yanking each of its ends backward even a good hickory pole might snap like a twig broken over a man's knee. The long tongue was only a little less vulnerable. If either of them splintered, the mustangs would come crashing into the wagon box. They must keep fighting the current, Caroline realized, if only to keep the wagon intact. *Swim,* she willed them, *swim.* But Pet and Patty were as frightened as she was. The creek had them in a chokehold. Their necks straightened, their noses pointed to the sky. Caroline could see the whites of their eyes.

"Take them, Caroline!"

The reins were in her hands and Charles's hat and boots on the floor before she understood what was happening. He stepped one stockinged foot up onto the corner of the wagon box and sprang from it into the creek. The wagon gave a terrible lurch behind him and—

Caroline's breath, her blood, stopped cold. The image of him leaping held itself frozen before her. It was as though her senses refused to register anything further.

But she had seen what happened next. Already she could feel the print of it on her memory.

The water had closed over his head.

Instantly the creek sealed itself as though he had never been there at all. Every ripple that belonged to Charles was gone.

Caroline waited with the reins in her hands and his name in her throat. She must not scream, must not frighten the girls, must not frighten the horses. Everything in her had dropped with him. She pulled back against the feeling and the reins tightened with her. She would hold the whole wagon afloat this way until Charles surfaced if she had to. Her eyes looked nowhere but the place where he had disappeared.

But it was not the same place, she thought with a cold flash, nor the same water. All of it was moving—creek and wagon and horses, water and wheels and hooves. And somewhere, moving with it or through it or against it, her husband. The creek might take hold of him—might already have hold of him—and sweep him away without her ever seeing.

Pet's collar jerked to the left and she seemed to stumble, though Caroline knew there was nothing solid beneath her hooves. Caroline pulled hard on Patty's outside line for balance. Patty's head swerved to the right and Pet's came with it, yanked by the crossline, but the collar did not right itself.

Something was snagged in the harnessing. The trace or the belly band or the breast strap—she could not be sure.

Caroline did not know what to do. She could not keep pulling—the bit was already notched too deeply into Patty's cheek—and she could not let up. Whatever it was had a firm hold. She could feel it herself in the lines. It took all her strength to hold them away from the drag. Then, oh then, the water beside Pet burst open, and there he was.

Charles.

Caroline saw his breath spray from his mouth in a mist of droplets and her own lungs unlocked. He had grasped the traces and was hauling himself up along Pet's side. His shoulder plowed up a swell of water before him.

He took hold of Pet's throat latch. All Caroline could see of him were his head and his fist, tight under Pet's chin. His own narrow chin barely breached the surface; the creek had him by the whiskers. Then she heard him speaking. Not the words, but the sound of them, so light and calm, they buoyed Caroline just enough that she could begin to think more than one moment ahead.

The mustangs must not give in to their panic. Not with Charles in the water beside them. She could not steer. Her arms were no match for the push and thrust of the current. But if she held the reins up high and steady, Caroline thought, Pet and Patty might not have to struggle so to keep their heads above the water.

Slowly, Caroline began to feed the lines out straight. She heard a rustle behind her and her attention splintered. Laura had come out from under the blanket. When, she did not know. Caroline did not turn around. She could not take her eyes from Charles. Until he was out of that water, there could be no room in her consciousness for anything else.

"Lie down, Laura," Caroline said, and Laura did.

Caroline honed all her focus back into the reins. Slowly she lifted the lines, searching for the right height, the right amount of tension. Too much would signal Pet and Patty to stop. Too little and they would flail. Higher, higher—there. Just below her shoulders their heads leveled, chins parallel to the water. *Now, steady,* she told herself. She pulled gently, firmly, backward until the graceful curve of the mustangs' necks began to reappear. The roar of the creek fell away from her ears as Caroline concentrated. Her arms measured the ever-changing tension in the lines and matched the two sides to each other. With Charles encouraging her, Pet was pulling harder now than Patty. Caroline slid to the left end of the spring seat, cocking the reins to soften Patty's bit so that she might swim ahead and match Pet's pace. Suddenly both reins softened in her hands. She wrapped them double around her fists, quick, to take up the slack.

Something had changed. Caroline felt it immediately in the lines. The leather in her hands was no longer taut with frenzy. It did not pull at her arms, but hung balanced between herself and the team. She had done it. The horses had regained control of themselves, and Caroline was driving—driving them up the center of the creek. They made no forward progress against the current, but that did not matter to Caroline. Pet and Patty had stopped straining skyward, and that alone was enough to thank God for. All the power it had taken to fuel the mustangs' panic returned to their chests and legs, and they charged stubbornly at the water.

There was no more time than that to be thankful. Again Caroline felt a drop in her stomach. This time the sensation hovered below her navel, rolling from side to side, unable to balance. It made her want to slip from the spring seat and spread herself flat across the floorboards. The whole wagon was moving in a way it had never done before. Two months of jolting and rattling, rocking and swaying, and this was both new and wrong, a sideways sort of teeter running right down the underbelly of the wagon. *Like driving down a ridgepole,* Caroline thought, and edged back toward the middle of the spring seat.

It happened too fast to brace for. The wagon tipped sideways and every muscle in Caroline's body snapped inward. Crates and boxes shifted behind her. The carpetbag on its hook swung out at her. Just as quickly the floor leveled, but Caroline did not release herself. Everything in her held its place, striving toward her own invisible center. Only her eyes dared move.

She could see no cause. Nothing had struck them. The water had not risen nor become more turbulent. She could even make out what Charles was saying to the horses.

"Come on, Pet. Gee over, Patty."

Charles. He was trying to coax the horses away from the middle of the creek. Of course. That was why the wagon had teetered. It was too light to stand upright with its broad side exposed to the strength of the current. But the wagon must be turned to face the bank if they were to make landfall safely. There was no other chance. The thought of all that water heaving again at the sideboards whitened Caroline's knuckles. It would either turn them or topple them—right over onto Charles.

Caroline repelled the thought. She would not, could not allow that scene to unfold—not in her mind or before her eyes. There was not even time to think of such a thing. Once the wagon began to turn, those horses must swim faster than the water flowed or the current would overtake them. Charles could not do that alone, not up to his neck in the creek. Caroline coiled up her courage and hauled the reins sideways. As the horses' necks angled toward land, Caroline felt her weight begin to shift from beneath and knew the creek's hold on the wagon was tightening. She slapped the lines hard, again and again. One crackling spray of water after another shot up from Pet's and Patty's backs. The little mustangs jolted and the wagon swung.

Caroline watched nothing but Charles, clinging to Pet. The willows blurred behind him. Water smacked and splashed at the boards, the overspray leaping up to strike sharp drumbeats against the thin canvas walls. Caroline prayed with her fists clenched and her eyes wide open.

> *Therefore will not we fear, though the earth be removed, and though the mountains be carried into the midst of the sea;*

Though the waters thereof roar and be troubled,
though the mountains shake with the swelling
thereof.

All at once the wagon and the creek ceased their
grappling. The wagon moved as though it were a bullet
careening down a rifle barrel.

"Haw!" Charles called out, and Caroline obeyed
quicker than the team, quicker than thought, pulling
the lines toward the western bank without knowing
why. She saw it then, a brown flat place a few rods distant. The break in the trees seemed to be racing toward
them. Instinct drew the reins toward her body. Safe
from capsizing, they must not now cripple the horses
or the wagon in landing. She could not slow the creek,
but she would slow the team what little she could.

The iron tires struck and bounced against the creek
bed. Caroline rocked forward, then sharply back.
Charles shouted, but Caroline could not hear what
he said. Sand and iron ground together beneath her.
Everything from the tin plates to the churn dash rattled. Then the sound of wood scraping wood as the
wagon tipped and it all skidded toward the tailgate.

Charles shouted again and there he was—rising,
running, out of the creek—shoulders, back, and legs
shedding water.

The shock of the wheels turning on solid ground sent Caroline's teeth clattering down on her tongue. Her eyes clamped shut against the pain. When she opened them, the wagon was still. So still. The rushing and the flowing and the roaring, all of it was over. Charles stood panting beside the shining wet mustangs with his clothes clinging to his skin.

Caroline found herself trembling so violently she could not let go of the reins. All the terror she had not had time to feel still had hold of her; everything that had not happened suddenly fanned out before her, bright and terrible. Her voice quavered, "Oh, Charles," and blood rose from her bitten tongue with the words. Had she been able to move, she would have had him in her arms.

"There, there, Caroline. We're all safe."

Better perhaps that she could not reach him, Caroline thought as she shivered and shook. There was enough thankfulness in her to crush him, and just the other side of that, a hot spurt of outrage. At him, at herself. She had known—they had both known—something was wrong, and because they could not put words to it they had gone into that creek anyway. With no one else to depend on, they had failed each other. There was no place in country like this for such mistakes, no place at all, and so she only half listened to Charles trying to soothe them all with his praise of the tight wagon box and strong horses. Brushing aside her fear had nearly just cost more than she could pay, and she would not do it again now, not if it shook her apart.

"All's well that ends well," Charles was saying, and that was so. But it would not have begun at all, Caroline knew, if they had listened to their own good sense. Even with creek water streaming from his whiskers, Charles could overlook that part of it. He was always facing forward, that man. Never back.

Laura's fingers filled the spaces between the boards at Caroline's back. "Oh, where's Jack?" she cried as she pulled herself up from under the blanket.

Jack. Caroline's shaking halted all at once. Her conscience bulged up so hard and solid, she could feel nothing else. They had left him. *She* had left him. It was not Charles who told Laura the bulldog could swim. Caroline remembered how Jack had growled at the Indians on the street, yet did no more than scrunch his eyes shut to brace himself for Laura's mauling hugs. He had asked nothing of them but to be allowed to follow behind his ponies, and she had abandoned that steadfast creature to the creek. She could picture him standing on that shore just as plainly as though she had turned to look. But she had not.

They waited better than an hour while Charles

searched, his whistle shrilling through the creek bottoms again and again after his voice would no longer carry. An hour with Laura so desperately hopeful that Caroline could not bear to look at her when Charles returned. Instead she saw Charles's face, saw him meet Laura's wishful gaze and know for the first time in his life he had failed his little Half-Pint. Caroline did not know how so much disappointment would fit inside one small wagon.

Charles said nothing to either of them. There was nothing to say. His clothes were dry, and there was no bulldog trotting behind him. It was past time for making camp. He climbed to the spring seat and flicked the reins.

It was a wasted meal. Not one of them could eat, yet they picked and pushed at their food until it was as good as sand on their plates. Her own looked like the creek bank, all grit and muddy molasses. Caroline's throat burned and swelled as she scraped the plates over the latrine pit. Even the scraps were wasted without Jack there to finish them.

God that doesn't forget the sparrows won't leave a good dog like Jack out in the cold, Charles had promised Laura when she begged for Jack to be allowed into heaven. The sentiment soothed the child, but it was no consolation to Caroline. Her conscience throbbed all the harder to think of it: After all her answered prayers for protection on this journey, she had left one of His creatures without so much as a backward glance. She could ask for nothing after this. Nothing but forgiveness.

"We'll camp here a day or two," Charles said when she came back to the dishpan. "Maybe we'll stay here. Good land, timber in the bottoms, plenty of game—everything a man could want. What do you say, Caroline?"

Everything a man could want. Caroline's hands stilled beneath the cooling dishwater. And a woman? Caroline did not dare look inside herself to ask such a thing. She did not want to be inside herself at all, did not want to be part of a person who had been so selfish. After this day, it would be mercy enough simply to arrive.

"We might go farther and fare worse," she ventured. Asking without asking.

Charles knew her better than that. He waited for the rest, watching her over the glow of his pipe as she scrubbed guiltily at the dishes. "Anyway, I'll look around tomorrow," he answered when she said no more. "Get us some good fresh meat."

Caroline nodded. She rinsed the dishcloth and walked out of the bright ring of firelight. When her hem rustled against the tall grass, she stopped and laid the dishcloth to dry over the long yellow blades. Caroline looked out into the wide open darkness. All this time, was this the place they had had been moving toward? She imagined the little campfire with a roof and walls around it, the heart of a small house with Charles smoking and the girls yawning drowsily in the flickering light.

A howl wavered into the air, the sound cutting a thin line into the blank space around her. Caroline felt it slide through her, too, tickling the gaps between each bone of her spine as though she were no more solid than the sky. As she turned from the prairie to the campsite the darkness became palpable against her back. Caroline refused to let it make her shiver, or hurry. The girls must not see their ma flushed from the grass like a frightened grouse, not by a sound as familiar as thunder. Anyway, she was not truly frightened. Charles's rifle and pistol were loaded, and there was the fire just steps away. She only wished again for something thicker than a shawl to mark the boundary between herself and all that dark and shapeless space.

"About half a mile away, I'd judge," Charles said.

Mary and Laura looked at each other. Both of them knew well by now how little time it took to cover half a mile.

"Bedtime for little girls," Caroline sang out softly.

Her fingers were down to Mary's fourth button when Laura cried, "Look, Pa, look! A wolf!"

Charles had the rifle butt notched into his shoulder before Caroline saw what Laura was pointing to. Two molten globes hovering in the long grass where she had just been standing, each reflecting the firelight like the brass disc behind a kerosene lamp. Eyes. Creeping closer. She heard the click of Charles cocking the rifle and held her breath for the shot. None came. The animal had crept another step, then stopped still—a perfect target.

Charles did not fire. He lifted his cheek an inch from the stock and peered over the tip of the barrel at those motionless eyes. "Can't be a wolf," he said, "unless it's mad."

Caroline hefted Mary into the wagon without feeling it happen. She leaned down for Laura and Charles shook his head. His finger was loose on the trigger now. "Listen to the horses," he murmured. Caroline cocked an ear. Nothing but their teeth snipping at the grass. Nor was she afraid, Caroline realized. Her body was poised for it, and yet she felt no sensation of fear. Alert, yes, and cautious, too, but though she kept herself and Laura held safely back, her mind seemed to lean forward, curiously drawn toward the riddle of what that creature might be. "A lynx?" she guessed aloud.

"Or a coyote," Charles said, picking up a scrap of firewood. "Hah!" he shouted, and pitched it toward the shining eyes.

Any sensible animal should have bolted. This one dropped to the ground. *To spring, or cower?* Quicker than bullets, Caroline put herself between Laura and the animal as slowly, inexplicably, it began to crawl toward Charles.

Caroline felt so strange. The animal's eyes seemed to scrape the ground. *Please,* those eyes said. It was pitiful enough to make her wince. No wild creature would humble itself so, unless it were sick or hurt.

Charles walked toward the edge of the firelight, the gun out before him.

"Don't, Charles." Whether she meant *don't shoot,* or *don't move,* Caroline did not know. The darkness around the creature began to thin as it continued forward. The swirl of a shining black nose took shape. Then a bone-yellow glint of teeth, pointing straight to the sky.

The burst of sound came from all around her. Charles shouting, Laura screaming. Everything moved in the wrong direction. Caroline reeled forward as Laura and the creature tumbled together in the dirt.

And then, "Jack! Oh, Jack!"

The surprise struck her like a blow. Only Jack, filthy and bedraggled and thrashing with glee. Caroline threw up her hands as though she might hold back the shock, fearful that she had not the strength to feel one more thing. She could not speak, could not laugh until all the guilt and worry rolled from her at the sight of his waggling stump tail. Then she wanted most to cry and could not do that, either. The instant Jack saw her he sprang to her, nearly bowling her over. He scrabbled and pawed until she bent down to try to touch him. But he did not want petting. He licked and licked her wrists and palms and plunged his snorting nose into all the folds of her skirt until Caroline knew—it was her smell he wanted. Wanted to coat himself in it, so that he might never lose it again. Somewhere out on the open prairie he must have scented her, standing alone in the tall grass outside the campsite, and he had followed.

She had led him home.

Thirteen

The morning breeze pushed Caroline's skirt to and fro as if she were a school bell. The fabric hugged her belly and the small of her back by turns as Charles strode away across the grass.

It ought to have made her feel small, alone on such a vast and empty plain. Instead she felt a fullness that had nothing to do with the outward billow of her skirt. The whole day stretched before her, with no wagon wheels cutting through it. Beside her the big washtub stood full and shining in the sun.

Without woods or walls to partition the space around her, the sense of that word—*alone*—blurred. The distance between them might expand until they lost sight of one another, yet they were all in the same place. Or rather, *on* it. The prairie did not contain them, but held them on its great open palm. Only the girls were small enough to make a forest of the tall grass and disappear beneath its surface. Their voices flitted up from the weed tops like the dickcissels', and for the first time she could remember Caroline did not fret to have them out of her sight. All she need do to find them was stand in the wagon box and watch for the dimpling of the grass.

Caroline's heels clicked lightly down the floorboards and her tongue mimicked the lively *tsk-tsk-tsk* of the little yellow-splashed dickey birds chirping around her as she straightened the boxes and slouching bundles. One jig-like call made her pause to listen with the half-gathered bedclothes in her hands. What must the bird who sang such a song look like—vivid as a crazy quilt or drab as a sheet? She finished stripping the linens from the beds and dropped the bundle over the side of the wagon. There lay the fiddle box on the bare straw tick, muffled between the pillows. In all these weeks they had not once reached into that box for music. Only greenbacks. She would ask Charles to play tonight, she decided, and tucked the blankets neatly around it. If he were not too tired. It had been too long.

It felt both right and wrong to use the day for a washing. Thursdays belonged to the churn, not the washtub, but after rattling across all those many miles the wagon itself felt so much like the inside of a churn that Caroline could not think of taking up the dash and pounding away at anything so delicate as cream. And anyway, there was none to be had. So it would be the laundry instead.

Caroline looked tentatively over the rim of the tub at the flat circle of water. Her own face looked back at her, just the same. The slightly uneven widow's peak beneath the neat white parting of brown hair. The lower lip that seemed always mournful or stern, no matter how sweet the thoughts behind it. Whatever changes this journey had wrought in her, they had not yet broken her surface.

Pleased, she smiled at herself and quickly blushed at the way her face bloomed back at her. Suddenly Caroline did not want to look away. The unexpected sweetness of her own modesty held her captive. This must be the smile that made Charles's eyes twinkle so when he teased her. She could feel the familiar contours of it, but had never seen the rosy flush, nor the dark ruffle of lowered lashes. No wonder he showed her no mercy.

Now she was too much pleased, and the charm of the reflection faded. Enough of that, then. Caroline rolled up her sleeves and tucked her skirt between her knees. She dipped her fingers into the pannikin for a smear of brown soft soap and began.

First the great bundle of sheets and pillowcases. Her

knuckles stung with cold as she plunged the fabric in and out of the water. With the handle of the rake she pried the yards of sopping muslin from the tub and wrung them out inch by inch before starting all over with the rinse water. Then towels, dishcloths, white underthings, and red flannel underthings. Last of all she carried the carpetbags out into the sun and stacked the heap of muddied winter clothes in the grass beside the washtub.

The folded dresses, pants, and shirts were stiff as canvas from weeks of wear. Caroline shook out her own everyday brown flannel and lowered it into the tub. The gray water crept hungrily up the hem, melting the caked dirt away. She threaded her hands deep into pairs of stockings and strummed them over the washboard until the dingy footprints disappeared from their soles.

Sweat ringed her underarms and collar. In her mind she fancied she could sketch the line of every blade of grass pressing into her knees. But never before had Caroline taken such pleasure in a washing. Everything she worked with her hands beneath the water came up softer, brighter, more itself.

She laid the drying clothes out like paper dolls on the grass. Caroline stood back thoughtfully taking in their colors and shapes: Charles in brown and green, herself and Mary in shades of blue, and Laura's little sprigged calico in just the bold shade of red Caroline longed to wear. Together all of them gently bent the grass, so that Caroline saw the soft imprint of her family on the land.

The image lingered pleasantly in her mind well after the clothes were ironed and folded away. When Charles came whistling home and the girls ran scrambling to meet him, the picture seemed to come alive. They rose out of the grass in a small billow of color and movement—Charles with Laura by the hand, Mary skipping alongside. Caroline smiled. Laura never could get enough of her Pa.

A pang of worry struck her. How might things change for Laura if this next baby were a son? Charles was not a man to play favorites, but there was no mistaking the softness in his eyes when he looked on something he loved. She had seen it kindling inside him these last days, as they drove across the prairie, and now she could hear it in his voice, telling Laura of all the bounty he had seen living in the grass and streams.

The game he carried did nothing to contradict his flourishes of excitement. Two fat fowl hung from his belt, and in his hand was a rabbit so outlandishly large its feet brushed the ground with every swoop of his arm.

Charles held up his catch to her and said, "I tell you, Caroline, there's everything we want here. We can live like kings!" The monstrous jackrabbit dangled from his fist, its long belly neatly silt. Where its vitals should have been, there was only a glistening cavern. A drop, then two, of rosy pink blood splashed the ground before her.

Caroline's viscera lurched. The dead rabbit loomed too large, a glory of waste and feast. She was thankful she had never seen it living. All the power and vibrance were gone from it, and what was left would feed them for no more than a day.

Be that as it may. Caroline shook the shudder of regret from her shoulders and took the rabbit by its ears. It was dead and they must eat. If she could not make the creature live again she would roast it up fine, wrapped in slices of fat salt pork, and they would take nourishment from every morsel.

Caroline scraped the bones from Charles's plate into the bake oven.

"Bet it weighed near seven pounds, field dressed," he said. Boasting, almost. She could not blame him. Not one fiber of the jackrabbit had gone to waste. Tomorrow there would be the good thick broth with dumplings for supper. The hide was pinned to the wagon box. She could hear Jack working over the head and feet beneath the wagon, and this once the rough sounds pleased her.

The sun nestled itself down into the horizon, tinging the water in the dishpan with shades of pink and orange. Caroline scrubbed slowly at the plates as the colors deepened. She was tired and sore from leaning over the washtub. But it was not the same weariness she had become accustomed to. Not the indifferent fatigue of travel, nor even the drain of childbearing. That never fully left her. Something she could not harness for herself was busy, always busy—building, feeding. At odd times she tired unaccountably, and that was when she was most conscious of the current of energy flowing past her to that teeming place. It was akin to the feeling of strength rebuilding after sickness. Even her thoughts were short of fuel, leaving her at times almost lightheaded.

This was earned, a vigorous sort of fatigue that came from doing, and the grateful cooling of muscles pulled and stretched under the sun, and Caroline greeted it with matching gratitude.

Behind her, Caroline heard the familiar snap of two metal clasps. She turned from the dishpan and found Charles with the fiddle box open on his lap. The whiskey-colored wood gleamed rich and warm in the firelight. Caroline left the tin plates to dry themselves and sat down by the fire.

One by one the strings twanged and wavered and then found their steady centers. Four pure notes emerged, and then with the tiniest twists of his fingers Charles sweetened them in a way Caroline had never yet learned to describe. Those sounds were a tune in themselves. They carried memories of firesides and corn-huskings and sugaring-off dances reaching all the way back to the threshold of her youth on the banks of the Oconomowoc. Her heart rose, tight and aching, to hear them at last. No matter what songs he played, those four notes always sang out first in welcome. That, more than anything, was the sound of home.

There was nothing to hold the music close around them, and so it rose with the smoke, higher and higher until each silvery note seemed to pierce the sky. Caroline wished for something to send out into the deepening night with it. Something sweet and fine and all her own. There was nothing but her voice, and she could not imagine her low contralto rising to meet the stars.

Yet Caroline felt a loosening in herself as the bow stroked the strings. Until the music began to release it she had not known that she had been holding on to anything at all. A space opened inside her as she listened, widening with each long note. Coaxed by the fiddle, she was opening herself to this place, for Charles's songs were not strutting out at marching tempo. They ambled and danced, not reaching beyond the horizon, but wheeling upward within it.

At last, then, he was settling. Caroline's throat swelled so fast the gladness nearly choked her. She pulled in a cool thin breath and held it. The song and the night air swirled through her, indistinguishable from one another. Nothing but the fiddle had spoken to her, and she was overcome. And Charles? He had eyes only for the strings, rocking so gently in time with the music that his contentment was unmistakable. Did he choose such melodies deliberately to match his spirits, Caroline wondered, or were his hands so connected to his heart that his mind did not enter into it at all? She watched his hands, now. The lightness of his fingers on the strings sent little tendrils of warmth through her. There was nothing in the world he touched more delicately, not even her own face.

All around them the blue-black bowl of sky throbbed with stars. The bow caressed the strings so softly they seemed to whisper, and Charles's voice, deep and mellow, melded with them:

None knew thee but to love thee,
Thou dear one of my heart . . .

Caroline lifted her eyes from his hands and found him gazing at her in the same way he had gazed at the fiddle strings. Delight bloomed all through her. She had no strength for modesty when he made his feelings so plain. She might hold her pleasure within herself, but she could not keep the effort from showing. The spread of her lips and the rounding of her cheeks gave her entirely away. And anyway, who was there to see? To have such a man, as content to hold her in his sight as in his arms, and never indulge him—well, that would be a waste. Selfish, even. Let him look as long as he liked, then, Caroline decided, and this once let him savor her pleasure, too.

Laura gasped and their eyes flickered toward the sound, breaking the spell. Caroline swayed to her feet and went to kneel beside her daughters. The girls had both slipped from the wagon tongue into tired little heaps of calico in the grass. "What is it, Laura?"

Her blue eyes were wide, full of the sky. "The stars were singing," Laura whispered.

Under her skirts and steels, the still and silent baby seemed to twirl like a key turning, as if it had been waiting, all this time, for this night and those words. A deep pulse of thankfulness radiated through her body before her mind could form the words. Caroline blinked tears from her lashes as she said to Laura, "You've been asleep. It is only the fiddle. And it's time little girls were in bed."

The firelight shone in their sleepy eyes and blushed all the round and dimpled places on their bare skins as they crawled into their nightdresses. Such plump and sturdy little girls. Anyone could see they had never known a moment's want, never dreaded the bottom of the flour barrel as she once had. Perhaps in a place like this they never would. Caroline tucked them into the wagon, leaving the canvas open so they might see the stars as they drifted off, and returned to the fire. She sat down close beside Charles, too full for words, and looked out into the wide open night. It was not hard to imagine that darkness stretching all the way back across the long way they had come. And the fiddle sang, low and rich now, its melodies swaying in an easy back-and-forth rhythm until the home they had left and the home they would make seemed within reach of each other.

Neither of them tied down the wagon cover. There was no need. The night was pleasantly cool even as they undressed, and Caroline had no desire to separate herself from it.

Nor did Charles. He lay down beside her and unfastened the yoke of her nightdress, tucking it back so her bare shoulder stood out white in the moonlight.

"Charles," she warned.

"Shhh," he said. "Just this." His hand traveled across her skin, stirring the downy hair along the peak of her shoulder. The inside of his wrist came to rest along the slope of her breast, and his warm pulse reached inward to meet her own.

Only his thumb moved now, so lightly Caroline felt as though she were rising like cream through milk. She opened her mouth to quiet her breathing and closed her eyes. Her fingers found a soft little gully between the corded muscles of his neck. With her thumb she stroked the whiskers along his jaw. "Caroline," he whispered, and she felt the word with her fingers. There was no need to answer.

Fourteen

Once more into the wagon, with the sun just peeking over the rim of the earth. All of them looked ahead now—not just Charles—watching as if the land that was to be theirs would be waiting to greet them. Charles whistled one tune after another as Pet and Patty strolled briskly through the swishing yellow grass. Away from the road it was tall enough to brush their bellies.

Caroline hummed along, her heart fluttering. Today was different. Each one of them down to the horses knew it. No road stretched before them, demanding that they strive ahead. They had been harnessed to that endless brown line, Caroline thought, just as surely as Pet and Patty were harnessed to the wagon. Without it the drudgery of trudging ever forward had lifted, and she felt such a lightness. Nothing pressed them—not the weather nor the time of day nor the distance—nothing but their own eagerness. They hurried, but only a little, only for the joy of it.

Before their breakfast had begun to wear off, Charles pulled back on the reins. "Here we are, Caroline. Right here we'll build our house."

Here. Caroline blinked at the suddenness of it. So many long weeks and miles, ended in a single syllable.

The others felt no such jar. Down Mary and Laura went, their bare toes curling over the spokes of the wheels. "Ready?" Charles held up his hands for her, as he always did. Caroline leaned down into them as though it were the first time. The house was not even paced off, yet she had the unmistakable sense of crossing its threshold as Charles put his hands to her waist and swung her to the ground.

No matter where the wagon stopped these last few days, there was always the feeling of being at the very center of the world. And now this would be their center, their world. It was beautiful, this pale, bright country with its blue-white sky, as beautiful as anything they had seen along the way.

Caroline turned slowly, looking all around her for something to mark this plot of ground off from the boundless land around it—something to fix in her memory and recognize as their own if she ever needed to find this place again, as the two big oaks and the sumac along the fence back home had done.

Here there were no marks upon the land itself. No fence or road, no hedge or furrow. Only bluffs rising to the north, an endless span of grass unrolling to the south. Between them, the rumpled line of a creek. Even the path the wagon had made through the grass was already melding back together.

For a moment she was adrift in the sameness of it all. There was nothing but the wagon to fasten to, and a wagon could never be trusted for such a task. Caroline swept her eyes across the breadth of the horizon. East to west, west to east, and back again. The more she looked, the more she steadied. No one thing had grasped her sight. It was everything at once, the whole contour of the view—the particular curve of the creek, the rougher edge of the bluffs against the sky—and the emerging knowledge that none of it could look quite the same from anywhere else. She could learn to recognize those lines the same way she recognized a familiar line of handwriting. It would only take time.

They unloaded the wagon right then and there, everything onto the ground with the canvas to spread over it. Then the wagon box itself came off the running gear and rested beside its freight. Goodness, it was small out in the open, all bare and swept and only a little more than knee-high in the tall grass.

Then, perched on the running gear, Charles rattled away toward the creek bottoms with his ax.

For most of the next two weeks there was little but the sound of that ax. Felling, chopping, hewing. The creak and tear of the bark and sapwood splitting away from the pale yellow heart of each log as he squared them off. They were lovely to look at, all neatly stacked and waiting to be joined together. The sun warmed the freshly hewn logs and every day Caroline could smell the smell of the house they would become, imagining it all around her. But she did not wait for the house to begin feeling at home. Each day the sun rose and set on the same sides of her bed. Good oak kindling piled up by the hour, and every bucket of water came from the same clean, sweet creek. And there was the unutterable luxury of a necessary, built of poles with a door and a plank seat.

With their daily movements they wore grooves into the land—to the creek, the necessary, the dishpan and washbasin, and around and around the growing stack of logs. Even Mary and Laura had their paths to their favorite little hills and hollows. First the grass parted, then it leaned and bent until at last it laid down in the dirt and was trampled under bare feet.

A day or two and the week returned to its accustomed shape. There were gaps where the churning and the baking ought to have been, gaps Caroline filled with the blandest of the preparations for the child. She cut squares of linen and painted them with boiled linseed oil to make fresh oilcloth, then fashioned flannel covers for them—one for each night of the week to guard the straw tick from leaking diapers. To protect her dresses she oiled rounds of silk trimmed to fit her breasts and backed them with linen. There was no wheat bran for filling, so there would be no proper pad to keep the leavings of the birth from soaking the bedclothes. More oilcloth would have to answer for that purpose. Caroline eyed the wagon cover briefly, then thought better of it. She boiled more linseed oil and painted the oldest of her tablecloths instead. In the scrap bag she found plenty of flannel rags to double her supply of sanitary towels.

Each of these small tasks drew her inward. Away from the land and yet strangely nearer it, for the child she prepared for would be a Kansan. Indeed, it already was so. Every time Caroline looked up from her work she could see the square Charles had paced off for the house, and inside that square was the place where the child would be born. Charles and the girls must work at making the land their own, but the child would emerge belonging to it.

In one day Charles built the house as high as Laura's head. Two dozen logs, notched and hoisted and fitted. After supper they leaned their elbows on the short walls, admiring the neat square space. Charles pointed out where the door and windows and fireplace would be, while inside Mary and Laura ran gleeful circles. Jack barked and wagged outside, trying to lick at them through the chinks. Caroline ran her hands across the topmost log. Good oak, just as their house in Wisconsin had been, but younger, slenderer. A youthful little house.

In and out went the needle. In and out and in and then the ax struck wood and she was looking up at Charles again. He stood halfway up the wall with his boot toes wedged between the chinks, chopping a notch into the topmost log. *Look, look, look,* the ax seemed to say each time it bit into the wood. *Watch, watch, watch.* Caroline pulled her needle through the flannel. In the time it had taken him to raise that log, she had sewn no more than a half dozen stitches. Perhaps if she sewed in time with the ax she could manage to keep her eyes on her own work. *Chop*-and-stitch and *chop*-and-stitch and *chop*-and-*whizz!* came a little chip of wood sailing down to land at her feet, and there she was, watching again. She forced her eyes back into her lap. Rags. Flannel rags she would not need for months yet. Impatience crackled in her elbows and all up and down her back. She could not do such tedious work. Not with the whole house going up ten feet from her face. She would fly apart. Caroline jabbed her needle into the half-finished pad and dropped it into her work basket.

Out of the scrap bag came the long curtain made of pillow cases she had fashioned for the wagon loft. Cut in quarters, it would likely serve as curtains for the new house. Caroline fingered the pretty red blanket stitching along the hem. That would just match her checked tablecloth. She rummaged through the bag again and came up with a handful of snippings from Laura's red summer calico. Enough, perhaps, for curtain ties—if she were careful. Caroline smoothed the pieces across her lap and smiled at the thought of crisp red and white curtains against freshly hewn oak walls. Her needle would fly so much faster if it were making something beautiful. Faster than Charles's ax. But she could not measure and cut curtains for windows that did not exist. Not with so little fabric to spare. Carefully Caroline folded the calico and muslin together and tucked them back into the scrap bag. She took up the flannel pad again and her throat swelled with frustration.

Always, the scale of Charles's work dwarfed her own. In the time it took him to build a wall or plant an acre, she might knit a sock or churn a pound of butter. One task was no less vital than the other; he could not build or plant barefoot and hungry. Charles knew that as well as she did and never failed to thank her for a new shirt or a good meal. But to have a hand in fashioning something that would not be consumed, worn out, outgrown—something as grand as a house? To be able to lean against that solid wall for years to come and know that she had helped put it there? Caroline thrilled at the thought.

But it was hard, muscled work, even for Charles. More so than the day before. Caroline could see it in his neck and shoulders, hear it in his swift exhale as he thrust each log upward. Yesterday his legs had borne the brunt of the lifting. He had only to squat down, take hold of one end of the log, and straighten himself up again. Today that was barely half the task. Now the height of the walls demanded the strength of his arms to hoist each log into place. His pace had slowed enough that even the girls' interest flagged until they finally wandered away to play. Up went one end of a log, propped at the corner where two walls met. Then, tentatively, the other rose as he worked, shuffling and grunting, to bring the whole timber level without dislodging the first end. One nudge too far and the wood lurched from its place, bumping its way down each of the logs beneath it. Charles staggered back, dropping his end without a word. He whipped out his handkerchief in a flash of red and swiped his face.

Caroline was beside him with the dipper and pail before he'd stuffed the handkerchief back into his pocket. "Let me help, Charles," she said as he drank. His eyes popped up from the dipper. One, then two drops of water trickled through his beard. Charles put down the dipper and wiped his chin in the crook of his elbow, still looking at her. Her empty hands reached for each other, then fled behind her back. She could not fold them before her as she usually did without drawing attention to her belly. There was no hiding it these days, but nor was there any need to proclaim it, either. Perhaps with no other women in sight he had grown accustomed to her shape. Perhaps, if she stood quite still and made no mention of it herself, he would not take it into account.

He considered so long her fingers began to wish for the needle and thread, if only to keep from fidgeting. She felt like one of the children, standing there so earnestly. Caroline watched the corners of his eyes narrow with thought and knew he was wondering how to accept without making more work for himself, as she did when Mary and Laura begged to lend a hand in her chores. She ought to have treated him to a jug of ginger water and sat back down to her sewing instead of trying to elbow in.

"I won't have you lifting logs," he said at last. "But do you think you could brace them while I lift the other end and square the join?"

Caroline did not say one word. All her childish excitement would spill out if she opened her mouth to say so much as *Yes, Charles.* She simply nodded and followed him to the west wall.

The logs that formed the northern corner jutted toward her like oversized pegs. Charles lifted the end of the fallen timber onto the highest one and propped it with the heels of his hands. "Hold it this way. Don't try to grip it when I lift the other end. It has to be able to move some while I position my side—just lean so it can't slip off." Caroline planted her feet and slanted her body forward to put her hands beside his. "That's it. The notch in the wall underneath will keep it from sliding the other way." He went to the south corner and hoisted the other end. "Now hold steady while I fit this into the notch." The log rocked, then wobbled and dropped squarely into place. Caroline pushed her-self back from the wall. As she did her end slid into its notch.

Charles propped his fists on his hips and bobbed his head in approval. "That's all there is to it."

Together they built the house one log higher, then another. Each time Charles squatted down and took the end of the log in both hands, levering himself back up with a thrust of his calves. Then he bent his knees and with a grunt, hoisted the end up to his shoulder. Caroline never tired of watching—the swoop of his knees, the spring from the balls of his feet, the deft flip of his palms as the log reached his chin. He grinned at her each time.

There were moments he was like something out of a book, that man, too grand and vivid to be fully real. With him, there were times when life had the feel of a story larger than themselves. All winter as he talked of going west, Caroline had caught glimpses of it as he saw it—a current pushing forward with purpose and momentum. What else could account for why she stood on this blank square of map with one end of a log in her hands? For his part, she did not know what he saw in a woman such as herself, what made him look at her the way he did, as though she were a song he had sung, come to life. Caroline shied a little to imagine what kind of song anyone could make out of her. It would be akin to exalting something as commonplace as a quilt, or a pan of milk.

Caroline did not see what happened. She only felt the jolt pass through the timber and down her elbows. Raw wood scraped, and suddenly the log was nosing down toward her.

She hitched herself sideways, going up on tiptoe to boost the log from beneath with her shoulder. Her foot caught in a hollow and one knee buckled. The log's weight shifted toward the notch of her neck, pressing her down. Caroline's thigh muscles surged upward. Too late—her knee could not straighten under the load. Her shin threatened to splinter like a matchstick. Every hinge in her body wavered as though it were on the verge of melting.

"Let go!" Charles called. "Get out from under!"

It was not a matter of letting go. Her hands bore none of the weight. It was her shoulder. She could not lift it from her shoulder. Her only hope was to throw her body down faster than the log could fall. Caroline let both knees buckle fully and thrust her hands up against the wood, hurling herself outward.

All the points of her body struck the ground—knee, hip, elbow, shoulder.

She lay waiting for the crack, expecting to be split

like a pitcher and feel herself spilling out onto the grass.

No crack came. Only the steady weight of the log on her foot, and, smothered somewhere beneath that, pain. She was not sensible of the pain itself, only a strange sensation pushing hard against the log, impatient to be felt.

"Caroline!" Charles was beside her, and Laura.

"I'm all right." Her voice was a gasp, the words nearly a lie. She was hurt, that was certain. How badly she could not tell. But she would mend or manage without; Caroline knew that already. Nothing vital in her had broken.

Charles lifted the log free. Pain bulged up into the space it left behind, so large for an instant she feared her shoe might burst. Caroline pulled herself tight. If she could hold her body tightly enough, she thought, she could shrink the pain down small enough to fit back inside her.

"Move your arms," Charles demanded. "Is your back hurt? Can you turn your head?"

Caroline did not want to move anything. Simply exhaling sent flames of hot and cold racing through her ankle. But she had never seen such a look on Charles's face. Not even with the creek rising nearly to his ears had he looked so horrified—white and trembling, and hardly an inch from tears. Gingerly she moved and turned. He looked to her middle, too frightened to ask aloud.

Caroline pulled all the awareness she could muster away from her throbbing foot. If anything had gone wrong with the child she could not feel it. The log had struck nothing else. That she was sure of. The rest amounted to no more than a stumble. Caroline tried to smile for him and managed mostly to wince.

"Thank God," Charles said. He cradled one arm behind her shoulders and another across her belly and helped her sit up. He looked at her, and his face seemed to shimmer with the effort of holding his relief in check.

Caroline laid a hand on his arm. "I'm all right, Charles," she said again, her voice far from steady. "It's just my foot."

With shaking fingers he stripped off her shoe and stocking and pressed into the raging flesh to feel the length of every slim bone and work each joint. "Does it hurt much?"

"Not much." A bald-faced lie, and no compunctions. Anything to make him stop.

"No bones broken," he said. "Only a bad sprain." The prodding stopped, but his eyes did not leave her foot. He stared at it, puffed and purpling in his palm—for once in his life overcome by what might have been. He ran his other hand over his forehead and up through his hair. His breath was shallow through his nose and open mouth.

"Well, a sprain's soon mended. Don't be so upset, Charles."

"I blame myself. Should have used skids." He still held her heel in one hand, his head in the other.

She could not sit on the ground any longer, or Charles would be the one to break. That was something Laura must never see. Caroline put her palms to the ground and pushed. Without a word between them Charles's arms were right where she needed them to be. Caroline felt him bracing for her weight and knew he would carry her, but she did not need Laura to see that, either. She pressed herself forward until his arms began to lift with her. Only a little wobble and she was upright on her good foot. Caroline stood still a moment, panting. Then she bent her grimace to resemble a smile and said, "Please bring my shoe and stocking, Laura."

Fifteen

There is nothing in the world but the weight—
pulling, tugging, dragging down. Not a log in
her hands, but her own belly, too heavy to hold. If she
lets go, it will break free, tearing her dress, her corset
strings, her very skin. Barefoot, she roams the prairie
for help. In one cabin, only men. In the next, Indians.
Her arms ache; her breasts weigh like sacks of coffee.
Her knuckles begin slipping past one another. Then
the sound of ripping—fibers of cloth or flesh?

Caroline blinked. Nothing had split apart but her
eyelids. The weight was only Charles's arm, hugged
down into the dwindling valley between her belly and
breasts. Caroline lay awake, feeling the throb of her
pulse against the rags bound about her ankle. Her mind
throbbed, too, making pictures in the dark: Charles

pinned under the fallen log instead. The dreadful creek she must cross to reach help in Independence. Caroline pinched her eyes shut. The pictures changed but did not dim. She saw her own high belly, and the empty foot of a bedstead looming from between her drawn-up knees. The place where Polly should be. "Oh, Polly," she whispered.

Caroline pulled as deep a breath as she could wedge under Charles's arm and willed herself to relax. That she could not manage. Her foot hurt, and the straw tick no longer smelled of home. It was thinner, and prickly in places with the new straw Jacobs had given them. Caroline tried to shift herself without rousing Charles and the child moved. A jerky little movement, as though she'd startled it.

She was caught between them. Sandwiched queerly from without and within. Resigned, she laid her arm over his, her palm brushing across the soft curling hairs that belied the firm muscles beneath. How different it must feel to be a man: built solid through, with everything beneath the skin belonging solely to yourself. Did he ever envy what she could take into herself, how much she could contain? Could he comprehend all it meant for a woman to hold herself open for her husband, her children? For all it demanded of her Caroline knew she would not trade the depth of those open spaces, those currents of life passing through her. No man could encompass another life so fully as a woman, except perhaps in his mind. Perhaps that was what made Charles clutch her so close now as he slept. He had felt her slip through his fingers this afternoon. It was providential, he had said, that her foot had not been crushed. She had not told him that the same hollow that saved her foot had caused the fall.

Caroline lost count of how many days passed before she could wear her shoe again, never mind lace it. Her instep swelled until the skin shone taut and yellow. Beneath the joint itself the side of her foot looked as though it were pooling with ink; a streak of black and blue and purple marked a line along the sole of her foot. Bands of greenish-purple ringed the base of her toes. The deep rosy smudges running up her calf seemed almost pretty in comparison. The smooth white fibers that joined muscle to bone in the stringy drumsticks of rabbits and fowl, these she could feel now in her own leg, and it was there that the pain lingered most stubbornly.

In the meantime she hobbled, and the house waited. Charles hewed out skids, and they leaned against the unfinished walls like a pair of crutches until the day he came up from the creek bottom calling, "Good news!"

An upward rush of hope surged through her and then leveled. He had not been to town—it would not be a letter or a paper.

"A neighbor," Charles said. "Just two miles over the creek. Fellow's a bachelor. Says he can get along without a house better than you and the girls, so he'll help me build first. Then soon as he's got his logs ready, I'll help him. How do you like that, Caroline?"

It was a trifle ridiculous that he should bring them seven hundred miles to be so tickled by the discovery of a neighbor. She smiled, almost without meaning to, and Charles was pleased. It was fine news, nonetheless.

He was there before the breakfast dishes were wiped—tall and scruffy, a weed of a man. His manners were quicker even than Charles's. "The name's Edwards, ma'am," he said without waiting to be introduced, and bowed so low that the tail of his coonskin cap brushed the ground. He looked at her almost in the way a woman would look—taking her in all at once, somehow acknowledging the evidence of her pregnancy without lingering on it or shying from it. Perhaps Charles had told him. Perhaps that was why he had come so willingly to help.

From the moment he bent down on one knee to shake her hand, Laura could not take her eyes from

Mr. Edwards. "I'm a wildcat from Tennessee," he told her, and she was charmed. Mary liked him, too, but seemed to think she shouldn't. Caroline saw the way she looked at his ragged jumper and watched her eyes widen with a mixture of awe and disgust when he spit a stream of tobacco juice from the corner of the house to the wagon tongue.

Caroline had to admit, if only to herself, that she had never seen a man spit so purposefully. With most of them it was like emptying a dishpan, the careless brown stream splashing forth just inches from their boots. Edwards took aim every time he pursed his lips and sent a neat line arcing straight toward his target.

Mary's instinct was to tame Edwards, to mend his jumper and perhaps ask Santa Claus to bring him a pretty brass spittoon for Christmas. Laura wanted to be Edwards, to climb the walls and sing and swing an ax until the chips flew faster than the music.

Charles and Edwards worked together like brothers, so fast and sure that it was bewildering to see. Caroline watched them singing and joking, riding the rising walls together and felt envy seeping into her gratitude. It had not mattered so very much yesterday when Charles had said their neighbor was a bachelor, but now Caroline longed for a Mrs. Edwards. Her girls helped, and eagerly, but it was not the same as working companionably alongside another woman.

And Edwards, who was he accustomed to working beside, back home in Tennessee? The way his movements harmonized with Charles's made it plain that he was used to being part of a team, and a good one, too. She and Charles could never have raised the walls in a single day. For that matter, neither could Charles and Henry, back home.

They would have dumplings with the stewed jackrabbit for their supper, Caroline decided. Never mind that there was no milk, no egg, no butter. White flour would show Edwards what his day's work meant to her. She dipped up a small cupful of broth and mixed it with bacon drippings, salt, and sugar. Then the soft, snowy flour, a full pint of it. She had not even opened the bag since . . . Christmas? Her eyes smarted at that, and Caroline shrugged one shoulder up to swipe her cheek. No use in summoning up thoughts of Christmas with Eliza and Peter.

Charles stood beside the newly fashioned doorway, grinning. The house was just as he had said, just as she had pictured it: a little more than twelve feet square, with windows east and west and space for a fireplace at one end.

But looking at it did not feel the same as imagining it, not even with the homey smell of a company supper wafting in. Her mind had limned the image with warmth and softness, as though it would become home the moment it existed. The reality was simply a house—fresh and welcoming, yet surreal in its blankness.

She had felt something very like this before, Caroline remembered, the first time Polly put Mary into her arms. All those months waiting for their baby, their child, their son or daughter—and what arrived was an infant. Bewilderment still overpowered every sensation of that moment. An infant in her arms, astoundingly complete and tangible, and as wholly unfamiliar as though Polly had lifted Mary out of a satchel instead of Caroline's own body.

Shyly, Caroline reached out and touched the slab that formed the doorway, then looked inside. She would sweep this space every day, sleep in it, wake in it. Bathe and dress in it. Come time, she would bear a child within these walls, and likely one day conceive the next. In the midst of it all, Caroline knew, the place would shift from house to home without her ever being able to pinpoint the moment of its happening.

Poised on the threshold, she pressed her fingertips gently against the bare wood but did not step inside. A notion had taken hold of her, too foolish to speak aloud and too firm to brush aside. *Not until we've properly introduced ourselves.*

They ate around the fire, halfway between house and tent—a respectful sort of distance that made Caroline wonder if all of them secretly shared her inkling to let the house acquaint itself with them. Or perhaps it was only that they wanted to sit back and admire it.

Edwards lay stretched out on the ground, her dumplings plumping his narrow middle, while Charles played the fiddle for the girls. Soon Edwards was up and dancing, and Mary and Laura clapped their delight. Charles's face gleamed behind the white flash of the bow, as though he were playing for a barn brimful of swirling couples.

Caroline sat back and smiled. *This,* she thought to herself. This was how it had felt to imagine themselves at home in Kansas. The particulars were different, with Edwards kicking up his heels and her own foot still too sore for tapping and the house only an outline behind them, but the glow of it, that was the same.

Caroline gazed beyond them, to the empty house with the pale ribs of its roof standing out against the sky. Tomorrow they would fill it.

Sixteen

Walls, straight up and down, and a ridgepole too high to touch. Caroline had not realized how much she missed the simple shape of a room. Her eyes could not get enough of the lovely squareness of the corners with their sturdy intersections. It did not matter that there was no door, no shutters, no curtains. Even with sunshine pouring through the chinks and the open roof Caroline felt sheltered, truly sheltered, for the first time in months. All this time she had held herself half-hunched against the elements, always ready to cock one shoulder against wind or rain or whatever else the sky might hurl at them. What a delight to turn her back almost defiantly to the sky as she swept the last of the chips from the floor.

Above her, Charles wrestled with the wind, stretching the canvas like a skin over the skeleton of roof poles. All those onerous yards of stitches had held so well that the wagon cover could serve as their roof until Charles raised a stable. That in itself was so immensely satisfying that the idea of a cloth roof did not dampen the pleasure Caroline took in the house. Already the space it enclosed belonged to her in a way the inside of the wagon never had, for the wagon never held the same space—it only flowed through a place, borrowing as it went.

A beguiling, radiant sort of shade fell over her. It was the canvas, suffusing the bright sunlight overhead. Caroline stilled the broom and pushed back her sunbonnet to watch Charles work. The wind was giving him fits, billowing and snapping the canvas and blowing his hair and whiskers every which way. He snorted and blustered so, she wanted to laugh at him. He would have that wagon cover lashed down in a jiffy. She knew it, even if he did not. Caroline pulled her bonnet into place and hurried to the bare tent poles to fold up the linens. The first thing she wanted to see inside the house were the straw ticks, all plumped up smooth.

"There!" Charles barked at the canvas. "Stay where you are and be—"

Caroline whirled, her arms full of quilts. "Charles!"

"—and be good." He blinked sweetly down at her.

"Why, Caroline, what did you think I was going to say?"

"Oh, Charles!" she cried. "You scalawag!"

He shimmied down the outer corner of the walls and scruffed up his hair until it looked like he'd crawled out from under a bramble bush.

The laugh she'd held back earlier tumbled out of her. Charles grabbed her up in his arms, triumphant. The rascal—no one else in the world could make her forget herself enough to shout and laugh like a schoolgirl.

"How's that for a snug house?" Charles asked, pulling her close against his side so they could both look at it.

The square yellow logs, topped with pale, smooth canvas, looked nearly golden against the soft blue sky. She could not begin to tell him how fine it looked. "I'll be thankful to get into it," she said.

"We're going to do well here, Caroline," Charles said. All the teasing had slipped from his voice. "This is a great country. This is a country I'll be contented to stay in the rest of my life."

Caroline's heart paused for an instant. There was a weight to those words she had not heard from him before, a fullness. "Even when it's settled up?" she ventured, scarcely daring to tilt her bonnet brim to look at him.

He squeezed her in against his chest with each syllable. "Even when it's settled up," he promised, and leaned his cheek on top of her head. "No matter how thick and close the neighbors get, this country'll never feel crowded. Look at that sky!"

It was so. Surveyors might come with their compasses and chains to mark the necessary range and township lines, but they would never square the curve from the sky.

Everything went where she wanted it—the broom in one corner, the churn in the other. Charles's gun over the door, of course, and the beds against the back wall, leaving space between them for the fireplace. Every decision belonged to her. Charles and Mary and Laura would not put one thing down without looking first to her for approval, as though the map of the inside of the cabin existed in her mind alone.

So she pointed out places for pegs to hang their clothing, the dishpan and dish towel, and Charles drove them into the walls. He hewed out narrow slabs for shelves and wedged those in between the logs in the corner that she designated as the kitchen. Caroline could have spent the afternoon admiring those plain, serviceable shelves. No longer would she have to bend double for a scoop of flour or cornmeal from a sack on the ground.

Nor would her neatly packed crates be jumbled and jostled into disarray. She had accommodated so many trifling inconveniences over such a long time that she had not felt their accumulating weight. Now, so many lifted all at once that it seemed she might rise from the floor. If not for the inevitability of cooking supper over the campfire, she might have.

But the campfire itself was more pleasant, too, because of the house. Because of the house, *outside* and *inside* had become distinct from each other once more. It was a rich feeling, sitting outside after supper for no better reason than because they wanted to. There was something absurdly delightful in the knowledge that behind those walls their beds lay ready and waiting, with the nightclothes hanging neatly on their pegs. Nothing need be dismantled or rearranged.

A warm, nectary scent glided by on the breeze. "I wonder," Caroline said, "if the cherry tree back home is budded out yet."

"I wonder what Polly will do for her cherry preserves if the Gustafsons don't share the fruit with her," Charles answered.

Caroline smiled. She could just imagine Polly scheming for her usual share of those good tart cherries. Perhaps she would simply send one of the children over with a basket, as she'd always done. Those poor unsuspecting Swedes would open their door to find three-year-old Charlotte beaming up at them. Wouldn't that be just like Polly. "Eliza and Peter's family must have increased by now," Caroline said. She ran her hands along her own sides. She was still not so big as Eliza had been when they left Pepin. Niece or nephew, Caroline wondered. Live or stillborn? In a few months, Eliza would be wondering the same of her. No, Caroline realized with a pang—she had not told Eliza before they left, had not told anyone but Charles.

"I should have had a letter ready to post when we stopped in Independence," she said aloud. All she'd been able to think about was whether any news awaited her. How selfish. The home folks would be lucky now to have word from her before snowfall. *Write*, Eliza had said that last morning. *Write.*

"I'll have to make a trip into town one of these days for nails to finish the roof," Charles said. "Soon as our stable and Edwards's house are raised, I'll tan those rabbit hides and take them in to trade. Be plenty of room in my pockets for all the letters you want to send."

Caroline nodded. It meant more weeks, but that could not be helped. At least now, with her trunk at the end of their bed, she could pull out her lap desk and pearl-handled pen any time she pleased.

She sat a few moments on that trunk after tucking

the girls into bed, taking in the feel of the place. Moon-light tinged the canvas roof a soft pewter. Already Caroline knew she would miss that luster when Charles finished the roof with wooden slabs.

"Come out here, Caroline, and look at the moon," Charles called softly. Caroline rose and ducked under the quilt Charles had tacked up for a door. He sat side-ways on the spring seat, arms open for her. Caroline sat down on his knee and settled in against him. Charles pushed the heel of his boot into the ground, bobbing the spring seat comfortably beneath them almost like a rocking chair. His thumb caressed her upper arm in slow harmony.

Caroline looked at the round white moon hanging free in the sky. Without trees or clouds to frame its light, there seemed to be no end to its reach, no end to anything at all. Darkness had melted the horizon; only the faint border of stars made it possible to sepa-rate earth from sky. Caroline closed her eyes and all of it melded together—the sphere of the child float-ing inside her, the circle of Charles's arms around her. Bounded and boundless.

Seventeen

"Mary! Laura!" Charles called. "Come and see what Pet has to show you."

Caroline followed them to the little log stable at a distance. She knew what it must be, but she had not expected it to be so new. The spindly black filly was still glistening, the meaty smell of the afterbirth unmistakable in the cool morning air.

The girls were oblivious, having eyes only for the creature's delicate legs and long, long ears. Caroline could smile at their wonderment, but she herself felt none of it. The sight of that pony, entirely unruffled, with her new little filly standing on one side and her own twin sister on the other turned Caroline all slack inside, disappointed, almost. For the hundredth time, she found herself wishing for Polly. Charles and Edwards had raised the stable in a single day, finishing only the night before. It was as if that filly had been waiting for the stable to be built—waiting until everything was ready to welcome her and then stepped out into the world the very next moment.

It would not be so simple when her time came.

Charles would have the cabin finished by then, of course. There would be a bedstead and a hearth and her own crisp-ironed curtains fluttering at the windows well before summer faded. All the same, Caroline knew she would rather lie on the floor, behind a quilt door and a canvas roof, if only Polly could be there with her.

Caroline did not say a thing when Charles saddled Patty and set off toward the bluffs. It was not that she wanted to gallop across the open prairie under that hot white sun. Given the choice she would much rather spread a quilt on the grass in the shade of the house and have a Sunday school with her girls. It was only that he had these chances to unhitch himself from everything, and she did not. There was never the extravagance of an afternoon all to herself, to do no more than sit down with her desk in her lap and write a letter to Eliza without a single interruption. Envy, pure and simple, and nothing she said to herself would snuff the resentful flicker in her throat. If she spoke aloud Charles would hear it, too, and so she only waved as he trotted away. No sense in marring his pleasure simply because she could not partake of it.

"What's the matter with Jack?" Laura asked.

Caroline looked up from the bake oven. The hair on the back of the bulldog's neck was bristling. Pet ran a nervous circuit and whickered for her foal.

It was as though a wind passed, touching only the animals. Caroline had felt nothing, not the least stir of unease. That in itself sent a little shiver across her arms. "What's the matter, Jack?" she asked. He seemed to raise his eyebrows at her. Caroline turned a slow circle. Nothing, as far as she could see. Nor a sound. She watched Jack's nose quiver into the wind. A scent, then?

Her first thought, always: *Indians?*

Could Jack's and Pet's noses perceive the difference between one race and another? More likely they could scent the dead things the Indians adorned themselves with—the skins and feathers, teeth and bone. Caroline had not seen an Osage since that day on the street in Independence, but she remembered the tufts of hair that fringed their leggings.

All this time in Indian Territory, Caroline thought,

and not one Indian. Even Charles had not seen them—only their deserted camping places. When she asked why, he had answered in that careless way of his. *Oh, I don't know. They're away on a hunting trip, I guess.*

And when they returned, Caroline wondered? Her breath shortened at the thought. Charles had made no proper claim on this land yet. They had not paid a cent for it, had not even filed on it. Supposing they did have papers from a U.S. land office—what weight would that hold with Indians? When the Osages found this house standing where nothing had been before, they would come for their rent as the storekeeper warned.

There was Jack, she told herself, already on guard. And she had the rifle, and the revolver, too, though Caroline could not think where it had been put. *Under the wagon seat,* her mind answered automatically, but that was not so anymore.

The pony came streaking up from the bottoms like a hawk diving straight for them. Caroline could not see the rider—only a brown blur hunched low against the animal's straining neck. Fear pinned her to the ground, a cold stake right down her backbone. It did not matter. She did not have time to move. Pony and rider tore past her before she saw that it was only Patty, Patty and Charles. Patty's hooves cut a great slash in the ground as he wrenched her to a stop just beyond the stable.

The pony shuddered and panted, dripping with sweat. Charles jumped down and spun around to scan the bluffs.

Caroline turned and searched the horizon, too, expecting a war party with arrows notched. Nothing but the wind moved through the grass behind him. "What is it?" she said. "Why did you ride Patty like that?"

"I was afraid the wolves would beat me here," Charles gasped. "But I see everything's all right."

"Wolves!" she cried. "What wolves?"

"Everything's all right, Caroline," he said. "Let a fellow get his breath."

Everything could not be all right, not with the way his hand was shaking as he mopped the sweat from the back of his neck and out from under his whiskers.

"It was all I could do to hold her at all," Charles panted. "Fifty wolves, Caroline, the biggest wolves I ever saw. I wouldn't go through such a thing again, not for a mint of money."

Caroline wanted to fold her ears shut, to pretend it was anyone but Charles describing how that pack of buffalo wolves had surrounded him, how he'd forced Patty to walk among them as they frisked and frolicked like dogs. If anything had happened to him, if just one of those wolves had taken a mind to— The thought loomed so large, she could hardly see around it. Widowed and pregnant like her own ma, his child a living ghost in her belly. Her whole life Caroline had carried the memory of how Ma had dropped where she stood at the news of Pa's shipwreck, as though the weight of that fatherless baby had yanked her to the ground.

"I was glad you had the gun, Caroline," Charles was saying. "And glad the house is built. I knew you could keep the wolves out of the house, with the gun. But Pet and the foal were outside."

Caroline bridled so suddenly the fear fell right out of her. Why had he gone off at all if he had reason to worry about the stock? Did it never occur to Charles that it might behoove them all to worry about himself now and again? "You need not have worried, Charles," she said, holding her voice exactly level. "I guess I would manage to save our horses."

"I was not fully reasonable at the time," he apologized, and some small part of herself Caroline hardly recognized was satisfied that he had been scared out of his wits. Perhaps he would remember that the next time he took it into his head to trot off toward the horizon.

"We'll eat supper in the house," she said.

"No need of that. Jack will give us warning in plenty of time."

If they ate inside there would be no need of warning, but she did not bother saying so. That sort of logic held no sway with Charles.

"Caroline." Caroline felt her mind stir, then sink back toward sleep. "Caroline. Wake up."

His voice made no sense. She could hear Charles breathing heavily beside her, yet the words came from above. She lay in the near silence, listening to that rhythmic *huff . . . huff* until something prickled her awareness.

Caroline's eyes sprang open. It was not Charles panting beside her. It was a wolf, the sounds of its warm breath leaking between the chinks in the logs.

Charles stood with the rifle over his bent arm. "There's a ring of them all around the house," he whispered. "Take this. Careful. It's loaded and half-cocked." The revolver. Caroline took the warm stock in her hand and leaned into a bar of moonlight to see the cylinder. All six chambers were full. Charles gestured toward the west window and went to stand beside the east window. Caroline knew he was watching the stable. She could hear the horses now, snorting and pacing.

Slowly Caroline crept to the end of the straw tick and began to raise herself from the floor. First to all fours, then she laid her free hand on the lid of her trunk and pushed herself to her knees. With the sound of the wolves' breath so near, she dared not put her fingers into the chinks for balance. Another shove against the lid brought her eyes level with the windowsill.

Caroline paused to look through the window hole and the revolver in her hand became no more menacing than a popgun. Those wolves, she saw at once, could do as they pleased. Charles had said he'd never seen bigger wolves in his life, but these creatures were so impossibly large they looked like bears crouched beneath wolf skins. She counted fourteen of them before the ring curved out of her sight. Between the rifle and the revolver she and Charles might be able to discourage them. That was all. If that pack set its mind on breaching the cabin, it would.

The thought did not frighten her. On the contrary— if the wolves had wanted to come inside, Caroline judged, they would have nosed the quilt door aside and devoured all four of them in their sleep. But they had not. Until they did all she and Charles could do was signal their intent to protect themselves.

Caroline sat down on her trunk and pulled her shawl from its peg. She propped the revolver's barrel on the windowsill, pulled back the hammer to full cock, and slipped her finger inside the trigger guard. So long as the wolves sat still, Caroline's thoughts kept still, suspended in an aura of calm. If the wolves came nearer, she knew her finger would squeeze the trigger before her mind formed the command, and so there was no need for her thoughts to go straying ahead.

The wolves made not a move, as though they sensed how near they could come without provoking a reaction. They sat, neither welcoming nor threatening, more acknowledging the boundary between them. Even Jack did not advance, did not so much as put his nose beyond the quilt hanging in the doorway. All of them silently watched one another. The moonlight glinted on the wolves' shaggy coats and made their eyes glow deep and green-gold. What part of her, she wondered, did the animals fix their gaze on? What feature most proclaimed her human—her clothing, her hairless skin? More likely her hands, Caroline decided, and the gun they held.

From the west side of the cabin came a long, smooth howl. As Caroline watched the wolves outside her window showed their white throats to the moon and a circle of sound rose up from them. The sound enveloped the cabin, reverberating all the way into the soft marrow of Caroline's bones until she felt it might lift her away. Was it music to them, she wondered, or prayer, the way it ascended into the sky?

Before she could rebuke herself for thinking something so profane Laura was up—straight up, clutching the quilt so tightly Caroline could see the little points of her knees and toes beneath the taut fabric.

At the sight of Charles with his gun Laura's grip on the bedclothes loosened.

"Want to see them, Laura?" Charles asked.

Laura nodded and went to him. Caroline knew she ought not take her eyes from her window, but she could not help it. The tableau of Charles lifting Laura to the windowsill captivated her in a way the motionless wolves could not. The child believed so wholeheartedly that no harm could reach her as long as her pa was near that her fear all but vanished in an instant.

That was as it should be, Caroline supposed. She herself had hardly any recollection of such a feeling. She had been five years old the last time she saw her own pa. Looking back, she remembered the terrible sensation of the earth rocking beneath her feet at the news of his death better than anything that came before the day the schooner *Ocean* sank. Caroline stroked the smooth metal seam of the revolver's grip with her thumb as the memories moved past her. Eventually the world had become stable enough that she could trust her footing again, thanks first to Papa Frederick and then to Charles, but the shadow of that dreadful day

lingered still. Ever after she lived alongside the knowledge that nothing on this earth could protect her completely.

Before they slept another night, Charles had built the
doors for the house and the stable both.

Then for three days he was gone, helping Edwards
raise his house and barn. Three days, alone with the
girls. He came home for supper, of course, slept every
night beside her and was there for breakfast in the
morning. Edwards's claim was only two miles away,
but it did not feel the same as when Charles was out all
day hunting or working the land.

Always before, their separate labors were bound up
in the same endeavor. With the straw Charles brought
her from the threshing Caroline wove the hat that
would shade his neck while he sowed the grain she
would bake into bread. From that harvest came yet
more straw, and round and round it went, like "The
House That Jack Built."

Now Charles was away, engaged in something apart
from her. Not that she begrudged Edwards. Not one bit.
If not for Edwards's help, they might have been sleeping in a tent the night the wolves encircled them. This
was a plain trade, a simple back-and-forth between two

men, and when it was over Caroline had no doubt she and Charles would resume their usual rhythm.

That was not the trouble. That was not what made her thoughts dreary and her smiles limp, even when the wind carried the sound of his approaching whistle up from the creek bottoms.

Caroline did not know quite what it was until after supper the second night, when Charles said, "Bring me my fiddle, Laura, I want to try out a song Edwards sang."

His eyes twinkled mischievously as he felt for the notes. It was a catchy melody with a good strong beat, well-suited for an accompaniment of swinging axes and hammers. Likely she would find herself humming it over the butter churn one day.

"What are the words, Pa?" Mary asked.

The bow gave a little squawk, and Charles colored ever so slightly. "Well, you know, I don't seem to re-member any more than the tune," he said quickly.

Caroline knew from his grimace that the words were not fit for mixed company. That in itself was no great shock. She could imagine Charles and Edwards indulg-ing in the occasional oath or bawdy song, just as there were things women would speak of only if there were no men within earshot.

Caroline rested her folded arms across the shelf of her belly. There, she thought. That was what she had been missing while Charles was away. Not her husband's company, but the chance to share her own. The girls had their games and giggles, the men their brash hijinks. Caroline had only herself.

Before the roof, before the floor, came the fireplace. Charles might have dug himself a well first and saved himself hauling water from the creek to mix the mud for plastering between the chimney stones. Instead he built the chimney and hearth, so she would not have to tussle with the elements to keep her cookfire going. That was the sort of husband Charles Ingalls was.

Caroline sat in the shade of the north wall, turning scraps of red calico into curtain ties and watching Charles stack the chimney stones while the child tumbled lazily beneath her ribs. It seemed to have discovered its limbs, its movements more purposeful now, more akin to a spoon stirring a pot than the tentative winglike flutters of the past several weeks. The straighter she held her back, the more room it gave the both of them, but her muscles were tired of bracing her spine like a ramrod all day long. Her corset helped only so much. The straw tick, with nothing but the dirt floor beneath it, did not help at all.

Truth be told, what Caroline wanted most in that house was a chair. Not an upturned crate or log to perch on, but a true chair, with a back and arms. She would cook outside all summer long, if only there were a chair to ease her weary back after supper. Her mind strayed to her rocker, and she smiled wistfully. But Charles, in his thoughtfulness, was building her a fireplace—and fairly wearing himself out in his hurry to please her, lifting stones and hauling water and clay for mud.

He stood back, smearing the sweat from his forehead into his hair and setting it all askew.

"You look like a wild man, Charles," she teased. "You're standing your hair all on end."

"It stands on end anyway, Caroline," he said, flopping down flat on his back beside her. "When I was courting you, it never would lie down, no matter how much I slicked it with bear grease."

He had tried, she remembered, valiantly. The slightest whiff of rosemary swept her back to their courtship, when every doff of his hat had filled the room with the smell of that herb-scented grease. Caroline combed her fingers through the unruly brown mass, remembering how her younger brother and sister used to hold their noses and tease, *Is Rosemary Ingalls coming to call?*

"You've done well to build that chimney up so high,

all by yourself," she praised him, twiddling a lock between her fingers.

His forehead shifted beneath her palm as he lifted his eyebrows to smile up at her. Just for a moment, Caroline let herself conjure a picture of the pleasurable diversions they might take, right here on the quilt, if there were not two little girls romping in the grass nearby. A sweet, warm current coursed through her at the thought. Caroline closed her eyes and turned her face to the breeze, letting the soft wind whisk it from her.

All of them waited before the new mantel shelf while Caroline went to her trunk and lifted the lid. Beneath the brown paper bundle that was her delaine, nested snugly between the good pillows, sat the cardboard box she had packed most carefully of all. She burrowed one hand deep into its center of crumpled newsprint until her fingertips brushed something cool and smooth. *Please,* Caroline prayed. If it were not in one piece—Caroline blinked away the thought. She would not cry over such a thing, not with Charles and the girls looking on. Gently she pressed the paper wrapping back, hollowing out a path until a glint of golden china hair peeped out. Once again Caroline tunneled down, wrapping her fingers protectively around the narrow china neck and waist. Up through the rustling papers, all in one piece, came her china shepherdess.

Caroline's heart gave a happy lurch. No matter that the painted lips could not speak, nor the tiny molded hands return the warm embrace of Caroline's palm. She was so bright and beautiful, so small and delicate, Caroline had never been able to get enough of looking at her. She flushed a little, feeling Charles and the girls watching. Here she was a grown woman with two dear girls of her own, and still she had as much affection for that china lady as Mary did for her rag doll.

Caroline wiped the dainty figure carefully with an apron corner, half cleaning, half caressing the smooth porcelain, then stood the china shepherdess right in the center of the mantel shelf, where she belonged.

Two words settled themselves comfortably in her mind: *Welcome home.*

Eighteen

If Charles brought home a prairie chicken, Caroline decided, she would lay a hot fire in the hearth and fry it up crisp and brown. She hummed softly to herself, half waltzing to the tune as she swept. The logs of the puncheon floor lay with their pale yellow hearts turned up to her. She almost hated to walk across them, they were so flat and new and even. But, oh, the sound of her heels on that thick floor. The swish of the willow-bough broom.

She leaned a moment on the broom handle, reveling in the shade of the new slab roof. Caroline missed the glow of the canvas as she'd known she would, but it was a welcome relief to have a place away, to close herself off entirely from wind and sun. That endless wind made her aware of every inch of her skin. It was too much, being touched so constantly. Once more Caroline gazed up at that good solid ceiling, silently thanking Mr. Edwards for the half keg of nails he had loaned so that Charles need not whittle pegs to secure the slabs to the beams. There had not been occasion before to consider the particular virtue of each fragment of a house. Apart from the occasional lashing of rain that made her fear for the shingles, their house had been a house, and she was thankful for it. Now Caroline harbored a separate admiration for the shutters, the hearth, even the chinking between the logs.

Every slab, every peg and nail inched them closer to owning the place. By the time the government opened a land office and offered the land, they would be firmly settled, and as settlers they would have first right to file a preemption on the quarter section they occupied. That was the law. The speculators and railroads must stand aside for the people who lived and worked on the land. The more she and Charles improved the land in the meantime, the more solid their claim, for the law had declared that a man's sweat contained as much worth as his pocketbook—more, even. Caroline looked out at the roll of prairie sloping off toward the creek. This time next year there would be a field of sod potatoes and another of corn taking root. Right beneath the window, a garden green with unfurling sprouts. This time next year, there would be a child clinging to her hip, sucking its fist and fussy with teething.

Outside, Jack growled. Caroline turned toward the open door. "My goodness!"

Two Osages stood in the doorway, their tufted scalp locks brushing the lintel. A narrow belt of colored wool held up their breechclouts. Above that, their lower ribs pressed faintly against their skin. Caroline flushed at the sight of so much bareness.

At each hip hung a knife and a hatchet. Her muscles tensed, as though she might spring at them if they came toward her, but she knew she could not move. A horse hair roach, black at the tips, made a ridge from their scalp locks down the back of their shining skulls. The broad base was a color so vivid Caroline had no name for it—neither red, nor pink, nor purple.

One of them went straight to the crate of provisions. The other looked at her so steadily in the face, it felt indecent. Caroline folded her hands tight against the crest of her belly, hugging her sides with her elbows. She prayed they would see and leave her be.

Outside, Jack's chain rattled and snapped against its iron ring. Caroline had never heard him so savage.

All at once the air seemed to shatter. She could not hear Mary and Laura—had not heard them since before the Indians came into the house. Alarm sluiced past her elbows and knees.

She could not look out the window without turning her back to the Indians. If anything had happened to her girls, Caroline told herself, she should have heard them scream. But she had not made a sound herself. She could not even call their names with her heart drumming at the base of her throat.

The first man set the sack of cornmeal on the checked tablecloth between them. Then patted it. Caroline shied from the sound. The Indian spoke—a low ripple of syllables. Caroline shook her head. She could not hear where one word ended and another began. The other man held out the sack, pointing it at her, then the hearth.

She understood, but she would not take the meal from his hand. Caroline forced herself to nod and point to the table.

Her mind pivoted back to Brookfield while her hands measured and mixed the cornbread of their own accord. She had been wearing her blue-sprigged calico the day the Potawatomi man walked into their house and took the peacock feathers from the vase beside the looking glass. Caroline could see him still, strolling away with those shimmering plumes gazing back at her from his hair. More vibrant than the feathered eyes was the memory of her ma's groan when they realized little Thomas had disappeared with the Indian.

The same sound was rising in her now, grating against the back of her breastbone as her whole body strained with the effort of listening for Mary and Laura. She started to press her palms into the top of the loaves, then jerked back. Her pulse stormed in her fingertips. She would not give these men the sweetening of the prints of her hands. That belonged only to Charles. Caroline wiped the grains of meal briskly on her apron and dropped the naked loaves into the bake oven. The iron cover rattled into place.

They looked at everything. Caroline watched the loops of beaded silver wire sway from their long earlobes as they probed through the cabin. Charles's tobacco pouch disappeared into one brown fist as though she had no more presence than the china shepherdess. They might take anything and she would not move, if only they had left her daughters untouched.

The Potawatomis had stolen only feathers, she reminded herself, not her baby brother. While the rest of the family watched the Indian decorate his hair with their peacock plumes, the little boy had toddled out of sight into the corn patch. She prayed these Osages might be as vain, that Mary and Laura were sheltered by Providence as Thomas had been.

But this was not Brookfield with its woods and corn patches. Through the window she could see clear to the willows along the creek—clear to the bluffs beyond—but she could not see her daughters. If she called their names, the fear in her voice would point the Indians straight to them. The baby thrashed against her bladder. Caroline's jaw clenched with the strain.

Suddenly Jack erupted into such a fury the Indians went to the window. Caroline could hear the bulldog lunging against the chain, scrabbling at the dirt. With each charge the metal links clattered and thrummed.

In a flash of calico the girls darted into the house. Caroline's relief frothed up like saleratus. Laura ducked behind the slabs Charles had left propped in the corner for the bedstead. Mary skittered barefoot across the length of the house and clung to Caroline's sleeve. The instant she felt Mary's hands around her wrist, Caroline closed her eyes and offered her thanks heavenward. Now she only wanted Laura's tangled brown hair under her fingers.

The Indians' eyes traced her gaze across the cabin, where half of Laura's face peeped from behind the slabs. They peered at her, bending down so that their hatchets dangled from their hips. One man spoke, and the other said, "Hah!" Laura jolted, cowering tight against the wood with nothing but her little white fingertips showing.

Caroline pulled Mary to the hearth and yanked the lid from the bake oven. "It's done," she announced. The Indians turned. Caroline thrust a finger toward the pale loaves and stepped back. The hot iron lid in her fist dared them to frighten Laura again.

The two men squatted low on the hearth, their legs bent like hairpins. Silently, each ate an entire loaf of the half-baked bread, pinching every damp crumb from the floorboards. By the time they finished, Mary's tears had warmed her sleeve.

The Indians stood. The shorter of the two pointed his chin at Mary and said, "Mi'-na." The other man smirked and nodded. Not a shred of malice slanted their expressions. Instead they looked amused, as though they had recognized something so plain they expected Caroline to see and join her smile with theirs.

She would do no such thing. Caroline shifted sideways, slicing through their view with her body. The lid to the bake oven was still in her hand.

The planes of the men's faces leveled. Without a word, they turned their backs and went out. The lid dropped from Caroline's fist and rolled on its edge to the stack of slabs.

Laura came running.

Caroline sat down hard on the straw tick, nearly pulling the girls with her. Relief corkscrewed through her.

"Do you feel sick, Ma?" Mary asked.

"No," she managed. Tremors welled in every joint; even her jaw quivered. "I'm just thankful they're gone."

"We thought they would hurt you," Mary said.

"We left Jack and came to help," Laura interrupted.

Caroline cupped their cheeks with her palms and cradled their heads against her shoulders. "My brave little girls," she said. Overwhelmed by their nearness, her breasts prickled, weeping warm flecks of foremilk into her chemise.

The table was set and a fresh mixing of cornmeal in the bowl when Charles came whistling through the grass. A jackrabbit dangled by its hocks at his belt, and he swung two headless prairie hens in one fist. The girls nearly toppled over each other in their scramble to tell him the news. Caroline was glad for their zeal. She did not want to recollect the Indians' visit any more than she must.

"Did Indians come into the house, Caroline?"

She held her voice even as a line of print as she told him about the tobacco and how much cornbread the two men had eaten. "They took the meal straight from the crate with me standing there. The way they pointed, I didn't dare refuse." The memory swelled her mind. "Oh, Charles! I was afraid!" Her chest constricted; she had not meant to tell him that part of it. Nor the girls, for that matter.

He assured her she had done right, that it was better to sacrifice a few provisions than make an enemy of any Osage, but she was not comforted. "The cornmeal was already running short," she added. It was petty; she had seen their ribs.

"One baking of cornbread won't break us." Charles lifted his fistful of game. The prairie hens' blunted necks wagged at her. "No man can starve in a country like this. Don't worry, Caroline."

She did not know what she had wanted him to say, but it was not this. He had not even looked at the sack of meal. Nor was he the one who would have to make it stretch. Her chin stabbed out like a child's. "If that's so, I don't know why they can't make do without our cornmeal. And all of your tobacco," she added, hoping to pry something more out of him.

Charles waved a hand. "Never mind. I'll get along without tobacco until I can make that trip to Independence."

Independence. The irony needled her. Two days she and the girls would be stranded on the high prairie while he went to town to replace what the Indians had taken. Maybe three. Three days with those men free to wander in and demand whatever else they liked of her.

"Main thing is to keep on good terms with them," Charles went on blithely.

Indignation burned through her like spilled kerosene. She could not hear a word he was saying until "band of the screeching dev—"

Her head snapped up. Caroline pressed her lips together and jerked her chin at him. The straighter she tried to hold herself, the harder she trembled.

"Come on, Mary and Laura!" Charles said. His voice was so bright, it sounded as if the words had been whitewashed. "We'll skin that rabbit and dress the prairie hens while that cornbread bakes. Hurry! I'm hungry as a wolf!"

Caroline sank down on a crate. There was nothing to do but collect herself. With the heels of her hands she slicked the perspiration from her temples into her hair. She heard Charles peg the rabbit's leg to the wall, then begin peeling the skin from the flesh while Mary and Laura pelted him with chatter about the Indians' visit.

Her ears followed only the ripples of their talk, until Charles's voice came down like the ax. "Did you girls even think of turning Jack loose?" Each syllable struck the same low note.

A spike of fear fell straight to Caroline's heels. What might she have done, had Jack come raging into the cabin? Likely stand by and watch the Indians kill the dog. That or shoot Jack herself.

Until this moment she had not thought about the revolver. What would the Osage men have done, as she drew the pistol and cocked it? Caroline began to tremble again. There was nothing she could use to protect herself or her daughters without inviting attack.

"There would have been trouble," Charles was saying. "Bad trouble."

There. He had said it, at least. But now the acknowledgment left her reeling. She listened to Charles reproach the girls and wished she could snatch his words from the air. That he should have been so cavalier with her, yet so grave with Mary and Laura was nonsensical. In Pepin they had been safe as buttons in the button box. Surely he could not expect them to comprehend the hazards of the Indian Territory.

"Do as you're told and no harm will come to you," Charles declared.

One objection after another crowded Caroline's throat. The girls did not understand. She could hear it in the shrink of their voices even as they whispered, "Yes, Pa." They were bewildered by his anger, and that was all.

Charles had not seen their fear, Caroline reminded herself. He had not felt Mary's tears soaking his sleeve, nor watched Laura try to press herself invisible behind the stack of slabs. He had only seen them boiling over in their eagerness to share the news of their encounter with the Osages.

But he was turning them in the wrong direction. They had not set the bulldog loose, and they had not been wrong to be afraid of the Indians, nor to want to protect her. Instead of being reproached, they ought to be praised for following their instincts. In a place like this, there could be no room for blind obedience. It was all the more dangerous to render them more wary of upsetting their pa than of the Indians. Their fear would guard them—if only Charles would leave them free to obey it.

Caroline swallowed all her protests back. She could not interject. Contradicting Charles would only muddy the girls further. She rose and went to the window for a breath of air. Alongside the woodpile, Charles had one of the prairie hens pinned by the wings under his boots. He pulled slowly upward on the thighs so that the bird began to stretch apart. The feathers shuddered, then the whole of the body tore free to leave the breast, pink and glistening, between the crushed wings.

———————

Charles nailed the provisions cupboard to the wall, to keep the Indians from making off with the whole thing. Caroline's shoulders flinched with every smack of the hammer. She could hold her thoughts in check or her body, not both. If she felt entitled to her anger, she might have turned it loose, but she did not. The fact that Charles had devoted the very next morning to building a cupboard complete with a padlock proved that he shared her concern over their supplies. But he would not say it. Caroline did not know why she needed him to; it was plain enough.

In went the cornmeal, the sugar and flour, coffee and tea. Charles flapped the lid shut and threaded a padlock through the slots he'd whittled into the wood. "There," he said, and held out the key. "String that up on a shoelace or what have you and wear it where the Indians won't see it."

"Wear it?" Caroline said.

Charles nodded. "That way if they take it into their heads to search the place, they won't find it."

Caroline stepped back. She could just imagine standing by with that key dangling between her breasts while those bare brown men rooted through the cabin. "You keep it, Charles," she said.

"No sense in you having to fetch the key from me

three times a day to do your cooking." He gave the key a little toss, fumbling to catch it when she did not. "All right?" he asked.

"That stands to reason," she said, and reluctantly put out her hand to accept it.

Caroline went to her work basket and retrieved a spool of red crochet cotton. If she was to wear the thing, it would not be on a scrap of shoelace. Then again, she thought, it must not be so fancy as to attract attention. So she worked an ordinary chain stitch with her crochet hook until the string of red loops was long enough to let the key lie securely behind the steel boning of her corset.

It would be a lie, to put herself between the Osages and the cupboard with the key around her neck, pretending to be unable to unlock it. How much easier on her conscience to simply put down her foot and refuse. Then again, she did not want to provoke them—only thwart them. So a lie it would be.

The first few days she constantly felt the scant weight of the key around her neck, felt it nudging her ribs when she bent or leaned just so. Even after she became insensible to the press of the cool metal teeth against her flesh, the brass left a faint green print like a brand on her skin.

Nineteen

How often the world seemed to bend for Charles, Caroline thought as she watched him crank the windlass, in a way it did for no one else. When they were mired along the Missouri, Mr. Jacobs had ridden up out of the trees to trade horses. The log fell on her ankle, and along came Edwards to finish raising the cabin and stable. Even the ride that had ended with Charles's terrifying encounter with the wolf pack had brought them, in a roundabout way, the man who now shoveled at the bottom of their half-dug well.

He was a round, squinting fellow, his fair skin scoured to peeling by the sun. No shirker, though, for every morning at sunup Mr. Scott was at the door, calling out, "Hi, Ingalls! Let's go!"

Scott was pleasant enough, but he was not convivial

like Mr. Edwards. After a polite "Morning, ma'am," he hardly seemed to notice her, or the girls. He swore mildly but absently during his spells down in the shaft, and Caroline tried all day long to keep Laura from straying near enough to hear the short blasts of execration echoing up out of the dirt walls.

At night, Charles was tired. Work with Scott was ordinary work—the bite of the shovel and the crank of the windlass. Occasionally a bark of laughter, but no rhythm, no real harmony between them.

Still, she was thankful for his work. Thankful even before the morning Charles said, almost in passing as he headed out the door with his shovel, "Scott said he spoke to his wife and she'll come for you. When it's time."

A flush crept up her neck to think of the men speaking together of such things.

"Did you thank him?"

Charles nodded.

Good then. It was done, however awkwardly. A space had cleared around her lungs, as though the news had loosened her corset strings.

Mrs. Scott would come. But now Caroline's greedy mind wanted to know what Mrs. Scott's voice sounded like, how many children she'd borne, whether her hands were large or small. Things Caroline did not know how to ask her own husband without betraying apprehensions that had no business intruding on such good news.

Mrs. Scott would come, Caroline repeated to herself. That alone told her something about the woman. If she could leave her own claim long enough to attend a lying-in, any children she had were weaned. There might be an older girl, big enough to keep up the housework and get the meals. She had volunteered to come, that much was almost certain. Caroline could picture Mr. Scott talking to his wife over supper, telling her about the Ingalls family from Wisconsin: a carpenter and his wife with two little girls, and the missus in the family way. A man who cursed the sun and wind—however mildly—in a woman's presence might not be so reluctant to say it right out, Caroline reckoned.

"No other kin?" asked the imaginary Mrs. Scott.

Mr. Scott would shake his head. Would he know why she had asked?

"You may tell them I'll come for her."

Charles's voice strayed into her imaginings. "Scott? Scott! Scott!" A pause. "Caroline, come quick!"

She might have scoffed at the words. Quick, indeed. Nothing she did felt quick these days. The sound of them was something else altogether. Caroline had never heard his voice like this. Dread billowed up around her so suddenly, everything else fell away—the sheets from her hands and the thoughts from her mind—and Caroline flew outside.

Charles was down on all fours beside the hole, peering into it. "Scott's fainted or something down there," he said. "I've got to go down after him."

"Did you send down the candle?" Caroline asked.

"No. I thought he had. I asked him if it was all right, and he said it was."

She had seen Mr. Scott shaking his head at the way Charles lowered a candle down the well to test the air each morning. *Foolishness,* he'd said. At once Caroline knew that blustering, impatient man had not done it. He had shimmied down the rope into who knows what kind of miasma while Charles finished his breakfast. She shaded her eyes and squinted into the hole. Not a glimmer of light, nor a glimpse of Mr. Scott's sun-bleached hair.

What shall we do? The words never reached her lips. Caroline looked up to ask, and Charles was tying a handkerchief over his nose and mouth. "Got to get the rope around him or we can't pull him out."

No. Her whole body pulsed with the word. *No, no,*

no. "Charles," she said almost tentatively, as though her voice were backing away from the idea, "you can't. You mustn't."

The triangle of handkerchief puffed out with each word. "Caroline, I've got to."

The wide black throat of the well gaped silently at his knees. Cold tingled in Caroline's belly at the thought of its depth. "You can't. Oh, Charles, no!"

"I'll make it all right," he promised. "I won't breathe till I get out." Caroline stood so still, the world seemed to quiver around her. What made him think he could promise such a thing? He could not climb back up that rope quickly enough to guarantee his own safety without someone to crank the windlass and draw him out of the earth like a bucket. For weeks, Charles had not let her carry so much as a pail of water from the creek. Now he asked this of her. No, did not even ask. She was so big she could no longer lift Laura onto her lap, yet he never considered for an instant that she would do anything but leap to the crank to help him save a man she hardly knew.

"We can't let him die down there," Charles said.

"No," Caroline declared. Better one man dead than both of them. There was no simpler arithmetic. "No, Charles!" she said again. Caroline watched, dumbstruck, as he sliced the top bucket free and tied the rope to the windlass as if she had not said a word. Her vow of obedience, broken, and it held no power over him. It did not matter whether she was willing to save Mr. Scott, Caroline realized in a dizzying rush, because once Charles stepped into that hole, there was not one fiber of her body that would refuse to strain at the crank to bring her husband back. He had not asked because she had no choice. Panic spurted into Caroline's limbs, pooling hot and syrupy in the crook of her arms and behind her knees. "I can't let you. Get on Patty and go for help," she pleaded.

He shook his head. "There isn't time." He reached for the rope and leaned over the pit.

"Charles, if I can't pull you up—if you keel over down there and I can't pull you up—" The way he looked at her, so earnest and determined, cracked her voice.

"Caroline, I've got to."

The ground swallowed him up, one silent gulp, and Caroline dropped to her knees. Above her the windlass squealed wildly, unspooling its last few feet, and thrummed to a sudden stop.

The rope trembled straight and taut, then went slack. He was at the bottom.

Oh, God, she prayed. *Dear God.* Her eyes reached and reached. There was nothing for them to fasten to but the moist brown walls of the pit. Sounds wafted up at her, sounds so muffled and magnified by their long ascent that she could not make them out.

Seven. Eight. Nine. If he did not shout, or tug at the rope within ten breaths . . . then what? Turn the crank? Run for help? *Twelve. Thirteen.* The rope jiggled and twitched. Caroline wrapped her fingers around it, felt the thin line of movement running through it. As long as it was moving, Caroline promised herself, Charles was alive. So long as it was moving, she would not let go of that rough jute, no matter how many breaths passed. *Eighteen, nineteen.*

Suddenly the rope twanged to the center of the well.

Caroline pushed herself from the ground. She took hold of the crank and yanked. It spun three-quarters of a turn and stopped so short, her shoulders jolted. She pulled again, wrenching the skin of her palms against the wooden handle. It wobbled but did not budge. There was not strength in her arms, nor the whole of her body to pull that crank.

I won't breathe till I get out. The last breath Charles had taken would be pressing behind his teeth by now. Caroline shook the image away. There had to be a way—Charles was not so gallant that he would have gone down unless there was a way out. Frantically she searched her mind, calling up a blackboard charted in her own hand with wheels and axles, pulleys and weights.

Caroline ground her heels into the dirt until her almost-healed ankle was a welter of old and new pain. She refastened her hands to the crank and heaved, leaning backward so the weight of her belly swung her nearly to the ground. The windlass creaked, following. Caroline's throat bulged with grunts she would not release as she propelled the leverage of her body up into the peak of the turn. Not one particle of energy would leave her unless she could direct it into the crank.

The crank reached the apex and continued moving— one full turn, then two, three.

Every strand of muscle in her arms burned. If they snapped or frayed before Charles reached the top— *No,* Caroline commanded herself. Only a few more turns and he would be out of reach of the fumes, high enough to risk a breath. Nothing mattered before that. Only give him time to breathe. So long as he could breathe, it did not matter how long it took to bring him to the surface. She could even stop to rest, once he breached clean air.

Caroline did not stop to rest. Her thrusting thighs and heaving back knew better than to surrender their momentum. She could picture his face, hear the echo of his voice telling Laura: *By jinks, you're as strong as a little French horse!*

Lit-tle . . . French . . . horse, lit-tle . . . French . . . horse, her mind and her muscles chanted together as the crank turned over and over.

The load lifted from the rope so abruptly, Caroline panicked at the thought it had snapped. Instantly the weight redoubled, and she cranked with a new fury.

In the same second a hand appeared on the ground; another gripped the leg of the windlass. Caroline's heart seemed to bloom past her ribs, brimming into her breasts and deep into her belly as she watched Charles spill himself onto the grass beside her. He slumped low over his knees, gasping, his boots still dangling over the edge. Caroline let go of the crank and put her hands to his back, feeling the air rush in and out of him. Above them the windlass squealed and spun. From the well's gullet came a heavy *whump.*

"Scott," Charles coughed, and tried to pry himself from the ground.

"Sit still, Charles," Caroline said. He had not caught his breath.

She could not hold him down. He staggered to the crank, pulling and panting. Caroline scrambled up and took hold of the crank again. Together it was simple as winding a spool of thread. Up ran the bucket, and, lolling on top of it, Mr. Scott. Caroline braced the crank while Charles hefted him onto the grass. Scott lay there, slack and rubbery, as if the fumes had half melted him. Charles put two fingers to Scott's wrist, then an ear to his chest.

"He's breathing," Charles said. "He'll be all right, in the air." A little shiver rattled him, then Charles dropped beside Scott, limbs splayed and eyes closed.

Caroline could not feel anything. The quivers of exertion in her muscles, the blood pounding through her limbs, the warm cascade of relief—all of it had been stripped from her. She blinked at him as he lay there, so very still. *Safe or dead?* The question drifted somewhere nearby, a puff of thought shadowing her mind as it passed by.

"I'm all right, Caroline." The words rushed out on a sigh. "I'm plumb tuckered out, is all."

The tips of her fingers began to tingle. Her palms burned where the grain of the windlass handle had bitten into the skin. "Well!" Caroline said, and a hot torrent came whirling up out of her. "I should think you would be! Of all the senseless performances! My goodness gracious! Scaring a body to death, all for the want of a little reasonable care! My goodness! I—" The child kicked, and the wobbly, watery sensation shattered her fury. Caroline snatched her apron to her face and sobbed.

Naked, she lies in the grass, the well a gaping hole between her splayed legs. A rope runs out from somewhere deep within her, down into the well. From the pit, the plaintive sound of Charles's fiddle rises. With each note the rope vibrates, as though it is strung across the neck of the instrument. Fibers of jute chafe her thighs, scour the delicate channel leading to the rope's source. She strains at it, the rope a writhing umbilicus between them, but Charles's head does not emerge from the hole.

A long, high wolf's howl melded with the wail of the note rising from the pit, and Caroline found herself awake. *Another dream,* she soothed herself as she twined her ankles together and tugged her hem back into place. Her nightdress had hitched itself halfway over her belly. *Only another dream.*

But the feel of it lingered. The sense of being tethered to that dreadful pit coiled around her in the dark. And the nakedness, calling her shame back to the very surface of her skin. What spiteful logic dreams dealt in: she would have been less ashamed to show her bare flesh than let Mary and Laura and Charles see the way she had abandoned herself to wailing and sobbing the moment all danger had passed. Worst of all was Mary offering her own dry hankie in place of Caroline's sodden apron. Fresh twists of shame wriggled through her at the memory, at the tentative pity on her five-year-old daughter's upturned face.

Caroline considered whether to close her eyes again. In daylight she could raise a bucket from the well and her mind strayed to nothing more troubling than keeping the water from splashing her shoes. Nights, though, she'd lived that dreadful morning over a dozen different ways, each bent into something more grotesque than the reality.

What was hidden between the folds of her brain that would not be content with the awful memories themselves, Caroline wondered, but insisted on conjuring them into such unearthly images?

The child shifted, as if it, too, were discomfited by such thoughts. Caroline fitted her hands around the mound of her belly and pressed, hugging inward with her palms. Poor thing. Not yet born, and already it had shared in each of her most fearful moments. What must it have felt when the dread and terror went coursing through her—did the same chilling-hot currents flood its budding limbs? Caroline winced at the thought.

No more, she promised it. *No more*. A promise she

could not hope to keep. She had no power to seal herself off from fear any more than she could conjure tides of happiness. If nothing else, Caroline suddenly chided herself, she might resolve to stop her mind from fondling the worst of her memories night after night. Her lip trembled at the thought of allowing herself to touch the store of fine things she'd locked in her heart the moment she'd begun packing her trunk in Pepin.

Caroline closed her eyes and imagined her rocking chair. The *swish-swish* of the runners across the floor, the gentle curve of the slats against her back. Her shoulders felt the soft embrace of her red shawl, its ends tucked around a swaddled bundle. The child's face still would not form in her mind's eye, but her arms summoned up its weight, its warmth against her body. Past and future, twined together.

In her mind Caroline fashioned a snug little haven for herself, entering it each night to call up the dearest of her memories for the child to feed on. The taste of her mother's blueberry cake and cottage cheese pie. The springtime riot of pinks in the sailor's garden up the road, all the way back in Brookfield. Her first week's pay as a schoolteacher, two dollar bills and two shining quarters. The cornhusking dances in Concord—the rich green swirl of her delaine skirt, the sound of

Charles's fiddle, the feel of his hands on her waist as they danced. Their first night together in their own little house in Pepin. Eliza. Henry. Polly. Ma and Papa Frederick. These memories ached, but softly, so that the ache itself became a pleasure. The ache hurt less than the blank places she had carved out by trying not to remember.

Nights passed, and Caroline found she did not need to reach so far back to find a memory that would unfurl into something so bright and warming that she thought surely the child must be sharing in her contentment. The child, after all, had been there, floating in the center of her every moment: Their first piping hot meal after the miring storm. The sky reflected in Laura's eyes the night she said the stars were singing. Supper with Edwards, with the newly built house outlined against that same starry sky. These recollections were not edged with wistfulness. They burned cheerfully, leaving no dim corners for darker thoughts of the creek, the Osages, or the well to congregate.

Then came the night after Charles finished the bedstead, when she could not think of one thing more comforting than the feel of that bed against her back. If she had not filled it with her own hands, Caroline would not have believed she lay on the same straw tick. The prairie grass beneath her was finer than straw, with a warm, golden-green smell somewhere between hot bread and fresh herbs, and it enveloped her like broth welcoming a soup bone. Her hips and shoulder blades, which always seemed to sink straight to the floor, floated above the rope Charles had strung between the framing slabs. She shifted deeper, and the rope sighed and the grass whispered. "I declare, I'm so comfortable it's almost sinful!" she said and closed her eyes, the better to savor every inch of the sheets cradling her body.

Twenty

At the sight of Charles and two cowboys leading a cow and calf up out of the creek bottoms, Caroline thought she must be back in her soft bed, dreaming. She had sat down on the end of the bed by the window with the mending, waiting for the fire to slack enough to put the cornbread on to bake, and the midsummer heat had lulled her to sleep. Caroline blinked, trying to sift the few fragments of reality from what she saw. It was already a stretch to make herself believe that a herd truly had chanced to pass by their claim, that the men driving it offered Charles a day's work keeping the longhorns out of the ravines instead of Edwards or Scott or anyone else in Montgomery County. Absurd as it was, that was real, and that itself—a day's work in exchange for a piece of fresh beef—had felt like a dream even as Caroline clasped her hands for delight. Now she closed her eyes and stretched her shoulders, waiting for the image to scatter and refashion into the familiar lines of the roof and walls.

Caroline opened her eyes and instead there was Charles, tying the animals to the corner of the stable and shaking hands with the two cowboys. "Well, Caroline?" he called through the window. When she did not answer he untied a fat packet from his saddle horn and held it up. The beef. *If that beef was real,* Caroline thought. Her mouth fell open. She felt a laugh go tumbling out of her, heard it meet with Charles's great rumbling peals, and knew it was not a dream at all.

Of course it was providential. It could be nothing else. But a slab of beef, a cow, and a calf was too extravagant, even for Providence. A cow. *And* a calf. She could not help repeating it to herself. There had never been a word so impossibly big as that *and.* A cow and a calf. Both rangy and unruly but goodness, milk and butter. Perhaps, Caroline thought, the hand of Providence had only been passing over them, on its way elsewhere with these fine gifts, and had somehow dropped them.

But the land continued to burgeon with gifts for them. Yellow-orange plums small enough to scoop up with a spoon. Walnuts, pecans, and hickory nuts still in their green husks, plumping for autumn. A queer purple flower with a turnip-like root that Edwards called Indian breadroot; Caroline could not get enough of its crisp, white flesh.

"Close your eyes," Charles said as he came through the door. It had become a game with him, bringing home little surprises to plop into their open palms. If not something to eat, then something to marvel at—a kernel of blue corn, a speckled green prairie chicken egg. "Now open your mouth."

Caroline hesitated. Last time it had been a sunflower seed, from the Indian camp. Charles had cut one of the great yellow flowers from its stalk and pegged it up on the side of the chimney to dry. She did not like to wonder what the Osages would think to see it dangling there, no matter how many times Charles told her the camp surrounding the crops was deserted. The idea of the Indians leaving their corn and beans and sunflowers to the mercy of weather and wild animals was nonsensical.

She could feel Charles waiting, daring her not to trust him. Caroline opened her mouth.

She smelled the juice on his fingers before it touched her tongue. A blackberry, hot and sweet from the sun. Caroline sighed as she crushed it against the roof of her mouth. The rapture of its smoothness, the burst of flavor like a pinch to her tongue. Nothing had tasted so bright since last summer's tart cherries.

"All along the creek," Charles said. "The fruit just about brushes the ground, the brambles are so heavy. You couldn't pick them all in a week."

Caroline salivated anew at the wealth of things she could do with them. Blackberry pie. Blackberries and cream. Blackberry jam. Dried blackberries, stirred into pancake batter and hasty pudding, or stewing over the fire. If she gathered them quickly, if the baking-hot sunshine held long enough to dry them, their rich, syrupy smell would brighten the cabin all winter long. And if Charles could find more prairie chicken eggs, Caroline thought, she could try blackberries in Ma's blueberry cake recipe. She would send one to Mr. Edwards, and to Mrs. Scott if it came out well, she decided. Just to be neighborly again, for its own sake. That would be as sweet as the fruit itself.

The next morning she dressed Mary and Laura in their oldest calicos and handed them each a pail. They gamboled around her, chasing rabbits and dickcissels all the way down to the creek. Caroline did not try to keep up. The hot wind made her skin feel dry and taut, as if moving too suddenly might split it open. Although there were only a few dwindling inches of lacing to spare along the sides of her maternity corset, she had not been so conscious of her increasing size lately. The child was not so much growing as ripening, so that most of what she felt now was the accumulating weight, and the straining of her body to contain it. And with better than a month yet to wait, Caroline calculated, panting a little. These last weeks she would spend both thickening and thinning, expanding outwardly while her own flesh stretched and narrowed itself to make room from within. The sensation made her thankful for her corset's firm embrace.

"Look, Ma!"

Charles had not exaggerated. A bounty of great, fat berries shone purple-black in the sun.

As Caroline and the girls clustered close to a tangle of brambles, swarms of mosquitoes billowed up then settled down to crouch on the fruit and pierce the skins with their needle-shaped tongues.

"Now watch." She showed Mary and Laura how to tease the darkest berries from their spongy white cores without bursting the tender black globes. "Put them gently into the pail," Caroline said, reaching all the way to the bottom before opening her hand. "The red and purple berries are not ripe enough to pull free."

Caroline watched them a moment. Mary picked just as Caroline had shown her, but Laura's pail would have to be made into preserves, or put into a pie. In her eagerness, Laura pinched the berries, then let them bounce by the handful onto the bottom of her pail. Caroline smiled in spite of herself. She ought to teach Laura how to keep from crushing the fruit, but Laura was having such fun. Already her short fingers were stained purple to the cuticles. There was little that pleased her more than helping, and blackberry jam was no less valuable than blackberries dried whole.

Caroline turned her attention to her own two pails and began to pick. It was lazy work, barely work at all with so many berries at hand, and heady with heat and the murmur of insect wings. Her belly snagged against the briars as she leaned to reach another cluster of fruit. A cloud of mosquitoes rose up sullenly at her approach, then crowded back in. They buzzed drunkenly, hardly aware of her fingers. Determined to pluck every berry within reach, Caroline stood in one place so long that her dress made a tent of heat around her. Sweat glossed the skin at her temples, dribbled between her breasts and down the backs of her knees. The key to the provisions cabinet clung to her damp skin, so warm that she could smell the tang of the hot brass. Mosquitoes pricked the back of her neck, her wrists, and even her ears. Purple smears streaked the girls' legs and ankles, marking the places they had swatted.

Breakfast wore thin as the sun climbed the sky, yet

Caroline did not indulge herself with mouthfuls of berries as the girls did. Hunger made a welcome pocket in her middle, and she did not hurry to fill it. As a child she would not have thought it possible that the empty rumble could be pleasurable, but now, brimming as she was, the feel of that space as it opened was a momentary luxury. Now and then she found a blackberry that was almost hot to the touch, and those went into her mouth.

If there had been this many blackberries in the thickets along the banks of the Oconomowoc, Caroline mused to herself, she and her brothers and sisters would never have feared winter's coming. Berry picking had been as much a necessity as a treat in those days.

With a smile she remembered little Thomas, silently scooping blackberries from Martha's bucket with a serving spoon he'd smuggled from the house, and how he had lied when Martha finally realized why she could not manage to fill her pail. "Honest, Martha," he said, clean palms upturned for her to inspect. "My fingers'd be all juicy if I stole your berries," he reasoned with big solemn eyes, not knowing that his purple tongue contradicted his every word. Martha was mad enough to whip him and sly enough not to bother. Thomas's comeuppance lasted all night long, running back and forth to the necessary. It had doubled them all over with

laughter then, but now, watching how her own daughters filled their mouths casually, almost indifferently,
Caroline's smile slumped. If Thomas had not spent
a winter making do with bread crumbled into maple
sugar water, perhaps he would not have gorged himself. It wasn't fair, she thought fiercely now, to shame a
child for greed when he had no memory of plenty. One
could not exist without the other. Children as small as
Mary and Laura ought never to feel their bellies gnaw-
ing at nothing.

"My pail is full, Ma," Mary said. "Can I go back
home? Please?" Her voice peaked into a whine.

"May I," Caroline reminded her.

"May I, Ma?" Strings of Mary's straw-colored hair
trailed through the sweat along the rim of her sunbonnet. Her face glowed pink and cross. Had they been in
Pepin, Caroline would not have hesitated. It was less
than a quarter mile back to the cabin. Mary could not
possibly lose her way from the path through the tall
prairie grass. But Caroline did not answer. She looked
toward the east, toward the Indian camp. It was not
that she did not believe what Charles had told her. If he
said the camp was empty, it was empty. It was that he
could not be sure where the Indians had gone, nor for
how long.

"You may help Laura finish her pail," Caroline said, "and then we will all go home together."

The next day Caroline laid a tarpaulin full of blackberries out in the sun beside the cabin and let Mary stay behind to guard it from birds and insects while Charles built a paddock for the stock. The drying fruit seemed to draw the mosquitoes up out of the creek bottoms and across the prairie. Long after the berries were picked and put up for winter, the insects lingered, indifferent to the smudges of damp grass Charles lit to smoke them from the house and barn. No amount of coal tar oil and pennyroyal rubbed into the skin discouraged the mosquitoes from biting. All day long the crock of apple cider vinegar stood open on the table, so they might dab each new pink welt the moment it began to itch.

Caroline could not say by any stretch that she was thankful for the mosquitoes. She could not be thankful for a pestilence that found its way under the sheets to prickle her unreachable feet with bites while she slept. Though she could not speak of it, there was a measure of reassurance in their nettlesome clouds. The land had become so bountiful she was almost wary of it. Here at last was proof that it was not too good to be true.

Twenty-One

It started low, and early. The cabin was still dim when Caroline woke to the warming ache behind her bladder. She levered herself from the bedstead and went to the door. The sun was not up, yet already the breath of the wind warmed her face. She stepped barefoot into the hazy predawn. Jack followed, perturbed.

Her waters broke just outside the necessary.

For a moment Caroline stood dripping on the path, thankful it hadn't happened in the new bedstead. The sight of the fluid soaking into the earth put a queer thrill high in her belly, at the spread of her ribs. This was something altogether different from emptying the family chamber pail along the roads of Iowa and Missouri. Had she been a papist, she might have crossed herself. Jack crept forward to sniff at the puddle and seemed satisfied. That was all the reverence Caroline needed, and she went about her business.

Charles met her at the cabin door.

"Caroline?"

She knew how she must look—barefoot, with her hair unpinned and the back of her gown wet and likely stained. "You'd best go ask for Mrs. Scott to come today. I should think before noon I will have need of her."

A shimmer of fear and excitement lit his eyes. "It's sooner than you expected. Isn't it?"

She tried to smile. "Only by two weeks. Maybe three." Perhaps even four.

"If I leave now, Scott'll be up for chores by the time I get there."

"And the girls?"

He nodded, shrugging into his suspenders. "I'll think of something to keep them busy."

All through the morning, the pain stretched steadily upward, tightening the hammock of her belly. By the time she'd cleared the breakfast dishes, it was cresting beneath her ribs. Under the waves flowed a tension that never eased. The dull heat of it rose upward until her throat was rigid from cinching back the sounds of her discomfort. Determined not to groan or whimper in front of the girls, she tried humming a little over the dishwater and found a sort of harmony in letting her voice drift above the drone of clenching muscle.

"One little, two little, three little Indians," Charles sang, pointing at Mary's and Laura's tanned faces, then wagging his finger in the air. "Nope, only two."

"You make three," Mary said. "You're brown, too."

Caroline had never cared for that song, but the pulse of the melody pleased her now. As long as she hummed, she did not have to remind herself to exhale.

"How would you girls like to go with me to see the Indian camp?" Charles asked. Laura danced up onto her toes, clapping. Even Mary dropped her dish towel and dashed to Charles's knee.

Caroline went cold. "It's so far, Charles," she said, clambering for words that would not show her fear. "And Laura is so little. She can't walk so far in this heat."

Laura's heels drooped to the floor.

"Then she shall ride Jack," Charles said. The lift of his eyebrows begged her not to press further. "Camp's been deserted for weeks," he added. "Not a whiff for Jack to trouble himself over."

Caroline nodded and turned back to the dishpan. There was nothing else for it; the girls must be away all day. She fetched the comb and sat down on the tallest of the crates with the small of her back pressed against the table. "Mary, Laura, you must be combed and braided. Indian camp or not, I won't have you going out with your hair wild."

The smooth strands coiling over and around her knuckles soothed her—such softness in contrast to what was happening within her body. While Laura stood between her knees, Caroline felt her belly go taut against the little girl's back. Laura spun around, her eyes wide. "Do it again, Ma," she asked.

"All done," Caroline said, shooing her along. "Mary's turn."

She tied their sunbonnets under their chins and handed the girls off to Charles, all brightly framed in calico. Her breath hitched, she wanted so badly to draw them up into her lap until Mrs. Scott came, but she made herself cheerful and followed them to the door. Charles lifted Laura onto Jack's back. Caroline smiled a little when the bulldog reached around to snuffle her bare toes.

"Now we'll all be Indians together," Charles said.

Mary turned in the dooryard. "Ma?" Her blue eyes looked like she very nearly understood.

Caroline softened her face as best she could and nodded toward the open prairie. "Go with your pa," she said.

A tremor of panic climbed Caroline's throat as the tall grass enveloped Charles and the girls. There was not a sound in all the world but the swishing of that grass and a rising whir of insects. She was alone, without even the bulldog. And this cabin was not fully home, despite the china shepherdess standing on the mantel. She laced her fingers beneath her belly and hugged herself. Her mother, widowed a month before Thomas's birth, had not been so forsaken as this.

Caroline blinked away the memory. There was not time to think of such things. Not with Mrs. Scott on her way, and work yet to be done before she arrived.

Sweat simmered out of her as she rubbed her night-dress over the washboard. She could not help feeling misplaced; leaning over a wash bucket at this hour on mending day skewed the rhythm of the week. If she could not be near Eliza or Polly or Ma this day, Caroline wanted to be busy with her work basket as she knew they would be. But her soiled nightdress must be washed. It ought to have been done sooner if it were to dry in time, but she had not known how to explain the stain to the girls.

Much as she concentrated on her task, Caroline could not rinse nor wring the images of her kin from her mind. She paused to wipe a wet cuff along her hairline as a pang took hold. There was no sense in missing Eliza and Ma, she scolded herself as she squeezed the water from the nightdress. Neither of them had ever lived near enough to attend her deliveries. Yet with every stricture of her womb the stretch of the seven years since she had last seen her mother seemed to broaden. And Eliza. The thought of her sister nursing her own little one in the rocker they had left behind watered Caroline's eyes.

The twisted nightdress creaked before she realized her elbows were trembling. Caroline shook the garment free of itself and stood a moment, letting the rising wind snap the last droplets from its hem. One still morning, Charles had pointed out the smoke from the Scotts' cabin to Laura. Now the blowing grass leaned toward the neighbors' claim, its thousands of bending fingers leading Caroline's eyes ever eastward. The air carried a hearth-like smell of hot clay and browning grain, but not a sign of habitation breached the horizon. Her low voice sidled shakily into the wind:

Come to that happy land, come, come away,
Why will ye doubting stand, why still delay?

Eyes combing the prairie, Caroline hummed through another spasm. The drone of the cicadas cut in and out of the melody. She scanned the blue-white edge of sky once more, then hurried inside to strip the good quilt and muslin sheets from the bedstead. The gray blanket and the old oilcloth must cover the straw tick, if only she could steal enough time between pains to manage them. First, she folded up the red-checked cloth and laid the table with everything Mrs. Scott would need: lard, linen and pins, clean rags, flannel swaddling, and the butcher knife.

All the while, the heat grew heavy and muscled as the spasms, which pulled against her back as if the child had rooted itself at the base of her spine. By the time the knock came to the door, each breath demanded Caroline's full attention. Panting a little, she smoothed her hair and blotted her forehead with the hem of the gray blanket before turning to the open door.

The sight of a stranger, stocky as a barrel, standing on her threshold with a fistful of wildflowers stilled her. Again the cicadas' whir surged and then fell, as if impelled by the swells of her homesickness. Caroline dabbed the corners of her eyes with her apron.

"Good morning," the woman said.

Caroline's womb clutched in response, echoing the words from Saint Luke: *For, lo, as soon as the voice of thy salutation sounded in mine ears, the babe leaped in my womb for joy.*

"Mrs. Ingalls?"

Caroline unstoppered her throat. "Good morning."

"I am Mrs. Scott."

"I am so—" Caroline's voice caught again. "So pleased to meet you, Mrs. Scott."

"Well now," Mrs. Scott said. "Looks like I didn't get here a minute too soon. I reckon you ought to trade that apron for a nightgown and leave the rest to me."

Caroline could not argue.

While Mrs. Scott made busy with the blanket and oilcloth, Caroline peeled off her corset and settled her damp nightdress around herself. She polished the key to the provisions cupboard free of her perspiration before handing it to her neighbor.

"What a very tidy house," Mrs. Scott said, helping Caroline into the bedstead. "It's good to see more of our own kind of folks settling the place up."

In the bed, Caroline's mind had nothing to attend to but heat and pain. The hearth crackled behind her in spite of the steamy wind barging through the open windows, for the fire must be kept high enough to scald the knife. Every crease of her body pulled the nightdress closer.

Amiably as she spoke, Mrs. Scott's voice crowded the cabin, while outside the insects' cry ascended without end. The sounds held Caroline teetering even as the clench of her laboring muscles released.

"Been here the better part of a year and I've never seen a one of those Indian women," Mrs. Scott was saying as she fitted the yellow flowers into a mug of water. "The men have so little modesty abroad, it makes a body wonder if the women wear anything at all in those huts of theirs. I don't blame you for locking up the foodstuffs with the likes of them prowling all over the countryside."

With the next spasm came a pressure so insistent, all Caroline wanted to do was scrabble backward out from under it. She pressed the heels of her hands against the straw tick and drew in all the breath she could hold. She did not want to push; she wanted only to put something between herself and that feeling. A picture of sausage-making filled her mind, how the filmy casings suddenly bulged and shone with each twist of the grinder.

She had forgotten this part of it, how the pain metamorphosed. With Mary, it had taken nearly two hours.

"Oh, Mrs. Scott!" Caroline cried.

"Yes?"

Caroline could not answer. She did not even know what she wanted.

The big woman clucked and nodded. "I was near about your age when I had my first. Yelled like a wild savage. Wasn't much quieter for any of the next four, either. Go on and shout if it does you good."

Caroline shook her head. She could not let go of herself, not with the whole world tilting and nothing else to hold on to.

With her next breath the momentum abated enough for her to feel that the child had loosed its moorings. Before Caroline could steady herself around it, an oncoming surge broke another cry out of her. Tears leaked down her temples, doubling her shame. She tried to hum quietly and faltered.

Mrs. Scott sat down on the edge of the bedstead and let her voice ring out:

There is a happy land, far, far away,
Where saints in glory stand, bright, bright as day;
Oh to hear the angels sing, Glory to the Lord, our
    King,
Loud let His praises ring, praise, praise for aye.

Caroline surrendered to the hymn and together they sang, each verse more loudly than the last. She ended the final chorus gasping, "Another, please." Her voice had become the only part of herself she held any sway over.

From one verse to the next of "On Jordan's Stormy Banks I Stand" the gait of the song quickened steadily until Mrs. Scott asked, "Shall we have a look, Mrs. Ingalls?"

"Please." The pain was fisted now, slamming itself downward. Still singing, Caroline parted her thighs and tented the gown over her knees for Mrs. Scott to see.

Filled with delight my raptured soul,
Would here no longer stay;
Though Jordan's waves around me roll,
Fearless I'd launch away.

The big woman nodded and patted her foot. "Any minute."

Mrs. Scott joined her for one more chorus, propping the quilt and pillows from Mary and Laura's bed behind her until Caroline was nearly upright.

She was full to quivering with the press of the child's head. Her nerves boiled and crawled around its shape, her flesh unable to cringe away. Desperate for movement, Caroline gripped her knees like the two handles of a plow and began to push.

With the hardening of her muscles the frisson ceased. Caroline's mind cleared as all at once she released herself into the pain. Breath by breath, she filled her chest with air and pressed it down against the bulge of her womb, down through her flanks to the end of the bed where Mrs. Scott sat coaxing. The force of each thrust bowed her spine and bunched the cords in her neck.

At the crowning, when it seemed as though the sun itself were boring its way out of her, Caroline lay back and held herself still as the seam at the base of her body unlaced, bracing for the snapping of the finest outer fibers. The hot squeeze of her heartbeat ringed the head and she felt herself stretched tighter and tighter until with a twist of lock and key the child bloomed into Mrs. Scott's hands.

For a moment she lay poised and panting. Her hips and knees were trembling and watery; her pulse thrummed between her legs. There was a tug and a sinewy slice as the cord was severed. Then the splutter of the infant's cry. It echoed deep into Caroline's own lungs and Caroline gloried in it, lifting her thanks to God.

Suddenly freed from the crush and strain, she went all but blank inside as Mrs. Scott tended to the child. The grip around her began to unknot, making Caroline's body her own again. She had not fully taken hold of the change before Mrs. Scott was laying the toweled infant across her chest.

"Here we are," Mrs. Scott said. "A fine little daughter, Mrs. Ingalls."

And there it was before her—the face her mind had been unable to conjure for all these months, so close Caroline felt the moisture of the baby's breath. Caroline inhaled, tasting it, and the world gentled around her, waking her blunted senses to glimmering sensitivity. Even the heat seemed softer, carrying the scent of the prairie into the cabin, ripe and golden.

Outside the shell of Caroline's body, the baby girl looked small and crinkled as a nut meat. Her skin glowed reddish-purple from its rubbing of lard. Caroline dipped her finger into the downy hollow below one delicate ear. The child rumpled into a squall.

"Ticklish," Mrs. Scott observed with a smile, but Caroline's heart jerked as though she'd been rebuked.

Caroline cupped her palms over the hunched shoulders and clenched bottom. "There . . . there now," she said as the firmness of her touch steadied them both. The child's eyelids unbuckled, immersing Caroline in a deep, slow stare. Chest to chest, they rode the lengthening crests and troughs of each other's breath. Caroline let her hands fill with the vitality before her—the gusting lungs, the bird-wing flit of heart. So much life throbbing within a space barely larger than a jelly jar.

Without breaking her gaze, Caroline unbuttoned the yoke of her nightdress and bared a breast. The baby nudged toward it after a time, mouth agape. Her limbs moved in small ripples, still accustomed to the watery press of the womb. Even before they reached her nipple the little gums worked, sparking fine grains of foremilk to life beneath Caroline's skin. Caroline closed her eyes and took her ease.

As the baby suckled, Caroline stroked the lines of her—the gully at the back of her neck, arms and legs folded tightly as a fresh handkerchief. The top of her head with its wisp of tar paper–black hair had a faint honeyed scent, like pollen. Within a few minutes, Caroline's womb constricted again and the afterbirth slicked out. The rich iron smell of it suffused the room. Mrs. Scott tied it into a cloth and carried it outside to bury.

Lying open to wind and sun, Caroline no longer felt bounded by her skin. Her heart beat deeper, rounder, thrusting her awareness beyond herself, as though its vibration melded with all that touched her. Every inch seemed to breathe and taste. Caroline soaked in the silky essence of the child nuzzled against her, the straw tick sighing beneath her, and reached for more. Putting a hand to the wall, she let the fibers of wood snag her fingertips, then smoothed them against the cool chinking. She turned her eyes to the rafters spreading overhead like open arms. All that sheltered them had been pulled, living, from the land. The whole of the house was a cradle of grass and timber and clay, proffered by the prairie and joined by the labor of Charles's hands. Caroline listened to the bite of the shovel and the fleshy thump of the afterbirth dropping into the ground. After all they had taken from it, it seemed fitting that this most raw and nourishing part of her should be swallowed by the land.

The strange flavor of that thought still wafted in Caroline's mind when Mrs. Scott came in to sponge her clean. With each cooling stroke Caroline's consciousness settled more deeply back into herself. Between daubings, she closed her eyes and waited for the singing of the droplets against the bowl. This water she so savored, Caroline realized as Mrs. Scott lifted the dripping sponge from the basin, had nearly cost both their husbands' lives. Her thankfulness that she should be beholden to her neighbor for this day and not the other flowed like her milk, so free and warm Caroline could not bind it into words.

It made no matter; there was no space between them that wanted for talk. To Caroline it seemed as though drawing the bucket from the gullet of that well had subdued Mrs. Scott. For all the earlier stridence of her voice, she spoke only with her hands as she guided the band of linen around Caroline's middle and pinned it firmly in place. Mrs. Scott squared the heaviest pad of flannel-covered oilcloth beneath her to take up the bleeding, then evened the nightdress over Caroline's knees as neatly as Caroline might have done herself. All the while she worked, Mrs. Scott kept her face turned steadily to her tasks, as though she understood that this birth had uncovered more of the meat of Caroline's soul than of her body.

She was skirting the edges of sleep when Charles and the girls returned.

Before Mrs. Scott could hush them, Laura and Mary cascaded through the doorway, their hands and feet tinged pink from the sun.

"Ma!" Laura cried. "Look, Ma!" Caroline's chest stirred to Laura's voice as though her affection were a living thing. It was nothing new to be called *Ma*, but the sound of the word was fresher now, and larger.

At the sight of her ma in the bed in the middle of the day and a stranger at the hearth, Laura pulled up short. Mary had not moved. Charles wove between them, agleam. The naked shine of his pride made Caroline feel shy as a little girl with Mrs. Scott standing by. Modesty tucked her face down so that her nose touched the baby's forehead, but Caroline could not mask the breadth of her smile as Charles drew near. He crouched along the edge of the bedstead and looked at the child coiled in the crook of her arm. One tiny hand was flung upon Caroline's breast. The constellation of pink fingertips dimpled her skin. Charles rubbed a thumb over the back of his daughter's hand, then leaned in to kiss

Caroline's cheek. The tenderness in his eyes touched her before his lips, and the empty bowl of her womb fluttered.

"Look what Ma has for you to see," Charles said to Laura.

Neither of the girls moved until Caroline turned back the sheet so they could look. Mary's lips parted in delight. She came, bringing Laura by the hand.

At Charles's elbow Laura broke loose and hung back. She peered warily at the bundle of black hair and red skin, then laughed. "Another Indian!" Charles twinkled at her. Caroline could hardly return their smiles for the trembling of her lips. All her months of apprehension had blinded her to this sparkling flock of moments. She had not savored their coming, and now each one settled only long enough to brush her with its wings before another took its place.

Mary had gone down on her knees beside the bed, gazing at her new sister as though she were a stick of candy too sweet to lick. "Such a tiny, tiny baby," she breathed.

"Hardly bigger than a prairie hen," Mrs. Scott agreed.

Caroline's passion flared. Mrs. Scott's every word about this child seemed too vibrant with meaning, but Caroline checked herself before speaking. *Least said, soonest mended.* "She will soon be big enough for you to play with," she assured her daughters instead.

"We'll call her Caroline, for you," Charles said. "Carrie for short."

Caroline recalled how this baby had twirled inside her that night on the prairie, the night Laura told her the stars were singing. Her spine tingled with the memory. "Caroline Celestia," she said.

"Carrie can have my beads," Mary said.

Before Caroline could ask, Charles reached into his pocket and drew out his handkerchief, knotted at both ends. Two pools of Indian beads glittered inside.

Laura stirred her portion slowly with her finger. "And mine too," she offered, not taking her eyes from them.

"That's my unselfish, good little girls," Caroline praised them, though her chest blossomed with sympathy for Laura. Mary was always so quick to show off her goodness. It was hardly fair to expect such a little girl to keep up. But Laura must learn. "Give them a strong thread, Charles, and they may string them." She touched Laura's cheek and felt the burn of the child's disappointment. "There are enough to make a little string of beads for Carrie to wear around her neck," she said. Laura was not consoled, but she nodded politely and went to join Mary.

Caroline closed her eyes, veiling herself from all of them as best she could. Not one fleck of emotion had entered the cabin without leaving its print upon her, and she thirsted for a space out of reach. Beside her in the bed, the soft movements of Carrie's breaths shifted and settled like whispering embers. In her newness, and her nearness, Carrie did not yet seem a separate creature unto herself, and Caroline welcomed the small animal comfort of her.

Caroline waited for the sounds of the cabin to carry her toward sleep—the *plick-plick* of the girls stringing their beads, Charles whistling "Daisy Deane" as he went to tend the stock, the jingle of Jack's chain. Mrs. Scott's tempo with spoon and mixing bowl was quick and steady. Beneath it all, Caroline silently strummed the notes of Carrie's name.

The smell of Mrs. Scott's good supper was still in the air when Caroline woke. The baby lay curled up tight as a bud beside her; Mary and Laura were already tucked into their small bed, their freshly combed hair lustrous against the white pillow cases. Her body felt loose, open. There was nothing taut and pressing inside, though she could feel where the weight and the pressure and the pain had been. Every inch of it hurt yet, but the remnants of the pain were so subdued as to

be almost pleasurable. Caroline took a deep, languorous breath, treating her lungs to their first leisurely
stretch in months. There was not a thing in the world
that she wanted.

"I'll sleep in the stable," Charles was saying. He
looked around the room. "Where's the gray blanket?"

Mrs. Scott grimaced. "It wants washing," she said.

Charles colored a little. Then he knelt down by the
bed and fitted his hand like a bonnet over Carrie's
head. His thumb roved over the baby's black hair as if
it were a grain of wood finer than any he had touched.
The look in his eyes was still too rich to meet; even
with all the newfound space inside her, there was not
room in Caroline's chest for the affection he was stirring. Without a word, he squeezed Caroline's hand and
kissed her knuckles.

"Come wake me if you need for anything at all," he
said to Mrs. Scott. The door shut behind him. Mrs.
Scott did not pull in the latch string.

Caroline closed her eyes and listened to the sounds
of Mrs. Scott undressing: the creak of shoe leather as
she eased her feet free, her loosed corset strings sighing
through the eyelets, the click of the metal busk unfastening. Then Caroline felt Mrs. Scott crawl up over the
foot of the bed, settling into Charles's accustomed place
by the wall.

They lay alongside each other, politely still. Only Mrs. Scott's voice moved toward her, softer yet than Caroline had heard her speak. "My Robert . . . he told me how you helped Mr. Ingalls pull him from the well," she said. "My family and I—we're much obliged."

Guilt sliced through Caroline like a scythe as her own panicked voice reverberated in her memory: *No, no, Charles! I can't let you. Get on Patty and go for help. If I can't pull you up—if you keel over down there and I can't pull you up* . . . She could not bear to hold such selfishness alongside Mrs. Scott's gratitude. "Please," she started. "It wasn't—"

"Don't say a thing," Mrs. Scott said. "Please. I don't have words deep enough to thank you as it is."

The words Mrs. Scott would not let her speak bulged Caroline's throat so that she could not swallow. Silently she prayed for forgiveness, though she knew it could not come swiftly enough to keep the guilt roiling behind her breasts from tainting her milk.

Caroline smiled grimly at the ceiling. If Mrs. Scott would not allow her to beg pardon, there was no choice but to make do with the consolation of penance. Tired as she was, she must lie awake and make certain her shame had wholly subsided before the child next woke to feed. Suckling on such agitated passions would likely give a newborn convulsions. A fitting punishment,

Caroline thought with rueful admiration. The more she fretted over what she might have cost Mrs. Scott and her family, the longer she endangered the blameless babe asleep beside her.

Mrs. Scott stayed for two days.

Caroline kept quietly in bed, letting herself reknit outside and in. When she sat up to sip a mug of Mrs. Scott's velvety bean soup, long threads of soreness flared through the muscles beneath her ribs. Inside, Caroline felt as though she needed a good tidying up. Everything had become so accustomed to leaning aside to make room for Carrie that the space where the baby had been still remained, an entity of its own. It was a queer, hollow feeling, not unlike the sudden emptiness of a room after a dance, with all its furniture pushed against the walls. The passage Carrie had traveled had a lingering warmth to it, like a fever slowly fading. Caroline felt its tender outline no matter how still she lay. When she passed her water, the soft ring of swollen flesh radiated in protest.

She woke when the child nuzzled at her breast, drawing out a few teaspoons of broth-colored fluid at a time. As she nursed, Caroline watched Charles and Mary and Laura as a stranger might see them. What she saw captivated her. *Just like Charles*, she was forever saying of Laura. A certain crinkle of Laura's snub nose as she laughed or the set of her chin when she was vexed was enough to make Caroline think, *Just like her pa.* Yet to someone like Mrs. Scott, who had not spent years tallying their similarities, Laura was simply Laura—a boisterous, eager little girl, shy, yet given to impulsiveness, where Charles was genial and even-tempered. Mirror images of each other, Caroline mused: the same, yet reversed.

Mary was no less a revelation. Proud at first of the way Mary laid the table and swept the floor without being asked, Caroline began to notice how Mary put herself always within Mrs. Scott's view as she worked. *Busy getting underfoot,* Caroline so often said. But the way Mary paraded about with the broom, it was suddenly clear the child was not so much eager to help as to be *seen* helping. The floor was clean, and still Mary swept doggedly at the boards, glancing at Mrs. Scott more and more pointedly. With a sorrowful pang, Caroline realized that her little helpmeet cared not at all for the household tasks she performed so willingly. Mary mimicked them only for Caroline's approval.

Caroline's fingers worried the hem of the baby's swaddling as she watched the vignette playing out before her. Mary swept on, incapable of understanding that Mrs. Scott might have no praise for her at all. A flush of mingled shame and pity crept up Caroline's neck as she grasped her own mistake: in trying to keep Mary unconscious of her beauty, Caroline had instead marred it with another kind of conceit. Her eyes retreated to the little one in her arms, unwilling to watch her eldest daughter grope so openly for admiration. Likely Mrs. Scott had seen Mary's performance for what it was right away and did not care to applaud it. Every swish of the broom in her ears swept the blush further across Caroline's skin. She could see it as well as feel it now, spreading down her chest toward Carrie. *It must not reach the baby,* she chided herself. Her embarrassment did not feel strong enough to put the child in peril, but all the same Caroline would not risk tarnishing her. But she could not stop it at Mary's expense. Caroline herself had cultivated Mary's pride with her unstinting praise. Showing her approval now, with Mrs. Scott looking on, would only worsen it. Yet at the same time Caroline could not bear the possibility that the bulk of Mary's pleasures had become secondhand, her smiles from others' satisfaction rather than her own delight. Anything less than a compliment, no matter how gentle, would cut the child bone-deep. Caroline's chest tightened as she fumbled for a solution, and she knew Carrie should not take one more swallow.

Caroline slipped a fingertip into the corner of Carrie's mouth and broke her lips from the nipple. "Mary," she said as Carrie's mouth worked in confusion, "would you like to hold the baby?" The broom stilled. Mary's face went round with awe. Caroline propped Charles's pillow into the corner beside her and patted the mattress. Mary came scrambling so fast, Caroline almost laughed. Mary arranged herself with her feet jutting straight out and her elbows bent, palms up, as if she were about to receive a stack of planks.

Caroline laid the baby across Mary's lap. Mary sat stone-still, as though so much as a blink might make Carrie cry. Paralyzed with wonder and terror, Caroline thought, just as she herself had been the first time Polly laid Mary into her arms.

Bemused, Mrs. Scott came to stand over the bed with her fists sunk into her hips. "Well?" she asked Mary. "What do you think of your baby sister?"

"She's heavy," Mary said.

Caroline felt her cheeks dimple. Carrie weighed a scant five pounds, she guessed, but for a child accustomed to a rag baby made of cotton and wool, Carrie's heft was considerable. Mary looked and looked. Carrie was such a small baby, but Mary studied her as though there were too much of her to see all at once. Carrie's face wrinkled, then puckered, and she gave a cry that struck the air like a splatter.

"Here, now," Mrs. Scott said, leaning across the bed for the baby. But Mary put her face beside Carrie's crinkled red ear and whispered, "Shhhhhhhhh." Carrie did.

Mrs. Scott chuckled. "She'll make a good little mother herself one day," she said, and Mary glowed.

Mrs. Scott would have stayed Saturday, to get supper and help with the children's baths, she said, but Charles presented her with an enormous jackrabbit and insisted she head home in time to roast it for her family. "I can manage the supper and the bathing," Charles promised.

And he did. He fitted a spit into the fireplace and turned two plump prairie hens on it until their skins glistened and the juice ran hissing into the coals. Then he carefully carved a breast from the bones and brought it to Caroline on a plate, alongside a heap of sliced Indian breadroot and a bowl of blackberries bobbing in fresh milk. Mary and Laura washed and wiped the dishes while Charles brought in the washtub and put water on to boil.

Caroline watched him line the dishpan with a towel,

then mix hot and cold water and dip his elbow in to test it. He set the pan down on the hearth and came to the side of the bed. She started to shift the baby toward him, but Charles reached up over her head, into the crevice formed by the meeting of the wall and the roof and brought down a bear grease tin. He opened it and laid a tissue-wrapped packet in her palm. "For you and Carrie," he said.

Caroline turned back the soft blue wrapping. Inside lay a creamy cake of pressed soap, pale and smooth as butter. The faintest whiff of roses brushed her nostrils. Her lips parted in wonder. "Charles, where did you ever—"

"On our way through Independence."

Months ago. She saw herself sitting on that wagon seat outside the store, wary of the Indians, wishing that Charles would only hurry. And all the while he had been inside, picturing this moment in his mind and choosing something small and fine to mark it. With all his worries over prices and land offices, he had thought of this—of her. She looked up at him, her eyes welling. "Oh, Charles." It was not much more than a whisper. He rubbed at the back of his neck, sheepish and pleased, then bent to gather up Carrie for her bath.

Carrie squalled until she vibrated with fury, perfectly incensed by the touch of the water. Mary and

Laura scrunched up their shoulders and covered their ears. Charles was not perturbed. He bathed Carrie with the sweet white soap, toweled her dry, and folded her into a clean flannel blanket, humming as he worked. "Clean as a hound's tooth," he pronounced, fitting the baby back into the hollow of Caroline's arm.

Caroline touched her lips to Carrie's fine black hair and breathed in. The scent of pollen still tickled her nose, but the raw newness of it was gone, shrouded by the smell of the store-bought soap. She kissed the baby's head, smiling over the pinch of disappointment in her throat. "Thank you, Charles," she said.

When the girls had had their turn in the washtub— they'd splashed more than they'd scrubbed, but Charles made sure to soap their hair and kept the suds from their eyes—Charles refilled the tub and draped the wagon cover between the bedstead and the mantel, screening off the hearth for her.

Caroline stood gingerly, her feet wider apart than usual. Between her legs it felt as though there was not enough space for what had always been there. One foot, then another went into the washtub. She gripped the rim and crouched slowly into it.

The water was so soft and warm, it felt like part of her. "Oh," she breathed, more quietly than the crackling fire. She sat still a full minute, letting it touch her.

Then Caroline unpinned the broad linen band Mrs. Scott had put around her the day Carrie was born and unwrapped herself. Her middle eased out like a flounce, the skin shirred around her navel. She sighed. The delaine, folded in tissue in the trunk at the foot of the bed would not fit her now, nor for months to come. A frivolous thought—there was no call for such a dress in this place. She washed herself tentatively, wondering whether the soap would mask her own smell the way it had changed Carrie's newborn scent. The blood turned the cloth and then the water faintly pink.

Carrie's voice sputtered on the other side of the canvas, and Caroline felt the tingle of her milk. In a moment it ran in hot rivulets down her wrinkled belly. It was true milk now, white enough to cloud the water where it dripped. She felt an easing in her breasts, the relief of a pressure so gradual that the building of it had barely registered. Caroline gazed fondly at the tub, the fire. There could be no pleasure in lingering now. It was a shared thirst. Carrie cried, and Caroline's chest opened like a moistened sponge, as if to absorb the child back into her.

Caroline stood and peeked over the wagon cover. Charles was perched at the foot of the bed, swaying forward and back to soothe the baby as best he could with no chair to rock her. "Hush, Carrie," he chanted.

"Hush-hush-hush. Ma's coming; Ma's coming just as soon as she can." Carrie took no comfort from his assurances. Her voice turned gravelly and her fists balled.

"Unbutton your nightshirt," Caroline whispered as she toweled herself. He gave her a dubious look. She nodded encouragement, and Charles did as he was told. "Lie down and put her across your chest," Caroline said. He laid the baby with her head over his heart, just as a woman would do. "Now nest your hands around her. She's used to being held tight as a bean in its shell."

His hands blanketed Carrie's little body. One breath, then two, and the tempest subsided. The baby hiccoughed and blinked, as if shocked by her own contentment. Caroline smiled to herself, knowing the feel of those hands spanning her waist. A flicker of envy warmed her skin at the thought of what it would be like to fit entirely within them.

She stood, pressing the towel to her breasts, her feet reluctant to lift from the water. Carrie would wait, cozied up that way on her pa's bare chest. With luck the baby might even fall asleep. But Caroline did not sink back into the tub. Moments ago she had wanted to stay in that warm, soft water, to pull it over her like a quilt and soak until morning. Seeing Charles and Carrie together, Caroline wanted only to be beside them.

She slipped her nightdress over her damp skin and fitted her body back into the hollow it had left in the straw tick. Between them was the little peak she and Mrs. Scott had made, lying so deferentially side by side. Caroline leaned across it and pillowed her head on Charles's shoulder. She could not see his face lying this way, but as they gazed at the baby she began to see his features reflected in Carrie, as though Carrie were a little mirror tilted sideways. His narrow chin was there with no whiskers to hide behind, and his high hairline.

"She has your eyes," Charles said.

She did, poor thing. "Newborn babies always have eyes like slate. They'll brighten in time. Mary's and Laura's did."

Charles's whiskers brushed her forehead as he turned. She could feel him looking quizzically down on her. "Is that what you think of your eyes?"

"Ma always said they were gray as the December day I was born." His were like a woman's, such a delicate blue as she'd only seen painted on fine china.

He traced her brow bone with his thumb. "Your ma was wrong," he said. "Your eyes are gray like flannel, and there's nothing half so warm and soft in the world as flannel."

Caroline's eyes flickered up, then her face ripened with a smile as the compliment swirled through her.

She pressed her cheek, red and round as an apple skin, into his shoulder.

He chuckled softly at her shyness, rumbling under the baby. Carrie crinkled awake.

The sounds the two of them made, his bass and her tremolo, rippled beneath Caroline's skin. Her pulse burgeoned through her body, and a fresh burbling of blood warmed the path Carrie had made through her.

Caroline sat up and inched herself as far toward the headboard as the flannel pad allowed while the child gritched at the air and began to sputter. "Here, Charles," she said and uncovered her breast. "Let me."

Charles lifted the fussing baby from his chest as though her flinty cries might strike fire. Carrie's lips buttoned onto her. Charles watched as the frantic movements of Carrie's jaw subsided into contentment.

"Caroline Ingalls, you are a wonder."

She looked down at the child, drawing its current of sustenance through her. Most any woman in the world could do as she had done, but Caroline could not deny his wonder. There was nothing Charles could not fashion, given the wood and tools to do it with, but she had formed this child—this creature of breath and bone—out of nothing but a spurt. She had not even begun with an intention. And now when the child cried, there was milk.

Charles looked out the window and then back at her. "I feel like a man who's found Canaan," he said.

The land of milk and honey. She saw it as he did, in the prairie grass, honey-gold in the wind, the running creek, the cow and calf, and now in the flow of her own milk. They had never wanted for shelter or game in the Big Woods, but this land was different. It seemed to lie with its arms open, inviting them to suckle freely of its bounty. When spring came she would trust her seeds to the good, rich ground. If this land would feed her children, it would become another sister to her. *We came unto the land whither thou sentest us . . .* , she thought, as if speaking to the place itself, *and this is the fruit of it.*

Twenty-Two

"You be Ma and I'll be Mrs. Scott," Mary said to Laura. "My rag doll will be the baby."

Caroline's cheeks ached from holding back her smiles. The new center of Mary's world lay nursing in Caroline's arms. Overnight Mary had become a miniature nursemaid: earnest, attentive, and entirely unconscious of how darling she was as she bustled about the cabin. When she could not fuss over her new sister, she practiced with her doll. It would only be a matter of time, Caroline supposed, before Mary tried to suckle that poor cotton baby. Caroline's lips twitched at the thought. All day long, she wanted to let the delight tumble out of her, but she could not let Mary realize that her grown-up airs only made her more childlike.

Laura was braced against the doorjamb, having a tug-of-war with Jack over a stick of firewood. "I don't—want—to play—inside," she said, as though Jack were jerking each piece of the answer out of her.

"I'll let you hold my rag doll," Mary promised.

Caroline's eyebrow arched. That was a sacrifice, coming from Mary. Laura was tempted, and her grip faltered just as Jack's playful growl changed. He let loose the stick, and Laura plopped onto the ground. "Jack!" she cried as the bulldog turned from her, his throat rumbling. Then, "Oh! It's a man coming, Ma!"

"You mustn't shout, Laura," Caroline reminded her. "Is it Mr. Edwards?"

Laura shook her head. "A new man."

Caroline shifted to look outside. A bay dun, mounted by a sandy-haired man, was trotting up the path from the creek. Sunlight glinted off a pair of round spectacles, giving the rider the look of a schoolteacher. Jack erupted into a fury of barking, and the horse shied. Charles's voice followed, calling off Jack and hallooing a welcome from the stable.

Mary ran to soothe her rag doll from the noise. Caroline tugged at her open bodice, trying not to dislodge Carrie from her feeding. The calico made a poor shield. "Close the door, please, Laura," she said.

"Aw, Ma!"

"You may stay outside if you keep well out of Pa's way. Close the door behind you."

Wishing again for her rocking chair, Caroline resettled herself onto the crate with her back against the wall and her ear cocked to the window. The wind seemed to blow the centers from the men's words, so she could hear only where one ended and another began. The tempo of their conversation was absurdly clipped: three words from the stranger, one from Charles, another from the stranger, two more from Charles. Perhaps the man spoke no English, Caroline decided. She gave up making sense of it and returned to the task at hand.

The baby's attention had drifted, too. Her eyes were closed and her tongue poked lazily at the nipple, sending a thread of warmth trailing below Caroline's hips, to the place that belonged to begetting and birthing. Caroline tickled under Carrie's chin to remind her, and the thin red lips resumed their muscular kneading. Neither of her older girls had taken to idling at the breast as this new baby did. She suckled in short spurts, tugging at the nipple half a dozen times, then slackening, content to make a meal of each swallow. It put Caroline in mind of the dainty way Mary sipped at the tin cup she shared with Laura, but it troubled her, too, that a child so new would be willing to make do with so little. "Take your fill, baby girl," she coaxed.

She did not speak to the baby by name, as the others did. To Caroline, *Carrie* was a word whose meaning was still forming. The child herself had left her body, but was still so small and near as to seem a part of Caroline—a cutting grafted back into her side. Sharing her name with the baby only blurred the lines further.

Mary, being the first and only child in the house, had been *Mary* straightaway, though after the five years it had taken to become *Ma,* Caroline had loved even more to hear herself say *the baby, my baby, our baby,* as though saying it somehow made it truer than holding Mary in her arms. This child was spending her first days as Laura had—an anonymous little creature, barely beginning to peel away from the mold her sisters had left behind.

For now, Caroline contented herself with looking at the child and thinking *Caroline Celestia,* as though it were the Latinate name for spindly, black-haired baby girls native to the Kansas prairie. Even if such a taxonomy existed, she mused, it could tell her only so much, for although a seed called *Ipomoea purpurea* would always unfurl into a morning glory, it was anyone's guess whether the blooms would be pink, purple, or blue.

Mary came to stand beside them and peeped over

Caroline's elbow. "Ma?" she said. Caroline knew what the question would be. She had promised Mary could mind the baby when she'd finished feeding. *Minding* meant little more than sitting on the big bed, watching her sister sleep, but Mary reveled in the responsibility.

"Is Baby Carrie full?" Mary asked. She said the name as though it were a single word: *Baby-Carrie.*

Caroline tried it for herself. "Baby Carrie is nearly finished." She liked the bridge it made so well, she said it again to herself. *Baby Carrie.* "You may fetch a clean flannel and lay out a fresh diaper while you wait."

Laura came scampering in with Jack trotting behind her. Charles followed. "He had a great big book, Ma," she said, breathless with the news, "and he wrote my name in it, and asked me how old I am, and put that in, too. He's going to send it all the way to Mr. Grant in Washington."

"My goodness," Caroline said to Laura. "That sounds very important. What is all this, Charles?"

"Census taker." Charles fanned his forehead with his hat. "Amiable enough fellow," he said, with a nod toward Laura. "Funny thing, though—he didn't mark anything down for property value. Whole column's left blank."

Caroline raised Carrie to her shoulder and leaned her cheek against the top of the baby's head. It fitted neatly as a teacup into a saucer. "We don't own it, Charles," she said gently.

"Not yet, but that doesn't make it worthless."

Twenty-Three

C aroline knew the moment the sickness touched her. It had been all around her—first Mary and Laura, then Charles, all within a single afternoon—but the moment it breached her own body was different.

"Oh," she said, and sat down on the end of the bedstead. She was panting. Her nose tingled with something more than the smell of scalded broth, and her eyes were warm beneath their lids as they roved over the disheveled room.

The chamber pail needed emptying, the water bucket had to be filled, the soup pot must be emptied and scrubbed before she could begin supper again, and Caroline knew—knew with her whole body—that she could do precisely one more task. She pushed herself up, and her shoulders rattled with a chill. *Sit,* she told herself. *Get a minute's rest, then try.* She had hardly sat for two days.

Charles had still not taken to his bed, but Caroline was not fooled. He had not so much as lifted his gun from its pegs. Not even in the depths of a Wisconsin winter had he huddled by the fire making bullets in the middle of the afternoon, much less for two days straight. She'd seen the sheen of cold sweat on his brow in the firelight and watched his hands tremble. It had been all he could do not to spill the molten lead onto the hearth. She did not know how he was managing to keep the stock fed and watered.

Caroline looked again at their own water pail. From where she sat, she could not see past the brim to gauge what little was left. They must have more. To drink, to make more broth, to sponge the perspiration from Mary's and Laura's fevered limbs, to rinse the baby's diapers and her own flannel pads. Just the sight of the pail waiting there by the door made her skin prickle with unease. Charles had not taken it out to fill when he left for the stable, as he always did. That alone told her he was not well. She did not know if she could ask him to go out again, with the chores already taking him so long.

Caroline stopped to think. How long had he been gone? The girls had been so fretful in the meantime, she could not begin to guess. Their fevers and chills never coincided. One was hot and the other cold. She had finally made each half of their small bed with a separate quilt, so that they might stop pulling and kicking at the one they shared. That, at last, had soothed them enough so they could sleep—Laura muffled in her quilt and Mary cringing away from the slightest touch of a sheet. Charles had not been in the house during any of it, or he would have saved the broth from scalding.

In her nest of pillows in the middle of the big bed, Carrie began to snuffle and kick at the air.

"Oh no," Caroline begged. "Please don't wake yours sisters. Here." She opened her bodice, but the fastenings on the flap of her nursing corset would not yield. Her fingertips felt . . . the word would not come to her. *Dumbed,* she thought, but that was not right. Her mind worked slowly as her hands, fumbling for something she could brush against but not quite grasp.

Caroline leaned down onto one elbow and stretched herself toward the baby, her other hand still working at the stubborn fastenings. "Shh-shh-shh," she insisted. "I'm coming. Ma's coming." The flap had moved only partway. Carrie was on the verge of a squall. Caroline could see her color rising, and all the points of her little face sharpening. She would have to manage. Caroline lay down alongside the baby, letting as much of herself spill through the gap as possible. It was enough.

The steels pinned awkwardly under her body prodded at her, but Caroline did not try to move. Carrie was feeding. Carrie was feeding and the girls were asleep, and all was quiet. There was so much that needed tending to, before the girls woke again and needed her most of all. *Rest,* she told herself. *Rest until Charles comes back from the stable.*

Darkness, wavering like a dream all around her. Hot hands, hot fingertips tingling. Hot breath curling over her lips from nostrils like stove holes. She'd never felt such heat—heat that made her skin crackle and shiver. The soles of her feet were papery, as though they'd been peeled down to dry bone. The darkness advanced and receded, expanded and contracted, as though the thick black air meant to crush her, or inhale her. Caroline closed her eyes and the world went mercifully, mercifully still.

A sliver of gray light. *Twilight or dawn,* Caroline wondered muzzily. The air around her had thinned and cooled, stopped its pulsating, but her limbs, her head, her very eyelids might have been filled with sand for all that Caroline could move them. She felt a scrabbling between her body and her arm, and knew it was Carrie who had woken her. Caroline turned her head to look.

The effort made her gasp, made the room reel. Her breast still protruded from the half-opened corset flap, but sometime in the fevered night she had shifted, and Carrie could not reach. The baby had fastened herself to a button on Caroline's open bodice and sucked until she'd pulled the calico into a pointed wet teat. Carrie tugged and batted at it, confounded.

Tears blurred Caroline's eyes. "Carrie," she said, but there was no sound. Her throat was like bark. Caroline prized a quivering hand from the straw tick and managed to loosen the hard twist of fabric from Carrie's mouth. Carrie instantly raged. Caroline whimpered at the shock of the sound striking her ears and at their own mingled frustration. She gripped the side of the bedstead and pulled. A chill shook her so fiercely, her joints rattled. She pulled again, and her body spasmed. The momentum of it rolled her sideways to meet Carrie, and there Caroline lay, gasping on her side, while Carrie took her fill.

She woke to the smell of filth rising up from the straw tick beneath Carrie. The cow bawled in the stable, and the sound and the smell whirled together. Pain buzzed under her corset, taut and swollen. *A wasp sting?* Carrie's lips gave a little pull, and the throbbing doubled. Caroline groaned at the realization. Pinned between herself and the oak slab, Carrie could nurse only from the left breast, while the right slowly filled, caged beneath the steels. The weight of it burned so that Caroline yearned to roll onto her back, but she did not trust her strength to pull the baby with her if she turned over. She could only grip the side of the bedstead to keep herself within Carrie's reach.

A wail rose up from somewhere beyond the bed. "I want a drink of water, I want a drink of water."

Mary. Her patient Mary, begging. Caroline's eyes smarted, but no tears came. Her body had no moisture to spare for anything so frivolous as tears. She felt a bump and a shudder against the board under her hand, and understood that Charles was on the floor beside the bed, trying to rise. His movements sent a cascade of aches through her body. Even the soft knot of her hair probed painfully into her neck. Caroline closed her eyes and gritted her teeth. She would bear it, if it meant he could manage to get up and tend to Mary. But the bed did not move again. Jack pawed, whined, howled. Then all was still—all but Mary's voice ebbing into sobs so dry, Caroline could hear the thirst scraping at Mary's throat. Hot needles of milk dampened the right side of her corset.

Caroline levered her head up, just enough to see over the slab. Her arm shook, and her heart seemed to flicker instead of beat. Laura was awake. Her face was dry and yellow, a tired corn husk of a face, but Laura was awake and looking back at her. "Laura," Caroline whispered, "can you?"

"Yes, Ma," Laura said.

Caroline dropped down beside the baby. Sounds moved back and forth across the cabin. Jack's nails on the floor. Dragging, dragging, dragging. A rattle and splash. Then nothing. She could not tell whether Laura had done it, or collapsed trying—only that Mary stopped crying.

Twenty-Four

Caroline woke softly. So softly. Everything was exquisitely still—the air, her skin. Her toes brushed against cool sheets and she smiled dreamily to herself. Nothing had ever felt so fine as that crisp muslin against her skin. For a moment she could not make herself understand why it all felt so singularly different. Everything was as it always was. Charles lay on one side of her, snoring lightly. Caroline turned her head to the other side and found . . . nothing. She stared, unable even to blink, at the space where the baby should be.

Nothing but her mind could move, and the sudden speed of it dizzied her. The sheets, her nightdress, the sense of comfort itself—all of it was wrong. Her memory groped backward and found Mary crying for water, the sound aswirl in a dreamlike haze of heat and inertia. Joining that moment and this one—nothing.

The memories stopped so short, Caroline's mind seemed to plummet. Anxious to dispel the sensation, she fixed her eyes to the row of buttons up the yoke of her nightdress. White, round buttons. Their smallness and their neatness made a foothold for her thoughts, which came creeping up out of the void.

What had become of her shoes, her dress, her corset? Had she only dreamed the sobs and the howls, the throbbing in her breast and the terrible, shimmering heat? Had anything in that nightmarish whirl happened at all? Caroline concentrated harder yet on the small white buttons as another realization worked itself free of the void. *Even if none of it had happened, Carrie should still be in the empty space beside her.* Caroline shivered. A pinprick of fear, first cold, then white-hot, pierced her belly. Deep inside her head, a thin specter of a voice dared to whisper: *Was the baby herself even real?*

Caroline's heart stuttered, too weak to pound. "Carrie?" The word was a creak. Her mouth tasted bitter and shrunken.

Suddenly Mrs. Scott's face was over hers. "Don't fret yourself, Mrs. Ingalls. The little one's asleep in the washtub. Snug as a bug, next to the fire."

The dreadful thoughts released her so suddenly, Caroline felt as if she were floating.

Mrs. Scott brought a mug of cool water and held it for Caroline to drink. The water rippled as it touched her trembling lips. She lay back on the pillow and her body continued to vibrate, softly, steadily. Not the ague, Caroline thought. Fear. It had lasted only an instant, but it had permeated her entirely. She could feel it melting away now, passing through her skin and lifting, harmless, into the air as Mrs. Scott used her knuckles to brush the matted tendrils of hair from Caroline's forehead.

"Now you're awake and the fever's passed, let's get this straightened out," Mrs. Scott said. Her big nimble fingers coaxed the tangled hair pins loose as she talked, until she had Caroline's long braid unfurled across her lap. "There's fever and ague all up and down the creek," she said, "all from watermelons, of all things. Some fool settler planted watermelons in the bottoms, and every soul that's eaten one is down sick this very minute, with hardly enough folks left standing to tend to them. I've been going house to house day and night, but yours is the worst case I've seen. It's a wonder you ever lived through, all of you down at once. Dr. Tann—he's a Negro, doctors all over this side of the county, settlers and Indians both, heaven help him—was headed up to Independence when that dog of yours met him and wouldn't let him pass. And here you all were, more dead than alive!"

"How long has it been?" Caroline asked.

"Couldn't say for certain. I've been here since yesterday, and Dr. Tann stayed a day and a night before I came." Her hands worked the braided strands slowly apart, all the way to the scalp. "No telling how long you'd all been down before that. Dr. Tann said by the way the stock went after their feed, he guessed another day or two anyhow."

Three days, at least. Caroline tried again to call up some recollection. There was Mary's voice. Then Laura's face, and the sound of her crawling across the floorboards, and the next thing Caroline knew she was waking into that blessed stillness. In between was something abrupt as a ravine, the likes of which she had never encountered within her own mind.

Hidden in that deep, blank void were all the things Dr. Tann and Mrs. Scott must have done for them, Caroline thought—every one of them, down to the cow and calf. What state they had all sunk to by the time the doctor found them, she did not like to imagine. All of it was set to rights. Even the square of flannel between her skin and the straw tick was fresh and dry.

Caroline turned her head and covered her mouth,

396 · SARAH MILLER

but Mrs. Scott heard the sound that slipped between Caroline's fingers.

"Now," said Mrs. Scott as she combed her hands through Caroline's hair, "there's nothing to be ashamed of."

But Caroline was not ashamed. She was so grateful, her throat throbbed with it. Things she could not have asked of anyone but her own blood kin, these people had done for her. Such a debt could not be repaid, except perhaps to Providence itself.

Mrs. Scott combed and combed, not untangling now, but soothing Caroline with her long, slow strokes. To think that Mrs. Scott had it in her to be kind after everything she had already done. It was almost too sweet to bear, but Caroline had no strength to resist. The fever had wrung her so dry, she felt brittle, inside and out.

Most of all, she wanted to see Carrie, but she did not want to ask. To ask would be the same as confessing that she had believed the absurd notion that had risen out of the fever-addled coils of her brain. Mrs. Scott had told her the baby was safe, and Caroline did not doubt it. Yet her body was unsatisfied. Her arms begged for the re-assurance of the weight and shape of the child, the per-fect fit of her, belly to belly and cheek to breast. She felt the insistent press of her milk—Carrie's milk—against her upper arms and took what comfort she could from its undeniable link with the baby.

While she waited for Carrie to wake, Caroline swallowed the powdered bitters Dr. Tann had left behind, puckering like a child at the way it drew every atom of moisture from her mouth. She lifted the mug for more water, but Mrs. Scott brought a spoonful of cream instead. "Don't swallow it right off. Hold it in your mouth a minute." Caroline obliged, and her entire face relaxed at the touch of that thick cream. It was silky-sweet and sank into the roughened surface of her tongue as softly as a kiss. Caroline's eyes rolled up blissfully to Mrs. Scott, who burst out laughing. "My mother's trick," she said. "Never fails. Most folks put their dose of quinine right into a mug of milk, but it's not nearly the same."

The laughter stirred Charles, who roused long enough to down his bitters and roll over. Presently a thin complaint rose from the washtub.

With the prick of the child's cry came a gentle bursting behind Caroline's breasts, and two warm, wet spots bloomed on her nightdress. She craned her neck, and there was Carrie, curled on Mrs. Scott's bosom like a little pink snail. Caroline's whole body seemed to smile as her eyes fell across the baby.

Mrs. Scott laid Carrie in her arms and helped her

with the buttons. Caroline touched Carrie's wan little cheek with a fingertip. Carrie reached toward it, her lips poised in a taut pink oval. She briefly mouthed Caroline's finger, then found her proper place and sucked so hard and fast, Caroline hardly recognized her.

In the time it took for their shared astonishment to register, Carrie's face buckled. Her tongue darted in and out as she spluttered. Caroline wiped the milk from Carrie's chin and tickled the child's lips with her nipple. Carrie took another great gulp, then arched backward and squalled.

"That'll be the quinine," Mrs. Scott clucked. "I imagine she'll taste every dose of bitters same as you do, Mrs. Ingalls."

Caroline pressed her cheek to Carrie's forehead, stroking her back as she shrieked. Carrie's skin felt loose, a garment too big for her spindly frame. At the touch of those tender wrinkles, a tremor rose up out of Caroline's chest. A feeble sob, or a last rattle of fever, she could not tell. The baby's cries were so penetrating, Caroline felt as though she were dissolving into them. "Poor thing," she said.

"You'll be squalling yourself unless you drain some of your milk," Mrs. Scott remarked. "It's a wonder you haven't already come down with a case of bad breast on top of everything else. My sister-in-law uses cabbage leaves to take the swelling down, but there won't be a cabbage in these parts for another month at least."

Anger crackled between Caroline's ribs so abruptly, she gasped at its sudden sharp heat. To lack something so simple as a cabbage! The baby would never have suffered so if they'd been struck with fever and ague in Wisconsin. None of them would, not with Henry and Polly so near.

"Why, Mrs. Ingalls!" Mrs. Scott exclaimed. "You look feverish all over again."

"It's only—" Caroline stopped and shook her head. She could not lie, any more than she could tell the truth. "It's too much," she managed. "Everything." She looked helplessly down at Carrie, then at Mrs. Scott, ashamed to ask aloud for her to take the baby back again. But there was not one thing Caroline could do for her daughter.

Mrs. Scott understood what she wanted, if not why she wanted it, and scooped Carrie up. "I'm not surprised," she said over Carrie's screams. She gave Caroline's elbow a knowing squeeze. "I saved back some of the cream for her, just in case. Don't you waste your strength worrying." Caroline nodded dumbly, aware only that her milk had become unspeakably bitter.

———————

"I don't know how I can ever thank you," Caroline said to Mrs. Scott. It could not be done. Both of them knew that. Caroline refused to so much as contemplate what sort of misfortune would have to befall the Scotts before she could repay her debts to them. Two more days Mrs. Scott had stayed. Even after Charles staggered up from the bed, she insisted on getting the meals and spoon feeding the baby in the wee hours so they both might rest through the night.

"Pshaw!" Mrs. Scott scoffed. "What are neighbors for but to help each other out?"

Caroline nodded. It was so. She had not fully known it, living alongside family most of her life. Caroline thought of embracing her, as she would have embraced Polly or Eliza, but did not know how to do it. Instead she contented herself with imagining the momentary feel of her heart pressing its thanks against the big woman's chest.

Caroline leaned against the doorway, thankful for its support as she watched Mrs. Scott go. She raised an arm to bid a final goodbye, and her pulse guttered like a candle flame. She had made too much of a show that morning, making up the bed and laying the table and wiping the dishes to convince Mrs. Scott it was all right to go. The bed ought to have waited, Caroline silently admitted. She was not fully well, none of them were, but she was well enough to do the things that must be done. That much and no more, she reminded herself.

Caroline sat down on one of the crates beside the table and surveyed the cabin. The wash was ironed and folded, the milk strained and the pan scalded. Mrs. Scott had given the floor one final sweep before leaving. Carrie lay freshly diapered in the center of the big bed. Caroline pondered a moment over what day it was. Wednesday. Carrie was five weeks old, and it was mending day. Both thoughts overwhelmed her. She smiled weakly at the scrap bag as if in apology, dazed at the realization that even so much as threading a needle required a precise sort of energy and focus she had not yet regained.

"Will you set one of the crates by the fireplace, please, Charles?" she asked. Charles did and walked her to it. Then he tucked a pillow into the washtub and laid Carrie in it, so that Caroline need not move from the crate to reach her. And there Caroline sat all morning, tending the soup Mrs. Scott had put on the fire to simmer for their dinner and supper.

Thursday, Friday, and Saturday, Caroline felt the slats of those crates pressing against her thighs whether she was sitting, standing, or lying down to sleep. Standing for any length of time brought on a queer fizzling sensation in her limbs, as though she could feel her strength being eaten away, so she sat to help the girls dress and undress, to mix the cornbread, to lay the table and wipe the dishes, to feed the baby and change her.

As Caroline's daily doses of bitters decreased, Carrie conceded to nurse again. Each time Caroline put her to the breast, Carrie's small black eyebrows furrowed with concentration, tasting before settling in to feed. Caroline could not begrudge Carrie her wariness. She had tasted her milk herself, and while it was not so bitter as she'd feared, there was an odd, metallic cast to the flavor. But the way the child shrieked and writhed when her feedings came too close upon the quinine, Caroline's breasts might as well have been filled with kerosene. Try though she might to down the bitters when Carrie was least likely to notice them—as soon as the baby finished a feeding or laid down to nap—Carrie's fickle appetite seemed to thwart Caroline's efforts.

"You can't be hungry now," Caroline said, perilously close to a whimper herself, though it was plain from the shape of Carrie's mouth and the tone of her cry that Carrie was. Caroline sighed. She could still taste the last dose of quinine, there at the back of her tongue where it was hardest to dislodge. She unbuttoned her bodice and resigned herself to the coming reaction.

Carrie squirmed. She scowled. She jabbed at Caroline with her small sharp fists, determined that the good milk she had found in the same place not an hour before must still be there. Such a flood of warm sympathy filled the space behind Caroline's breasts at the sight of Carrie's consternation as would have drenched the child, but Caroline could not communicate it, except perhaps through the milk Carrie would not take. Defeated, Carrie threw back her fists. Her face flushed and her chest spasmed with a silent scream. The tiny body in Caroline's arms seemed to beg for movement, but every speck of Caroline's energy was rationed, with none to spare to walk the floor with her daughter. Again Carrie cried and Caroline's milk answered, wetting the both of them.

"It's an ill wind that doesn't blow some good," Charles called from the dooryard.

Her impulse was to hiss at him to hush, that Carrie was asleep, as anyone with the consideration to look before hollering out that way could see. Caroline looked up from her mixing bowl and saw him backing through the open door, carrying what seemed at first glance to be a strangely graceful armload of willow kindling. Charles stopped in the center of the room and put it down. "Didn't have the strength to cut firewood, so I sat myself on a stump behind the woodpile and built this for you instead."

A chair. A rocking chair.

Caroline could not speak. For a terrible instant, she thought she might burst into tears. She had never asked, never complained of leaving anything behind, yet he had known, and made her the thing she longed for most. And she had nearly scolded him for it. Now and again she had heard the sounds of his ax and hammer, and thought nothing of it.

"Should I show you how it works," Charles teased, "or are you happy enough just looking at it?" She was, nearly. It was such a lithe-looking thing, its frame a single swooping curve, its back and seat good plain wickerwork. Caroline reached out to touch the narrow willow arm. No further. She would make herself feel as lovely as the chair itself before sitting in it, she decided.

First, she smoothed her hair and took off her apron, as though her momentary flicker of anger were a stain she could strip from herself. Then she went to her trunk and brought out her gold bar pin and fixed it to her collar. Charles put the pillows from Mary and Laura's bed onto the chair, and draped the whole thing over with their small red and blue quilt. Then Charles took Caroline by the hand and led her to the chair with the girls prancing like puppies.

Through the pillows, the woven willow strips cradled her back. She tested the chair's easy backward sway and thought of the cool willows swishing like hoop skirts along the creek. Caroline closed her eyes. "Oh, Charles, I haven't been so comfortable since I don't know when."

How well he knew her, shape and size. When she rested her elbows on the rocker's arms, they did not pry her shoulders upward. The seat's depth precisely matched the span between the small of her back and the bend of her knees. Beneath her the floor seemed to rise to meet her feet at each forward swoop. Even the Big Woods rocker she had mourned all this time had not fit so well.

That chair Charles had fashioned as much out of awe as wood, honing and polishing until he had created a frame worthy of the image he carried in his mind of his wife and child-to-be. Empty, it had been a beautiful thing to look at.

This chair was another kind of gift. Five years had passed, and Caroline knew he had never stopped looking at her. Indeed, he had only looked more closely. He had seen—and remembered—how she rocked on tiptoe, the way she sometimes slipped her elbows from its arms to rest her shoulders as she nursed or sewed. From those memories he had woven a chair that held her as effortlessly as a pitcher holds water. And he had done it by measuring with nothing more than his gaze.

Charles lifted Carrie from the bed. Caroline reached for the baby, hands already curving to her shape, softening in welcome. When their skins touched, it was like a kiss.

As she leaned back Caroline's elbows settled into the curling arms of the chair. All the crosspieces of her body seemed to loosen. With a sigh she looked at Carrie, and the child smiled up at her. Caroline's breath hitched. Carrie's eyes were still so big in her peaked little face, but her cheeks had shown a flicker of roundness. A feeling like a spreading of wings brushed Caroline's womb and she pulled Carrie closer, rocking deeply now, as if the motion might keep all that she felt from spilling over.

With a thud, the floorboard bounced beneath her feet. Caroline nearly spilled the dishpan. She whirled toward the sound and saw a watermelon rolling just inside the doorway. Charles sank down beside it.

"Charles! Are you all right?"

"Thought I'd never get it here," he said, slapping the melon. "It must weigh forty pounds, and I'm as weak as water."

A strange mixture of dread and desire fluttered Caroline's stomach. "Charles," she warned, "you mustn't. Mrs. Scott said—"

He only laughed. "That's not reasonable. I haven't tasted a good slice of watermelon since Hector was a pup. It wasn't a melon that made us sick. Fever and ague comes from breathing the night air. Anyone knows that."

Caroline tucked her fingers into her palms. They itched to spank that fat melon as Charles had, to hear its delicious green thump. In her mind she could already taste watermelon rind pickles, with lemon, vinegar, and sugar; cinnamon, allspice, and clove. Her thoughts seemed to cartwheel over each other, she was so eager to talk herself into it. She only half believed Mrs. Scott's proclamations about watermelons and ague, and Charles's logic could not be denied. None of them had so much as laid eyes on a melon since Wisconsin. Caroline glanced at the girls, and all her eagerness fell flat. The very fact that they were playing quietly indoors on a day such as this reminded her of all the ague had cost them already. The consequences were more than Caroline dared chance. "This watermelon grew in the night air," she countered, then bit her lip. The argument was so weak, it had the ring of a joke.

"Nonsense," Charles said. "I'd eat this melon if I knew it would give me chills and fever."

Caroline knew that tone. There would be no persuading him. "I do believe you would," she said.

He heaved the watermelon up onto the table and sank the butcher knife to the handle into its deep green skin. He steadied it with one hand and levered the knife downward until his knuckles brushed the oilcloth. The melon creaked apart and lay rocking on the table, red and sparkling. The broken edges of its flesh looked crinkled with frost. With his jack knife, Charles prized a perfect little pyramid from the center and offered it to her.

Caroline shook her head. "No, thank you, Charles. And none for the girls, either," she said.

"Aw, Ma!" they cried together.

Caroline did not scold them. They were so disappointed, she could not stand to look at them. Never in her life had she denied her girls good, fresh food. Caroline hated the sound of every word: "Not so much as a taste. We can't take such a risk."

Charles shrugged and licked a dribble of juice from his wrist. Then he popped the whole piece of melon into his mouth. It bulged his cheeks and made him purse his lips to keep the juice from spurting out. The sound of his teeth crushing each cool bite was more than Caroline could bear. "Take it outside, please, Charles. It isn't fair for the girls to watch." He went, Jack trotting behind.

The girls returned to their play, but they were quiet and sullen about it, not quite sulking. Caroline knew they could picture Charles as well as she could: sitting on the stump behind the woodpile with his elbows braced on his knees, hunched over a giant crescent of melon. With no one watching, he would spit the seeds, gleefully as a boy. Caroline stopped herself. Her mouth was watering. Another minute of that, and she'd be glowering like Mary and Laura. She swallowed and blinked the image away, finished the dishes, then mopped the puddles of juice from the table and wrung out the dishcloth. She picked up Carrie and went to her rocker.

It was hard to feel bereft of anything in that chair, with the baby in her lap. Caroline pressed her thumb into Carrie's palm and rubbed a slow circle. It was a trick she had learned early on, when she could not get enough of touching Mary's silken hands and feet, that made all of her babies go limp with pleasure. But now Carrie grabbed hold of Caroline's finger and pulled it to her mouth. She gripped fist and finger with her gums, testing the strength of her jaw. Then her eyes widened and her toes splayed. She gave a little chirrup and sucked and sucked at Caroline's fingertip.

"What in the world?" Caroline wondered.

Mary came running. "What is it, Ma? Is Baby Carrie all right?"

"I declare, your baby sister is sucking my finger as if it were a stick of candy."

Mary offered her own waggling fingers, but Carrie would not be distracted. She was still at it when Charles came back, wiping his chin with his handkerchief. "The cow can have the rest of it," he announced. He kissed her, and Caroline tasted the sweet juice on his mouth. She licked her lips. So sweet after days and days of bitter quinine, she shivered. And then she knew. It was the juice from the dishcloth that Carrie tasted on her fingers. Caroline looked again at Carrie and saw that she was happy. Happy, perhaps for the first time in her life.

She waited until after supper, excusing the girls from wiping the dishes so that she might slip a spoon into her pocket unnoticed. Without a word, Caroline went outside. First to the necessary. No one had asked where she was going, and this would render their assumption true; no need for questions meant no need for lies.

From the necessary, the woodpile beckoned irresistibly. The voice in her mind seemed not entirely her own. It chanted and whispered at her as she walked,

"I am," she whispered to Carrie. But gratitude, Caroline had learned in childhood, was too often the feeblest of pleasures; gratitude was nothing like what she had been waiting to pass between herself and her daughter. Carrie gave her another squeeze, and this time Caroline smiled softly into the darkness in spite of herself. And then there was another, larger hand. Charles. He fitted it over her free breast and stroked softly, the way she would finger a fine length of silk. Drops of milk beaded up on the nipple. He caught them with a fingertip and brought it to his lips. "Sweet," he whispered to the curve of her neck, and kissed her shoulder. A lump bobbed hard in Caroline's throat. *Sweet.*

Twenty-Five

The wind whipped the fringe of Caroline's shawl against her elbows as she stood waiting for the wagon to disappear. Behind her, Jack whined and pulled at his chain. The pressure against her corset told her it was time to wake the baby for her morning feed, before Carrie cried and woke Mary and Laura, but Caroline would not turn her back on the wagon.

Forty miles to Oswego. A span better measured by time than by distance. A day and a half, two days to get there. An afternoon or a morning to trade. Then back again. Charles could not accomplish it in less than four days. Four days, and no way around it. If there were to be enough provisions to see them comfortably through the winter, as well as repay Mr. Edwards the nails he had lent to finish the roof, they must be bought in Oswego.

She could feel her awareness expanding as the wagon dwindled from sight, much as it had the day Mary had learned to creep across the floor, and Caroline had fully realized the perils of the stove, the woodpile, the washtub. Just as she placed herself daily between the children and the hazards of the house and yard, Charles stood between all of them and everything beyond the bounds of their claim. Now, with Charles away, Caroline became conscious of that greater perimeter, of listening for sounds from the stable and the path to the creek as well as the house. Anything that approached—from an Indian to a jackrabbit to a hailstone—would come first to her.

So when Jack barked just before milking time that night, snarling so that Caroline could hear the snap of his teeth from inside the house, her eyes darted from the bowl of cornmeal in her hands to the pistol box, high up on the ledge above the bedstead. Wood clattered and the bulldog's chain rattled. Someone yelped—a man.

"Call off your dog!" At the sound of English, Caroline exhaled. Another clatter of wood.

"Call off your dog!" the man yelled again, and Laura shouted, "Mr. Edwards!"

Caroline dropped the bowl and dashed out the door. Mr. Edwards indeed, crouched atop the woodpile, scrabbling backward from Jack and scattering stove lengths onto the ground. "He's got me treed!"

Caroline grasped Jack's chain as best she could with her meal-dusted hands and reeled the snarling animal toward her until she could reach his collar. "No, Jack," she said with a jerk that cut his wind. The slant of the bulldog's brow seemed to challenge her judgment, but he obeyed. Resentfully. "I'm so sorry," Caroline said to Edwards as Jack continued to grumble. His collar vibrated beneath Caroline's fingers so that she did not trust letting go. She twisted awkwardly to try to meet Edwards's eye. "I declare, Jack seems to know Mr. Ingalls isn't here. He's gone to town. Oswego," she added.

"Yes, ma'am, I know. Mr. Ingalls passed my claim this morning and asked me to come by these next few days and see that everything was all right. If you don't mind, I'll see to the stock for you while I'm here."

"Mind?" was all she could say. Caroline was so taken by surprise, Jack seized the opportunity for one last half-hearted lunge at Edwards.

Edwards grinned, dancing backward from Jack's teeth. "I didn't suppose you would."

The next day the knock came just as she was finishing the dinner dishes. Caroline's heart bobbed, lifting and sinking almost simultaneously. Because Edwards was not Charles. And, if she was entirely honest with herself, because he had come too early for the milking. *Of all things!* she scolded herself. Caroline took a moment to smooth her face into a welcome. She had no right to show Mr. Edwards even a speck of disappointment for his trouble, no matter what time he arrived.

"Oh," she said as she opened the door, "Mrs. Scott!" Caroline thanked her lucky stars Jack hadn't treed the woman on the woodpile. Mrs. Scott did not reply, and Caroline recognized that she was out of breath. "Is everything all right?" Caroline asked, scanning the horizon off toward the Scotts' claim.

Mrs. Scott waved a hand. "Just windblown," she puffed. "Thought I'd stop in and see how you folks was making out." She looked up and smiled. "My, but you do look well, Mrs. Ingalls."

Caroline's cheeks felt as though they might split with pleasure. A visit. Mrs. Scott had walked nearly three miles for no other reason than to pay a friendly call. "Come in," Caroline said. "Come right in and let me fix you some ginger water."

Theirs was a singular blend of ease and formality, Caroline thought as she mixed sugar, vinegar, and ginger into a pitcher of cool water for her guest. Mrs. Scott behaved as though she had never seen Caroline bare and trembling with pain or fever, never sponged blood from her thighs or rinsed her chamber pail, never shared her bed. Yet the knowledge of those things permeated their every word and action, for they knew almost nothing else of each other. They had never met on level ground before, and every comfort Caroline could provide Mrs. Scott now, from hanging her lavender sunbonnet on the peg by the door to inviting her to sit in the new willow-bough rocker, gave Caroline the greatest of satisfaction.

"I'm sure she's grown since I saw her last," Mrs. Scott exclaimed over Carrie. "Heavier than a pail of blackberries."

"How heavy am I, Mrs. Scott?" Laura interrupted.

"Laura," Caroline murmured, with a subtle shake of her head that said *Mind your manners.*

Mrs. Scott raised an eyebrow at Laura, even as she answered, "Oh, I'd guess you're almost as heavy as a bushel of cotton." To Caroline she said, "My husband's people raised cotton in Kentucky. Mr. Scott and I tried our hand at it in Missouri. We kept ourselves quite comfortable for a few years. Up until the war, anyway. After that there wasn't money in it anymore," she added. Pointedly? Caroline wondered. Or was that her own ears, hearing more than what was said where the virtue of the Union was concerned, as she was so apt to do after her brother fell at Shiloh? The sound of Mrs. Scott's voice dimmed as Joseph's soft smile, so much like her father's that she could no longer distinguish between the two, appeared in Caroline's mind. How strange to think she was older now than her eldest brother had ever been. Or ever would be. She had long ago become accustomed to his absence, but not to these odd reminders of her lifetime eclipsing his.

"Mr. Scott reckons he'll try planting a few acres here, too, if the Indians ever clear out," Mrs. Scott continued, oblivious. "No telling what they'd do if they came across a field of cotton. They've just got no sense of personal property. The way they come in and out, it makes a body feel as though you didn't own the place."

"It was different in Wisconsin," Caroline ventured. "In Pepin the Chippewas kept to themselves. When I was a girl in the eastern counties, even the Potawatomis weren't so bold as the Osages."

Mrs. Scott's brow furrowed. "Pepin County? How far were you from the Minnesota massacre?" she asked, continuing without an answer. "I've heard the stories.

Like to scare me to death. My brother wrote me how they—"

Caroline cleared her throat, cutting her eyes toward the girls.

"Anyway, I hope to goodness we won't have trouble with the Indians," Mrs. Scott said. "I've heard rumors." She raised her eyebrows to show that she would not speak of them in front of the children and gave a smart nod.

Jack would not lie down. His fur bristled and flattened, as though the wind were blowing inside the house. He circled and paced, sniffed at the windows and whined at the door. When Caroline opened it, he would not go out.

"Jack's afraid of something," Mary said.

"Jack's not afraid of anything, ever!" Laura declared.

Even as Caroline admonished Laura for contradicting, she wondered which of them was right. She had never seen Jack frightened, but there was no doubt he was uneasy. All of them were. The girls were mostly impatient. Every minute Charles did not come disappointed them. They had counted four long days without complaint, eager for the first hour that they could begin to hope for his return. All the care Caroline had taken all day long to say *might* and *maybe* each time they asked if Pa would be home tonight did not matter once the sun began sloping toward the horizon. Insensible to the rising wind, Mary and Laura huddled shoulder to shoulder at the window, peering down the creek road with an intensity that might have parted the grass.

For all her own eagerness, Caroline could not keep from watching Jack. It was as though he were stirring some intangible something with his body, trying to smooth it, or herd it from the house. Perhaps, she thought, they both were roused by the same vague apprehension. Her mind had circled in the same way for two days, veering around the invisible forms of Mrs. Scott's unspoken rumors. "Indian trouble" could take so many shapes; without one to fix upon, Caroline felt as though her head were clouded with smoke. Something dark and shifting passed continually along the edges of her internal gaze, so persistently that when she unlocked the provisions cabinet for supper, she did so with a furtive glance out both windows. The treeless vista was a comfort and a worry, both. Any man or beast intent on doing harm would have to belly crawl twenty rods or more through the grass to avoid being seen. Why, then, was Jack so restive? *The wind?* Caroline wondered. Perhaps it carried some far-off scent only Jack could detect, as it had the day Charles out-ran the wolf pack. *That was a mistake,* Caroline chided herself, *thinking of the wolf pack.*

Jack kicked up a clamor of barking, and all of them jumped. "Someone's knocking," Mary said over the racket. Caroline hesitated. Jack's nose pointed to the roof and the force of his baying had lifted his front paws up on tiptoe, yet his tail waggled and he did not snarl. It could not be Charles, for the latch string was out. Caroline had not made up her mind before the door flapped open and there was Edwards, thrust across the threshold as though the wind were shoving him forward.

"You snuck up on us, Mr. Edwards," Laura scolded. "We've been watching the creek road for Pa all after-noon."

Edwards's answer came so readily, Caroline wondered if he had rehearsed it. "I was out hunting jackrabbits for my supper, and came up the Indian trail instead."

"Did you get any?" Mary asked.

"Nope." He shifted his eyes toward Caroline, add-ing, "Didn't see anything big enough to aim at."

The way he said *anything*—with a tweak of empha-sis that made it seem a sentence in itself—Caroline felt a tingle at the back of her neck. Nothing on the Indian path. Likely he meant to reassure her, but the knowledge that he had felt compelled to look there made her wonder if she ought to coax the girls from the window and bolt the shutter.

Edwards shook himself almost like a dog. "That wind!" he said. "You might be bundled up tighter than a sausage in its casing and it'll still find a way through."

"Warm yourself a minute, Mr. Edwards," Caroline said. He took no more than that before trudging out for the chores, pushing back into the wind with his chin tucked to his collar. Caroline went out behind him to draw an extra pail of water for the night. The instant she passed from the lee of the house, the wind submerged her. Like the current in that terrible creek, Caroline thought with a shudder. Her shawl whipped around her, pulling as the wind pushed. When she turned back to the cabin after tussling with the pail and the rope, she could feel the wind splitting across her face as though her nose were the blade of a plow.

Edwards was not long behind. He set the pail of milk on the table and stooped down before the fire, putting his palms out to the blaze.

"I wish I could contrive a way to send some of this milk home with you," Caroline said. "It's been so kind of you to do the chores while Mr. Ingalls is away."

Edwards ducked his head in a kind of nod and did not answer. Had she embarrassed him? Caroline won-

dered. No. She could see him thinking, turning something over in his mind as though debating whether to
bring it out into the room.

"The Osages are camping in the shelter of the
bluffs," he said at length. "The smoke was rising up
out of there when I crossed the bottoms." Caroline
did not permit herself to react. She simply took in the
words, as though by saying nothing she could force
the space they had occupied to seal itself over, leaving
the room and everything in it undisturbed. Edwards
rubbed his hands fast. They seemed almost to hiss. He
spoke again, without changing the tone or volume of
his voice: "Do you have a gun?"

"I have Mr. Ingalls's pistol," Caroline answered.

Edwards nodded. "I reckon they'll stay close in
camp, a night like this."

"Yes," Caroline said, as if saying it would make it so.

A furrow appeared between Edwards's brows. "I
can make myself right comfortable with hay in the
stable. I'll stay there all night if you say so."

Did he know she was afraid, Caroline wondered,
or only presume that she must be? She glanced fur-
tively at the children. Laura's face had brightened at
the thought of Mr. Edwards staying all night, but the
offer had made Mary wary. Her china-blue eyes were

measuring Caroline, as if she were considering whether or not to be scared.

A little more fear toward the Indians would do Laura no harm, was Caroline's first, rueful thought. But if by accepting Edwards's offer she might be teaching her daughters to be fearful inside their own house—with the door latched and the pistol on its shelf and the bull-dog keeping watch—simply because Indians existed? If they realized their ma was not certain she could protect them as their pa did—what then?

Caroline had no choice but to make the words brisk and calm. The way he had asked her about the gun, Edwards would surely understand. "No, thank you, Mr. Edwards, I won't put you to that trouble. Jack will look after us. I'm expecting Mr. Ingalls any minute now."

He looked at her long enough, Caroline wondered for an instant if she were making a mistake. Mary and Laura and even Carrie trusted her implicitly to keep them safe, without regard for how she accomplished it. Was it a peculiar strain of vanity that made her insist upon doing it herself?

"I don't guess anything will bother you, anyway," Edwards said, standing.

"No," Caroline answered.

He crossed the room and put his hand on the latch, but he did not open the door. Caroline did not know him well enough to make out what he was thinking now. By his outward appearance alone she would never have suspected what kind of a man Edwards was. Tobacco stained the corners of his lips. His hair looked as though he'd been cutting at it with his razor rather than a pair of shears. It was long and fine and inclined to snarl, a lustrous golden brown halfway between Mary's and Laura's. He had been towheaded as a boy, Caroline reckoned, and not so terribly long ago. She rubbed her finger and thumb together, imagining the feel of it.

"Mr. Edwards?" She paused, sure of her intentions, yet unable to gauge how he would receive such an invitation.

"Ma'am?"

"Mr. Edwards, I know it is quite some time off, but I wonder if you would consider having your Christmas dinner with us. Our family would be proud to have you."

She saw how the words touched him, how he wanted to smile but could not trust himself to do it. He swallowed once before speaking. "Yes, ma'am," Edwards said. Solemn. The muscles at the corners of his mouth jerked, once. "I should like that very much."

Caroline shut the door behind him and pulled in the latch string.

It was too late for Charles to come home. There was no sense in sitting up, no call for him to drive so late, in the dark and the wind. By now he would be camping somewhere, surely. But Caroline was every bit as reluctant as the girls had been to go to bed—more so, even.

The latch clattered in the wind, and she forbade herself from turning to check the latch string again. It was pulled in. She had not laid a finger on it since letting Edwards out. No one had. The shutters were bolted. Jack lay between the lintels, his belly against the threshold. There was nothing to fear.

There was only the wind, which was certainly nothing to be afraid of. If Mary or Laura woke, frightened, Caroline would tell them so, and it would be true. The wind itself was no threat. Yet two facts remained: the wind was blowing, and Caroline was discomfited.

The way it touched the house—slapping the walls, snatching at the latch and rattling the shutters, like something trying to get inside—Caroline could not help thinking it was punishing them for standing in its way. And the sound. If anything living had shrieked that way, she would have rushed outside to assuage it. *Or inside for the gun,* Caroline thought as another gust crashed against the shutters. It did not matter how many times she assured herself that the sounds signified nothing. Every nerve in her body reacted to them, insistent that something was amiss.

Caroline rocked in her chair, thankful for its movement, and trained her eyes on the fire. One by one, she conjured up images of the things Charles would bring back with him: salt meat, linseed oil, sacks of flour and oats and beans, a keg of nails to repay Mr. Edwards, perhaps a jar of pickles for herself. Of course, there would be a treat for Mary and Laura to squeal over. She pictured Eliza, and Ma, and Martha, and Henry and Polly reading the letter she had sent, and felt her face soften momentarily.

But the pictures were no more than a haze; Caroline could not hold them before her for even a minute without the thing she did not want to think of showing through. Her eyes strayed to the shelf that held the pistol, and she closed them. *There is no need,* she told herself, rocking deeply. *Only stop thinking about Indians.* But her mind would not obey. It rubbed and rubbed at that thought until it shone too brightly to ignore.

Caroline went to the bed. For a moment she stood, watching Carrie sleep. Her little fists lay flung open on either side of her head. *Anyone with sense would stop fretting and climb into bed beside that baby girl,* she thought. But the baby was not what Caroline wanted. She put one hand on the mantel shelf, stepped onto the bed rail, and reached up over Carrie's sleeping form. Her fingers touched the cold metal barrel first. Then the stock, polished smooth with use. Her thumb found a scratch in the wood she had not noticed before.

Caroline did not look at the gun. She did not need to. She went back to her rocker and laid it in her lap, half-cocked. Its barrel she pointed toward the fire. The weight of it seemed to draw her shoulders down where they belonged. At the same time her eyes lifted, found their way to the china shepherdess, and settled.

The fear was not gone. She had only made a place for it, invited it to sit alongside her. That was less wearying than refusing to acknowledge its presence. For a time she was aware of nothing but the gun in her lap and the shepherdess on the shelf. Both of them cool, still, and shining. Both of them a kind of assurance.

The wind wailed long and high, and Caroline rocked, letting the sound pass through her as though she were an instrument. She thought of how the fiddle screeched on those rare occasions when Charles struck a wrong note and wondered if it felt the way she did now.

Something gasped, something inside the house, and

Caroline's fingers were around the pistol's stock, her thumb poised over the hammer.

It was Laura, sitting straight up in bed. Mary lay beside her, eyes wide open. Caroline froze. She had not meant for the children to see her with the gun in her lap. It would not be at all like the familiar sight of Charles with his rifle. She could see Laura's eyes following the firelight up and down the pistol's silver barrel. It was then that Caroline realized she had not frozen at all. The chair still rocked, as though it rocked itself.

Don't be afraid.

Caroline could not say it, not when her only comfort had been to subsume her own fear.

"Lie down, Laura, and go to sleep," she managed instead, with only a hint of a quaver.

"What's that howling?"

A flutter of panic pierced Caroline's belly. Could they see her hands trembling, how her jaw clenched as she struggled to answer? Silently, she uncoiled her fingers from the stock and flattened them against her thigh. *Don't frighten them,* Caroline willed herself. She imagined the way her voice needed to sound before saying the words. Gentle enough to soothe. Firm enough to end Laura's questions. "The wind is howling," Caroline told her. "Now mind me, Laura."

Laura inched back under the quilts, and Caroline refastened her gaze to the china shepherdess. She wanted to smile back at that serene china face and felt a strange urge to apologize for being unable to do it. Caroline looked and looked at the painted blue eyes, and tried to wonder what the shepherdess would see through them if she had the power of sight. The single room she faced, day and night, with only a glimpse through the open door now and then? Caroline winced at the idea. Perhaps her painted gaze would turn inward instead, to someplace entirely different and belonging only to herself. The faraway shelf she had occupied, in Detroit or Chicago, before Henry Quiner had chosen her to carry home to his not-quite-four-year-old daughter. Could the little china woman remember what Caroline herself could not—did she recall the moment Pa had placed her in Caroline's hands?

Caroline nearly smiled then and began to sing softly. To herself, to the shepherdess, to the children, still wide awake behind their closed eyes.

There is a happy land, far, far away.
Where saints in glory stand, bright, bright as day.

The jolt against the door ought to have frightened her, rousing Caroline as it did from a fretful doze. But she recognized the sound as surely as if Charles had called out to her. The instant she heard it Caroline wondered how she could have taken the wind's purposeless clattering for anything human.

"Didn't you think I might have been an Indian, Mrs. Ingalls?" Charles's voice scolded as she flung open the door.

He was teasing—she could hear the twinkle in his eyes even if it was too dark to see beneath the brim of his hat—but Caroline's mouth dropped open at the thought of her own foolishness. "No," she said just as suddenly, and bold as brass. "Jack wasn't growling. He knew it was you, too."

Charles grabbed her up in his arms and laughed. His coat was stiff with cold. Clumps of frozen mud dropped from his boots and iced her toes. She did not tell him she had been afraid; the half-cocked pistol lying on the seat of the rocker spoke more freely of that than she ever would.

Charles knew. He would not speak of it any more than she would, not with the children suddenly awake and eager to claim their places on his knees, but Caroline heard it in his cheerful boom as he told Mary and Laura about the wind and the rain and the freezing mud that had seized the wagon wheels and slowed Pet and Patty to a crawl. *Everything is all right,* his manner was saying, even as Caroline picked up the pistol and laid it on the mantel shelf without a word about it.

And it was so. The little house was full in every way it could be filled—with the scent of coffee bubbling on the hearth, the sound of her husband and daughters, the sight of all the provisions Charles piled on the table. Oh, those fat, heavy sacks. Cornmeal. Salt pork. Coffee and tea, flour and sugar, molasses and lard. Everything, down to tobacco and nails. Even, Caroline saw with a smirk and a shake of her head, a pound of sparkling white sugar, as if Charles could not help thumbing his nose at the prices in Independence. Caroline put her hands on each keg and sack and parcel, patting the way she patted Carrie's little belly after a feed. With the milk and dried blackberries and the game, it would surely be enough see them through the winter.

Enough. Caroline had never yet tired of the word, perhaps never would. As a child, *plenty* had been too grandiose a term for anything but berrying time, but when Ma had had occasion to pronounce *There will be enough,* even when it was just barely true, that was a feeling ofttimes more delicious than the food itself.

"Open the square package," Charles said over the girls' heads.

It was wrapped so neatly, with its crisply folded corners and a knot of white string. Her first thought was of a book, or writing paper—extravagances that made no sense. She lifted it and the weight puzzled her. Even Charles's big green book was not so heavy.

"Be careful," he said. "Don't drop it."

A thrill went through her, of delight and dread as she understood. It could be only one thing. "Oh, Charles," she gasped, aghast at the expense, "you didn't." She laid it back down on the table, fearful now of damaging what must be inside.

"Open it," he insisted.

Caroline untied the string and folded back the paper. Eight panes of window glass.

She could not keep the figures from chalking themselves up in her mind. Eight panes of glass could not be less than twelve dollars back East. But here—a place where white sugar went for a dollar a pound? No, she assured herself. That was why Charles had driven forty miles to Oswego. That was why she and the girls had spent four days alone on the high prairie. He had saved the overland freight, at least. Still, the cost amounted to no less than the equivalent of nine and a half acres. The single square pane in her hands represented more land than it took to hold the house and stable and well. It was a foolish, frivolous thing to do with so much money.

But gracious, it was beautiful, that glass. Clear and cool and smooth, and ever so faintly blue, like ice. Caroline lifted the top pane to the firelight, and the edges seemed to glow. She put a hand to her chest, to keep from floating away. Four panes for the east, four for the west. He had bought her sunlight and moonlight, sunrises and sunsets. She would be able to see clear to the creek road and the bluffs beyond, all winter long. Come spring she could look out at her kitchen garden and see Charles working the fields of sod potatoes and corn.

He should not have done it. Every cent he had saved by going to Oswego had surely gone into this glass. Caroline could not get air enough into her to properly thank him.

Twenty-Six

Had she known how many Indians she would see through those window panes, Caroline thought as she glanced toward the Indian trail for the dozenth time that day, she might have quelled her delight. She tried to tell herself that it was only the novelty of looking through the glass that made her more aware of the passing barebacked riders, but that was as good as a lie. She told herself that the way they rode, without ever so much as glancing askance at the cabin, there was nothing to worry over. But that did not feel much like the truth, either. They might as well have turned their heads away entirely, they pointed their eyes so resolutely forward. *I refuse to see you*, that posture proclaimed.

It seemed an indecent thing to envy an Indian, but Caroline did. No matter how she tried, she could not replicate their willful indifference. Every Osage on that trail claimed her attention. And Jack—Jack plain hated to see an Indian pass. All day long he snarled and barked and scrabbled against his chain, until the bare ground was scored with slashes. Charles had to nearly drag the bulldog in for his dinner, he was so reluctant to leave the trail unguarded.

"I can't say I blame him," Caroline said. "I declare, Indians are getting so thick around here that I can't look up without seeing one."

Charles leaned down at the window to survey the trail. It ran almost through the dooryard before angling away to the northeast. "I wouldn't have built the house so close if I'd known it's a highroad. Looked like nobody'd ridden it in months when we got here. They must not use it, spring and summer."

Caroline would not say that she did not mind. But there was no use in complaining, either. "That can't be helped now," she said. She put a bowl of jackrabbit vitals on the floor for Jack, then dredged the remaining pieces with flour, salt, and pepper. The lard in the skillet had begun to crackle. She turned, lifting the plate of meat, and nearly dropped it.

An Indian stood in the doorway. "Goodness," she gasped. Jack looked up from his bowl and lunged. His jowls were bloodied with jackrabbit, his teeth bared. Charles leapt forward and snatched the dog back by the collar. The Indian had not moved one step, but Caroline saw him draw himself up, his chin and chest both lifting in a kind of internal backing away. "Ho-wah," he said.

"How!" Charles answered.

The Indian seemed to smother a smirk at Charles's reply and stepped into the house. He was tall, taller yet than Charles, so that he reached up to gently bend back the feathers on his scalp lock as he crossed the threshold. He walked the length of the house and squatted down beside the fire as though he'd been invited. Charles pulled his belt from its loops and used it to buckle Jack to the bedpost by his collar. Then Charles squatted down alongside the hearth. The two men said nothing. Behind them, the melted lard gave a pop. Mary and Laura sat on their little bed with their backs against the wall, watching.

Caroline stood completely still for a moment before she realized that she was not frightened. She was not entirely at ease, but she was not afraid. In fact, she thought, having the Indian in the house was not so very different from sitting down to milk a new cow for the first time. Caroline had the same sense now of being nominally in charge and at the same time acutely aware of her own physical disadvantage. If the man poised on her hearth had a mind to, he could spring up and harm any one of them. Yet if he had a mind to, he gave no indication of it. The silence between Charles and the Indian seemed almost amicable, and gradually Caroline understood that if she did not carry on with her task, her hesitation would tip their tentative accord out of balance.

So she picked up the plate and a fork and strode to the fire. One by one she laid the raw pieces of rabbit into the hot fat. Everyone watched. They listened to the frying meat bubble and snap. They watched her turn each piece up golden brown and dish a helping onto five plates. She gave one to Charles and one to the Indian. She handed Mary and Laura their portions, as though they ate dinner on their bed every day of the week. Then Caroline picked up Carrie from the big bed and held the baby in her lap while she ate one-handed at the table. No one spoke.

When Charles finished eating, he slowly unkinked his legs and took his pipe and a new paper of tobacco down from the mantel shelf. He filled his pipe and offered the packet to the Indian, who did the same. Thin tendrils of smoke rose up from their two pipes. Caroline wished the smoke might spell out the men's thoughts. They puffed at the tobacco until the rafters were hazy and their pipes were empty. Then the Indian spoke.

Caroline tilted her head in surprise. He sounded nothing like the two men who had come into the house before. These sounds were so smooth and languorous, they seemed a single long word. *French?* she wondered.

Charles shook his head. "No speak," he replied.

The Indian lifted a hand in acknowledgment, and no more was said. After a moment, he stood and walked out the door. Jack pulled against the belt that held him to the bedpost, straining forward with his nose and teeth, but he did not growl.

"My goodness gracious," Caroline said. She stroked Carrie's back again and again, as though it were the baby who wanted comforting.

"That Indian was no common trash," Charles remarked.

Caroline looked around the cabin. Her dredging boxes of flour and salt and pepper all sat on the table in plain sight. The door to the provisions cupboard stood partway open, revealing its cache of bulging sacks and crates. The Indian had not peered inside, but Caroline had no reason to suppose he had not seen them. "Let Indians keep themselves to themselves," she said, "and we will do the same."

"There's nothing to worry about," Charles said. "That Indian was perfectly friendly. And their camps down in the bluffs are peaceable enough. If we treat them well and watch Jack, we won't have any trouble."

Caroline agreed, but she did not say so. She did not know how to explain to Charles how she could be thankful they were friendly and still not want them inside her house. It did not seem a thing that should need explaining.

"Ma, Baby Carrie's hungry."

Caroline did not argue. Mary knew. She had set to learning her baby sister's signals by rote and could decipher them nearly as well as if Carrie were her own. This once, Caroline was grateful for the interruption. Her fingertips ached from pushing the needle through the rabbit skins. Mary and Laura could hardly wait for their caps to be finished. Each time Caroline laid aside her sewing, they came to kneel beside the work basket and stroke the fur. She herself favored the beaver pelts. Their rich brown underfur was deeper than the lushest velvet; you might sink a finger to the first knuckle into its improbable softness. But those pelts, along with the mink and wolf, they could not afford to keep—not if they were to have a plow and seeds for planting.

Charles had done well, so early in the season. The stack of pelts reached nearly to Laura's knees. If Charles's traps kept yielding this way, all the cash in the fiddle case might go toward proving up on the claim.

Caroline stood and stretched and went to stand a minute in the doorway. The air was pleasantly brisk, yet lacked the familiar scent of leaves bronzing in the sun. Autumn here had a golden, grassy smell, dry and soft, like a haymow. She reached for her shawl—its red the color of a sugar maple at full blaze—and pulled it comfortably about her shoulders. This was the welcome stretch of weather that turned the fireplace into a boon companion. Soon enough it would become a ravenous mouth to feed. For now, though, it demanded little in return for the comfort it gave.

Behind her, the baby fussed. Caroline let her. Carrie had nearly grown out of her newborn cry, and Caroline enjoyed listening for the little voice that was beginning to emerge between the growls and shrills. Next autumn there would be no leisure, not with corn and sod potatoes to pick, and Carrie to mind. Next autumn, Carrie would be walking.

Caroline tucked her pinky into the corner of Carrie's mouth and gently broke the baby's grip on her nipple.

The little mouth yawned as Caroline eased her from the crook of one elbow to another.

At the sound of footsteps Caroline looked up, expecting Charles, anticipating his smile at the sight of her in her rocking chair, the way his eyes would sweep across her face, down her neck and open bodice, to Carrie.

"Gracious!" she cried.

Two brown men stood in the doorway. They headed straight toward the locked cupboard as though the smell of flour and lard had lured them in off the prairie. Quickly Caroline buttoned up. Her fingers fumbled, mismatching the holes. They must not see the key on its string.

The baby was only half-fed. She whimpered and squirmed. This day of all days, her appetite chose to be impatient. Caroline put her finger in Carrie's mouth. Carrie sucked and bawled, and Caroline felt the prickle of her milk letting down. Her cheeks flared as the stain warmed the calico of her bodice. Furious with shame, she slipped an arm between herself and the baby, clamping the heel of her hand against her breast to hold the leak steady.

The injustice of it was scathing—that she must withhold food from one child to protect the provisions for the others.

444 • SARAH MILLER

At least the children were all within sight this time, within reach, even. The girls were at her sides, Mary with her rag doll—Caroline did not know how or when she had gotten it—and Laura clutching her half-finished fur cap. She heard a quick hiss of pain from Laura and knew that the needle she had left poised in a seam had stabbed her daughter's palm. Laura did not make another sound.

One Indian, the one wearing a dingy green calico shirt above buckskin leggings, lifted the corner of the dishtowel from the pan of cornbread on the table. Green Shirt motioned to the other man, who came over and snatched the towel away so sharply it cracked against the air. He laid it out and tied the loaf of cornbread in it, to take. The Indian's dusty hands snagged the fabric as he knotted it to his belt.

Caroline swallowed hard. Mother Ingalls had given her that towel, its corner embroidered with a pine tree that had once been green. It was so threadbare now it was good for nothing more than screening leftovers from the flies, but she did not want to let it go this way. *If that is the most valuable thing they take,* she promised herself.

Caroline did not finish the thought. As she watched their eyes probed every niche of the house. She saw them study the mantel shelf, the windowsills. Green

Shirt squatted down to reach into her work basket. Mary and Laura skittered backward. One by one he inspected every one of her crochet hooks and knitting needles. *Looking for the key,* Caroline thought, and hugged Carrie closer. They had not seen it on her neck, she realized. If they were looking for it, it was because they did not know where it was.

Before she could feel any relief, Green Shirt made an exclamation and held up a triumphant hand. Caroline jolted at the sight. The key to her trunk.

"Oh," she said without meaning to. The Indians' faces lit up as her hand flew to her lips. Without a word they set upon the lock of the provisions cupboard.

The key would not fit. The shaft was round instead of flat. The tip would not reach far enough inside to give them even the satisfaction of a hopeful jiggle. Towel Thief smacked the padlock so hard the hasp rang out. Green Shirt made a sound that sounded like swearing. *Could they swear,* Caroline heard herself wondering somewhere far inside her mind, *in another language, against a heathen god?*

Green Shirt turned, the key pinched in his fingers. Looking for the hole that it would fit into. He raised his eyebrows at her, and his wrist pivoted in the air. Back and forth, back and forth. A question.

If she so much as exhaled in the direction of her

trunk, he would go to it. Caroline lifted her chin to point her eyes straight over his head. *I will bake them a cake,* she thought. *A cake with white flour and sugar, and a roast prairie hen apiece if only they will not open that trunk.* Both men turned, following her gaze. She saw their attention move to the empty pegs over the door, and she watched their lips spread wide as they understood that Charles's rifle was not in the house. Caroline shivered as though a bead of hot lead were rolling down the back of her neck. They might take anything they wanted now.

Green Shirt gave his wrist a violent flick. The key flew, glanced off the basket, and clattered against the toes of Mary's shoes. Mary yelped and ducked behind the rocker. Carrie screeched, and Caroline's stomach chilled with the realization that her grip on the baby had tightened so hard, she could feel Carrie's thigh bone.

One of them—Towel Thief—picked up the pile of pelts.

No. Caroline was on her feet. She did not step toward them, did not speak, only let the force of the thought vault her out of the chair and billow from her skin like steam until it filled the room.

Carrie stopped crying. The men stopped moving. They spoke in what sounded like half words. Towel

Thief shook his head. Green Shirt struck his palm with the side of one hand, swiping as though he were brushing away an insect. Towel Thief glowered. Green Shirt jabbed a finger in Caroline's direction. The entire core of Caroline's body recoiled as he spoke, his hands making motions she did not want to interpret. Towel Thief dropped the furs in a heap and stalked out the door.

"All's well that ends well," Charles said when she told him what had nearly happened.

No, Caroline thought, *it is not.* She could not say so. If she opened her mouth, she would cry. Her every muscle was fixed with the task of holding the corners of her lips steady. The very sight of a man in green calico, even her husband, wearing a bright, clean shirt she had made with her own hands, made her almost dizzy. The only scrap of consolation was the absence of Charles's usual blitheness. But the resignation Caroline heard in his voice instead was no comfort. The Indians would come and go as they pleased. Charles would do nothing about it, because there was nothing to be done.

Caroline tried to imagine the scene as it would appear to Charles: the Indians had not hurt her, had not even touched her, nor made off with anything of value. On the surface the encounter did not sound consider-

450 • SARAH MILLER

ably different from the first two men who had come into the house months ago.

But it was. She had been wrong to be afraid of those first men. Caroline could see that now. Everything that had frightened her that day had risen out of her own dread of what they *might* do, not from anything they had actually done. Her fear had blotted out the subtle expressions and gestures that ought to have signaled civility, and so she had not understood that they were asking, not demanding. Green Shirt and Towel Thief's behavior had been crude enough to violate not only her own standards but the Osages' customs as well. There was no one thing she could point to as proof, yet Caroline was certain. All the courtesy she had been incapable of understanding before was entirely absent in them.

"If you had seen the way they looked at everything," Caroline began. Charles's face stopped her. All the sympathy she had wanted so desperately after her first encounter with the Osages was there in his eyes and mouth. It was so genuine, it hurt, and all the more because it was misplaced.

He believed he understood: his wife was afraid of Indians, the way a child fears the dark, and she had been left alone in the dark.

It was as if he had no concept of malice, Caroline marveled. He would trust anything, man or beast, until it gave him reason not to. *And,* she thought with a sudden gust of understanding, *he takes for granted that the same is true of the Osages.* No wonder then, that he could leave her alone, that he was so imperturbed by the Indians' intrusions. Charles knew that she and the girls would do nothing to provoke them, and so in his mind they were safe. The realization made her woozy. *Perhaps if he had gone to war,* Caroline thought, *he would know better.* Charles Ingalls was something out of a world that no longer existed—or a better one yet to come. She felt the flicker of a smile even as her breath hitched. More often than not, that was one of the things she loved best in him.

Charles simply could not comprehend that she was at their mercy each time an Osage walked into the house. One Indian was like another to him. Unless there were weapons drawn Charles would never feel what she had felt, half-unbuttoned, with the baby clutched in one arm and the key all but burning a hole through her corset as those men pointed at her. Caroline tasted acid in her throat, remembering.

If she did not put that scene out of her thoughts, it would score her mind with ruts too deep to pull herself out of. Caroline closed her eyes and made a picture of nothing—only the softly moving darkness behind her eyelids.

She could banish the image, and that was all. The residue of everything she had felt remained, thick and unfamiliar in her chest. A sort of anger without heat, without focus. She did not want to aim it at Charles, but there was nowhere else for it.

Charles sensed it. He spoke and moved carefully, as though she'd been bruised and he dared not jostle her. The instant Carrie began to flail and bleat after her bedtime feed, he picked her up, eager to spare Caroline anything that might further trouble her.

He bounced and walked and patted. Tickled the baby, sang to her. Carrie was tired to a frazzle. Caroline could hear it in the breathy whine before each cry. *Hweh, hweh*, Carrie whimpered. *Hweeeh-heh.*

Caroline closed her eyes, touched her fingertips to her forehead, rocked in her chair. Still, the baby fussed. *Leave them be*, Caroline urged herself. *Let him find his own way.* But Carrie. Carrie could not say more plainly what she wanted, any more than Caroline could pretend not to understand.

"She can't be hungry," Charles protested as Caroline rose from the rocker. "And she's bone dry." If he had

seen the thumb-shaped bruise on Carrie's thigh when
he diapered her, he had said nothing of it.

Caroline held out her arms. Charles seemed to shrug
as he lifted Carrie into them.

Caroline nestled Carrie into the space between her
breasts, fitting the little round cheek into her palm. The
baby's ear lay over her heart. Caroline enfolded herself
around her daughter, so that every soft part of her body
pressed gently against Carrie's skin. "Shhhhhhhh," she
whispered, holding almost still. "Shhhhh." Caroline
began to sway, more gently than a breeze. The baby
shuddered, panted, quieted. Out of the corner of her
eye Caroline saw Charles's expression, his half smile
betraying a medley of admiration and hurt. Caroline
leaned down to nuzzle her own cheek against Carrie's
hair and felt at once how the singular fit of their bodies
excluded him. She was sorry for Charles, yet could not
bring herself to separate herself enough from Carrie to
open their tight circle to him. *Selfish,* she thought, *selfish and spiteful,* and closed her eyes so that she would
not see if she had pained Charles further.

Into the long silence came the snap of the fiddle
box's clasps. The bow glided through rosin, then there
were the hollow woody plunks of the fiddle itself being
lifted from the felt and into its place beneath Charles's

chin. The bow sighed tentatively across the strings, then sang out.

"*Blue Juniata.*"

Oh, Charles, Caroline thought, helpless. And there she was again, back at the cornhusking dance when Charles had looked out across his fiddle strings and seen that she was looking back at him—and only him. He'd seen her face and known that his own furtive, hopeful gazes had not been wasted. Caroline could still hear the laughter, the thrum of dancing feet swirling around her. She remembered the blush blooming on her cheeks and her pulse tingling in her fingers and toes. And his eyes, those twinkling, teasing blue eyes that were known on both banks of the Oconomowoc—how those eyes had shone. They might well have said their marriage vows right then and there, Caroline had thought ever after.

The notes could just as well have been his hands, the way the music touched her. He was sorry. He could not have made it plainer, nor more sincere, with his own voice. Likely he did not know quite what he was apologizing for, Caroline thought. It did not matter to Charles. He would not hold to anything if it meant he could not also have her.

Caroline let out a little puff of air, the tiniest signal of defeat, and began to sing:

Wild roved an Indian maid, bright Alfarata,
Where flow the waters of the blue Juniata.
Strong and true my arrows are, in my painted
     quiver,
Swift goes my light canoe adown the rapid river.

She sang it his way, adopting all the trifling mistakes she had so boldly chided him for that first time she heard him sing it—*girl* became *maid,* and *snowy* turned to *sunny*—every verse, just as he had written it into the little poetry booklet that even now was locked safely inside her trunk.

Her words met his music, and the two joined to form one seamless sound.

Twenty-Seven

It sounded, at first, like the wind. High and long and wavering. Caroline had tugged the quilt over her shoulders before she woke enough to realize the chill that made her shiver was not from cold.

She sat up in bed. Charles stood at the door in his nightshirt, lifting his rifle from its pegs. A feeble gray light fringed the curtains. An hour or so remained until dawn.

"Is it wolves?" she whispered.

Charles shook his head. It was too early in the day for wolves.

Caroline drew her knees to her belly, gathered two fistfuls of quilt under her chin, and listened again.

The sound traveled on the wind, but it was not the wind. It was shrill, and arrow-sharp, as if it had been aimed at them. At intervals it was punctuated with bursts of speed and volume that made Caroline's shoulders jerk.

It was human, she realized, and female. Women. The pitch told her that, though she had heard bull elk reach notes as high.

"How far is the Indian camp?" she asked.

"Two, three miles northeast."

Two or three miles. How could they hold their throats open so wide that they could be heard at that distance, even with the wind to carry their voices? Caroline could not imagine what it would take to make her turn loose such sounds—what immensity of grief, or rage. Ma had not made sounds like that when Pa had drowned, nor when Joseph was killed. Yet it was not unbridled wailing. Each tone had been honed into a particular shape. Though Caroline could grasp neither rhythm nor meaning, she perceived that there must be notes and words. A song?

If it were a song, it bore no resemblance to anything Caroline could call music. It had no beat. They did not seem to pause for breath. Now and again Caroline thought she caught a semblance of melody, but it followed no pattern she was familiar with. This was continual, and alien. All she could be certain of was that the sounds did not signal fear. The women were not being savaged, at least.

Mary and Laura woke, saw Charles standing guard in his bare feet, and soundlessly crawled into the big bed. Caroline tried to hum to them, but it only accentuated the strangeness of the Indian song. She held them and was thankful for the firm press of their bodies, which kept her from shivering. When it was time for Carrie to feed, they shifted to make room. Otherwise they stayed still and quiet.

At sunup, the sound stopped.

"What was it?" she asked.

Charles propped the rifle barrel against the wall and wiped a sweaty palm across his nightshirt. "Never heard anything like it," he said. "Never even heard a story of anything like it."

It began earlier the next morning. Caroline felt it before she fully heard it. Her nerves quivering at the same high pitch, Caroline pulled the quilt from the bed and took Carrie with her to the rocking chair. Charles sat with the nose of his rifle resting on the lip of the east windowsill. They said nothing. There was nothing to say. Caroline put the baby's head under her chin, so she could feel the rhythm of the small fast heart against her own, and cupped her hand over Carrie's ear. When Mary and Laura woke, she motioned for them. They came with their quilt and hunched against her knees to hide their faces in her lap. The harder she tried to be still, the more her body trembled.

Her throat ached with inarticulate frustration. If the sound was a warning, a threat, they did not know how to heed it. It was not screaming or singing or yowling or wailing. And yet it was all of those things. It rose and rose, dipped for a merciful instant and then rose again so sharply that Caroline flinched. Even weeping had a cadence. This had none. Caroline closed her eyes and rocked, counting a deliberate tempo for each gentle sweep of the rockers across the floorboards.

One-two-three, *one*-two-three, *one*-two-three.

She dozed without any awareness of being asleep, for the sound penetrated her dreams. When she woke the sound had ceased. The vague fragments of her dreams evaporated as she blinked into the silence, but the count of the waltz, and the hot stricture in her throat, remained. *One*-two-three, *one*-two-three, *one*-two-three. As she braided Mary's and Laura's hair, stirred milk into the cornmeal, walked from the table to the fireplace. The rhythm circled her every movement until she was half-dizzy with it.

All day, her mind replicated the Indians' strange high notes at the slightest provocation. She heard them in the whinnying horses and the squeaking of the windlass and the ring of Charles's ax at the woodpile.

Anything pitched above a whine snatched her entire focus, leaving her feeling foolish and lightheaded when she realized its source. Yet when Jack broke into a deep rolling growl, Caroline went absolutely still. She knew down to her bones that this sound—the opposite of everything her senses had been attuned to—signaled something actual.

Her eyes darted to the latch string, then to the girls. They had seen her look. If Mary and Laura had not guessed already they knew now that she was afraid.

But they shall not see the depth of it, Caroline silently declared, and resisted the impulse to take the pistol down from its shelf before going to the window. With her shoulder to the wall she peered out sidelong, so as not to move the curtains. Jack was up on his back feet, straining on tiptoe against the chain on his collar, snapping at the air. Charles had put down his ax and stood with his rifle pointing east. He was not squinting down the barrel yet, but his thumb was poised to cock the hammer. Caroline's breath fogged the glass in quick bursts as she watched and waited.

A voice called out. Male. Then another.

"Eng! Gulls!"

"Eng! Gulls!"

Charles lowered the gun as two men came into view. Caroline's long exhale blanked an entire pane as she fit the syllables together: *Ingalls.* Both held rifles, the barrels propped against their shoulders.

"It's Mr. Edwards," Caroline said, "and Mr. Scott." Mary and Laura came to peep out. It could not be so bad, Caroline reasoned to herself, if Mr. Scott had left his wife and children at home. They lived to the east, nearer the Indian camps.

Scott and Edwards did not come into the house. Nor did they rest the butts of their rifles on the ground. They stood together outside the stable, talking. Their talk was at once intense and distracted. Caroline saw each of them survey the eastern horizon in turn. Jack had returned his attention to that direction, too. Edwards caught sight of her and the girls, pressed up against the window glass, and favored the children with a nod. Mary and Laura waved, but Caroline had seen the look on Edwards's face. It was more wince than smile.

When they had gone Charles called to her through the latched door. "Caroline, will you come give me a hand with the milking?"

A cold tingle threaded up Caroline's spine. He was an hour ahead of milking time. Whatever news the men had relayed could not be said inside the house. "Yes, Charles," she answered. "Mind the baby, please, Mary. I won't be long. Laura, will you pull the latch string in behind me and open the door when I come back?" Laura nodded eagerly. Caroline wound her shawl across her chest and went out.

Charles was standing in the stable, waiting. He kneaded the back of his neck as he spoke. "The removal act passed the House and the Senate in July," he said. "The Osages were granted a reservation south of the Kansas line. This land will be sold at $1.25 an acre, just as we were promised."

News they had waited months to hear. News that should have made Charles whoop and grab her up in his arms. Now he said it with a grimace.

"July," she repeated. And then, when he did not explain, "Why haven't they gone?"

"The Osages only just approved the act. They were late returning from the summer hunt and took five weeks to think it over."

That, too, was good news. Caroline peered at him. He spoke as though he were confessing a sin.

"Charles," she said. "Tell me."

"Fifty Osage warriors went into town a week after they'd approved the act. They stood in the middle of Independence and put on some kind of fancy garb and painted their faces." Caroline's skin began to creep as she pictured them undressing in the street, streaking their faces and heaven knows what else with slashes of red and black. "And then they danced," Charles said.

Caroline blinked. She could not adjust the scene in her mind to match what she had heard. "Danced?"

Charles nodded. "Scott heard it from a man who was there."

"What does it mean? Is that what they've been doing these nights?"

"I don't know. Neither did Scott. The Indian agent has called in troops."

"Thank heaven for that, at least."

Charles swallowed. He would not look at her. Caroline clutched her shawl closer about her neck even as her center filled with heat. Anger or dread would overtake her in a moment—she could not tell which.

"Charles?"

"Scott said their orders are to protect the Indians."

"The Indians?" Her voice was shrill. She spun so that he could not see her face and stood panting with shock. She would break apart. Caroline could feel it happening. Every tiny grain of her was loosening, preparing to fly apart.

"Caroline, we don't know—"

She shrugged his hand from her shoulder. "I have to get back to the girls."

Caroline did not undress that night. She craved the feel of the barrier, however slight, that her corset and stockings and shoes made between her skin and the vibrating air. She sat up in the rocking chair while Charles squatted before the fire, making bullets. Her mind roiled with unwelcome thoughts.

Why had they come? Why, when the mention of Indians made her mind recoil, had she consented to bring their children to a place called Indian Territory? Charles, of course. Charles, who made life seem like a song—a song so sweet and heartfelt she sometimes failed to hear its words. But to think that Charles would have foreseen something like this? Caroline would have laughed at the idea had she been able.

She tried instead to feel nothing. There was no room for it. In a single room with two little girls near enough to watch every blink, without even a pantry door to hide behind, there was no space for anything like anger or tears. The only place to cry was the necessary, and Caroline would not go out where that raw sound might touch her.

Again and again she watched the thin silver stream of liquid lead flow into the bullet mold, then pop out a moment later, hard and shining. If only she could do just that—pour all her scalding thoughts into a tight, smooth ball capable of piercing the very thing she was most frightened of.

Caroline imagined herself sighting down the barrel of a rifle loaded with such a bullet. Toward what would she fire? Images of Towel Thief and Green Shirt faded before fully materializing; she could no longer picture their features. Charles's face came into focus instead, and Caroline jolted back so that the rocking chair creaked.

No. She did not want to take aim. She wanted only to fire, to feel the hard recoil of the stock against her shoulder as the anger and fear were propelled outward into the empty black air.

They sat up all that night without a word passing between them. When the first cry finally sounded, Caroline gasped, as if inhaling the sound. Carrie cried, too, and would not be soothed. The harsh union of Carrie's shrieks with the Indians' made Caroline tremble with the effort of holding her own voice at bay. She pressed her forehead into the heel of her hand and plunged her fingernails slowly into her scalp. The child was hungry, yet Caroline would sooner scream herself than unbutton her bodice. It was more than the habit of concealing the key while Indians were abroad. Even with the door latched and the curtains drawn, she still did not want to bring her bare breast out into the open. As though there were any real choice in the matter. The milk would come. Caroline felt the hot pricking, half pain and half pleasure, as it corkscrewed downward, and submitted.

They did not recognize when it was over. The fifth morning came and silence rang in Caroline's ears. The sensation was oddly discomfiting. It was as though she could feel the space where the sound used to be—a space that now felt too large and open.

Caroline had been so intent on deciphering its meaning that she had lost sight of the one crucial piece of information the wailing-song had imparted: where the Indians were. Now, it seemed, they might be anywhere.

But they were not. For a day and a night she and Charles stood at the windows with weapons loaded and cocked, rebuking the children for the slightest whisper that might muffle an Indian footfall—and saw nothing. Jack paced and peered and sniffed, and did not find anything to growl at.

Near midday a quick burst of barking signaled the approach of something from the north, out of the creek bottoms. Caroline glanced first at the pistol, to be sure, yet again, that a bullet was in the chamber. She closed her eyes for an instant, peering inward for courage, before looking out.

A rider. A white handkerchief was tied to the muzzle of his rifle, which he waved in the air. Scruffy curls of golden-brown hair glinted in the sun.

Edwards. She and Charles recognized him at the same moment and flung open the door to meet him.

Edwards pulled his horse up inches from the threshold. "They're gone," he announced.

"Gone?" Charles and Caroline asked together.

"Packed up their camp and left. I went there, to see," he said.

"Mr. Edwards!" Caroline exclaimed. "They might have—" Her tongue hovered half-curled, groping for the next word. Her mind seemed to have lost its footing. They might have enacted any number of the horrors she had envisioned these last several days and nights. Plainly, they had done none of it.

Edwards nodded. "I know. I couldn't stand it any longer. Seemed like risking a look was better than sitting in my cabin, bracing for a tomahawk between the eyes every time a stick of kindling popped. I crawled on my elbows the last hundred yards," he said, tilting a forearm. The dirt was rubbed so deeply into the fabric that it shone softly, like leather. "When I finally worked up the nerve to lift my head over the grass I never felt so foolish in my life. Hardly anything there but ashes and sunflower shells and gnawed-over buffalo bones."

"Where are they now?" Caroline asked.

"South's all I know," Edwards said. "The tracks all pointed south. Winter camps, maybe, or the new reservation."

Caroline stood in the white-gold afternoon sun. *Gone.* Day after day she had listened to the world being torn asunder, and it had not happened. Every blade of grass and every atom of the broad blue sky remained as she had left it. Nothing but the terror and the ire had been real, and all of it of her own making.

It was still there. Caroline could feel it within her, a thick, dark inner lining, suddenly stripped of its purpose. A tremor came over her, clutching her by the gut and radiating upward. Her breath tasted of acid. Her body, preparing to purge itself. Caroline walked to the necessary and emptied herself of it.

Twenty-Eight

"It has to snow," Laura said. "It has to."

Caroline had given up polishing the girls' nose prints from the window panes. Their breath misted the glass until it ran in narrow streams that mirrored the rain falling just beyond their fingertips.

"Even if it does," Mary asked, "how will Santa Claus find us, so far away in Indian Territory? Ma?"

Mary had used different words yesterday, and the day before, but it was the same question. *Patience*, Caroline told herself. They would never learn to have patience for others if she could not first be patient with them. "I don't know," she said. "I expect he'll find a way. Santa Claus knew where to find my stocking when I moved from Brookfield to Concord," she added.

"That was back East," Laura said, as if it were another country. And so it was.

Caroline scrabbled for a reply. "Well, we are not the first family to move to the Indian Territory. You don't suppose all those other pas and mas would stay where Santa Claus couldn't bring presents to their little boys and girls?"

Caroline looked up from her work, ready to show them a buoyant smile. Two sets of narrowed blue eyes met hers. The difference amounted to the width of a blade of grass, but it was enough to put a twist in her conscience. Caroline squirmed. Her daughters had never looked at her that way. Was it any wonder, she asked herself, when all she gave them were answers that would not hold still?

Perhaps they would find some contentment if she said no, Santa Claus would not come this year. He would go to the Big Woods and find them gone, and bring all their presents to Kansas next year. But Edwards. Caroline could not discount the slim possibility of Mr. Edwards. He still had the nickel Charles had given him over a month ago to buy Christmas candy for the girls in Independence. What he did not have was a horse.

"You'll tell us if you run short of anything," Charles had said when Edwards came to warn them to lock their stable. Edwards had not even heard the horse thieves. He could not say whether they might be Indians or white men, though his missing saddle pointed away from Indians.

"Anything we have, you're welcome to," Caroline added.

"I'm well provisioned," Edwards assured them. "And I can still get to town so long as my boots hold out," he'd said, knocking one heel against a fencepost. None of them had given a thought to anything so trifling as Christmas candy.

Now, though, she and Charles had room in their minds for nothing else. Caroline gazed out over the girls' heads at the blurry gray morning. She longed for snow almost as much as Laura; there had never been a Christmas Eve so leaden. If the rain did not let up, it would not matter whether Edwards had fetched the girls' Christmas treats from town. Twice this week Charles had tried to reach Edwards's claim, and the rising creek had held him back.

The rain stopped as if by magic. Mary and Laura bit their lips and grinned at each other. Then Caroline opened the door to the sunlight, and their faces fell. The wild *whoosh* and tumble of the flooded creek, inaudible over the rain, now filled the room. They had not considered the creek a barrier. Of course they hadn't. Winters in Pepin, the frozen Mississippi River became the smoothest road in the county.

When Charles came in bearing a great wild turkey, Caroline looked past it to his pockets, searching for a telltale bulge.

"If it weighs less than twenty pounds I'll eat it, feathers and all," he announced.

The false boom in his voice was unmistakable. Caroline knew there was no bag of candy hidden in his coat. "My goodness, it is heavy," she said, trying to be cheerful over the turkey. Its oil-colored feathers still glistened with rain. The girls watched, disinterested, as a puddle of rainwater formed on the floor beneath the bird's dangling wattle.

"Is the creek going down?" Mary asked.

With a little sigh, Charles abandoned the charade. "It's still rising," he answered.

The news sank hard and fast. No Christmas for Mary and Laura. No company to share their turkey. Caroline blinked back the memory of how Edwards had been too pleased to smile when she asked him to dinner. "I hate to think of him eating his bachelor cooking all alone on Christmas Day."

Charles shook his head. "A man would risk his neck trying to cross that creek now."

With their chins in their hands, Mary and Laura watched her pluck and dress the turkey. Caroline wished they would go back to fogging up the windows. Their eyes had gone flat. At least with their fingers smudging the glass, they had been hopeful.

"You are lucky little girls," she said as she trussed up the bird and rubbed it with lard, "to have a good house to live in, and a warm fire to sit by, and such a turkey for your Christmas dinner." She looked up, smiling. The girls had wilted further yet.

Caroline's smile went slack. The words might have come out of her own mother's mouth. True though they were, it was she who ought to have been grateful— grateful that her children had grown up without want, that they had never felt the sort of cold and hunger that made it impossible to take food and warmth and shel- ter for granted. Instead she had as good as rubbed her daughters' noses in their disappointment. Caroline did not know how to make them understand, short of tell- ing them things she hoped never to speak of, stories that began *After my pa died . . .*

The fire popped and hissed into the stillness. The girls lay in their bed with their eyes to the rafters, obedi- ently waiting for the day to end.

"Why don't you play the fiddle, Charles?"

He looked into the fireplace. "I don't seem to have the heart to, Caroline." His words might have been made of water, he was so sodden with disappointment.

Caroline could not stand it. "I'm going to hang up your stockings, girls," she declared. "Maybe something will happen." They looked at her with such wonder, Caroline's heart did not know whether to break or swell. She strode to the mantel and hung their two limp stockings beneath the china shepherdess. It was thanks to Edwards that she could do even this much, Caroline thought as she threaded the wool over the borrowed nails. Silently she wished him a happy Christmas. "Now go to sleep," she said to Mary and Laura. "Morning will come quicker if you're asleep." Eager now, they squinched their eyes shut and tunneled deeper into the quilts. Caroline lingered there with her fingertips still on the mantel. Her thumb brushed the head of one nail as she looked down on her daughters. It was so easy to forget, now that there was Carrie, how little Mary and Laura still were. Quickly she bent and kissed them good night a second time and returned to her chair.

Caroline heard herself humming faintly as she rocked. She gave no thought to the tune. Her mind scoured the cabin, pondering what sort of Christmas she might patch together. It must be something new and fresh, or Mary and Laura would not be fooled.

Nothing from the scrap bag or the button box. Paper dolls might lift a rainy afternoon, but she could not expect them to bear the weight of Christmas morning. There could be no molasses candy without snow, nor vanity cakes without eggs.

Charles's voice was hardly a murmur. "You've only made it worse, Caroline."

Caroline's stomach seized at the thought of them waking to empty stockings tomorrow morning. She had been careful to say *maybe*, but by hanging those stockings she had made them a promise, no matter the words she used. Something in that cabin must have the power to delight two little girls, her mind insisted, especially two little girls whose entire afternoon might have been altered by something as simple as a snowflake.

"No, Charles," she said as an idea shaped itself. "There's the white sugar." Together with what was left of the white flour she would make two sweet white patty cakes, drifted with sugar.

He scraped at a hangnail. "Walked two miles in both directions, looking for a safe place to cross. Should have thought of Christmas candy when I went to Oswego," he said to his knees. "I took for granted there'd be time for another trip to Independence."

"Charles," she said. He raised his head. The look on

his face belonged to a child. Caroline felt her center go soft, as it did when Carrie whimpered. "I can manage," she promised. His expression eased some—grateful, and at the same time ashamed of his gratitude. That could not be helped. For all his looking ahead, this once Charles had failed. Rain and horse thieves did not disguise that plain fact. Caroline could not tell him otherwise. But she would do what she could to shelter the children from his oversight.

White flour, white sugar, lard, and milk. Saleratus, and a pinch of nutmeg. The white flour was so silky and cool, Caroline mixed the dough bare-handed until it was warm and smooth as her own skin. She rolled it into a thick circle as large as the pie plate, then neatened the rough edges with the heels of her hands. With a knife she cut out two hearts and dredged them with white sugar until they glittered faintly in the lamplight. Quietly, she placed a layer of stones in the bottom of the bake oven, laid the heart-shaped cakes carefully into the pie plate, and lowered the plate into the oven.

It was an extravagance, all that white sugar and flour. And yet it felt paltry. There ought to have been layer cakes, and cookies, and squiggles of boiled sugar candy, Caroline thought as she sat vigil by the bake oven. Swedish crackers, vinegar pie, dried apple pie.

The cabin should be heady with brown sugar and clove, and the rich velvety scent of beans and salt pork lazily bubbling in molasses. At the very least, a dried black-berry pie. Even without a cookstove, Caroline knew she could have contrived to make some of it.

We have left undone those things which we ought to have done.

Caroline's skin prickled at the gravity of the words. *An empty cookie jar is not a sin,* she assured herself. But still her throat grew hot and tight. Charles had been merely remiss, while hers was a disregard so sly she had been unable to recognize it. It was as if she believed she could keep Christmas from coming, Caroline thought, pressing an apron corner to her nose, as though without the sweet smells and tastes to remind her, she would not think to miss Eliza and Peter, and Henry and Polly. Or, she thought with a deep-belly resonance that signaled the greater truth, it was as if she believed the special things they'd so enjoyed to-gether should not be enjoyed apart.

Caroline Ingalls, what nonsense! That's what Eliza would say. Caroline could hear her sister's incredulous laugh, see her starry-black eyelashes blinking back tears at the very idea. And Polly—Polly would be too heartbroken even to scold at the thought of such a be-reft Christmas. Caroline shook her head, thankful that it would not occur to either of them to imagine what she had done. For oh, how it would hurt them to see her like this.

I'm sorry, she thought to Eliza and Polly, and to Charles and the girls. *I'm sorry.*

Silently Caroline unlocked her trunk and pulled out the blue tissue paper she had saved from the cake of store-bought soap. A trace of rose scent still clung to it. She teased the two thin layers apart and laid one patty cake in the center of each, taking care to keep the surface that had touched the soap to the outside as she wrapped them. The paper would rip when the girls pulled their gifts from their stockings, no matter how gentle they were. She was not sure herself whether she could nestle the little packets into the stockings without tearing them. Caroline touched her fingertips to the frail tissue one last time.

Jack growled, rousing the hairs at the back of Caroline's neck. She shrugged, trying to rub the sensation away with her collar. It was only what Caroline thought of as his grumbling growl, the sound he made to let them know there was someone passing outside. She cast about for something to hush him—a scrap of salt pork or a dab of leftover stew—before he woke the girls. But the bulldog's growl deepened, shifting into a warning aimed at whatever was approaching the cabin door. He gave one sharp bark.

Caroline panicked. The girls were already stirring and their stockings were still empty. She snatched up a dishtowel and tossed it over the presents.

"Ingalls! Ingalls!"

Her head snapped toward Charles. His face mirrored her own bewilderment.

Charles blocked Jack with his boot and threw open the door. There stood Edwards. Edwards, fairly jingling with cold, the ends of his hair crackling with half-formed ice.

"Great fishhooks, Edwards!" Charles cried. "Come in, man! What's happened?"

Edwards stepped gingerly, as though his boots were lined with frost. "Carried my clothes—on my head—when I waded the creek," he gasped.

Caroline's mouth fell open. That icy, raging creek. She shuddered at the thought of all that cold water rushing past her own bare skin and did not imagine any further.

"I'll be all right, soon as I get some heat in me."

"Oh!" said Caroline, and ran for the kettle and the stew pot.

Charles shook his head. He was still trying to picture it and having no better luck than she. "It was too big a risk, Edwards," he said, heaping the fire with fresh wood. "We're glad you're here, but that was too big a risk for a Christmas dinner."

"Your little ones had to have a Christmas," Edwards replied with a cock of his head. "No creek could stop me, after I fetched them their gifts from Independence."

Caroline's heart stopped beating. If he were joking about such a thing, she would not know how to forgive him.

"Did you see Santa Claus?" Laura shouted. She was up on her knees in the bed, like a dog begging.

Caroline stilled every thought, trying to imagine how she might absorb the words from the air if Edwards's answer was not what her children needed it to be.

"I sure did," Edwards said, matter-of-factly. Mary and Laura erupted into a flurry of questions. "Wait, wait a minute," Edwards laughed. He opened up his coat and brought an oilcloth sack from an inside pocket. Caroline took it dumbly. The stiff fabric was creased with cold. Then Edwards sat down cross-legged on the floor beside the girls' bed, and leaning forward with his elbows on his knees, he spun Mary and Laura a tale tall enough to rival the likes of Mike Fink and Davy Crockett.

Caroline opened the mouth of the sack and everything else melted from her consciousness. Two gleaming tin cups. Two long sticks of peppermint candy as big around as her thumb. And winking up from the bottom of each cup, a new copper penny. Her throat burned and her eyes swam. How many months had it been since he'd seen Mary and Laura sharing their single tin cup, and he had remembered. The sudden burst of affection she felt toward Edwards was too big for her heart, too big for her chest. She filled the stockings with shaking fingers, then sat down on the edge of the big bed and scooped up Carrie. Carrie's warm body filled her arms. Caroline held the baby close, pressing gently, gently, with each grateful thud of her heart.

"We shook hands," Edwards told the girls, "then Santa Claus swung up onto his fine bay horse and called, 'So long Edwards!' And I watched him whistle his way down the Fort Dodge trail until he and his pack mule disappeared around a bend." Edwards leaned back with a smart nod that said, *There!*

Mary and Laura regarded Edwards as though they were not sure he was fully real. A man who had spoken to Santa Claus—shaken his hand!—sitting near enough to touch. They had entirely forgotten their stockings.

Caroline waited a moment, savoring their awestruck faces before she prompted, "You may look now, girls."

Half a second passed before they understood. Then they flew to the hearth in a tumble of bare feet and red flannel. There had never been such squealing and laughing. Right away Laura wanted to feel and taste everything about her gifts. She pretended to drink from her empty cup, licked her peppermint stick, nibbled the underside of her patty cake. Mary held each object with utter reverence, reluctant to touch their surfaces overmuch and mar their aura of newness. She only stood, utterly transfixed by the brilliance that now belonged to her: the cool polished tin, the twirling red stripes, the bright white sugar.

The way Edwards watched the both of them—smiling, yet subdued, his eyes far away as if he were envisioning faces other than the ones shining before him—made Caroline wonder. Were there little boys and girls somewhere in Tennessee, lonely for their Uncle Edwards this Christmas? Once her mind had invented them, Caroline could not think otherwise. Silently she thanked Edwards's nieces and nephews, real or imagined, for the loan of him.

"Are you sure your stockings are empty?" Caroline asked just when the girls' giddiness had begun to dwindle.

They blinked at her—all of them but Edwards, even Charles. Caroline nodded toward the stockings, and

Mary and Laura obediently snaked their hands down to the toes. Caroline watched the puzzlement drop from the girls' faces as their fingertips brushed smooth, cold copper. They froze, wide-eyed, and looked at each other. Both of them knew what it must be, yet could not believe it. Even as the coins emerged pinched between thumb and forefinger, they could not fathom possessing such a thing. They held their pennies wonderingly in the palms of their hands, as if the coins might melt like snowflakes if they dared turn away.

Caroline smiled so broadly, her temples ached. Who but a bachelor would think to give two little girls a penny apiece? Only a man without children would think so broadly, unhampered by any limits as to what kinds of things could come out of Santa Claus's sack. At the Richards brothers' dry-goods store in Pepin, those cups could not have cost less than four cents each. What he had paid for them in Independence, and the candy besides, Caroline did not want to suppose. And yet it was the pennies that dazzled them. After all that she and Charles had fretted, believing they had nothing worthy of their daughters' Christmas. It was like a parable, acted out before her own hearth.

Laura plunked her penny into her cup and jingled it round and round. Mary studied hers, making out the numbers stamped on its face. "One. Eight. Seven.

Zero," she read, triumphant. Caroline nodded her praise, happy beyond speech.

They would never, never forget this Christmas. None of them. Already Caroline could feel the morning embedding itself in her own memory. Her mind was bottling it whole, so that it would remain fresh and glistening as a jar of preserves.

Charles gave a little cough that was not a cough at all. He pumped Edwards's hand up and down, broke loose to give his nose a quick swipe with his cuff, and took Edwards's hand again, holding it so firm and steady that Caroline could feel the gratitude passing between them. She stood to offer her own thanks, and Edwards's hand disappeared into his coat pocket. Out came a sweet potato. Then another, and another, each one a full handful. Caroline did not have arms enough to hold them. Edwards piled them into her apron until the knotted ties at her back strained with the weight. Nine fat, knobby sweet potatoes.

There was no name for what she felt for Edwards then. She had never felt this way toward anyone. Her husband, her brothers. There was not a reason in the world for Edwards to have been so generous. Never in all her life had there been a Christmas so rich.

"Oh," Edwards said, and patted his shirtfront. Something rustled partway down. He undid a button and drew out two envelopes. "Mail," he said simply. One went to Charles, the other he held out to Caroline.

At the sight of Eliza's handwriting on the envelope, Caroline felt her face crumple. She could not get her breath; she was crying without tears. The paper was warm, the envelope so fat it could only be the circulator. Eliza and Peter, Ma and Papa Frederick, Henry and Polly, Martha and Charley. All of them had put their hands to these pages. Caroline pulled a hairpin loose and slit open the envelope where she stood.

Ma had begun the letter as she always did: *Dear Children . . .*

The words filled her chest. One person at least knew she was yet a child in this world. *Oh, Ma,* she thought as comfort rained through her. Caroline's lips fluttered as she read the first lines—scolding them all, as ever, for not writing more and sooner—holding her suspended between laughter and tears. *Save some of it,* Caroline urged herself. *News won't spoil; don't gorge yourself all at once.* Only she could not fold it back up without treating herself to a glimpse of Eliza's section. What Caroline saw there sent a warm shiver through her, as though her sister's news had reached out and brushed every inch of her skin.

"Eliza and Peter had a boy in April," she told Charles, "named for your father."

"That's fine news," Charles said. He held a twenty-dollar banknote in his hand. "First payment from Gustafson," he explained. "Sent it on the third of September." Almost a year since they'd left, and Gustafson had sent what amounted to two dollars a month. A spark of unease nipped at her, then winked out as soon as her eyes returned to Eliza's news. *Lansford Newcomb Ingalls arrived April 5, 1870.* Caroline touched her fingertips to the baby's name, imagining a boy with Eliza's bright eyes and Peter's gangly limbs; the soft Quiner mouth, the untamable Ingalls hair. She looked at the date on Eliza's portion of the letter and marveled at the passage of time. The nephew in her mind was only a few minutes old, yet by now the real Lansford Newcomb Ingalls must be crawling.

The dipper jangled in the water bucket—Laura, trying out her new cup. Caroline blinked once before realizing that of course she was still in Kansas. For the briefest flicker of consciousness, she had been wholly elsewhere. Not so far away as Wisconsin, Caroline was too far grown for that sort of make-believe, but someplace both high above and deep within, where distance was of no consequence. That was as much a gift as the letter itself.

She turned to Edwards, ready to lavish him with thanks. His face, both wistful and sated, stopped her.

She could not escape the sense that it was he who was trying to repay them for kindnesses already given. Had a plate of white flour dumplings and a half dozen fiddle tunes by the fireside meant so much? Caroline regarded her neighbor more thoughtfully, recalling how he had settled his shivering self right down on the floor alongside the girls and launched into his Santa Claus tale without taking a sip of hot coffee or turning his palms toward the fireplace. That alone gave her cause to believe that Edwards wanted no more than to feel at home with family. To laud his generosity and enthrone him as a guest of honor now? That would almost certainly spoil his pleasure.

It was a guess, and one she was willing to hazard aloud. "Charles," she said, "why don't you and Mr. Edwards see to the stock while I warm the stew and set the breakfast table for five?"

Charles looked at her as if she'd blasphemed. But Caroline saw the happiness soak Edwards straight through. He buttoned up his coat, loped to the milk pail, and called, "C'mon, Ingalls!"

Caroline could not remember the last time she had been so full. Of food, of affection, of gratitude. The cabin was redolent of tobacco, peppermint sticks, gravy, and browned sweet potato skins. She had allowed Edwards the satisfaction of gallantly refusing the rocking chair, and so she rocked Carrie in her lap while the men leaned over the table with their pipes and picked at what remained of the turkey.

"What's the news from town, Edwards?" Charles asked.

Edwards glanced at Mary and Laura's bed. "Little ones asleep, ma'am?"

Caroline nodded. Laura was snuggled up with her new tin cup.

"Is there trouble?" Charles asked.

Edwards nodded. "Up in Cherry Township. A young doctor from Pennsylvania tried to run a half-breed and his family off his claim. Fella's name is Mosher. Guess he's part Osage, but he married a white woman. Been there four years, even raised a few fruit trees. A week ago yesterday Doc Campbell's posse ordered Mosher and his wife and child out of their beds in the night and torched the cabin. Pistol-whipped the lot of them right there in the yard while the place burned." Edwards's eyes flicked toward Caroline. He dropped his voice further. "I hear Mrs. Mosher's in the family way."

A twinge of horror iced across Caroline's middle. "Mercy on us," she said.

"Yes, ma'am." Edwards turned a turkey rib in his hands as he spoke. "Marched the whole family into the woods in their nightclothes. Those Campbells must have threatened him something fierce."

"Are they all right?"

"I hear Mosher was well enough to register a complaint with the Indian Board, but beyond that I don't rightly know. A few days after that, another half-breed's cabin was torn down."

The news was so at odds with all that had happened that day, Caroline could not make a place for it to lodge in her mind. It hung outside of her, like something that had happened in a book instead of two townships northeast. The men seemed ashamed of it—Charles for asking and Edwards for telling. They scraped silently at the turkey carcass until Charles asked with a note of cheer so deliberate it was jarring, "Did I ever tell you about the time my father took a sow sledding on the Sabbath?"

"Twice," Edwards said. Caroline burst out laughing.

"I'm sorry, Charles," she said, then buttoned her lips between her teeth so that they could not smile.

Charles grinned and shook his pipe at her like a schoolmaster brandishing a pointer. "Caroline Ingalls, you are not the least bit sorry."

"Did I ever tell *you* how I got the coonskin for my cap?" Edwards countered.

Charles shook his head.

488 · SARAH MILLER

"Well," Edwards said. "I wasn't but eight years old, and I treed a fat old daddy raccoon one Saturday night at twilight, right in our own front yard. My mama said it'd be a sin if I shot and dressed one of God's creatures on the Sabbath, so I asked her for my blanket and my catechism and sat under that chestnut tree all night and all day Sunday, studying the sacraments and waiting to shoot that varmint. I kept the Sabbath and the raccoon, both." Charles leaned back against the wall and chuckled. "He was so big, Mama made me two caps—one boy-sized and one man-sized. When I outgrew the one, she lopped off the tail and sewed it onto the other."

Caroline watched the smoke from the men's pipes twine together as they all laughed. She blew out a long, silent exhale, envisioning how the smoke of her breath would meld with the tobacco smoke were they sitting outside before a campfire instead of under the good roof Charles had built with Edwards's nails. It was moments like these that she had envied when Charles had gone to help build Edwards's house, moments when the thread of one story joined into the next, forming a lattice of shared memories. The thread extended toward her now, well within reach, if she dared unlock her store of memories to grasp it.

"I remember—" Caroline ventured. The men turned toward her, the lift of their brows encouraging. "It was the year we were married, Charles. Thomas and Papa Frederick strung up a swing on the big maple tree beside the riverbank for Lottie. My half sister," she explained to Edwards, "she must have been six or seven years old. It was a perfect place for a swing, all smothered in shade, and the river so near, you felt as if you might sail straight over it and land on your feet on the opposite bank." The smell of that place wafted through her mind, green and silvery and dappled with yellow sun. "We called it Lottie's swing, though the big boys and girls used it just as much as she did, never mind that every one of us was at least ten years older than she. Lottie never complained, until the day one of the cows decided to take a swing." Edwards's face twitched. He squinted at her, to see if he were being teased. Caroline went on without a stroke of embellishment. "That cow walked up to the plank seat, put her front feet through, and she was stuck. She couldn't walk more than three steps before the swing scraped her udder, and she didn't know how to back out. Oh, how that cow bawled." The men snorted with laughter, even Charles, who knew the story as well as she did. She might have stopped there, but the memory, once loosened, begged to be stretched to its full length. "Lottie just shrieked, she was so taken aback. That was the only time in my life I saw Papa Frederick come running. It winded him so, he wheezed like a broken penny whistle when he laughed. Thomas had to cut the ropes to get the cow out. Lottie cried and cried. She declared she wouldn't drink a drop of milk until Thomas fixed the swing." Edwards shook his head and slapped his thigh, and Caroline feasted on the knowledge that he would tell this story by the light of campfires and hearths for years to come.

It was as fine a day as Caroline could remember. She felt it tapering to a close well before Edwards pocketed his pipe and looked resignedly at his coat. "Let me at least warm it by the fire," Caroline offered.

Edwards raised his palms to her. "I've stayed longer than I ought to already," he said, rising, "and I'm as warm as I'm likely to be. Once I get into the creek, it won't matter if you've set me ablaze, coat and all."

Caroline winced. She had forgotten the creek. The water would be black, its cold surface like a blade against the skin. The moon was no more than the width of an onion skin.

"You know you're welcome to stay," Charles said.

Edwards shrugged into his coat. "And I thank you."

"You'll come back if the current is too high," Caroline added. He wouldn't, she knew that, but it bore saying.

Edwards touched his mittened fingers to Carrie's belly and gave her a jiggle. "Next year it'll be your turn for a treat from Santa Claus, little miss," he told her. He looked at Mary and Laura, content in their beds, and nodded to himself. Their happiness bolstered him, Caroline mused, as if they were his own.

Had he been Henry, or Peter, Caroline would have taken hold of his arms and leaned her cheek against his then. Instead she laid a hand on his sleeve and pressed, gently. "Merry Christmas, Mr. Edwards," she said.

His long, flat smile all but cut his face in two. "Merry Christmas, Mrs. Ingalls," he replied.

Twenty-Nine

They prepared for the purchase of the plow, both she and Charles, as though it were an impending birth. When they ate from their first harvest, it would join them with the land, not unlike how Mary had joined them. Her existence had fused them in a way they could not otherwise achieve, even when their bodies were linked one within the other. So it would be with the plow and the prairie. The blade would part the soil, so that it could be filled with seeds. As soon as the crops had put down roots and began reaching up out of the ground, there would be no mistaking to whom this quarter section belonged. After that, the papers and the filing were a formality.

Every pelt nailed to the cabin wall, scraped clean, and worked soft before the fire was as good as a banknote, stacked up against the purchase. All winter long, the talk was of little else. While they worked, they spoke of the seeds Charles would buy, not only this year but the next and the next, and of which section of earth would best suit each variety. Charles had every acre mapped out in his mind, and he could twist and turn his plans for each one like a kaleidoscope. Hearing him talk night after night of the varying patterns, Caroline savored the knowledge that the plow was already rooting Charles to the land. From time to time he must hunt, of course, but the planting, watering, and hoeing required that he stay within earshot of the cabin. With luck, Caroline promised herself, she and the girls might never be alone with the Indians again.

There was no time for music that season. Instead there was the rhythmic slop and slap of brain slurry rubbed onto dried hides. Charles brought her the brains, which she screwed into canning jars until they were needed. If it was cold enough, they were put out to freeze. When it was not, she put the jars in a pail and lowered them down into the cool shaft of the well.

Once a hide was scraped and stretched and dried and soaked, Caroline heated a bowl of water on the hearth until it was just warm enough to bathe a baby. Then she unjarred a brain and kneaded it into the warm water, grinding the soft bits between her fingertips to form the milky slurry that Charles would rub into the rawhide to tan it.

With the head of a dulled hoe, Charles scraped the moisture from the brained hides until they were barely damp. Jack sat beside him, waiting to lick up the accumulated scum of liquid rawhide that Charles wiped from the blade every so often. Finally he wrapped the hides around the bedpost and worked them back and forth—as though polishing the toe of a shoe—to turn them smooth and supple.

All winter long, the house smelled of brains and skins and sweat. Caroline took to looking out the east window as she worked. There would be her kitchen garden. She could see it as clearly as Charles could see his fields of corn and sod potatoes: cucumbers, tomatoes, and onions, squash and carrots and beans, all drenched in the morning sun. In the afternoon, the cabin would shade the plants from the harshest heat. She would plant them as she always had, so that the rows of colors would meld from one to the next in a living rainbow. All those seeds had come from home. Wisconsin seeds bred in Kansas ground. Like Carrie, Caroline thought, and smiled. Alongside Polly's cucumbers there would be sweet potatoes, from Mr. Edwards, for she had saved one back from Christmas dinner. As soon as the ground softened and the sunlight grew less watery, she would bring in a few spadefuls of earth and start the sweet potato in a flat before the window. Perhaps when Charles went to Oswego for the plow, she could busy herself and the girls for an afternoon with that small task.

They were both of them giddy the day Charles set out for Oswego. Giddy and giggly, for Caroline had a case of hiccoughs that interrupted every attempt Charles made to kiss her goodbye. Carrie squawked in surprise with every spasm that jostled her. Caroline laughed herself breathless. Finally Charles kissed Mary and Laura all over their faces and said, "Give that to your ma!" They just about knocked her down with kissing her.

The next days were chill and muddy, but Caroline could feel a change in the cold, as though a warm breath had been exhaled into it. Each evening before supper the girls came in rosy-cheeked, a faint halo of sweat dampening the hair beneath their woolen wraps. In the morning, the lines of the hopscotch squares Caroline had traced in the yard for them the day before were crystalized with frost.

The first three days passed easily. On the fourth, the girls ticked like pocket watches, conscious of every minute. "Last time it was only four days," Laura complained on the fifth morning.

"Pa came home so late on the fourth night, it might as well have been five," Caroline reminded her.

Laura frowned as though she'd been tricked. "Today is five. That means Pa has to come home today." she declared. Caroline made no attempt to dissuade her. Charles would be home or he wouldn't; nothing she said would soften Laura's disappointment if he did not arrive on time.

Neither could she pretend that her own anticipation was not buoyed higher and higher as the day passed. Every few minutes she glanced up from plucking the prairie chicken Mr. Edwards had brought the day before to glance down the creek road. The wagon would be brimful. Not only with the new steel plow and the seeds, but fresh sacks of flour, sugar, and cornmeal. Caroline thought of salt pork, fried until the fat had crisped, and licked her lips. That would be a treat to savor after so much lean winter game. She had not asked for anything for herself. There was nothing she particularly wanted, except perhaps a letter. With the expense of the plow, there might not be enough to spare for extras, though she hoped for Mary's and Laura's sakes that there would be. Surely a stick of penny candy, at least. Charles never forgot his girls.

As she admired the pictures in her mind, Caroline

found herself humming without regard for where the tune had come from. When she realized, she swallowed and stood still, listening, to be sure.

Indians.

It could not be. Their camps had been empty since before Christmas. But it was. There was no mistaking that sound. She let go of the fistful of feathers and wiped the sweat from her palms. Was that why Edwards had come calling the day before? She had been so pleased by the prairie chicken, she suspected nothing but neighborliness.

Caroline felt as she had the night on the prairie when they had lost Jack and Charles had nearly shot the bulldog by mistake as he approached the campfire. Her body had poised itself on the edge of fear, but her mind was not yet fully afraid. Her mind wanted to know more. She went to the window and listened again.

It was music, at least. The melody was unlike any song she had ever sung, but Caroline could find the pattern in it. The beat was choppy, like the sound of the girls jumping in and out of their hopscotch squares. Perhaps that was why she had not recognized its source sooner. This song was the opposite in every way of the sounds they had heard in the fall. Even as she cautioned herself that she could not be sure, Caroline ascribed joyfulness to it.

What sort of song would they sing after killing a man?

Caroline stepped back, bewildered. That thought had come from her, as if her mind had no concern for the consequences of its thoughts. "Stop that," she said, as though one of the children had talked back to her. It had no business asking such questions of its own accord, questions she did not want asked, much less answered.

A little more than two hours after that, Charles was home. Laura yelped and Jack whined, but Caroline did not let them outside to greet him. She went alone to help him unload. Together they hefted the new plow into the stable. Charles locked the door.

The Indians were still singing.

"I thought they'd gone," Caroline said.

Charles sighed. He had expected this, though Caroline could not tell whether his reaction was composed of relief or dread. "So did I. Word in town is they've come back from the winter camps one last time," he said. "The Indian agent will lead them south to the new reservation in a few weeks."

She felt herself calculating the time as if it were an absolute measure—as Laura had calculated Charles's absence. Not a couple, not several. A few. Three weeks, then. Twenty-one days. She would allow them that much without complaint. Every day of it, she would pray morning and night for their departure.

Inside the cabin all was smiles and jollity. Charles had traded well. Everything they needed and more was piled on the table, down to coffee and seed potatoes. Instead of white sugar he had bought all manner of treats. Out of a paper sack came a packet of crackers and a jar of cucumber pickles. Caroline's mouth and eyes both watered at the sight of those little green gherkins bobbing in their brine. It had been nearly a year since she had asked him to look for pickles at the store in Independence, and all that time he had not forgotten.

From beneath the flour sack Charles drew an oblong package, wrapped in paper and tied with white string. He dropped it onto the table with a soft slap and raised his eyebrows at her. It could only be fabric—enough for a new spring dress. Caroline pinched her lip between her teeth as she untied the wrapping. Charles had only once come close to choosing a calico she did not like, but his indifference toward the proprieties of fashion always carried a certain amount of risk. He would have bought yards and yards of brilliant Turkey red, if he thought she possessed the gumption to wear it.

Caroline exhaled at the sight of it. The softest lavender ground, like lilacs, with a spray of feathery gray fern leaves. In the center lay a fat coil of narrow gray braid to trim the hem. Had there been a woman at the store to help him coordinate the goods? she wondered. They complemented each other perfectly: the trim, a few shades darker than the gray in the fabric, serving to accentuate the delicate pattern. The calico was Charles's doing, that was sure. Lavender was not a color she would have thought to choose for herself. It was a demure shade, fit for a little girl's Sunday best, and entirely impractical for an everyday dress.

Caroline loved it. Under the hot Kansas sun it would be gentle to the skin and refreshing to the eye. Already she could imagine how Charles would look at her when she wore it. He loved to see her wreathed in color.

"It's too much," she told him, as she always did.

His face told her it wasn't nearly enough, as it always did.

For the girls there were cunning little black rubber hair combs that fit like bandeaus, with a star shape cut out from the center and backed with ribbon. Blue satin for Mary and red satin for Laura, just as if Caroline had picked them out herself. The girls were enraptured. They gazed at each other, then swapped combs so they could see their own. Laura put hers on Jack and squealed with laughter at his dubious face, crowned by such finery.

"Charles, you didn't get yourself a thing," Caroline said. His eyes twinkled at her. Both of them knew that was not true.

Thirty

Caroline stirred one more half spoonful of sugar into the pot of stewed dried blackberries, smiling to herself. Charles would not expect a treat at noon, in the middle of the week. She could hear him calling to the mustangs: *Gee up now, Pet. Come on, girls! Straight and true, straight and true.* Below his voice, the blade of the plow went sighing through the earth. Caroline smiled inwardly. Charles handled that plow as though it were another wife, as though he had never owned such a thing. She suspected he had named it. In a minute she would send Laura out to wave him in for dinner. Mary was laying the table, and the cornbread needed only to brown.

Caroline watched Carrie kicking her feet in and out of a sunbeam. She was so different than her sisters had been at this age, with their dimpled knees and deep creases of fat like furrows encircling their wrists and ankles. Carrie was lean and narrow, a little jackrabbit of a baby. Yet Caroline could not look at her puncturing the air with her small sharp heels and think that she was not beginning to thrive in her own hardy way.

The sunlight dimmed between kicks. Carrie lay poised, her feet ready to strike. Slowly her kinked legs sank toward her belly as she bored with waiting. Caroline lifted her eyebrows and made an *O* of her mouth, in hopes the baby would mirror her surprise rather than be vexed. Carrie gurgled in agreement. The sunbeam had played a fine trick, melting into the air. The firelight seemed to brighten by contrast while Caroline stirred the pot of blackberries, until it might have been dawn instead of noon.

"I do believe it's going to storm," she said to the girls. But the light was wrong. Rather than clouding, it had shrunken somehow, turned down like the wick in a lamp. Yet through the west window, the sky was clear. A dissonant twang sounded in her mind. Caroline put down the spoon and went out to look. Halfway across the room, she saw. To the south, the sky was black.

The smell reached the cabin at the same moment as Charles's shout: "Prairie fire!"

For one crystalline moment, it was beautiful. Like silk, like water. Orange and yellow, a perfect saturation of color writhing over the prairie. The great curve of flame caressed the earth, its long arms slowly undulating outward. The fire itself did not appear to move forward at all. The black spume of smoke billowed so high and wide, it seemed instead as if the landscape were surging forward, passing into it.

Her eyes feasted on the blaze, unable to deny its splendor, but Caroline's mind made no concession. The radiant vista before her did not simply burn; it consumed. It fed on all that was put before it with the indifference of a threshing machine. If they themselves passed through it, there would be nothing left on the other side but the empty chaff of their bodies.

Caroline ran.

Bucket after bucket of water. Up from the well, into the washtub. Burlap sacks snatched from the stable, pressed down into the tub. The burlap would not take the water fast enough. It bubbled up around her hands, tried to float, even as the water beaded over the coarse fabric. All manner of creatures fled past her as she struggled. Rabbits, prairie chickens, snakes, and mice, dashing toward the creek. From them rose a nameless sound, a frantic rush of panting and scurrying.

"Hurry, Caroline!" Charles cried. He was tying the

team to the stable, plow and all. "That fire's coming faster than a horse can run."

Caroline opened the mouth of one sack and dragged it through the tub like a dipper, scooping the water into it. Then Charles was beside her, taking up one handle of the washtub. Together they staggered toward the fire line. *Faster!* urged her legs. *Mustn't spill,* warned her brain. Everything in the world moved in the opposite direction, even the fire itself. A jackrabbit leapt over the tub right between them, fearless in its panic.

A crooked gash in the earth framed the house and yard. Two slashes slanting south from the half-plowed field and a third joining them east to west. "I couldn't plow but one furrow; there isn't time," Charles panted, and dashed back to the house.

One furrow. Fifteen inches of bare dirt to wall them off from the fire. The torn sod lay belly up, the exposed roots splayed in every direction. Those fine white threads would burn quick as hair, Caroline thought. She stood before the advancing curtain of smoke and flame, aware now of its warmth against her skin. Its roar was such that there was no other sound, almost no sound at all—only the faintest of crackling as it licked and chewed its way over the grass. One furrow, and one tub of water.

Charles came out of the house at a run with a stick of

firewood held like a candle in one fist. His other hand shielded the small flame. He stepped over the furrow and touched flame to grass. Behind him the air shimmered.

The fire Charles set was so small, Caroline could have held it in the palm of her hand. It seemed made of a different element from the blaze that engulfed the horizon. These flames were not enough to cook over. They only lapped placidly at the blades of grass within their own circumference, oblivious to their freedom. "Burn," she urged. Whispering, as though the big fire might be the one to hear and obey. "*Burn.*" Charles lit another, and another. The grass began to hiss and seethe. One by one, the little fires seemed to reach out and join hands. A thread of orange spread itself around the house. *Ring around the rosy,* Caroline's thoughts sang. *Ashes, ashes.*

A hot current of air gusted from the south, and the little flames bowed down. Caroline watched as a clump of roots lit up. They looked like fine wires, all gold and copper. Like Charles's whiskers in the light from the hearth. Then the flames were on her side of the furrow.

Put it out.

With the swing of the wet burlap, Caroline felt her mind unhitching itself. *Shuuush* went the sack through the flaming grass. Again. And again. She heard the sounds of her own exertion as she swung and stamped, felt the heaving of her chest as she grunted. Her heels bit into the soil as she ran to the next fire. When it was gone, there was another—two more, three. Where her thoughts had been, there was only clean space. Beyond that space was an awareness that the fires north of the furrow must not be allowed to spread. The children were north of the furrow. And the house, and the livestock. The command hung suspended in front of her, where she could not lose sight of it. The fire could penetrate her skin with its heat and her lungs with its smoke, but it could not touch that edict.

A dickcissel, wing tips flaming, streaked to the ground. Breast to the sky, it flapped, spattering flames into the yard. Caroline's sack swooped down. The little bulge pulsed, heart-like, beneath the burlap. Caroline brought her heel over it and stamped. Beneath the crunch a single desperate squirm, then nothing. She ran to the next small blaze.

Her cheeks were dry and taut. Her feet were wet, and the hem of her dress. The line of sweat down her back met with the spray from the swinging wet sack. None of it had significance. There was only awareness. Each sensation briefly registered and then was dismissed. Only those things that might prevent her from beating out the next fire were retained. The lightening of the sack as the water evaporated. The blurring of her vision and the cough that cut her breath if she lingered downwind of the smoke.

The change did not sink in immediately. No more than one surface of her body had felt the approaching fire as it loomed up out of the south in a flat, pulsating wall. The heat intensified as it neared, but its shape never altered. No matter which side of her body faced the blaze, it met her squarely. Then Caroline's cheeks felt the heat bend incrementally. It crept along the curve of her face, but her skin did not communicate the meaning of that fact to her mind until she became aware of the hot waves beating against both of her temples at once.

Caroline looked up and saw the fire breaking in two, the sky a blue-white knife between the wedges of flame. There was no backfire now. The two had fused some half-dozen rods south of the furrow, then split sideways, plain as a square-dance call. *Forward and back, bend the line!* Two lines of flame meeting, rotating, and parting.

Two flanks, east and west, rose on either side of the break. The cabin stood in a valley of orange and yellow. Above it, a narrow streak of pale, pale blue. Charles's voice shouted: "West!"

Caroline flew to the washtub, doused a fresh burlap

sack, and ran with it to the western furrow. She beat and beat at the ground. She trampled the grass, slashed at the bare roots with the heels of her shoes. That it was not yet burning did not matter. She would allow the flames no easy place to roost.

The first spark alighted in her hair. Caroline raked it loose and smothered it in her fist. There was no pulse or squirm like the dickcissel. It ceased to burn and was gone. More sparks, and more dropped from the sky as the western flank of the fire swept alongside the furrow. One and another and another, slow to burn, yet accumulating faster than she could extinguish alone. She ran and panted and swung, while all around her the heat built into something so dense it felt liquid. Beside her the flames roared and vibrated and reached.

The sack was no longer a sack, but a ragged, sooty flap. Her exposed skin seemed on the verge of blistering.

Then up from the south came a rush of cold so startling, it struck her like a splash of water. Caroline whirled.

Nothing there. Nothing at all—the fire was passing, leaving the air so cool against her skin, she might have been naked. As she watched, the head of the blaze reached the plowed field north of the house and veered off to the west. Away.

Four or five small fires remained inside the furrow.

Caroline walked to them and put them out. As she did so, each shred of muscle in her shoulders throbbed to life. She lifted an arm and pressed her closed eyes into the crook of her elbow. They were gritty with soot, and the sweat stung. Cool air seeped into a torn seam where her sleeve joined her bodice.

When she lifted her head the land smelled scorched, like burnt bread. Through the haze of smoke she saw Charles moving toward the washtub. A flicker of red caught her eye, and Caroline's body snapped toward the house, her sack raised. Red calico, and above it, two small white faces peeping round the doorway. As they moved cautiously forward Carrie appeared, dangling like a puppy from one of Mary's forearms; in the other Mary clutched her rag doll.

Caroline felt a swelling within herself. It pressed against every edge of her body, so light she was utterly weightless. Relief.

She crossed the yard to the house and went down on her knees before them. Her fingers touched their cheeks, but her hands, sodden and dulled with the sting of burlap, could not feel them. Caroline put her lips to each of their foreheads in turn, poised in the shape of a kiss. With her lips she felt their presence. When she pulled away she saw the smudges where her chin had brushed their noses. The slight lift of her cheeks as she smiled squeezed two fat tears past her swelling eyelids. "The backfire saved us," she assured the children. Her voice trembled as she said it. "And all's well that ends well."

Mary's eyes welled. "I let the dinner burn," she said.

Behind them Caroline saw the cookware on the hearth. The cornbread was charred, the pan of berries blackened beyond smoking. That was all they had lost to the fire. Her laugh came out a dry bark. It scraped her throat and watered her eyes. Caroline hugged Mary close, kissed the salt from her cheeks, and smoothed her hair. "You didn't let your sisters burn," she whispered.

Caroline put her hand over the keyhole to muffle the click as she turned the lock. If Charles or the girls stirred enough to ask her what she was doing, she could explain, but she had no desire to. She opened her trunk and drew out the Bible and turned its pages until she found the words she was looking for.

And after the fire a still small voice.

From her apron pocket she drew out a sliver of wood so narrow, its tip tapered into a delicate curlicue. After supper she had walked the length of the stubbled line of grass until she found the stick of kindling Charles had used to light the backfire and pried a splinter from it with her fingernails. Now Caroline laid it across the paper, so that it underlined the verse. It would be impossible to see those words without remembering this day.

She had hardly spoken all evening. "Smoke," she rasped with a tap of her fingertips against her aching throat, and that had satisfied them. It was only a portion of the truth. Behind her breastbone something like a small ember glowed softly, and Caroline did not want to douse it with talk. It was as though she harbored a tiny portion of the fire, and to her surprise, she wanted it to remain within her. So she kept silent, holding herself still around the fleck of warmth.

Carefully Caroline closed the Bible around the splinter and slipped it back into the trunk. She felt the way she had felt when her brother died, and when her children were born. Open, so that everything reached straight through to her heart. Entirely conscious of the current of life coursing through her. Until this day she had not noticed the concordant notes between the two. This was the feeling that came over her each time the veil between this world and the next was lifted. Today that veil had very nearly torn, and though no one had passed through it, Caroline still sensed its nearness and its thinness.

The scent of smoke wafted upward as she stepped

out of her dress and hung it on its nail. Likely that smell would never fully leave the fabric. She wrapped her shawl close around her nightdress and went to stand a moment in the doorway. The bare, burned prairie stretched out beneath the moon, all black and silver. Like an ambrotype, Caroline thought, and wished that her mind could preserve the sight as clearly. It was not a scene that would lend itself well to a pressed metal frame propped against a mantelpiece. In the dark the line that separated the brown earth from the black all but vanished. Yet to Caroline it was as perceptible as the outline of her own skin.

That was how near the fire had come. That close and taken nothing. Rather, it had left something. Caroline rested her fist against her chest. With each beat of her heart her consciousness of the burn line seemed to momentarily intensify, as if her own blood were pulsing through it. Quietly she walked out from the house until the grass beneath her feet became stiff and dry. She crouched down and touched her palm to the earth. Warm.

Caroline let go of her shawl and put both hands to the ground, as though her cool skin might soothe the burned places—as though the prairie were a fevered child, and she its mother. A small portion of the heat entered her hands, and Caroline felt her body soften, as it did when she held her husband or her children. When she stood, she did not brush the ashy soil from her palms. She balled her two fists together, knuckle to knuckle against her chest, and held them that way all the way back to the house.

Inside, she bent over Charles and put her hands to his face. He stirred, half waking, and murmured something indistinct. Caroline climbed into the bed beside him. The sooty, sweaty smell of the fire still clung to his whiskers. She ran a toe lightly, so lightly, along the sole of his foot.

A sound, something less than a syllable, passed through his throat—the sound of everything else dropping softly from his mind. He turned toward her, slipping a hand across her ribs, his thumb settling just below her breast. Two bones, set farther apart than the rest, left a space where he could feel the flicker of her heart beating beneath the skin. Their feet slipped past one another again and again, the rough and smooth places crisscrossing in ticklish shivers. Caroline put her fingers into his whiskers. Charles kissed their tips as they brushed by his lips. Each kiss wakened the tiny spark of warmth deep within her. *Kindling,* she thought.

He lifted his body onto hers, forearms framing her head and shoulders. She closed her eyes as his hands burrowed into her hair. His long brown whiskers skimmed over her chin and collarbone, their tips grazing the bare skin along the yoke of her nightdress. She so lost herself in the feel of his fingers and thumbs kneading her temples and scalp that she felt that sweet unfurling, like a fist opening, even before Charles nudged his way into her. Caroline opened her eyes to watch the twinkle in his diffuse. It made her think of daybreak, the way the stars seemed to melt into a soft haze of brightness. From their very first night together it had become one of the things she relished most.

That first time had taken her by surprise, though not in the way she had expected. She had not known fully what to expect, aside from the surety that she must relinquish herself to her husband. Charles, she knew, would be gentle and so she had little fear of pain. Nevertheless, what she prepared for was a loss, however intangible. As he spread his weight gingerly over her, there had been one quick beat of panic she could not keep from rising to meet him. *It is only Charles,* Caroline had reminded herself, and resolved to be still and trust him to take whatever was his right as husband, and no more.

Instead she found herself slowly beginning to rock with him, astonished to see what her body could do to this man. Once within her he became like a boy in her arms, giddy and grateful, then nearly tearful with plea-sure. What she felt was only an indistinct probing, not so much unpleasant as unaccustomed. Twice he moved just so and there were quick flickers of heat, glimmers of the brilliant flashes he himself seemed to be experi-encing. The second of them had made her gasp at the delight telegraphing beneath her skin.

He'd stopped, drawing back as though fearful he might have burned her. "Are you all right?"

Caroline was panting softly. She could see it in the faint rise and fall of her breasts beneath her nightdress. "Yes, Charles." And then, "Go on."

He descended again, tentatively. This time the over-whelming sense was of enveloping him, of embracing him entirely, and all at once the last of her apprehen-sions fled. Her body yielded, a sudden ripening, wel-coming him deeper.

Charles had sensed the change and his pace had quickened until he whimpered and shuddered. Caro-line felt a hot spurt and then it was done. He shivered all over and sank down around her. Caroline lay still beneath the pounding of his heart, listening to the *luff-luff* of his breath falling into her hair. In a few min-utes he raised his head to look at her, a little abashed, and she had ventured a smile.

"It was all right?" Charles asked. "I didn't hurt you?"

She'd wanted to tell him no. Nothing he had done had put his own pleasure above causing her pain. There had been a fleeting sting at the outset, but Caroline did not see how he could have prevented that. Likely he had felt it himself, so she shook her head. It eased him considerably, but there was still something pinched in his expression. If not for the fact that he was able to meet her eyes she might have mistaken it for shame. Perhaps, she'd thought as she studied him, she did not know Charles Ingalls well enough yet to decipher these ever-so-slight anglings of lips and brow. And then with a warm rush she recognized the shape his features made.

Beholden. He had looked for all the world as though he felt beholden to her. Caroline herself perceived nothing of the kind. He had taken nothing from her. Indeed, to have him feel that way was a gift in itself, a kind of power she had never anticipated. Caroline put her palm to his cheek and coaxed his head down onto the crocheted yoke of her nightdress. With her fingers she combed his whiskers.

As she'd lain there with him beached upon her an unexpected sense of pride welled up within her until she felt nearly regal. That he could lose himself so fully in her was a revelation.

Now his body planed against hers, shaving away thin curls of pleasure. He had learned, in the ten years since, to give, and she to take all that he offered. Rare were the times when it was not enough. Charles had never knowingly left her hungry for more. And yet, Caroline thought as she moved with him, she did crave more—of everything. All her life she had longed to breach that pale and hazy boundary between *enough* and *plenty*. All her life she had forbidden herself from wanting to reach toward it, telling herself in her mother's voice that enough is as good as a feast.

It is not so. The heat in her chest flared into her belly and beyond as the traitorous thought broke free. *It is not so.* It was only something Ma had desperately needed her children to believe.

Tonight she would feast, Caroline promised herself, and with the tilt of her hips and the clutch of her thighs she made plain her desire. Charles gave a luxuriant sigh and nuzzled his cheek against her neck. Emboldened, Caroline murmured to him of how often she imagined his fingers, so nimble on the fiddle strings, plucking the same sweet chords from the softest folds of her body. She felt his skin flush and the swell of his excitement. Caroline let go of herself, of everything but Charles. He did not use his hands, but the cadence of his movements became so fluid and familiar, Caroline could not escape the notion that he was enacting a melody upon her. With her eyes closed she could picture the matching strokes of the bow across the strings. Charles moved in that same smooth pattern until her every nerve was honed to its brightest, keenest edge, the rhythm building until at the last her body trembled in a final vibrato.

When he had caught his breath Charles whispered, "None knew thee but to love thee, thou dear one of my heart."

The chorus of "Daisy Deane." She had not imagined it, then. The music had been in his mind and in his flesh. Caroline smiled broadly into the darkness, anticipating the memories her mind would conjure the next time he played that song. The day had consumed every ounce of her, yet Caroline could not remember the last time she had felt so vibrantly alive.

The next day was not washing day, but Caroline filled the washtub and brought out the clothes she and Charles had worn the day before. There were two small black-rimmed holes on the back of Charles's shirt, just at the shoulder blade, that she would have to patch. At the front of her own dress, the skirt was scarred with places where fire had eaten into the braided trim along the hem. Beneath that the calico itself was badly scorched. Caroline sighed. The trimming could not be salvaged. Nor could the dress be worn without fraying the remains of the hem further. And it was her new dress, made from the lilac calico Charles had brought back from Oswego. To mend the skirt properly would require more braid or ribbon—yards of trim she did not have.

Look at what you do have, her mind insisted mechanically. Her chest and throat tightened in resistance. *No,* said another part of her, equally frustrated that she could fall back so easily into that old habit.

Caroline made herself pause, the way she did before speaking to the children when they were at odds with each other.

Might it be possible, she asked herself, *to mourn the one while rejoicing in the other?* The loss of a dress was a small one. It did not compare with all the irreparable things that might have gone up in smoke. But it was a loss, and she would allow herself to feel it. She touched the charred fabric lightly, so as not to break the fragile threads. It was so new, she had not yet memorized the pattern of the soft gray leaves printed across the lavender ground.

The sorrow was as sweet as it was fleeting. Caroline had barely acknowledged it before it had passed. *Like rinsing away a stain before it has time to set,* she thought as she set to work.

She took up the soap—lye soap, itself made of ash from good Wisconsin hardwood—and rubbed it into the smoke-darkened places. "Ashes to ashes," she murmured.

By the time Charles returned from the Scott claim she was squeezing the last of the suds from the clothes. The stains were not gone, especially where the smoke and the sweat had mixed, but they had faded enough that Caroline was satisfied the garments would not appear marred.

"The Scotts are all well and safe," Charles said. "They'd seen Edwards as well. His place wasn't touched. The fire never crossed the creek."

"I'm thankful for that." She held out his shirt so that he could see the holes.

"Close call," he said. "Never felt a thing. There was talk," he added, fingering the burned places, "that the Indians set the fire to drive off the settlers."

Caroline let the news settle, working it over in her mind as she pressed the fabric against the washboard.

Then she spoke as though the idea were of no consequence. "They've already agreed to leave."

Charles nodded. He dipped up a bucket of rinse water from the well for her before replying. "I didn't say I believed it."

"But Mr. Scott does."

"Yes."

"And Mrs. Scott."

He did not answer that. Likely he couldn't, but Caroline knew. The way Mrs. Scott had spoken of the Indians before the fire left no room for doubt. For all her kindness to her neighbors, Mrs. Scott had seemed to savor the thought of what depredations Indians—any Indians—were capable of, as though it vindicated her hatred for them. Caroline could not say whether she herself hated them any less, but she found nothing to relish in it. Nor was it a conviction she cared to cultivate any more deeply.

She sat back on her heels to look at him, her hands submerged in the cold rinse water. "If I am to live here, Charles, it cannot be under the cloud of what the Indians might have done, or may do." She said it without force. It was not a threat—only a fact. "I've seen enough that I can already imagine more than I care to."

He understood. Or rather, he agreed. He did not understand. Charles would never share her sentiments toward the Indians. He could stand before an Indian man without feeling his viscera clench and his bowels shudder, without the fine hairs on every surface of his skin rising up in a feeble attempt at protection. Caroline's body told her to be afraid, and she obeyed it; there need not be a reason. Charles's did not.

Caroline could not change his response to the presence of the Osages any more than she could change her own. Yet Charles was willing to abide by her condition. He had agreed with only a moment's consideration, without coaxing or scoffing. Warmth swarmed suddenly around her heart, and Caroline surprised them both with a smile. Charles smiled back without knowing why, happy, as always, to have pleased her. She would let that be enough. Caroline heard her thoughts and spared another smile, for her ma this time. *More than enough.*

"Come here, Caroline. And you, Mary and Laura."

Something to see, Caroline guessed. Perhaps an animal, by the way Charles called out to them—low and slow, so as not to frighten whatever it was away. Unless there were a bison grazing in the yard, she could not think what would make him interrupt her work. Caroline gave a scolding smile to the crochet thread in her hands. It was not work, really. The mending was done, and the half-finished row of scalloped lace she had begun so long ago in Wisconsin had been so tempting, there at the bottom of the work basket. So she had let herself pretend it could be used to disguise the burned hem of her lavender calico, even though its pattern was far too elaborate for an everyday dress. Her hands delighted in the intricate movements, so unlike braining hides and wringing laundry that she was not vexed each time the thread snagged on the rough tips of her fingers. How long since she had made something beautiful for its own sake?

And now Charles's voice was boring a hole through her concentration. With a sigh, she realized she had lost count of the stitches. She set the lacework back into the basket and stood, treating her back to a luxuriant stretch. "Let's go see what Pa has to show us," she said to Mary and Laura.

The girls ran outside ahead of her, scampering over the board Charles had propped across the doorway to keep Carrie indoors. In the weeks since the fire she had begun creeping across the floor, pulling with her hands and scooting her knees along behind. Soon she would be crawling. Now Carrie followed her sisters as far as she could, then gripped the board with hands and mouth. "We'll have to ask your pa to tack a strip of canvas to that edge," Caroline told the baby as she hitched up her skirt to step out. Otherwise the child would chew off a mouthful of splinters.

Caroline reached up to shade her eyes against the sun. When she could see, she stopped short. Her hand dropped to her chest. At once she understood why Charles had called her name first, before the girls. Never in her life had she seen so many Indians. Scores of them, mounted and on foot, with baskets and bundles, all pointed west.

"Oh, the pretty ponies! See the pretty ponies!" Laura cried, clapping her hands. "Look at the spotted one."

It was plain from the way the ponies were packed that the Indians were leaving. Blankets, hoes, cookpots. They had left nothing behind. "Mercy," Caroline heard herself say. She had not expected to watch them go—only to learn one day that their camps were empty, that they had fulfilled their agreement with the government and moved south of the Kansas line.

"Thank God," Caroline said. She meant it, but she did not feel it. Not yet. Here before her eyes was an answered prayer, and she could neither rejoice nor reflect, only witness its happening. Now that it was happening, Caroline wondered what she had supposed she would feel. Glad, relieved? She felt so little, she could not put a name to it. The moment flowed by without seeming to leave a mark.

Near the head of the procession rode the Indian agent, a white man of about forty, with a dark beard and eyelids that sloped gently downward at the outer corners. A ghost of a memory grazed Caroline's thoughts as he passed. Not so much a recollection, but a sensation, as though for a fleeting instant she inhabited the mind and body of a child who was accustomed to looking up into a face like that one.

Pa, she thought with a warm shiver, and her feet carried her to within a few yards of the procession. Not Papa Frederick, but her own father. In all the years he had been gone, she had never seen eyes so much like Pa's. Her brothers had inherited fragments of his smile, his hands, even his voice, but not one of them had his eyes. Had she known the agent's name, she would have called out to him, just to see those eyes looking down on her once more.

Instead the man rode on, and Caroline stood suspended in her memory as one Indian after another passed through the space he had occupied. For the first time Caroline felt safe enough in their presence to observe them with no other thought than to see what they looked like. The shape of their faces fascinated her. They were unmistakably different from her own. The planes were flatter, the lines straighter. Even the plumpest of cheeks appeared oblong instead of round. If their skin were white and their hair done up in curls, Caroline thought, she would still know the difference, just as she would know a spaniel from a bulldog.

It was Mary who recognized one of them. She gave a little gasp and took Caroline's hand, hiding her face behind it as though she were a bashful toddler. Caroline saw the faded green calico shirt and a sizzle of fear crossed her own belly. That was the man who had flung the key to her trunk at them when it would not fit the lock of the provisions cabinet. She remembered the sound of it as it careened off the toe of Mary's shoe and skittered across the floor.

At his knee he wore beautiful fringed garters, woven in bold zigzags of green, blue, and black. Had he been wearing them that day in the cabin? Caroline could not recall anything beyond his glare and the movements of his hands.

He did not acknowledge them now, did not so much as look in their direction. Caroline straightened her back and thrust out her chin, determined that he should notice them. He would look her in the eye and see that she was not afraid now. But he did not. He rode by, gesturing with his free hand as he talked with the man riding alongside him. Caroline felt as though she'd been slighted. Was it possible that what had happened inside their cabin did not hold enough significance to stand out in his memory?

She scanned the line of Indians, looking to see whether the first two men to frighten her were here, too—the ones who had come asking for food before Carrie was born. Caroline could recall nothing of them but swaying silver earrings and prominent rib bones. A dozen of the men riding past might fit that description. Some of them looked toward her. Others did not. Caroline recognized none of them.

She turned her attention to the women. Nothing the men had done had frightened her so much as the sounds the Osage women had made last autumn in the early hours before dawn. Those endless, wailing notes had come from their throats. Their voices were so quiet now, it did not seem possible. Each one that passed carved a hollow feeling deeper into Caroline's center. In all this time, as Caroline longed for her sisters and her mother, Mrs. Scott had been the only woman she'd seen. Now, dozens. Sisters, daughters, mothers, grandmothers, none of them with the slightest link to her.

No, Caroline realized, that was not so. Some of them must be wives or mothers of the men who had come into the cabin. Was there one among them who had received a loaf of cornbread, tied up in a towel with a pine tree embroidered at the corner? Perhaps that towel was folded carefully into one of the bundles tied to the horses, or incorporated into a garment. Caroline studied the women individually as they passed. Their hair, so smooth at the parting it looked wet, was so enticing that Caroline put her hands into her pockets to keep her fingers from fidgeting over the imagined strands. Their clothing was an assemblage of deerskin and calico, in vibrant hues she had not worn since she was a child. Rich yellows, reds, and violets, decorated with beads, fringe, and ribbon work. Through the fabric Caroline could see the shape of their uncorseted breasts against their chests and the way they puddled on the women's laps. One woman, a little older than herself, lifted her blouse to nurse an infant, and Caroline could not avert her eyes from that bare brown breast. She had never seen a nipple so dark.

What did Charles think, looking at such women? Was he imagining running a hand over that sleek black hair, as Caroline herself was?

"Pa," Laura said, "get me that little Indian baby." Caroline turned in surprise. She had never heard such a tone from her daughter. Laura was not asking, she was commanding. Beneath the firmness, her small voice quivered with desire. Coming from a man's mouth, that timbre would mean avarice, or lust.

"Hush, Laura," Charles said.

She only spoke faster, her voice rising, "Oh, I want it! I want it! It wants to stay with me. Please, Pa, please!"

Laura did not look at Charles as she begged. Her eyes were fixed on what she wanted. Caroline traced Laura's gaze and saw an infant tucked into a basket that hung over the flank of a piebald pony. There was nothing to set it apart from the other Osage children, except that it seemed to be looking squarely back at Laura. "I declare, I've never heard of such a thing," Caroline said.

"Hush, Laura," Charles said again. "The Indian woman wants to keep her baby."

"Oh, Pa!" Laura said. Her voice cracked. Tears spilled down her face and dripped from her chin.

Caroline did not know what to say. Some of the Indians were looking at them now. What would they think—what might they do—if they heard Laura and understood what she had said? "For shame, Laura," she chided, and regretted it immediately. Laura had lost all hold of herself. She could hardly breathe enough to sob. Caroline crouched down beside her daughter and asked, softly, "Why on earth do you want an Indian baby, of all things?"

Laura panted and hiccoughed before she managed to answer. "Its eyes are so black," she whimpered, looking past Caroline through a blur of tears. As if she were no more than coveting a dress for its buttons. It made no sense. Laura knew it, too, and grimaced with the effort of trying again. Caroline wiped Laura's cheeks with her apron, hoping the touch itself might help her grasp what Laura was trying to convey. It did not. Whatever Laura felt, she did not have the words for it. It was too large, and she was so small she could neither contain it nor release it. All she could do was look up at Caroline with eyes that begged to be understood. *Beseeching.* Caroline knew the word well enough, but she had never seen it like this. Laura's misery was so raw, Caroline could feel the throbbing of it herself.

"Why, Laura," she said, and suddenly she was the one pleading. "You don't want another baby. We have a baby, our own baby." The rest of the words caught in her throat. She gestured toward the doorway, where the crown of Carrie's dark little head was visible above the board.

Laura tried for an instant to agree. Then her face crumpled. "I want the other one, too!"

Her outburst struck Caroline's face like a wind. She sat back on her heels, too bewildered to try anything else. "Well, I declare!" she said.

"Look at the Indians, Laura," said Charles. "Look west, and then look east, and see what you see."

Laura obeyed, and Caroline with her. The line of Indians seemed to rise up out of the grass to the east, then sink back into the west, as though they were as much a feature of the prairie as the creek and the bluffs. When Laura turned back, the black-eyed baby was out of sight. Caroline braced herself for a fresh surge of desperation and protest. Instead Laura accepted the blow as if she were grown. The expression slid from her face until her features were slack. Her shoulders jerked with jagged, silent sobs. However incomprehensible its cause, Laura's grief was real. The sight of it left Caroline staggered, as though something had been taken from her, too.

Caroline took Laura's hand and held it until the last of the Indians had passed. She wanted Carrie more, to turn her back to the Osage procession and take the baby up in her arms so that Carrie might feel how vital she was, no matter how many black-eyed Indian babies might pass through the dooryard. But it was Laura who needed her, not Carrie, though Caroline could think of nothing to do but stand by the child until Laura had absorbed the brunt of her loss.

"Are you ready to go inside?" Caroline asked when

the Indians were gone. Laura shook her head. "All right. We'll sit on the doorstep awhile."

Caroline sat down with her back propped against the doorway and pulled aside the board that separated them from Carrie. The baby scooted out and found her place in Caroline's lap. Caroline's body eased some as Carrie settled back against her. Carrie knew perfectly well where she belonged. Caroline stroked Carrie's plump knee with her palm—round and round, as though she were polishing it.

It was time for dinner, and Caroline could not compel herself to move. "I don't feel like doing anything," she said to Charles, "I feel so—" She did not know how to say what she meant, any more than Laura had. There was no single word for it. The weight of the Indians' departure, balanced against the lightness of her relief, had left her blank inside. Everything she could feel was outside of herself—the smoothness of Carrie's knee under her palm, the curve of the baby's spine against her chest. "So let down," she finished. That was not it, but it was as near as she could manage.

"Don't do anything but rest," Charles said. Caroline did not have it in her to smile, but her cheeks rounded at his tone. He had not spoken to her that way since she was pregnant.

"You must eat something, Charles."

"No," he said, looking at Laura. "I don't feel hungry." He went to the stable then and hitched the mustangs to the plow. She and Laura and Mary were not hungry, either. Together they sat, watching the path the Indians had worn across the yard. Blade by blade, the grass would grow up through the footprints and horse tracks. There would be no trace of their leaving.

Thirty-One

Caroline set down the pails and lifted the back ruffle of her bonnet so that the breeze could find the nape of her neck. Three rows remained to be watered: the carrots, the sweet potatoes, and the tomatoes. One thing never changed, and that was the everlasting heaviness of water. Pail after pail she pulled from the well and toted to her kitchen garden. Each dainty plant must have its dipperful if it was not to suffer during the long afternoon.

The soil here was sandier than she was accustomed to. It was warmer to the touch and easier to work, but did not hold water in the same way. Water splayed outward over the surface of the ground before sinking in, leaving only a thin layer moistened. Caroline had shown Laura how to carefully press a little dimple into the earth around each stem, so that the soil might cup the water long enough to soak the thin white roots. Twice a day Caroline bent double all along the length of each row, emptying each dipper of water where it could do the most good. Laura begged to help, but Caroline diverted her to digging a shallow trench around the perimeter, to ensure no rainwater fell out of reach of the seedlings. Careful as Caroline was with the dipper and pails, her hem was always damp and gritty by the time she finished. Laura would no doubt douse herself to the kneecaps.

Mary sat on a quilt spread over the grass, minding Carrie and sorting out remnants of calico from the scrap bag to sew her own nine-patch quilt. Caroline shook her head fondly, watching Mary arrange her favorites into pretty patterns. Five going on twenty-five, that child.

A gleeful squeal came out from under the sun canopy Caroline had contrived out of a pillowcase draped across two crates. The string of Indian beads dangled from one of the wooden slats, and Carrie lay in the shade, jabbering at the brightly colored beads. Caroline considered the three rows of plants still waiting for water. They would not wilt in five minutes' time. She sidled down on the edge of the quilt and propped herself on an elbow at Carrie's feet. The hair that had been fine and black as soot had given over to a warm golden brown. Her knobby little knees and elbows were rosying up like crabapples. A smile ripened Caroline's cheeks to see it. Caroline reached up to tinkle the beads with a fingertip. Carrie flapped her arms at the air and squealed. Caroline put her hand to the baby's belly. Its warm curve reached up to fill her palm.

"Letter for you, Ingalls," Mr. Edwards's voice called.

Caroline bounded up from the quilt, lightened with hopes for the circulator. "Mind the baby, Mary," she said as she smoothed her hair and strode out to the edge of the field where Charles and Edwards were meeting. "It's good of you to remember us at the post office, Mr. Edwards," she said.

"Just got back from Independence last night," he replied, handing Charles the envelope. "News should be pretty fresh. The clerk there at the post office said it hadn't been sitting but a week or two yet."

It was addressed only to Charles, in a hand she did not recognize. Caroline felt fidgety as a child while she and Charles and Edwards exchanged pleasantries: news from town, an invitation to supper, a polite refusal. Edwards had hardly turned his back to head home before Caroline was holding out a hairpin for Charles to slit open the envelope. "Who is it from, Charles?"

"Couldn't be anybody but Gustafson."

A single sheet of paper. He read it once, then Caroline saw his eyes return to the top of the page and begin again. He said nothing.

"Does he send any news of Henry and Polly?"

Charles turned the letter over, then looked inside the envelope. "I don't know."

"Charles?"

Charles licked his lips. "He's reneged. Can't make the payments, so he's moving out—moving on. That twenty dollars he sent last summer is the last money we'll see from him. The property defaults to us."

No more payments. Caroline's mouth went dry. Every dollar and a quarter the Swede did not send was an acre lost. "How much is left in the fiddle box?"

"Not quite twenty-five acres' worth. Thirty-one dollars and twenty cents." He turned to the plow and slapped it gently with the letter. "Could have had forty acres for what this cost. Don't that beat all. Traded fifty dollars in furs for a steel plow and the only land I can afford to till is seven hundred miles away."

"The land office wouldn't have traded furs for acreage," Caroline said gently.

Charles whipped his hat down onto the freshly turned furrow. "Damn it all."

Caroline winced at the strike of his words. She

glanced back at the girls. They were watching. Not scared yet, but alert that something was happening. Caroline moved so that they could not see Charles's face and lowered her voice. "If we raise a crop—"

"This ground won't raise anything but sod potatoes and sod corn until the grass roots have rotted out." Charles pronounced *sod* as though it were a vulgarity. "We can't raise anything of value in time to make payment."

"We've lived here a year without paying." Caroline trailed off, unsure where that feeble thought was headed.

He spoke fast, already impatient with the figures— figures she knew just as well as she did. "Government allows thirty-three months from the time we settle to make proof. That leaves less than two years to raise two hundred dollars beyond what we need to live. Plus two dollars just to file our intent to preempt. I don't see how we can do it. Thirty-one dollars isn't even enough to see us home, much less through two more years."

Home. The word sent a sort of tremor through her, as though a stout bone, long ago broken and mended, suddenly began to bend.

Charles was still talking. "I'll have to find work along the way. Someone between here and Wisconsin's bound to need a carpenter or a field hand."

Caroline's head spun like a weathervane slapped by a sudden gust of wind. All year long she had faced herself firmly in one direction. Now a single sheet of paper demanded she turn completely around. Charles sneered at the envelope in his hand. "Takes six weeks or better to get word of anything. If I'd known sooner—" Caroline heard the brittle quiver in his voice and knew the moment for words had passed. If she spoke, even to comfort him, he would snap.

She looked at the cabin. Her eyes lingered on the half-watered kitchen garden, the open door, the low fire in the hearth, but her mind had not the strength to take hold of any of it. A hungry spot that did not want for food had opened itself at the parting of her ribs. Caroline pressed the heel of her hand into it. It was soft, yet unsatisfied, as though she had tried to slake herself with cotton bolls. She left Charles and walked toward the cabin, approaching it as if it were a structure out of a dream she might wake from before crossing the threshold. Caroline stopped in the middle of the single room, slack of thought. When the log had fallen on her foot, there had been a moment like this. The pain existed—she could feel its presence encircling the wound—but the weight of the news blocked the sensation from reaching her. There was no safe place to look: the glass windows with their curtains trimmed in red calico, the fireplace built of creek stones. And beside it, the willow-bough rocking chair. Her hands rose up in surrender and she sank down into the chair. She rocked herself, eyes closed.

Outside, Carrie sputtered. Caroline heard Mary's voice and Laura's, trying to hush her. "Carrie, see the beads? The pretty-pretty beads, Carrie?" Then a cat-like whine as Carrie protested. They were trying to jolly her with tones so fawning they made Caroline's jaw tighten. The baby was having none of it.

"Bring her here, Mary," she said.

Mary and Laura crept across the threshold together. Carrie was pushing her hands into Mary's shoulder and her knees into her sister's belly. She rarely consented to be carried now that she could crawl. Caroline took her long enough to kiss her, then set the baby down on hands and knees so that Carrie could move freely. Caroline closed her eyes and resumed her rocking.

"Ma?" Mary asked.

Caroline opened her eyes. "We're going home."

The girls looked at her, at the china shepherdess on the mantel, the rifle over the door, and finally at each other. Caroline understood without their asking. The meaning of the word had shifted for her, too. Like theirs, her mind no longer reached backward at the thought of *home*. "Back to Wisconsin," Caroline said. One dry, soundless sob clutched her throat, and then another. Caroline turned her face and drew her emotions inward, to the very center of herself. She exhaled, slowly, until her face relaxed. "Everything is all right," she told Mary and Laura. It was the falsest truth she had ever spoken.

Charles lay in the bed beside her, his eyes fixed on the ceiling. He had spoken only two and three words at a time since coming in for supper. Through the window, Caroline could see the plow where he had left it standing in the field. The gentle swoop of its blade shone out white in the starlight.

"Charles," she whispered. She touched his whiskers. He was mute. Likely fearing what might come out of him if he tried to speak, Caroline thought. So in need of comfort, and utterly unable to ask for it.

She could grant him his silence. Words could not be relied upon to soothe him. But she would not leave him embedded in his own grief.

Caroline turned to face him and drew her long brown braid across her body, stroking the thick length of it as he so loved to do. With its tip, she brushed his hand. He did not reach for her. His eyes continued to move up and down the ceiling, as though he were counting and recounting the beams and nails it had taken to fashion the roof.

I opened to my beloved; but my beloved had withdrawn himself, and was gone, Caroline recited to herself. *I sought him, but I could not find him; I called him, but he gave me no answer.*

She slid a hand beneath his nightshirt. She caressed the narrow seam of soft hair up the center of his belly, ran her fingernails along the crease of his thighs. His body had no choice but to respond. She heard a small, defeated groan, and felt the sheet inch back ever so slightly as it began to tent below his navel.

He rolled sideways, meeting her in the middle of the bed. Their foreheads touched, but his eyes would not rise above her collarbone. As though what had happened to them today were something to be ashamed of.

She took him in, hooking her heel into the crook of his knee and pulling him close. His belly touched hers and she drew him closer yet, until she could feel his heartbeat against her ribs. His embrace was wooden, as though he dared not let himself feel anything at all. Caroline closed her eyes. The only thing she would deny him was a place for his shame to roost.

She held him as she rocked him with her hips, coaxing and coaxing until she felt his body begin to yield up its burden of sadness. She felt it break, as though it were a solid thing, felt his body clutching at itself as he resisted letting the pieces go. Caroline pulled him deeper, whispering, "I remember how you looked at me, driving into our first Kansas sunset." His muscles clenched and shuddered and his breath went ragged. He could not cry, but his movements became a sort of sobbing. Caroline rocked and rocked, milking the sorrow from his flesh.

He gave a muffled cry and she paused with her belly pressed to his, holding herself open for him while he spasmed.

If there were a child to come of this, Caroline wondered, would it bear a trace of the sorrow that had made it? Her heart throbbed softly at the thought of a small woebegone creature—a boy, perhaps, with Charles's blue eyes and long fingers. She surfaced from her thoughts and Charles was looking at her with those very eyes. The shadows at his mouth remained, shallower now.

"I'm sorry," he said.

It pained her to smile. "So am I," she answered.

He brushed the edge of her face with his knuckles slowly back and forth until they slept, joined.

Eliza, Henry, Polly, *Ma and Papa Frederick.* Caroline said their names to herself over and over again as she emptied the cabin into the wagon. And there would be Eliza's new little boy. *Lansford Newcomb Ingalls.* To see them again in this world would be . . . what? Caroline knew no word to encompass it.

Then shouldn't the thought of their faces when the wagon arrived back in Pepin be enough to spur a smile? she asked herself once more. Caroline had a letter already written to drop at the post office on their way out, but there was every possibility that they themselves would arrive in Wisconsin before news reached the family. Imagine knocking on Polly's door, with Carrie in her arms, and asking to borrow a jar of pickles as though no more than a day had passed. Imagine Polly Quiner, speechless. That scene raised one corner of her mouth. It was all the joy Caroline could summon.

Think of the pantry, she told herself as she crouched before the little provisions cabinet to pack a crate with small bags of flour, cornmeal, coffee, and sugar. *Think of cooking on a stove again, with an oven and enough room to boil and fry and bake all at once. Think of cooking and eating in one room, and sleeping in another.* All of it made her want to be happy. None of it did.

"It all fit on the way in," Charles said when she handed the crate up over the tailgate. "Seems like it ought to all fit on the way out." He stood stooping with the crate in his hands, surveying the inside of the wagon.

"There's plenty of space, here," she said, patting the empty boards at the rear corner—the same place the crate had just vacated.

Charles shook his head. "Saving that for your rocking chair," he said.

Oh, how she wanted to smile just then.

Caroline turned numbly from the wagon and there was her kitchen garden. She had neglected to water this morning. Though the plants were not truly wilting yet, she could see they were beginning to suffer. The leaves had a soft look about them, almost like cloth. A few more hours and they would be slumped, the thin rib down each center pliable as a hair. She went to the well and filled one pail, then another. There was no time for it, no sense in it. It was almost cruel. Tomorrow they would wilt again, and there would be no respite.

Caroline could not talk herself out of it. Tenderly she watered the tomatoes, sweet potatoes, and carrots without risking a glance toward the wagon or the cabin. If Charles or the children asked, she would answer simply that the plants needed water. She did not need them to understand any more than that. Halfway through the cabbages she paused to look back over the ground she had covered. Already the jagged edges of the tomato leaves were tilting gratefully upward again. Caroline knew then that she could not abandon these plants to the mercy of the sun and the jackrabbits. Not after she had carried the seeds all the way from Wisconsin.

She moved more quickly through the beans, cucumbers, peas, turnips, and onions, more conscious now of both the time she had used and the time she still needed to accomplish her task. Then she went around back of the cabin, where the flat she had used to start the sweet potatoes stood propped against the chimney. Caroline counted the square partitions along two edges, multiplied, and divided. Room for only four plants from each row. By the numbers, it was not worth the effort. And her rocker was already straining the capacity of the wagon box. She dared not ask Charles to make room for one more thing. Caroline picked up the trowel, undeterred.

Hurrying around the corner of the house, she met Charles on his way to the stable. He carried a small coil of rope. If he took notice of the garden implements in her hands, he gave no indication. Perhaps he thought she was carrying them to the wagon, to pack. "If you don't object, I'd like to take the cow and calf over to the Scotts' claim," he said. "The mustangs will outpace the calf if we try to bring the cattle along. Maybe the cow, too." He slapped the rope against his thigh and said with a faint note of petulance, "Even if they could keep up we can't afford feed for all of them."

Caroline nodded. It was fitting, after all the Scotts had done for them. "That would be a fine thing, Charles. You'll give Mrs. Scott my thanks?" she asked. "For all her kindness. She has been . . . ," Caroline's lips tightened, tugged by a pang of loyalty to her blood kin. Yet it was true. Though the threads were of different fibers, her tie to Mrs. Scott was as firm as the knots that joined her to Eliza, and to Polly. However true, it was more than she could ask Charles to relay. "We'll always be beholden to them, cow or no cow," she finished.

"I'll thank her as best I can," Charles promised. "I want to offer Edwards the plow," he added. "I can't figure any way to pack it. The plow we left in Pepin ought to be there in the barn yet, unless Gustafson made off with it."

"Yes," Caroline said. "I would be proud for Mr. Edwards to have the plow. He'll want to pay you," she supposed.

"He will, but I won't let him." The challenge of compelling Edwards to accept such a gift seemed to buoy him so that he came within a fraction of smiling. "Can you be ready when I get back—say an hour or so?"

"I think so. Yes."

That satisfied him. Caroline waited while he went into the stable. He came out leading the cow by her long twisting horns. The calf followed, untethered.

"An hour, then," he confirmed. He grimaced as if drawing a fine distinction. "Probably a little more. Scott's a talker."

"An hour," Caroline repeated. He made no move to leave. His eyes went over and over her face. Seeking something? A flush crept up her neck. Did he guess what she intended to do with the flat and trowel after all? Suddenly he ducked forward and kissed her cheek, then strode off to the east, the calf trotting behind.

Caroline allowed herself a moment's bewilderment, then set to her task. With the trowel she dug around the hardiest-looking plants, taking care not to sever their roots if she could avoid it as she prized them loose and fitted them carefully into the small wooden partitions. One by one she lifted them free and felt the tug and snap of the almost invisible fibers still clinging to the soil. When the flat was full, her neat kitchen garden looked bedraggled as a mouth full of pulled teeth.

She went to the wagon and unlatched the tailgate. For the first time, her resolve flagged. There was no-where, not even if she could have stood the flat on its end and slipped it into a crevice like a book onto a shelf. Though it was filled with every tangible fragment of their lives, the wagon box looked unfamiliar. Unopened bags of seed Charles had brought from Oswego bulged into the aisle, narrowing it considerably. Their winter wraps, which would not fit into the carpetbags, hung draped over the churn handle. The displaced provisions crate balanced on the seat of the rocker. Caroline put her hand to one of the arms and gave it a gentle push. The chair replied with a short lurch and a disconcerting creak. She bent to peer under the seat to see whether it oughtn't to be wedged, to keep the pliant willow runners from stressing.

"Oh," Caroline said.

The space between the runners was empty. She lifted the wooden frame filled with Kansas soil and Wisconsin plants and slid it easily between them. It was as though the rocker had been holding a place for it.

By the time Charles came up the creek road, the empty coil of rope dangling at his side, Caroline had herself and the girls all freshly washed and braided, with their sunbonnets tied under their chins. "Come, girls," she said. "Pa's ready to go."

Charles held up a hand to slow them. "Edwards will be along soon," he called.

"For the plow?" Caroline asked.

Charles shook his head. "Not yet. Creek's still too high from the spring thaw to get it across, even for Edwards." He pulled a padlock from his hip pocket. "He gave me this, to put on the stable door so he can come for the plow when the water's gone down." Charles tossed the lock an inch or two into the air and let it drop heavily into his palm. "He wants to say goodbye. To you and the girls."

"That's kind of him," Caroline said. A slim strand of sympathy twined around her heart at the thought of how it would pain the children. She shifted Carrie to her hip and rested a hand on Laura's back. Mary and Laura both understood, in a way they had not before, how long and how far a goodbye might stretch. A year ago they had stood in the snow and kissed their cousins dutifully, without feeling the weight of it. Now the significance of the looming farewell made their faces long and sober.

"I'll hitch up," Charles said.

They waited in the shade of the wagon. The girls leaned against the wheels, holding the spokes as though there was comfort to be found in the smooth lengths of hickory. Caroline stood with Carrie in her arms, trying not to take it all in, trying to keep the freight of this single day from engraving itself upon all her memories of this place.

Jack growled so softly it was almost a purr. Caroline stepped into the sun to watch the creek road. The girls crouched, peeking under the belly of the wagon. A moment later, Edwards's long gangly shadow came loping toward them.

First he shook hands with Charles. "Goodbye, Ingalls, and good luck." Caroline knew from the jolly way he tried to say it that the men had already had their true goodbye. As Edwards approached, she saw the expression in his eyes that belied the smile he had determined to wear. Pleading she would do the same. She smiled back. For the children's sake. That was what Caroline told herself, though she knew better. In truth they were playacting for one another, she and Charles and Edwards, only pretending the children were their audience.

"Goodbye, ma'am," Edwards said, and his relief called a genuine smile to her lips. "I sure will never forget your kindness."

"Nor I yours, Mr. Edwards. I don't know how we would have done without your generosity," she answered, wishing he could see all the memories that gleamed bright in her mind as she said it.

He gave her a quick little nod, almost curt, and set his jaw. Then Edwards crouched down on one knee and shook the girls' hands as though they were grown-up ladies. First Mary, then Laura. Mary said, "Goodbye, Mr. Edwards," as though she had rehearsed for days. Laura, Caroline knew, would not be able to speak. That child's heart was too near her throat. Edwards's lips bunched up tight as he and Laura regarded one another, helpless.

What her girls had meant to him, Caroline could only imagine. When they left, she thought to herself, he would be rootless.

It made no sense—he had come to Kansas without family, of his own accord—but Caroline knew it was so. Without feeling it happen, they had grafted him into their family tree, and he had done the same. And now they would leave him.

The impulse rose so clear and strong, Caroline did not question it. She passed Carrie to Charles and hurried to the back of the wagon to unlatch the tailgate. There in the corner beneath the rocker was her miniature garden, the dozens of tiny pairs of leaves reaching up like small arms. She chose one sweet potato seedling and plopped it into Mary and Laura's old tin cup. Then she hefted the flat of plants and carried it to where Edwards waited, standing before him as though offering a tea tray filled with dainties.

"My best seedlings," she explained. "Tomatoes, carrots, cabbage, beans, cucumbers, turnips, onions, peas."

Her voice hitched. "And sweet potato." Her vision blurred, but she held her chin firm. "I'd thought to take them with us, but . . . ," Caroline trailed off. She could not say what she wanted to say: *They belong here.* "They would stand a much better chance if you would care for them," she finished.

"I'll miss your good dumplings and cornbread, Mrs. Ingalls, but come fall these vegetables will brighten up my jackrabbit stew just fine." He took the flat carefully, propping it against his hip like a baby so he could offer a free hand for her to shake.

Caroline took his hand in both of hers, clasping it for a long moment. "Mr. Edwards." She steadied herself and spoke the thought one piece at a time, so that her voice would not falter: "You have been—as fine a neighbor—as we have ever had." She gave his hand an extra squeeze at *ever.* "As we ever will have," she amended.

His thin lips fought for the words. "Yes, ma'am."

"Oh, Mr. Edwards," Laura cried out, "thank you, thank you for going all the way to Independence to find Santa Claus for us."

Caroline's chest gave an almighty heave. Edwards's hand broke from hers and he was away, striding through the long prairie grass.

Caroline put her hand on the lip of the wagon box and stood a moment, looking. The place itself tugged at her. All of it. From the bluffs and the creek road to the north, to the thin blue-white lip of the horizon to the south. It had never belonged to anyone before. It had not even belonged to them.

Eliza. Henry. Polly. Ma and Papa Frederick, her mind coaxed. *Lansford Newcomb Ingalls. A stove and a pantry and rooms with doors.*

Caroline climbed up and took her place on the wagon seat. Charles handed Carrie up to her.

Edwards, she thought. *Mrs. Scott. The smell of the grass on the wind, and the everlasting blue vault of the sky.*

Her heart was full and heavy behind her ribs, like a breast in need of suckling. She pressed Carrie close, trying to suffuse its deep beats as Charles boosted Mary and Laura onto the straw tick.

Another moment and Charles was beside her, the reins in his hands.

"Ready?"

No, she thought. *Never. And yes. Quickly, before it breaks me.* "Let's go," she said.

"Pa, I want to see out." Laura's voice. "Please, Pa, make it so I can see the house again."

Caroline looked straight ahead, wishing he wouldn't and sure that he would.

The wagon lurched as Charles jumped down, then shuddered with the loosening of the rope at the back so that Laura and Mary could peep out through the wagon cover. For a long moment it was still. Then Caroline heard Charles's footsteps, receding instead of approaching. She did not trust herself to look forward again if she looked back, but she turned. Laura and Mary crowded the small keyhole Charles had made in the canvas. Past their heads, a narrow swath of the cabin was visible.

Charles stood in the doorway. Or rather, at its edge. He did not step inside, but stood with one hand on the lintel, the other on the latch. In her mind she could see all the things he would be looking at. The empty mantle. The place beside the hearth where her willow-bough rocker had stood. The glass windows.

Caroline could not watch any longer. She put her cheek to Carrie's head and closed her eyes. She inhaled deeply, drawing the smell of the baby's hair through the clean cotton bonnet. When she felt the wagon lurch again with Charles's weight, she lifted her head. A small dark circle dampened the pink calico.

"Left the latch string out," Charles said. "Someone might need shelter."

Caroline nodded, grateful for the bonnet brim that hid her wet cheeks from him.

He chirruped to the horses. Caroline angled her face into the warm prairie wind. Before the first mile had passed, it would dry her tears.

It was to be a piecemeal farewell to Kansas itself, Caroline realized as they drove northeast. That was a mercy. Mile after mile, the grass still rippled and the sky extended beyond the reach of her eyes. Tomorrow they would drive into the sunrise, across the same hills that a year ago had beckoned them west. The symmetry of it pleased Caroline in a way she could not account for.

"Something's wrong there."

Mary and Laura stood up on the straw tick and grasped the back of the wagon seat to balance themselves while they looked. "Where, Pa?"

"There," Charles said again, pointing with the reins. "Look right between Patty's ears. See it?"

It was a fleck. A pale, still fleck in a sea of swaying grass, perhaps a mile off. Caroline narrowed her focus and the shape became a wagon. A wagon, motionless by the side of the road in midday. No smoke meant no cookfire.

"Sickness?" Caroline guessed, keeping her voice low. Or worse.

A smaller, darker smudge gradually appeared at the stilled wagon's front as the distance closed between them. Where horses should be, yet too small to be horses. People. They were as motionless as the wagon.

Charles guided the mustangs off the road, approaching cautiously.

A man and a woman sat on the wagon tongue. They were young. Little more than twenty, the woman, perhaps less. Caroline could not see past the woman's bonnet brim to her face, but her milk-white hands were so profusely freckled, they could belong only to a redhead. Her dusty hem did not obscure the fact that the dress was new. It was an everyday work dress, but the sleeves were shaped in a fashion that Caroline had not seen before, and every line of the paisley pattern stood out crisp. A few months in the Kansas sun and the sage-green print would hardly be distinguishable from the fawn-colored ground. Both of them looked so morose that Caroline began planning what she might cook for their supper while Charles helped the man dig a grave.

"What's wrong?" Charles asked. "Where are your horses?"

"I don't know," the man said. "I tied them to the wagon last night, and this morning they were gone."

Stranded. A subtle wave of nausea trickled through Caroline's stomach, cold as well water.

"What about your dog?" said Charles.

"Haven't got a dog," the man said. He sounded like a child. A shamed child, angry and embarrassed at not having known better.

"Well, your horses are gone," Charles said, as though the man had not fully realized it. "You'll never see them again. Hanging's too good for horse thieves."

"Yes," the man agreed.

Charles inclined his head toward her. Caroline knew his question as plainly as he knew what her answer would be. She nodded.

"Come ride with us to Independence," he offered.

"No," said the man. "All we've got is in this wagon. We won't leave it."

Charles's breath came out like a punch to the air. "Why, man! What will you do?" he blurted. "There may be nobody along here for days. Weeks. You can't stay here."

"I don't know," the man said.

"We'll stay with our wagon," the woman declared. Caroline turned back the brim of her own bonnet to look at her more closely. Was that small hump of calico behind the woman's folded hands the beginnings of a child? Or was it only her slumped posture?

"Better come," Charles insisted. "You can come back for your wagon."

"No," the woman said. Her tone signaled an end to the conversation.

Charles's lips worked silently, flummoxed. Caroline touched her fingers to his thigh. "Let's go, Charles," she said. "Leave them be."

"Tenderfeet!" Charles marveled under his breath as they rattled back onto the road. "Everything they own, and no dog to watch it. Didn't keep watch himself. And tied his horses with ropes!" Charles shook his head. "Tenderfeet!" he said again. "Shouldn't be allowed loose west of the Mississippi!"

It stung to hear him speak so harshly, as though they had done him some personal offense. In a way, they had. He, who had done everything right, must leave the land he so loved, while they had shackled themselves to it out of pure foolishness. "Charles," Caroline said. Tenderly, as though they were lying side by side on the straw tick. He sighed and leaned back a little. "Whatever will become of them?" she ventured.

"I'll leave word tomorrow when we pass through Independence. Someone will have to take a team and go out after them."

They spoke no more of it. Charles drove until the

mustangs' lengthening shadows leaned eastward. They had come seven or eight miles all told when he turned the wagon from the road to an overgrown trail. "I think this is the place," he said. "Doesn't look quite right, though. There's a good well a little ways off the road," he explained as the horses nosed through the brush. "A young bachelor from Iowa staked his claim right near here, if I'm not mistaken. I made his acquaintance on my first trip to Oswego." Charles cocked his head as he tried to align his memories with the landscape. "He'd just finished the well and was eager to show it off, so I humored him and stopped to water the horses. Nice enough fellow, talked a blue streak. Lonely, probably. He told me three or four times I was welcome to rest my team on his land any time."

A quarter mile down the trail, Caroline spotted a chimney. "There?" she asked.

"Must be," Charles said, "though I would have sworn the chimney was on the other side of the house."

The jagged outline of a burned claim shanty emerged around it as they approached, blackened and spindly against the sky.

Charles whistled a low note of astonishment. "Fellow said he was headed back East in the spring to fetch his sweetheart. Next time I passed by he was gone, but the house still stood. Shall we make camp here, or . . . ?"

Caroline considered. The ruined shanty lent the place a hollow feeling that did not invite attachment. That suited her. She made an attempt at cheerfulness. "We don't know where we'll next find good water."

Mary and Laura circled the shanty, collecting fragments from the tumbledown walls that would burn, while Caroline mixed cornmeal with the sweet, cool water and endeavored to keep from thinking about what might have happened to the people who had once lived here.

If she wanted to, Caroline could have made herself believe they were headed in, not out. Everything was the same. The unruly little cookfire hissing in the wind, the sinking sun setting the surface of her dishwater aflame with pink and gold, tucking the girls into their little bed in the wagon box. Everything down to the homeward pull of her heart was the same. Only the direction of that pull had changed.

Before returning to the fire she paused over the crate of tin dishes to stroke the leaves of the sweet potato seedling. *What if,* she thought, wrapping her fingers around the mug of sandy soil, *everything that feels like home is contained in this single tin cup?*

Home is where the heart is. That was what the samplers said, spelled out in small, neatly crossed threads. But her heart no longer knew where to roost. It was as though it had moved into the wrong side of her chest.

"Do you know, Caroline," Charles said as she sat down on the wagon seat, "I've been thinking what fun the rabbits will have, eating that garden we planted."

The pain was quick and deep and entirely without malice. He had not taken aim; he had taken a stab at fooling himself into cheerfulness and pierced her most tender spot instead. And he had done it with an echo of her own well-worn adage: *There is no loss without some small gain.* Caroline waited for the throb to subside, then said gently, "Don't, Charles."

He was quiet a moment, looking into the fire with a brittle smile. He did not seem to sense her hurt, only that his own had not dwindled as he had hoped. Then his mouth curled mischievously. "Anyway, we're taking more out of Indian Territory than we took in."

Caroline detected the sly undertone of a joke, but lacked the energy to guess where it was headed. "I don't know what."

"There's the mule colt. And Carrie."

Caroline's burst of laughter took them both by surprise, it was so out of proportion to the remark. He grinned at her, eyebrows cocked wonderingly. Caroline covered her mouth and shook her head. She could not explain. Only a man could miss the absurdity of such a notion. He had not felt the weight of a half-formed child sloshing in his belly as the wagon clattered over every rut and stone in seven hundred miles, nor vomited his breakfast into the ditches of five states.

Caroline wiped her eyes and found that he was gazing at her, his fist propped against his temple. The laughter had scoured her almost clean, and a soft, deep ache filled the space where the pain had been.

Charles leaned down and slid the fiddle box from under the wagon seat. He plucked the strings, coaxing the four familiar notes to their round, sweet centers, and Caroline shivered with a tremor of emotion too rich to name.

In that sound was the feel of her green delaine, whirling about her waist at the cornhusking dance; the scent of rosemary and pipe smoke and the shine of a crochet hook, flashing before a fire of stout Wisconsin hardwood. And now it was imbued with the first flutterings of a black-haired baby girl, and the unexpected delight of Edwards, dancing and whooping in the starlight. Caroline ached for all of it at once. The fiddle sang out high and sweet, as though it were pulling the notes from her chest, and Caroline remembered: It had been the sound of the fiddle that first awakened her heart to this country.

Now her heart seemed to spread, to peel itself open so that it could span the full breadth of the memories contained in those sounds, and Caroline marveled that her body could hold them all, side by side.

Her left hand slipped around her waist, her right settled over her breast.

Here, she thought. *Home.*

Author's Note

Caroline is a marriage of fact and Laura Ingalls Wilder's fiction. I have knowingly departed from Wilder's version of events only where the historical record stands in contradiction to her stories. Most prominently:

- Census records, as well as the Ingalls family Bible, demonstrate that Caroline Celestia Ingalls was born in Rutland Township, Montgomery County, Kansas on August 3, 1870. (Wilder, not anticipating writing a sequel to *Little House in the Big Woods*, set her first novel in 1873 and included her little sister. Consequently, when Wilder decided to continue her family's saga by doubling back to earlier events, Carrie's birth was omitted from *Little House on the Prairie* to avoid confusion.)

- No events corresponding to Wilder's descriptions of a "war dance" in the chapter of *Little House on the Prairie* entitled "Indian War-Cry" are known to have occurred in the vicinity of Rutland Township during the Ingalls family's residence there. Drum Creek, where Osage leaders met with federal Indian agents in the late summer of 1870 and agreed peaceably to sell their Kansas lands and relocate to present-day Oklahoma, was nearly twenty miles from the Ingalls claim. I have therefore adopted western scholar Frances Kay's conjecture that Wilder's family was frightened by the mourning songs sung by Osage women as they grieved the loss of their lands and ancestral graves in the days following the agreement. In this instance, like so many others involving the Osages, the Ingalls family's reactions were entirely a product of their own deep prejudices and misconceptions.

- Though Wilder blamed her family's departure from Kansas on "blasted politicians" ordering white squatters to vacate Osage lands, no such edict was issued over Rutland Township during the Ingallses' tenure there. Quite the reverse is true: only white intruders in what was known as the Cherokee Strip of Oklahoma were removed to make way for the displaced Osages arriving from Kansas. (Wilder mistakenly believed that her family's cabin was located forty—rather than the actual fourteen—miles from Independence, an error that placed the fictional Ingalls family in the area affected by the removal order.) Rather, Charles Ingalls's decision to abandon his claim was almost certainly financial, for Gustaf Gustafson did indeed default on his mortgage.

The exception: Unlike their fictional counterparts, the historical Ingalls family's decision to leave Wisconsin and settle in Kansas was not a straightforward one. Instead it was the eventual result of a series of land transactions that began in the spring of 1868, when Charles Ingalls sold his Wisconsin property to Gustaf Gustafson and shortly thereafter purchased 80 acres in Chariton County, Missouri, sight unseen. No one has been able to pinpoint with any certainty when (or even whether) the Ingalls family actually resided on that land; a scanty paper trail makes it appear that they actually zigzagged from Kansas to Missouri and back again between May of 1868 and February of 1870. What is certain is that by late February of 1870 Charles Ingalls had returned the title to his Chariton County acreage to the Missouri land dealer, and so for simplicity's sake I have chosen to follow Laura Ingalls Wilder's lead, contradicting history by streamlining events to more closely mirror the opening chapter of *Little House on the Prairie*, and setting this novel in 1870, a year in which the Ingalls family's presence in Kansas is firmly documented.

Acknowledgments

I am indebted to:

William Anderson, for kindling my interest in Laura Ingalls Wilder by so willingly sharing a number of uncommon resources. Had that information not been so easily accessible, the idea for this book might never have fully germinated.

Christopher Czajka, for reading the manuscript with a keen eye for accuracy and an impeccable instinct for authenticity.

And to Little House Heritage Trust, for entrusting me with Caroline Ingalls. I have never been, and never will be, unconscious of that honor. My time with her, and my partnership with you, has enriched my life in more ways than I could have hoped to foresee.

SARAH MILLER began writing her first novel at the age of ten, and has spent the last two decades working in libraries and bookstores. She is the author of two previous historical novels, *Miss Spitfire: Reaching Helen Keller* and *The Lost Crown*. Her non-fiction debut, *The Borden Murders: Lizzie Borden and the Trial of the Century*, was hailed by the *New York Times* as "a historical version of *Law & Order*." Sarah lives in Michigan.